THE

ROYAL TWINS;

h

OR,

THE SISTERS OF MYSTERY.

BY THE AUTHOR OF

"ELA THE OUTCAST," "THE SMUGGLER KING," "THE OLD HOUSE OF WEST STREET," ETC.

———————

LONDON:

PUBLISHED BY G. PURKESS,

COMPTON-STREET, SOHO; AND ALL BOOKSELLERS.

PREFACE.

THE following tale has been so favourably received while appearing in numbers, that the author's task is reduced to little more than returning thanks for the patronage already granted.

It may not be out of place, however, to call attention to the manifold mischiefs which have arisen out of the statute known as the Royal Marriage Act, which deprived the princes of the blood royal of the privilege, which is accorded to the meanest subject, of bestowing the hand where the heart has been already given. George the Third himself, and his sons, the Prince of Wales and the Dukes of Clarence and Sussex, were sufferers from the cruel state policy which forbids an alliance with a subject of these realms, no matter how nobly born, how distinguished for beauty, or admired for the practice of every virtue.

But if oppressive to the Prince, how much more painful was the fate of the lady who became a victim of this unnatural law. The lives of Mrs. Fitzherbert, and of Mrs. Jordan, have come before the public, and the incidents described in our tale are not more mysterious or surprising than those recounted in the authentic histories of those unfortunate ladies.

It is certainly one of the misfortunes attached to the highest rank in. this country that its possessor is surrounded with conventionalities, and forbidden the honest and unrestricted exercise of those feelings which nature has implanted in the human breast; and it may be beneficially borne in mind by those in an inferior sphere of life, that if deprived of the advantages of wealth, they possess in some important respects a liberty of action which is denied to the monarch on the throne.

London, April, 1848.

THE ROYAL TWINS;

OR,

THE SISTERS OF MYSTERY.

BY THE AUTHOR OF "ELA, THE OUTCAST," "THE GIPSY BOY," &c.

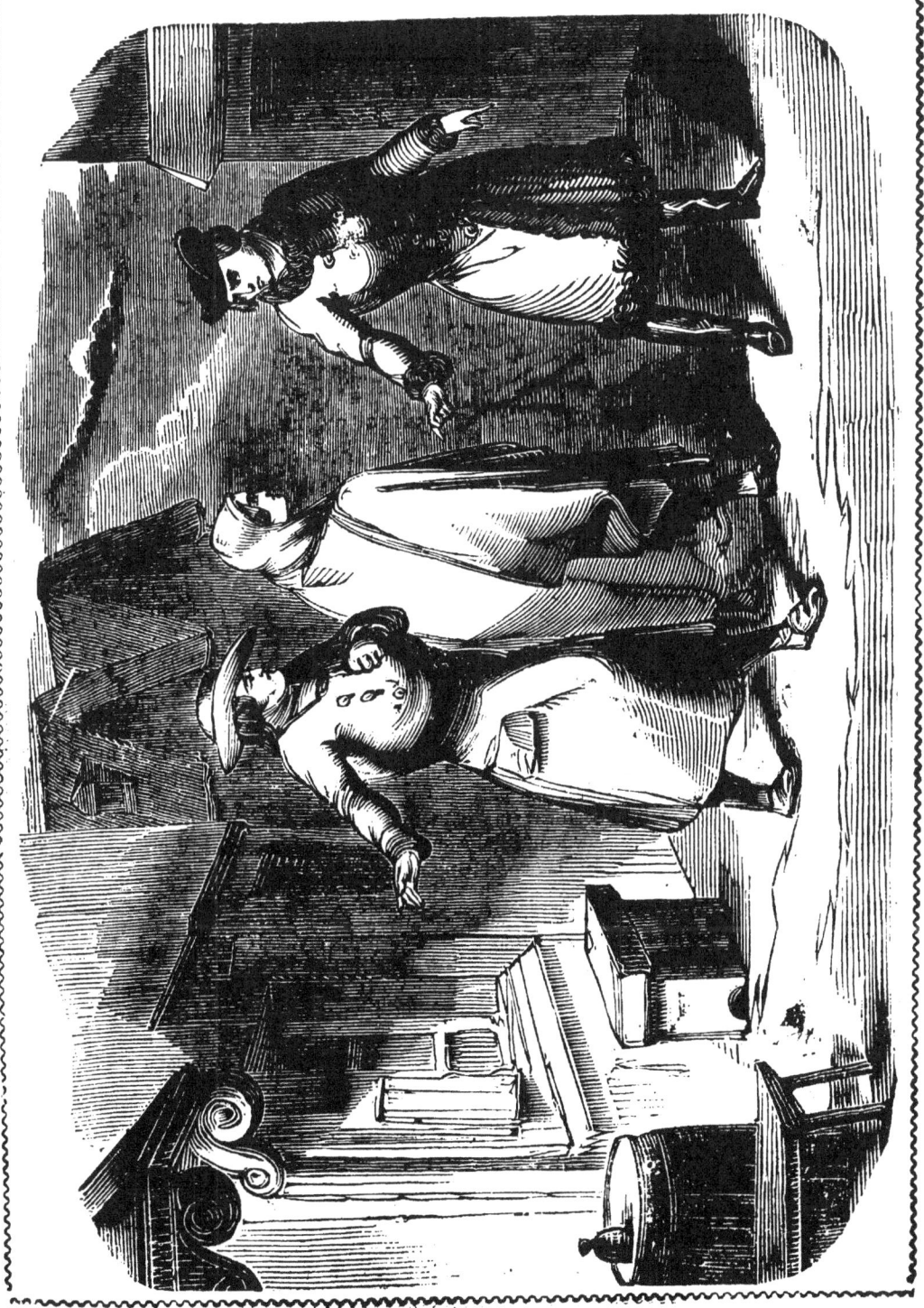

INTRODUCTION.

READER, we have not wandered into the regions of fiction for the subject of the present narrative. The extraordinary events recorded in these pages are all matters of fact, as several distinguished persons could, if necessary, fully testify; especially *the offspring of the illustrious heroines*, who furnished the author with the documents upon which he has founded the present tale, and by whose authority they are now published to the world.

The real names of the principal persons who figure in these pages, for obvious reasons, are concealed, as it is far from the wish of the editor to wound the feelings of any one member of the numerous distinguished families connected with the facts related in this history; but the localities in which the various scenes are described to have been enacted, are perfectly correct. The editor has, in fact, adhered as closely as possible to the plain and simple truth, knowing that it needed little embellishment of his own to give it interest, and perfectly agreeing with the immortal bard, that

> " Truth is strange—
> Stranger than fiction."

CHAPTER I.

THE OLD STREET IN WHITECHAPEL.—THE OPENING OF THE PLOT.—THE APPOINTMENT.—AN AFFAIR OF MYSTERY.

RATHER more than sixty years ago, a filthy street, or alley (the name of which we forget), of crazy and tottering ruins of houses, which had evidently been erected at a very remote period, wormed its pestiferous way from the Whitechapel-road to that classic region known at the present day by the somewhat uninviting name of the " Dog-row," appalling to the eyes of the spectators from their tottering condition, and dangerous to the wretched, squalid passengers who alone ventured through the street, threatening, as they did, to topple down every moment, and to bury all beneath their ruins.

This filthy avenue was very narrow—indeed, so particularly so, that it would have been no difficult matter for individuals living on opposite sides of the way to have shaken hands with each other out of their windows. The effluvia which arose from this miserable place was sufficient to breed a pestilence in the neighbourhood, and no doubt was the cause of hundreds of lives being sacrificed yearly; and to add to the abominable nuisance, there was an open sewer in the immediate vicinity, into which all the poisonous filth of the neighbourhood emptied itself.

Sanitary measures were not even dreamt of at that period, and human life was recklessly sacrificed, without any one being bold enough to suggest a remedy for the fearful evil; and, indeed, if any one had been daring, or rather humane enough, to suggest such a thing, he most undoubtedly would have been set down by the wiseacres of " the good old times," as a decided madman.

This wretched alley might be said to be no-man's-property. It had been in the same state as we have described it as far back as the recollection of "the oldest inhabitant" could go. No one claimed it; no one knew to whom it belonged; and every one did as they liked with it, without receiving the least check from those in power. Not a casement was there in that decrepid street which, for many years, could boast of a pane of glass; not a door which had not long since rotted from its hinges, and been applied to the purposes of fuel for the poor starving beings who thronged the locality; and rats and mice sported undisturbed, although, from their attenuated appearance, they certainly did not appear to be in much of a sporting condition. It was marvellous that they did not emigrate in disgust to some more promising land.

These wrecks of houses had been for some time "condemned;" but, as is often the case with condemned criminals, they were respited, not during the royal pleasure, but that of the parish authorities. It could hardly have been supposed that any persons could have had the hardihood to venture to seek a shelter in these tottering ruins; but such was the fact. Some hundreds of miserable beings had no other local habitation and a home, and the parochial authorities never, for a moment, thought of interfering with them. It saved them a deal of expense, inconvenience, and trouble, by not having to shelter many of them in the workhouse; and, good, kind, charitable, humane men,— as all parish officers, from time immemorial, ever have been, and we suppose ever will be,—there was another chance which they had their eyes to, no doubt,—the crazy buildings could not prop each other up for ever; they must fall some day or other, crushing and annihilating their miserable tenants; and surely that would be a most excellent way of " decreasing the surplus population."

This condemned rookery might with truth be called a free colony of vagrants, cadgers, street-beggars, squalid, starving poverty, and thieves. It was a ghastly refuge for the destitute and abandoned on the broadest scale. Here the guilty might hide themselves from detection, and even the midnight assassin find a refuge from the officers of the law, without the least fear of interruption.

But not only did crime and vagrancy find a retreat in this wretched place, but many of the deserving, uncared-for poor, whom misfortune had struck down, sought an apology of a shelter within its poisonous precincts, rather than seek the tender mercies of the parish authorities. Oh, the appalling, the heartrending scenes that might have been met with among this class of unfortunates, if the eye of charity could have deigned to contemplate them—to have ventured to visit and pour the balm of consolation and unostentatious relief into the bosoms of their afflicted, starving fellow-creatures!

The weather was cold, wet, and miserable—in fact, it was as miserable as it could possibly be in that most cheerless of months, November, and that we conceive will be a sufficient description for our readers. A thin, misty rain had been incessantly drifting down for days, and the atmosphere was choked with a suffocating fog. Mud and filth were in their glory in every narrow avenue; the only sounds that saluted the ears were the clattering of pattens on the wet pavement, the consumptive cough of the pedestrian, the half-stifled cry of the drowsy watchman, or the sullen moan of the wind at intervals, as if it was grumbling at the fog for not permitting it to roar out and bellow with all the strength of its lungs. It was night (about eight o'clock), though from the gloom which had prevailed, it could scarcely be said that there had been any day.

The rookery which we have taken such pains to describe, was buried in profound darkness, except where here and there a faint glare of light forced itself through the fog, showing that some of the miserable tenants had found means to provide themselves with a little firing to impart some degree of warmth to the shivering limbs of themselves and their emaciated children. To gaze into the dark alley at that time, was indeed to look into the black subterranean cavern of despair. But we doubt much whether there were many who were bold enough to do so.

In one of the houses, which was perhaps not quite so ruinous as the rest, two or three families, whose only crime was that of being miserably poor (a very heinous crime, indeed, by-the-bye, in the estimation of many *disinterested* persons), had for some time located themselves, existing Heaven only knows how, and to one of the rooms in this house we must now direct the attention of the reader.

It was a large and cheerless place, with broken, blackened walls, decayed flooring, and a huge fireplace, which had not often seen the rousing fire which at present blazed upon its hearth. There was an old mattrass in one corner of the room, covered with a tattered rag, but perfectly clean; a tottering table stood in the centre of the room, on which was a teapot without the spout, two broken cups and saucers, the remains of a quartern loaf, &c., which showed that the inmates of that gloomy room had been fortunate enough to procure a meal!

On two ricketty chairs, and huddling themselves close into the chimney-corner, to secure to themselves all the warmth of the fire (which was so great a novelty to them), were seated a man and woman, the former occupied in smoking a short pipe, which, from its blackened appearance, had evidently seen considerable service.

The woman was very thinly and sparingly clad, but remarkably clean; she had an infant at her breast. Her figure was thin, but bore all the traces of former grace; and her countenance, which was pale, wan, and melancholy, showed all the signs of former beauty. It was no common expression of countenance; in its sad lineaments might be traced a volume of misery and suffering.

The man's attire was equally mean, but marked by the same scrupulous cleanliness as that of his wife. He seemed to be about thirty-four years of age, and the ravages of

a

want and misery were stamped upon his brow.   His countenance was open, manly, and expressive, and his figure still retained the appearance of having once been fine, muscular, and dignified.

This was James Milford (as he now chose to call himself) and his wife, Mary.   They had once been in affluent circumstances, and nothing could be brighter than the prospect before them; but cruel fate, and not their own misconduct, had reduced them to their present wretched state, and terrible indeed were the sufferings they had for some years past been enduring.

How they had existed at all they scarcely knew; two of their children had died for the want of the common necessaries of life, and it seemed as if that must ultimately be their own fate, unless Providence, in its infinite mercy, sent them some speedy relief.

Milford for a short time after the dreadful change in his fortunes had obtained employment as a labourer, upon the most miserable wages; but at length that failed, and himself and his wife were driven upon the wide world, without one friend to whom they could apply for assistance.   At the workhouse they were cruelly refused relief, and what else was then left them but to beg, or steal, or starve?   Steal they could not; to see his beloved wife perish for want was more than James Milford could bear to contemplate, and, therefore, to beg was their only resource.   We will not attempt to describe the sufferings, the insults, the cruelties they had to undergo in this wretched condition; but they bore it all with the most Christian fortitude, and were even resigned under afflictions which would have driven many persons to the most desperate acts.

Unable to find the means of providing themselves with shelter, they sought refuge in the miserable place we have described at the commencement of this chapter, and, although they kept themselves as much apart as possible from their vagrant neighbours, they would have been driven entirely from that frightful apology for an asylum, had they not partly associated with them.

The George, in George-yard, Whitechapel, was always a notorious haunt for street cadgers and vagrants of every description.   Here the sturdy beggar who had imposed upon the public as "suffering every ill that flesh is heir to," as a maimed sailor, or a respectable mechanic out of employment, during the day time, and by his piteous appeals seldom failed to reap a rich harvest, to the injury of the really distressed, met of an evening to feast, carouse, and make merry with his fellows, and to concoct fresh schemes to prey upon the purses of the public; and scenes of the most revolting description were nightly enacted.   Milford was sometimes compelled to join them, and how disgusting, how degrading was it to the feelings of one who had been born and educated a gentleman, and in whose breast still glowed every generous and honourable feeling!

By chance, Milford, the day before that of which we are writing, encountered a gentleman who had known him in his days of prosperity, but about whose character there was a great deal of mystery.   He would have shunned him, but the gentleman, notwithstanding the painful alteration in his looks and personal appearance, knew him in a moment, and detaining him, expressed his sorrow at seeing him in such a wretched condition, and his anxiety to assist him, for the sake not only of the respect he had always borne towards him, but his late aged relative, who had met with so dreadful and untimely a fate.

At the mention of this circumstance Milford exhibited great emotion.

"Ah, sir," he said, "you were on intimate terms with my unfortunate grandfather."

"I was," replied the gentleman; "we were connected together by circumstances of no ordinary character; but let us waive that subject.   We will retire up this dark passage, where no one can observe us.   I have something to say to you, and I am glad that fortune has thrown you in my way."

They retired into the passage accordingly, and Milford awaited what the gentleman had to say with considerable impatience.

The gentleman was apparently between fifty and sixty years of age, but his fine, tall, portly figure, retained all the elasticity of youth.   His appearance was military, and his countenance was still handsome and prepossessing.

"Is your wife still living, Clavering?" asked his companion.   Milford, or rather Clavering, which was his real name, replied in the affirmative.

"And your children?"

Milford sighed deeply, as he replied,—

"Two of my poor little innocents died of hunger; my Mary has now another infant sucking at the breast, which alas! I fear it is not unlikely will share the same fate."

"Oh, no, that shall not be," said the gentleman; "since you have the good fortune to meet with me, I will take care to prevent such a calamity taking place."

After a pause, during which he looked stedfastly in the face of Milford, he added,—

"I have a proposition to make to you, Clavering, which, if you agree to, you will be greatly serving me and others, and will at the same time place yourself in comfort and independence."

Milford started, and stared at his companion with amazement, scarcely able to trust the evidence of his senses.

"Oh, sir," he exclaimed, "name what it is you want me to perform, and if it is anything that I can do without a dereliction from integrity and honour, you will find me most ready to comply with your request."

A slight frown passed over the stranger's brow.

"You surprise me, Clavering," he said, "by supposing that I could wish you to perform anything derogatory to honour and integrity."

"Pardon me, sir," said Milford, "I did not mean to insinuate anything offensive; in what, pray, can I serve you?"

"This is not the time or place to mention it. We might have listeners, and it is a business on which the greatest secrecy must be maintained; but still no time must be lost. I must see you again to-morrow night, and I must also see your wife; where do you reside?"

"Alas, sir, it is a wretched hovel, where other poor unfortunate creatures like myself herd together, for we have not the means to pay for a lodging."

"Where is it, Clavering? Tell me, and I will not fail to visit you there to-morrow night at nine o'clock."

"Oh, sir," replied Milford, "you cannot—a gentleman like you cannot venture into that haunt of misery, pestilence, and crime. There are wretches there who would not hesitate to take your life for the purpose of robbing you."

"Tush!" said the gentleman, impatiently. "I have been into many such places in my time; and, therefore, entertain no fear. My business will admit of no delay. So tell me at once where I may find you and your wife to-morrow night; and then I must leave you, in order that I may lose no time in making my arrangements."

Milford, more and more astonished, gave him as correct an address as he possibly could, to the place where he was to be found, which the gentleman entered in his pocketbook; and then taking out his purse he placed a couple of guineas in Milford's hand, saying,—

"Provide yourselves with present necessaries; and mark me, you and your wife must prepare yourselves for a journey."

"A journey, sir," said Milford, in amazement; "where?"

"We will talk further of that when we meet again; remember, at nine o'clock to-morrow night I will be there; and that if you comply with my request, your fortune is made. Good night."

Without saying another word the gentleman walked away; Milford saw him step into a hackney carriage; and he then slowly bent his steps towards his wretched hovel in the Rookery, revolving in his mind the singular adventure, and in vain endeavouring to conjecture what could be the nature of the business the gentleman wished to engage him in.

CHAPTER II.

THE APPOINTMENT KEPT.—THE STRANGE JOURNEY.—THE MYSTERIOUS CHARGE.

RETURN we now to the miserable room in which we left Milford and his wife. Nothing could exceed her astonishment when her husband made her acquainted with what had taken place between him and the gentleman; and she awaited the arrival of the following night with the most eager impatience. The mention of the gentleman recalled some painful recollections to her mind; and she could not refrain from tears.

It was now half-past eight; and Milford sat in silent thought and expectation. A drizzling rain continued to descend; and the night remained all the same that we have previously described it.

"It is not likely that he will come on such a miserable night as this, James," at length said Mrs. Milford; "and, after all, perhaps it will be as well if he does not."

"Why so, Mary?" asked her husband.

"Because I always look upon that with suspicion where there is so much mystery attached; and poor as we are, I would sooner that we should remain so, than that we should be entrapped to assist in any dishonourable plot."

"And think you, Mary," said Milford, "that all the gold in the universe would tempt me to assist in the accomplishment of that which was dishonourable? No, Heaven knows, I have had enough to try me, and to tempt me to crime; but thank God! I am the same James Clavering as I was before fortune withdrew her smiles from me. Besides, he is a gentleman, I believe, and a man of honour, and cannot contemplate anything of a guilty character."

"And yet," said Mrs. Milford, "although he was on such intimate terms with your grandfather, and so frequently visited him, you never knew his name or rank."

"True," said Milford, "I have often wondered what could be his reason for concealing it so carefully, and frequently questioned my grandfather upon the subject; but I could never get any satisfactory answer from him; and he seemed vexed at my importunities. However, I feel satisfied that he is a person of some consequence, though what could be the nature of the business they were so frequently privately engaged upon, I never could fathom."

"I am lost in astonishment," said Mrs. Milford; "oh, Heaven grant that some honest means may present itself to extricate us from our present miserable and degrading situation."

"He promised me," said Milford, "that if I acceded with his request, that I should be placed in comfort and independence."

"It must be something of very great importance to induce him to hold out such promises. But did he not say that we must prepare ourselves for a journey?"

"He did."

"Whither can he wish us to go? And surely he cannot expect us to travel on such a night as this?"

"He stated that his business would not admit of any delay," said Milford; "and probably the journey is not a long one. But I dare say he will explain everything when he comes."

"If he does come," said Mrs. Milford; "but I do not think it likely on such a miserable night. Besides, does it not seem most improbable that a gentleman like him will venture into this wretched and filthy place?"

Their conversation was interrupted by the sound of footsteps ascending the creaking stairs; and the next moment there was a gentle tap at the room door, which Milford opened, and the expected visitor entered. He glanced a hasty glance around the wretched apartment, and then greeted Mrs. Milford with much politeness.

"I am sorry, Clavering," he said, "to see you in such a deplorable situation, and regret that I knew not where to find you before, that I might have rendered you some assistance in your difficulties."

"I feel obliged to you, sir," answered Milford, "for the sympathy you are pleased to express in my misfortunes; mine has, indeed, been a chequered life, but still I have the consolation to know that my troubles were not brought upon me by any misconduct of my own."

"I am satisfied of that," said the gentleman; "but now to business. Have you well considered the proposition I made you last night?"

"I have, sir; but surely you cannot but think that I expect some further explanation of the business before I make any agreement."

"That you shall have at another time and place," returned the gentleman; "but I repeat, that it is nothing which will at all compromise your character. You are now in poverty and wretchedness, the opportunity is offered to you to extricate yourself from it, and once more to become comfortable and independent; and I cannot believe that you, Clavering, will be so foolish as to reject it. Come, what say you?"

Milford looked at his wife, and hesitated what answer to make.

"You, Mrs. Clavering," said the gentleman, "I am sure, will see the necessity for your own sake, for the sake of your child, of your husband accepting the offer I now make to him."

"I do not doubt the honour of your intentions, sir," replied Mrs. Milford (for by that name we will still continue to call them), "but I must say that some further explanation would be more satisfactory."

"That I promise you shall both have before many hours have elapsed. But time is stealing on, and my business is urgent; are you ready to accompany me?"

"Whither?" demanded Milford.

"Excuse me, but that question I must also decline to answer. No doubt you are much astonished that I should think so much secrecy necessary; but my business, and that which I wish to engage you in, is of that peculiar nature that it is actually indispensable. The journey, however, will not be a long one."

"But is it necessary that my wife should accompany us?"

"Undoubtedly, we can do nothing without her; besides, I do not intend you to return again to this wretched place; I have provided a small house for you, furnished with every comfort, whither I will conduct you after our business is satisfactorily settled."

Milford and his wife looked at each other in perfect amazement and bewilderment.

"But consider our appearance, sir," said Milford; "you surely would not like to be seen with us in the public streets, and the night is not a fit one for my wife and her infant to be exposed in."

"I have a carriage in waiting a short distance off," returned the gentleman; "quick! the business, as I have frequently observed before, will admit of no delay. Have you decided?"

Milford looked at his wife; the offer of a comfortable home, when put in contrast with the wretched hovel they had for so many months "dragged" out their wretched existence in, the promise of independence, were temptations not easily to be overcome. Then the degradation to which they were subjected by being compelled to associate with the vilest and most abandoned of wretches, to be obliged to be "hail fellow, well met," with them, to have to tolerate their ribald jests, and coarse rhodomontade, were surely reasons more than sufficient to urge them to agree to the gentleman's proposal.

Such were the thoughts that were passing in the mind of Mrs. Milford, when her husband put the question,—

"What says my Mary? I will be guided entirely by your decision, my dearest love."

"Then, James, we will trust ourselves to the gentleman's honour," replied Mrs. Milford; "and trust to Providence that our determination may not prove wrong. Oh, how happy shall I be to be removed from the contagion of the misguided and abandoned individuals with whom we have latterly been compelled to associate, and of rescuing my poor, innocent boy from that vortex of ruin into which he must be plunged should we be compelled to remain in our present miserable sphere of life. James, we will, with your permission, accept of the gentleman's offer."

"Enough, my dear Mary," said Milford; "I think you have made a wise decision; and Heaven send that our wishes and motives may not be thwarted or disappointed. Sir, we are ready to attend you. Mary, wrap that rag around you and our boy, for the sudden exposure to the inclemency of the night might otherwise be productive of the most dangerous consequences."

"There is no occasion for that," said the gentleman, taking off his military cloak, and throwing it around the thinly clad limbs of the mother and her infant; "this will shield your wife and child from the cold and rain, and the humble articles you leave behind will be of service to any unfortunate persons who may seek an asylum in this wretched place. And this," he added, removing from his person a heavy top coat, and giving it to Milford, "will also protect you from the weather."

Milford was about to make some reply, but the stranger (for such was he in name to them, although not in person) waved his hand, and Milford having adjusted himself in the coat, said that they were ready.

"Enough," said the gentleman, with a look of satisfaction; "you will have no reason to regret having come to this decision. You now, if you accede to the proposals I shall have to make to you in an hour or two, quit this tottering abode of misery for ever, and in future live in comfort and independence."

Sudden hope and confidence sprang up in the bosoms of Milford and his wife, and they quitted the dismal den in which they had suffered all the tortures of poverty and self-degradation, with feelings which the reader will easily imagine.

They descended the creaking stairs with as much caution as possible, lest they should arouse the attention and curiosity of the other unfortunate inmates of the house, and soon found themselves in the street, without attracting any observation. The gentleman walked on at a rapid pace, and beckoned them to follow him as quickly as they could, and Milford, supporting the feeble limbs of his wife, and whispering a word of hope and comfort in her ear, obeyed the instructions of their conductor, and in another minute they had emerged from that sink of abomination and pestilence, in which it had been their hard lot so long to be located, into the Whitechapel-road. The gentleman walked on at a rapid pace, so that Milford and his wife found some difficulty in keeping up with him, and owing to the darkness of the night, they would frequently have missed his course altogether had he not turned back and pointed out to them the way he was proceeding.

The fog was still as intense as ever, and the rain continued to descend in the same misty manner as it had done throughout the day and evening. The light emitted from the lamps had no effect whatever, except to render confusion worst confused; in many instances they were completely extinguished, and those that remained, twinkled with no more radiance than so many rushlights, unworthy even of a comparison with will o' the wisps, although, like them, they only twinkled to lead the pedestrian astray. The wind had increased in strength, and blowing from the north-east, drifted the mizzling rain in their faces. But it was not many minutes that they were exposed to these unpleasantries, for just before they had reached the corner of Osborne-street, the stranger came up to them, and taking the arm of Mrs. Milford urged her on, at the same time observing—

" It is fortunate that the fog is so dense that it is impossible for any one to take any particular notice of us. Ah, Robert, you are there!"

" Yes, your grace," was the reply. Mr. Milford and his wife were startled at the title, but before they had time to think, or to recover themselves from the confusion into which their discovery of the exalted rank of their conductor had thrown them, they beheld a carriage drawn up to the pavement, and a servant waiting at the door to hand them in ;—the unknown assisted Mrs. Milford into the vehicle, saw her husband take his seat by her side, he then followed himself, the blinds were drawn closely down, and the carriage proceeded as fast as it was safe to do through the fog, to the place of their destination. It was some time ere Milford or his wife could recover themselves sufficiently from their embarrassment to speak, and the gentleman did not seem to be inclined to break the silence. The whole affair, so far as it had proceeded, was so extraordinary, that it appeared to Mr. and Mrs. Milford more like a dream than anything else, and what would be the result of it they in vain puzzled their brains to conjecture. That the individual in whose hands they had placed themselves, was a nobleman, they had now every reason to believe, but what could be the nature of the business he had engaged them in, and what cause there should be for so much secrecy, they were perfectly at a loss to conceive.

The carriage, in consequence of the fog, could only proceed at a slow pace, which seemed much to annoy the gentleman, and the blinds being carefully drawn down, Milford and his wife had no opportunity of discovering the route they were pursuing, although, from the frequent turning of the vehicle, it seemed to be a most intricate one, and there could be very little doubt that the plan was so formed to prevent them from being able to discover it again.

" Have we far to go, sir?" at length Milford ventured to inquire.

" Some five or six miles only," replied the man, " and but for this confounded fog we should soon accomplish it."

" You are a nobleman," said Milford, " if I may judge from the way in which the coachman addressed you."

" Ay, ay," impatiently replied the unknown; " but it matters not what or who I am; suffice it to say I am a man of honour. Ask no further questions, for I cannot answer them, and depend upon it the engagement into which you have entered with me, will cause you no regret, but will be of every advantage to you, if you only act with prudence."

There was something in the tone of the unknown's address, notwithstanding the mysteriousness of the whole affair, which inspired Milford and his wife with confidence, and

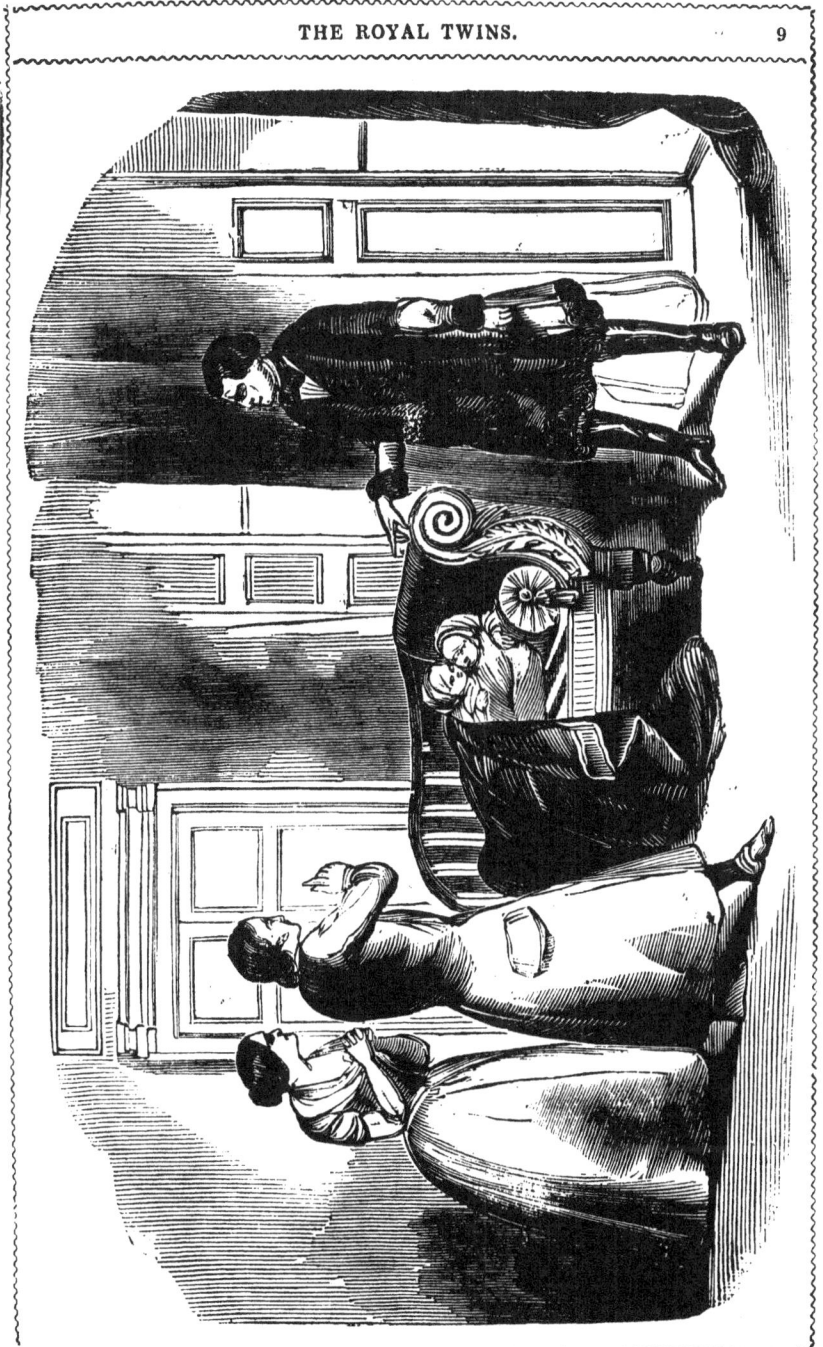

they put no further questions to him, but awaited the result of the adventure with the utmost anxiety.

The gentleman threw himself back into one corner of the vehicle, and seemed to give himself up entirely to thought, and it would have been quite evident to any person who could have observed the expression of his countenance at that time, that those which were busying themselves in his mind were of the most important and weighty description.

The reflections of Milford and his wife were of no less intense a character. What was the nature of the business they had entered upon? What would be the result of the adventure? What new scenes were they destined to take a part in? Who was the individual with whom they were now seated? These were questions which very naturally suggested themselves to them, but which they found themselves totally incapable of answering. He had promised them comfort and independence, but what could be the nature of the service he would require of them in return, they were completely at a loss to imagine.

The carriage no longer continued to rattle over the stones, but was evidently making its way over a level road; they could also hear a rustling sound, like the whistling of the wind among the leafless branches of the trees, and the absence of all the noise and bustle of the different passing vehicles convinced them that they had left the busy heart of the metropolis, and were pursuing their way along a suburban or country road.

"Whither are we going, sir?" again asked Milford; "surely there cannot be any necessity for all this mystery?"

"There is," answered the gentleman; "but I beg that you will not be alarmed; there is no harm intended you; I can have no motive for such a design."

"We are now in the suburbs of London, are we not?" inquired Milford.

"We are," was the answer, "and shall shortly arrive at the place of our destination. With this answer I request that you will be contented, and put no further questions. It must be evident to you that I wish you to remain ignorant of the road we are travelling, or the place to which we are going. I have strong reasons for so doing, which it would not be prudent for me to explain."

Milford put no further questions, but he was far from satisfied, and his wife was even more uneasy and anxious than himself.

In this manner they continued to travel for about half an hour longer, in the most profound silence, when suddenly the vehicle stopped, and the coachman alighting opened the door, and the stranger having descended from the carriage, assisted Mrs. Milford out, and her husband followed her.

The fog had in some measure cleared off, and they were enabled to distinguish immediate surrounding objects.

They found themselves standing before a large pair of folding gates or doors, which seemed to open upon the grounds of an ancient and spacious mansion, whose dark outline they could dimly perceive in the background, from the lights which glimmered from its various windows. A long and dreary road was behind them, which they had traversed; on each side of them the open fields, and immediately opposite to the building another road, or rather avenue of trees, the termination of which the darkness would not permit them to see.

They were not, however, permitted long to look about them; the gates were already opened, when the gentleman, advancing to Milford and his wife, said,—

"We have arrived at our journey's end, so far, but you must submit to have your eyes bandaged for a few minutes."

"I like not so much mystery and precaution," remarked Milford; "what necessity is there for it?"

"It may and doubtless does appear strange to you," replied the gentleman; "but, at the same time, there is every necessity for it. I again assure you that you have nothing whatever to apprehend; there is not the least harm intended you."

"I think it is quite time that you should explain to us the nature of this most extraordinary business," remarked Milford.

"In a few minutes everything shall be explained," said the gentleman; "if you will but have patience."

"Where are we, sir?" demanded Mrs. Milford, with much anxiety, and looking eagerly around her; "I do not remember ever to have seen this place before."

"I do not suppose that you have," said the gentleman, "and I do not wish you to recollect it again. But come, we waste time. Will you consent to what I require?"

"We have proceeded so far," replied Milford, "that it would be almost useless now to retreat; but remember, sir, that nothing whatever shall compel us to act in any way which our conscience cannot approve of."

"You will be put to no such test," was the reply; but Milford and his wife thought it was not spoken in such a tone of firmness as that in which the stranger had previously addressed them.

Handkerchiefs were now bound across their eyes, and a servant and the gentleman led them along, and they soon found that they had entered the building, by the closing of the heavy doors behind them. All was silent around them, and they could hear nothing but the sound of their own footsteps and those of their conductors as they ascended the stairs. At length they seemed to be traversing a long gallery, and at last to enter a suite of apartments, in which the same silence prevailed.

At last they stopped; the bandages were removed from their eyes, and they were struck with astonishment at the scene which was presented to their observation.

They found themselves in a lofty and spacious apartment, brilliantly lighted up, hung round with landscapes and portraits in richly carved frames, and the whole of the furniture was of the most costly and *recherche* description. But what particularly attracted their attention, was an elegant escutcheon at one end of the room, on which was embroidered, in silver and gold, the royal arms. A portrait of his Majesty, George the Third, and another of the Prince of Wales, were also suspended from the wainscot. The floor was richly carpeted, and the effect altogether was dazzling in the extreme.

Milford and his wife were stupified with amazement, but the stranger seemed to witness their confusion with no surprise.

"What place is this?" at length demanded Milford; "and for what purpose are we brought hither?"

"Your first question I do not think it prudent to answer," said the gentleman; "you must remain in ignorance of it, at present, at any rate; as regards the other, you will soon be satisfied. But I must now request you both to swear that you will never, without my express permission, or through some extraordinary circumstance, reveal to mortal ears the transactions of this night."

"Oh, why should we bind ourselves by any such an oath?" said Mrs. Milford. "I regret that we were prevailed upon to engage in the business at all, and would much rather that we should now retire from it, and proceed no further."

"That must not be," said the gentleman, "and it would be madness on your part to think of doing so, when, for the performance of a simple, nay, I will say, a merciful act, fortune is offered to you."

"This secret is to me perfectly inexplicable," said Milford, still looking around the splendid apartment in complete bewilderment. "Why should we take an oath which may involve us in unknown difficulties?"

"I will pledge you my word and honour," answered the gentleman, "that not the least harm shall come of it. Be quick, and decide at once, for we are only wasting that time which is most precious to me."

Milford still hesitated, but still his curiosity was so great to become acquainted with the whole facts of this mysterious business, that it overcame his reluctance, and after whispering a few words to his wife aside, he said,—

"Well, sir, trusting to your honour, we will take the oath required of us."

"Thank you," said the gentleman; "you have come to a wise determination, and will have no cause to regret it."

The oath of secrecy was then administered in due form by the gentleman, after which he observed :—

"So far all has proceeded well, and I have not the least doubt but that everything will terminate to our mutual satisfaction. I must now leave you for a few minutes, but will shortly return; in the meantime you will find refreshments on yonder table, which you and your wife must much need after your journey."

With these words he retired from the room by an opposite door, which they heard him lock after him, and Milford and his wife were left alone to their own reflections, which the reader will naturally imagine were of the most bewildering description, and they awaited the return of the gentleman with the greatest impatience. They once more looked around the splendidly furnished apartment, and in vain endeavoured to form a conjecture as to where they were.

They now had the curiosity to go to the door, at which the gentleman had departed, and listen. At first they did not hear anything, but the light that glimmered through the crevices of the door, convinced them that some one was in the apartment upon which it opened, and soon afterwards they were confirmed in that opinion by hearing the low muttering sounds of some persons apparently in earnest conversation. This was followed by deep sobs, which seemed to proceed from a female, and then the light disappeared from the room, and they heard the retiring footsteps of two or three individuals.

A few minutes of further suspense followed, when the room door was suddenly thrown open, and the gentleman entered, followed by a middle aged female, bearing in each arm a lovely female infant, dressed in the richest manner.

Milford and his wife started at this unexpected sight, and looked at the gentleman for an explanation. He noticed their anxiety, and after telling the woman to place the infant twins (for such they were), ordered her to retire from the room until such time as he should require her attendance again.

"My friends," began the gentleman, "you behold these lovely innocents—twins in beauty as they are by birth. They are the offspring of noble, nay, of illustrious parents, but Fate has so ordained it, that for the present they must be separated from them, and brought up in ignorance of their real origin. The honour, nay, I might almost say the lives of several distinguished persons depend upon their remaining unknown. A handsome allowance will be given to those who will receive them under their care, and bring them up as their own, and they will have the satisfaction of knowing that they have probably been the means of preventing the lives of these two poor helpless innocents from being sacrificed. You, my friends, I have selected for the important task, and it was for that purpose that I brought you here. You have but one child of your own; I have engaged a wet nurse for you, whom you will find at the house I have taken for you, and which has been furnished with every necessary comfort; and you will, therefore, not find them any incumbrance to you, and may bring them up to believe that they are your own children, until such time as it may please Providence to permit their real parents to reclaim them. Here is money to the amount of five hundred pounds, which sum shall be regularly remitted to you every three years, and that will enable you not only to give them a fitting education, but also to keep yourselves in comfort and independence. Say, then, are you willing to undertake this precious charge?"

To attempt to describe the feelings of Mr. and Mrs. Milford, while the gentleman was thus speaking, would be utterly vain. They first looked at him, and then at the two lovely infants, in the greatest bewilderment; and for a few moments they were at a loss what answer to return.

"You need not be surprised, sir," at length said Milford, "that myself and my wife are utterly confounded at such an unexpected and startling proposition."

"I am not," returned the gentleman; "but still I hope that you will be induced to agree to it."

"Is it possible," said Mrs. Milford, "that these poor infants can have parents living, and that they can make up their minds to part with their innocent offspring, and resign them to the mercy of strangers?"

"It is stern necessity that compels them to do so, and, oh, you can but little imagine the heart-rending anguish they are now enduring, I beg of you, my dear friends, not to refuse my request, for I repeat, that the lives of these poor infants themselves, as well as others, may be sacrificed if they are not removed. In a few years their parents may be in a position to acknowledge them, and to release you from your burthen, and then how amply will you be rewarded, in the consciousness of having performed so generous, so humane, so noble an act, and in having been the cause of preventing ruin and misery to others."

"But who are the parents of these discarded children?" demanded Milford.

"They are of the highest rank," said the gentleman; "but more than that I cannot reveal."

"Are they born in wedlock?" asked Mrs. Milford.

"Pardon me, but I must decline to answer that question. I beg you not to keep me in suspense; but to tell me at once whether you are willing, on the terms I have mentioned, to become the protectors of the infant twin sisters?"

"And you even decline tò make us acquainted with your own name?" said Mr. Milford.

"You shall know that on a future occasion; at present, I have the most particular reasons for keeping it a secret."

"The task is a most responsible one," said Mrs. Milford; "and I am afraid to undertake it. Besides, should we not be guilty of a great crime in becoming parties to such a deception?"

"Oh, no," replied the gentleman; "do not suffer any such erroneous idea to trouble you. Instead of being guilty of a crime, you would be performing an act of mercy and benevolence. Decide at once, for the hour is now getting late; and we have some distance to go when we leave here."

A short silence ensued, during which time Milford and his wife consulted together in whispers. The mystery of the affair perplexed and rendered them doubtful; but the prospect of having once more a comfortable home, and being extricated from all those privations and anxieties they had for so many years endured, was a temptation which it was hard indeed to resist; they looked at the beautiful infants as they lay asleep on the sofa; and their scruples were at once overcome.

"And if we do consent to take charge of these lovely children," remarked Milford, "can you promise us that at some future period their real connexions shall be made known to us?"

"Unless unforeseen circumstances, involving their own safety and that of their relations, interpose to render further secrecy necessary, I assure you that they shall," answered the gentleman; "you will have the satisfaction of knowing that you have been the means of saving these two innocent sisters from a premature and unnatural fate; and also the honour, and perhaps the lives of more than one individual related to them. Oh, did you but know, or were I permitted to make you acquainted with the melancholy and peculiar circumstances in which their parents are situated, the excruciating anguish it causes them to be compelled to part with their offspring, you would not, I am certain, hesitate a moment."

"But must we bring them up in ignorance of their having no natural claim upon us?" demanded Mrs. Milford.

"Not without my permission," replied the gentleman; "or, unless the prospect of death should deprive them of your protection. As I have before promised you, ample provision shall be made for their support and your own."

"But what guarantee have we that those promises will be fulfilled, since we are ignorant of your name, and know not where to find you?" asked Milford.

"I can give you no other guarantee but my solemn promise. I repeat that they are children of the most distinguished individuals in the illustrious ranks of society; but more at present I am not permitted to reveal. Surely, Clavering, when fortune, a comfortable home, and the satisfaction of having saved the lives of the innocent are offered to you, it can require no second thought to a man of your good sense, to know which way to decide."

At this moment one of the infants, whom Mrs. Milford had been gazing at with the deepest sympathy, awoke; and a cherub smile greeted the attention of the fond parent and amiable wife, who had so long, and with so much patience, been enduring all the privations of poverty, and at once enlisted all her affections and generous solicitude. She felt as if she could love the poor unprotected little ones as fondly as if they had been her own; and turning to her husband, and fixing upon him such a look as only a mother can give, or a noble-hearted, generous-minded man can duly appreciate or understand, she directed his attention to the objects of her anxiety. Milford pressed her hand, and the expressive glance and action were not lost upon the gentleman, whose countenance brightened with hope and gratitude as he observed,—

"I see, my good and amiable friends, that I have no longer any occasion to plead to you in behalf of these two little unfortunates. I knew your kindness of heart too well to entertain much doubt that such would be the result of my negotiations with you; and I can never be sufficiently grateful to Providence, who caused me to meet you at so critical a moment, when my mind was distracted to know how to look after, or rather, how to provide for the safety of the tender ones. I presume I need not ask you, then, if you finally consent to my proposals?"

"May I ask, sir," said Milford, "if you are any relation to these children?"

"Excuse me, my friend," returned the unknown, with some confusion and emotion, "if I decline to answer that question; it is irrelevant at the present moment, and might be productive of serious consequences."

"But, if we take charge of these children, when shall we behold you again?"

"That I cannot say; but, depend upon it, I shall constantly have my eye upon them, and that I will faithfully perform my engagements."

"And this mansion," said Milford, once more looking around the magnificently furnished apartment with astonishment and admiration; "does it belong to you?"

The stranger shook his head, and his uneasiness and impatience increased at the questions which Milford put to him.

"Recollect," he remarked, "that time is waning apace; it is now not far from the hour of midnight, and, as I before observed, we have some distance to go before we reach the place of our destination, that is, if you agree to my propositions."

"Are the infants baptized?" asked Mrs. Milford.

"They are," replied the gentleman; "this," pointing to the one who had awoke, "is the eldest by one short half hour, and is named Augusta; her twin sister bears the name of Charlotte. I beg of you not to let us delay any longer."

"We will trust to your honour," said Milford, "and Heaven assist us as we faithfully, and from the purest motives, discharge the duty which has been so unexpectedly imposed upon us. We are ready at once to attend you."

"Oh, thanks, thanks, my good friends," said the gentleman, putting the pocket-book containing the money in Milford's hand. "Oh, did you but know the weight of care and misery you will be the means of removing from the connexions of these dear children by your compliance with my wishes, I am certain that greater satisfaction would be imparted to your minds than you have probably experienced for many years. You are now released from that abject state of misery and poverty in which I found you, and depend upon it, it will be no fault of mine if your future days are not those of prosperity and happiness. The female you lately saw will attend us to the house I have provided for you, in order to assist you in taking care of the infants, and I must request that you will put to her no questions on the journey. I have before told you that I have engaged a wet nurse (a very worthy and respectable young woman, I believe), whom you will find at the house; but she is perfectly ignorant of all the remarkable circumstances connected with these children; and, therefore, you will, I trust, see the prudence of not putting any useless interrogatories to her. Excuse me, I will be with you in a few moments, and then we will at once depart."

Thus saying, and without giving Milford or his wife time to make any reply, the gentleman quitted the room by the same door which he had done before, and which they once more heard him take care to lock after him.

Mr. and Mrs. Milford were so much confused and astonished by the extraordinary event, the mysterious character of the whole proceedings, and the change which a few short hours had wrought in their present circumstances and future prospects, that they could give expression to their feelings only by their looks. They gazed towards the infants, who were again both wrapped in a tranquil sleep, and their uncommon beauty excited their warmest sympathy and admiration; they felt as if they could already love them as if they had been their own children, and after what the stranger had stated regarding the peculiar dangers with which they were surrounded, they did not at all regret the responsible engagement into which they had entered.

They were aroused from the reflections to which this contemplation of their new charge naturally gave rise, by hearing a faint shriek, followed by heart-rending sobs, as if from some female in the greatest distress, and evidently proceeding from the apartment into which the gentleman had retired, and this was immediately succeeded by a second, as if of some dead weight falling upon the floor. All then was still, and Milford and his wife awaited in suspense and anxiety in the hope of obtaining some elucidation of the mystery. In a few moments the door was unlocked, and the stranger re-entered the apartment, followed by the female whom they had before seen, dressed for the journey.

The gentleman's countenance exhibited considerable emotion, and he sighed deeply as he turned to Milford and his wife, and in a tremulous voice demanded if they were ready. They answered in the affirmative, and the gentleman having motioned to the servant, she approached the sleeping infants, and wrapping a rich mantle around them, she took them in her arms.

"My dear friends," said the stranger, "ere we depart from this room, I must again request you to submit to have your eyes bandaged."

"What necessity, sir, can there be for all this secrecy?" demanded Milford.

"There is every necessity for it, I assure you," answered the stranger; "but it is useless to waste time in putting such questions; suffice it to say that I wish you not to have any recollection of this place again. Will you agree?"

"Well, as we have proceeded so far," replied Milford, "it would be useless for us to object; but I must say that I think there can be no absolute occasion to be so particular. We have sworn not to reveal the transactions of this night; we have also undertaken the serious and responsible charge you wished us to do; and surely there can be little harm in our being, at least, acquainted with the name and the locality of the place in which we have made so serious an engagement."

"Do not press the question, I beg of you; at some future period, it may,—nay, it will be answered."

"The magnificence of the place convinces me that it belongs to some most distinguished individuals."

"It does,—it does," impatiently and hurriedly returned the gentleman; "but let that acknowledgment satisfy you."

Milford and his wife cast another anxious and inquisitive glance around the splendidly furnished apartments, but made use of no further observation, and, submitting to have their eyes bandaged, as before, they were led from the room, and descending the stairs, were handed into the carriage waiting at the gates, which immediately was driven off at a most rapid pace, and it was evident was soon far away from the place where so singular a scene had lately been enacted. The handkerchiefs were then removed from the eyes of Mr. and Mrs. Milford, and the blinds of the carriage having been drawn up, they found themselves travelling along a dark and uneven road, with only a few straggling dwellings, of the humblest description, scattered on either side.

Milford had not the least recollection of the road; in fact, he did not think he had ever seen it before, and he knew it would be useless to put any questions to their mysterious companion after what he had said.

The stranger was sitting with his arms folded across his breast, and buried in profound meditation, and Milford could perceive, from the paleness of his countenance, that the thoughts which occupied his mind were of the most distracting kind.

The rain had ceased, but it was still very cold, dreary, and dark, and was calculated to have the most gloomy effect upon the spirits of the travellers. The infants still slept, and the female held them on her lap, and seemed to avoid notice as much as possible, no doubt acting from the strict instructions which had been given her by the gentleman. Milford was completely lost in amazement and perplexity, and so extraordinary were all the adventures of the night, that he could scarcely persuade himself that he was not labouring under the influence of a dream.

Mrs. Milford, who pressed her own child to her bosom, was overpowered by the unusual fatigue and excitement she had undergone, and gradually fell asleep, from which her husband did not attempt to disturb her, thinking it would refresh her, and enable her the better to enter into the business they might have to transact when they should arrive at the place of their destination.

The unknown frequently sighed deeply, and Milford was convinced that he was suffering much mental anguish. How anxious was he to penetrate into the mystery attached altogether to this affair! But he saw no chance of being able to do so; and he was compelled to leave it to the will of Providence, who, he had no doubt, would in time unravel all, and to his satisfaction.

After travelling along a narrow lane, they entered upon a more open and cheerful road; and Milford, looking from the window of the vehicle, could perceive the reflection of lights at a distance, which convinced him they were leaving the suburbs, and would soon enter the more busy scene of the metropolis. But still he had not the slightest recollection of the road, and was perfectly confident that he had never travelled it before.

"What road is this?" he at length inquired, breaking the silence; "and how long shall we be before we reach our journey's end?"

"A very short time will bring us to the place of our destination," answered the gentleman, starting from his reverie; "as for the name of this road, it is useless for you to know; and I must decline informing you."

" Surely, there is no occasion for all this precaution, sir."

" Indeed, but there is; and so you would say, if you knew all. No unfair advantage is intended to be taken of you, and therefore rest satisfied, and ask no further questions."

Milford looked doubtfully at him for a moment; but the stranger again relapsed into silence, and Milford saw it was utterly useless to put any further interrogatories to him.

At length they emerged from the road, and entering the town, after driving through several turnings, they entered a quiet and retired, but respectable little street, and the carriage finally stopped before the door of a small but extremely comfortable-looking house; and from one of the windows of the upstairs room a light glimmered, showing that the place was not only inhabited, but that, notwithstanding the lateness of the hour (for it was now past one o'clock), some of the inmates had not yet retired to rest.

" Is this the house?" eagerly asked Milford.

" This is the house I have engaged for you," answered the gentleman; " it is indeed yours, and you will find it very different to the wretched place you have for some time past been residing in."

Milford was lost in amazement and curiosity, and the astonishment and perplexity of his wife, who had now awoke, were equal to his own. They had not much time, however, given them for reflection, for the driver of the vehicle had alighted from his box, and knocked at the door, which was opened by a decent-looking young woman, with a light in her hand, and who looked at the carriage with evident anxiety.

The gentleman descended from the carriage first, desiring Mr. and Mrs. Milford to remain there for a minute or two. He then conversed a short time with the female, who came to the vehicle, and received one of the sleeping infants, which she kissed affection-ately. The female who had come with them from the mansion took the other and alighted, and Milford and his wife following, they entered the house.

CHAPTER III.

THE NEW HABITATION.—THE DEPARTURE OF THE STRANGER.—THE MYSTERY INCREASES.

THEY entered a parlour, in which a cheerful fire was burning, and the furniture of which was entirely new, and of the most neat and useful description. Refreshments were spread upon the table, and it was quite evident that every preparation had been made for their comfortable reception. So striking was the contrast it presented to that wretched, tottering hovel they had recently quitted, that Mrs. Milford and her husband were completely overpowered.

The gentleman, having desired the two females with the infants to retire till he should send for them again, they left the room, and he then sank on a seat, and, covering his face with his hands, remained for a few seconds wholly absorbed in thought. At length, however, he looked up, and addressing Milford and his wife, said:—

" My good friends, we have now arrived at our journey's end; this is your future home, if you think proper to accept of it; and here you may enjoy all those comforts of which you have been for so many years deprived. This has been a night of severe trial to me; and on you depends much more,—the happiness, the safety, of many individuals, but more especially that of the two sweet infants committed to your care. Tell me once more, I solemnly adjure you, are you resolved faithfully to fulfil the promises you have made to me?"

" As you keep your word, sir, so will we ours," answered Milford. You are not ignorant of our characters, and years of poverty and cruel suffering have wrought no change in them."

" I believe you, Clavering," said the gentleman, " or I would not have entrusted to you so precious a charge."

" We will watch over them and protect them with the same affectionate attention as if they were our own offspring."

" Guard them as narrowly as you would your own lives," said the stranger, vehe-mently; " for, oh! you can little imagine how much depends on their safety. Let not a word escape your lips to any one respecting the events of this night, or the consequences will be terrible."

THE ROYAL TWINS;

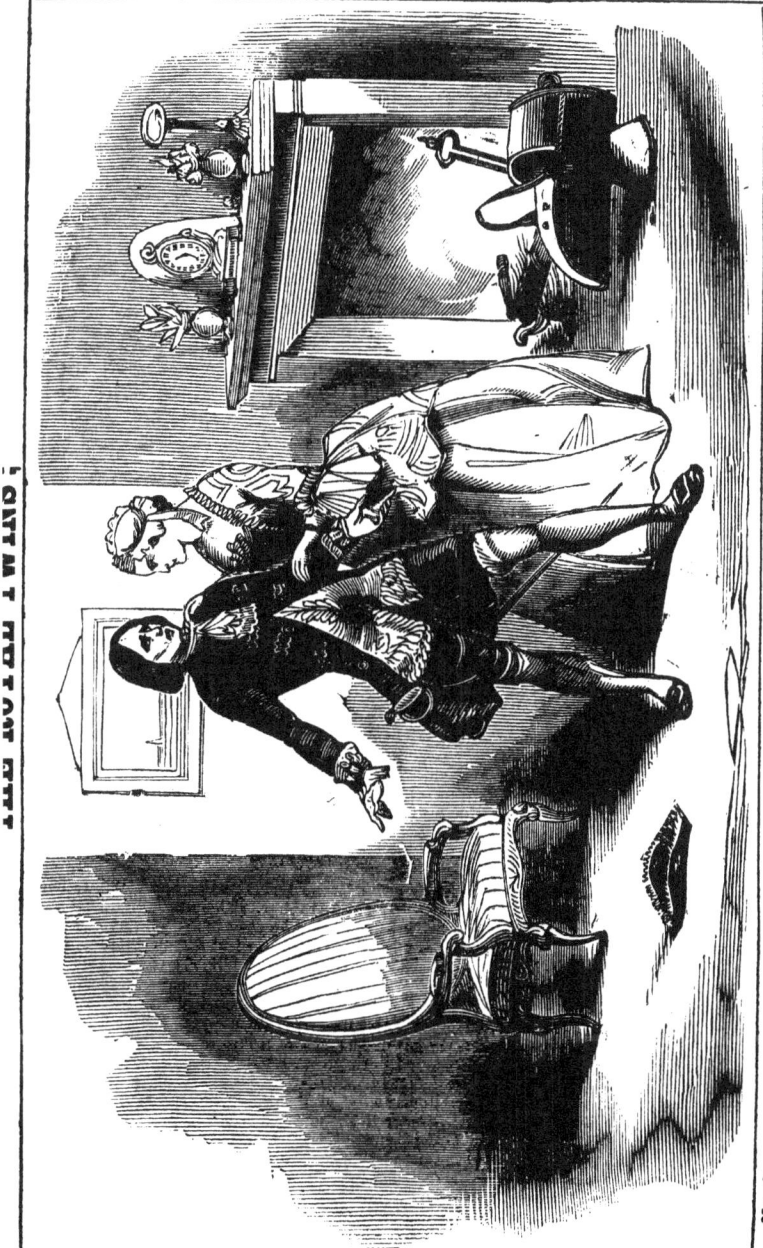

OR, THE SISTERS OF MYSTERY.

No. 3.

"We have promised,—we have sworn," said Milford, "and we will not break our oath."

"Then may Heaven reward you as you faithfully perform the important and sacred task you have undertaken. I must now bid you farewell. The time may come when I may deem it no longer necessary to conceal my real name and rank from you, or those of the parents of the infant sisters, Augusta and Charlotte; but until then you must remain content, and forbear to make inquiries that might lead to unspeakable danger."

"But when shall we behold you again?" demanded Milford.

"I have before told you that it is impossible for me to answer that question."

"But it is absolutely necessary that we should know where to find you, in case anything should happen upon which we ought to consult you."

"That I must also decline to give you any information upon; but rest assured that I shall be ever on the alert, and shall know all that happens to you and the children. The money shall be regularly transmitted to you at the periods I have promised; and, should I see it necessary, further assistance shall be afforded. Let the education of these two children be respectable, but humble; let them not encourage any ambitious hopes, and learn them to despise all the empty and glittering show of pride and ostentation, and may they be valued only for their own intrinsic virtues."

"Your instructions shall be strictly adhered to, sir," said Milford.

"I am satisfied," said the gentleman. "The servant I have engaged for you as wet nurse, it is useless for you to question; for she is not acquainted with anything connected with this secret. She was hired by a friend of mine, and has been made to suppose that the children are those of a deceased sister of yours, who was formerly in my service, and in consequence of which I have interested myself in your favour. Of course, I need not impress upon you the necessity of your being in the same story. She is also ignorant of my name. I have received the highest character with her, and I have no doubt you will find her every way agreeable and useful."

"Has she a husband living?" asked Mrs. Milford.

"Yes," answered the gentleman; "but he is a seaman, and his ship has just sailed. She has a young child at present at the breast, and therefore she is in every way qualified for the situation. And now, my dear friends, I must leave you, for the hour is very late, and I have far to go. You also need repose; and may the morning find you in a fit state of mind to enter with spirit upon your important task. As you hope for happiness yourselves, oh! guard, I beseech you,—watch, with affectionate attention and solicitude, the two innocent children committed to your care."

He arose from his seat as he thus spoke, and the females were again summoned to the room. With the deepest emotion he kissed the infant twins, and then once more pressing the hands of Milford and his wife, he beckoned to the woman who had accompanied them from the mansion to follow him; and before they had recovered from their confusion and astonishment, he had retired from the house, and they heard the carriage roll hastily away.

Mrs. Morton, which was the woman's name, seemed to eye the mean and scanty clothing of Milford and his wife with no little surprise; but, at length, she respectfully interrupted the silence by desiring to know whether they had not better partake of some refreshment, and then retire to rest, as they must be fatigued with their journey, and the hour was very late. The question aroused them from their lethargy of thought, and they gazed at Mrs. Morton with some degree of bewilderment, and scarcely knew what answer to make. They remembered the instructions the gentleman had given them, and knew they must use caution; otherwise, they would betray themselves.

"What is the name of this street, my good woman?" at length asked Milford.

Mrs. Morton informed him, and he found it was situated in the neighbourhood of Tottenham-court-road (at that time little more than a village), and he put no further questions to her on that subject, remembering the caution of the unknown, and fearful that he should excite some suspicion. Mrs. Morton was a most prepossessing woman both in her appearance and manners, and Milford and his wife at once became as familiar with her as if they had been on the most intimate terms for years.

"You had better partake of some refreshment," she observed, "and then I will show you to the chamber prepared for your reception, which I hope will meet your satisfaction. You are too much fatigued to have the charge of these sweet little cherubs to-night, so if it please you I will take them to my room where my own child is sleeping. They do not seem likely to cause much disturbance to any one to-night. Bless them, they are lovely children, and no doubt, as the orphan offspring of a relation so dear to you, you must feel the greatest anxiety towards them."

Mrs. Milford felt greatly confused at the remarks of Mrs. Morton, and the subterfuge they were compelled to practise; but her husband had more presence of mind, and replied,—

"Yes, Mrs. Morton, it is only natural to suppose that we should feel the greatest anxiety for these dear children, especially under the peculiar circumstances in which they have, through the demise of my dear sister, been placed under our protection. But more we cannot explain. No doubt you think it strange that we should be introduced to you in such an extraordinary manner; but that subject we must beg leave to decline entering upon for the present, at any rate."

"Sir," said Mrs. Morton, "that is no business of mine, and I have no wish to be inquisitive; I am satisfied with my engagement, and I trust that you will find me not unworthy of your friendship. But, will you not partake of some refreshment?"

"We will do so," said Milford, "while you are gone to place these dear infants to rest; and, when you return, we shall be quite ready to retire to rest, for indeed the fatigues of this night have been very great."

Mrs. Morton made no further observation, and Milford and his wife having tenderly kissed the unknown infants, who had been committed to their care in such a remarkable manner, the former retired with them from the room.

Mr. and Mrs. Milford sat in silence for some few seconds, and gazed around the room. The whole events of the last few hours were of that unusual description, that they completely bewildered them, and they could scarcely bring themselves to believe in their reality. They partook slightly of the repast which had been provided for them, and then Mr. Milford observed,—

"What an extraordinary adventure is this, my dear James; it has all the character of the wildest romance about it; but a few hours since, and we were in the most awful state of penury and distress, and it was only the anxiety we felt for the dear child at my bosom that made us cling to life; but now we find ourselves transported to a comfortable home, and in the possession of a fortune. Who this gentleman can be, and how he is connected with the infants, I cannot imagine; but it is quite evident, both from his observations, and all the circumstances, that they are the offspring of some most distinguished individuals. I almost trembled at the great responsibility we have taken upon ourselves."

"The responsibility certainly is great, Mary," replied her husband; "but it is useless to regret it now; we have undertaken the task, and we must endeavour to perform it to the best of our abilities."

"And, perhaps, we may never behold the gentleman again, or have an opportunity of discovering to whom the children belong. Oh, we were, indeed, wrong in taking them under our charge on such terms."

"Perhaps we were so; but we must make the best of it: trust to providence, who, no doubt, will in due course of time unravel this strange mystery. Was it possible that we could resist the appeal of this strange gentleman, when he so solemnly assured us that, unless we took them under our protection, the lives of these poor little innocents, and of others, would almost inevitably be sacrificed?"

"Oh, no," replied Mrs. Milford; "and yet the gentleman, from whom we received them, might surely have confided to us his name."

"Why, it would certainly have been more satisfactory had he have done so," said Mr. Milford; "but I feel certain that he is a person of distinction, and, as we have proceeded so far, we must trust to him as a man of honour."

"Heaven send, for these poor children's sake, my husband, that we may not be deceived; but is it not also remarkable, that, in all his visits to your grandfather, and the familiar terms upon which he was with every one, we could never discover his name or rank?"

"It is," coincided Milford; "but although it is certain that my aged relative was intimately acquainted with him, and was the confidant of all his secrets, he never addressed him by any other title than 'friend,' and that with extreme deference, as if he was fearful of taking too great a liberty; and you also know, Mary, that we could not—any of his friends and connections could not offend the old gentleman more than by questioning him upon the subject."

"True," said Mrs. Milford; "and what their transactions were together seem likely for ever to remain a mystery, as well as the perpetrator of the horrible crime by which your grandfather lost his life. You remember the painful anxiety the unknown gentleman evinced on that occasion, and the strange questions he put?"

"Remember it," said Milford; "oh, can I ever forget that awful night? Heaven pardon me if I judge any one wrongly, but there is one whom I must ever suspect to be the cowardly and monstrous assassin of my venerable relative."

"Ah, your uncle; he——"

"Hush!" interrupted Milford; "you are right in your suppositions, my dear Mary, but at present it would not be prudent to venture to whisper such a thing. Oh, God! what terrible reasons have I not to shudder even at the mention of the name of Ralph Clavering! It was his vices, temptations, and villany that brought my parents to a dreadful and untimely death. It was he who deprived us of fortune, my poor wife, and drove us into the most abject and degrading misery and want; compelled us to herd with wretches of the vilest character, and cast us forth as beggars upon the wide world. But I dare not trust myself any longer with this fearful subject. Heaven grant that our miseries are now at an end, and that, as our motives are dictated by rectitude and humanity, so may we be rewarded."

"Amen!" devoutly responded Mrs. Milford; "but," she added, "I cannot forget the mansion to which we were taken to-night. The costliness of the furniture, the noble portraits that decorated the room, and the royal arms so conspicuously displayed on the escutcheon, all afford matter for wonder and speculation. Certainly, that mansion must be the residence of some illustrious individual, and adds to the mystery of this most perplexing and extraordinary business."

Before Milford could make any reply, Mrs. Morton re-entered the room, and the expression of her countenance betrayed wonder and excitement.

"Pardon me," she said, "I wish not to appear curious or impertinent, but I am satisfied that yourselves and your sister must have moved in a most distinguished sphere of life, from what I have within the last few minutes discovered."

Milford and his wife started, and could not very well conceal their confusion.

"What mean you, my good friend?" said Milford, at last, as composedly as he could.

"I never beheld more costly clothing than that of the dear little infants," said Mrs Morton; "and I could not but look at it for some time in surprise and admiration."

Mr. Milford exchanged a significant glance with his wife, and then said,—

"True, true; the clothing of the children presents a strange contrast to the meanness of that of me and my wife, which arises from circumstances which it is not necessary to explain."

"I trust that I have not offended, sir," said Mrs. Morton. "I have no wish at all to appear inquisitive; I am engaged to perform a certain duty, which I hope to be enabled to do to your satisfaction; but, as I found this suspended from one of the infant's necks, and it seems of great value, I thought it best to place it in your hands."

As she said this, she delivered a brilliant gold locket, set round with diamonds, to Milford, who, together with his wife, started; but, knowing the necessity of it, they conquered their astonishment and confusion as much as they could, and Mr. Milford observed,—

"This is indeed a treasure, Mrs. Morton, that, owing to peculiar circumstances, we have a right to set the highest value upon. I am obliged to you for your attention, and perhaps, at some future period, you may be better acquainted with our singular history. We will now, if you please, retire to rest."

Milford carefully put the locket in his pocket, and taking the arm of his wife, they followed Mrs. Morton out of the room, and a short time afterwards were introduced to their chamber. Mrs. Milford placed her sleeping boy in a little cot by the side of the bed, and Mrs. Morton, having respectfully bade them good night, retired.

Milford and his wife gazed around the chamber with feelings which may readily be imagined, when the contrast it, like the other apartment they had just quitted, presented to their recent desolate and miserable abode, is taken into consideration. Mrs. Milford could not refrain from tears, and her husband, pressing her to his bosom, and raising his eyes gratefully towards Heaven, exclaimed,—

"Thank Thee, all bountiful giver of all good, for rescuing us from that starvation and poverty with which it has been thy will so long to visit us, and guide and protect us, I beseech thee, in the way we should act under the peculiar circumstances in which we are at present placed."

Nothing could be more neat and tasteful than the manner in which the chamber was furnished; every article was new that it contained, and it was quite evident that no expense had been spared. They found a wardrobe well stocked with male and female apparel, such as would become the most respectable classes of society to wear, with several suits for children of various ages; in fact, the mysterious unknown seemed to have not lost sight of the least thing that would be necessary for their use and comfort.

"How wonderful is all this," remarked Mrs. Milford; "and how powerful and important must be the motives of the party who has thus so generously and expeditiously made his arrangements. Oh, my husband, what a change is this from our late wretched circumstances! How many years it is since we had a comfortable roof to shelter us. But that locket!"

Milford took it from his pocket, and they were completely dazzled by its brilliancy and evident value, but more especially when they beheld the royal arms engraven in the most chaste and finished manner at the back.

Milford opened it, and the miniature of a lady, exquisitely painted on ivory, was then revealed. The countenance was dignified, and remarkably handsome, but there was an expression of melancholy about the eyes, which was peculiarly and painfully impressive. The miniature seemed to represent a female apparently about twenty years of age.

Milford gazed at it with feelings of astonishment and admiration, and neither of them, for a few minutes, had the power to speak.

"This miniature doubtless represents the mother of our tender charge," at length, observed Milford; "it is fortunate that it has been left with them, and has probably been done so in mistake. It may some time or other lead to a discovery; however, it is quite evident, as the gentleman informed us, that they are the children of parents in the most distinguished ranks of society. What extraordinary circumstances can have been the cause of their being obliged to part with them?"

"And then the royal arms engraven on the back of the locket," said Mrs. Milford. "What can be the meaning of that?"

"I am lost in bewilderment," replied Milford; "and am more than ever impressed with the importance of the task we have undertaken. We must take especial care of this locket, for there is no knowing what extraordinary discoveries it may be productive of."

"Very true," observed Mrs. Milford; "but I think, at the same time, it would be only prudent that we should not let it be known to the children themselves unless circumstances may seem to sanction such a disclosure."

"A prudent suggestion," said her husband; "but come, my Mary, let us retire to rest, for I fear that the unusual fatigue and excitement you have, on this eventful night, undergone, may have injurious effects on your health."

Mr. Milford carefully locked the valuable locket in a chest which stood in one corner of the chamber, and then having offered up their prayers to Heaven, and supplicated its guidance in their future conduct, they sought their pillow; but notwithstanding their extreme weariness, so altered was their situation, and so many were the thoughts that crowded upon their minds, that it was some time ere sleep descended upon their eye-lids, and it was then only to dream of the wonderful and almost incredible adventures of the night, a night which formed the most remarkable epoch in their otherwise eventful lives, and the result of which it was impossible for them to foretel, or in the slightest way to conceive.

The morning dawned; they awoke, and opening their eyes, gazed around them in amazement. Although the events of the previous night were, of course, vividly stamped upon their memory, they could scarcely persuade themselves that it was not all a dream; and they could with difficulty imagine where they were, or by what means they had come there. The whole facts, however, quickly rushed upon their memory; and they arose from their couch, anxious again to behold the infants who had been entrusted to their future care in so mysterious a manner.

They selected becoming clothes from the wardrobe, in which they attired themselves; and so great was the alteration made in their present appearance, that it would have been impossible for any of their late wretched companions to have recognized them.

As Mrs. Milford gazed upon her husband, who had suffered so much, and borne it all with such manly fortitude and resignation, she could not refrain from tears. Milford pressed her to his heart with all the affection of first love.

"Oh, my husband!" exclaimed Mrs. Milford; "can this be real? Are we no longer in that miserable state that we were yesterday, when gaunt hunger hourly stared us in the face, and enduring the scorn and insults of the multitudes, we dragged on a torturing existence only from the niggardly charity of strangers. Has fortune once more smiled upon us, and shall we be happy?"

"I trust in Heaven, Mary, that we shall," answered Milford; "and, therefore, let us endeavour to hope for the best. We have at present every means of comfort; and if the stranger fulfils his promise, we shall never know the tortures of poverty again."

"But should he fail," said Mrs. Milford, "even the money he has advanced to us, although it is a large sum, will soon be exhausted; and then what would become of us, with such an increase to our family?"

"Do not anticipate any such evil, Mary," remarked her husband; "for I do not think that it is likely to take place. I place every confidence in the promises of the gentleman; and the emotion he evinced on leaving us, and parting with his children, convinces me that he could never, by deceiving us, leave them to the misery which must be consequent on his neglect. God knows the purity of our motives, and will protect us through our arduous task. I already feel a most uncommon interest in the fate of these two innocent babes, and am resolved to cherish and love them the same as if they were my own. In this respect, the same as in all others, the unknown shall find me faithfully adhere to the promise I made him; and I know that you, my dear wife, will need no example on my part to urge you to do the same."

"Indeed, I will not," said Mrs. Milford; "all a mother's attention, assiduous care, and affection, they shall receive from me; but still I cannot help thinking that the gentleman need not have been so fearful of confiding more to us than he did. Some accident might befal him; life is uncertain, and ignorant as we are of anything that might lead to a discovery of the children's connexions, we should be left in a dilemma of the most awkward and perplexing description."

"No doubt the gentleman has made every necessary provision in case of that," returned Milford; "in fact, from the observations he made use of, we have a right to conclude he has; and if the parents of these children are as deeply afflicted at being obliged to part with them as he has represented them to be, they would, at every risk, take the earliest opportunity of communicating with us. But come, my dear Mary, compose yourself as much as possible, and let us go below, for I can already hear Mrs. Morton stirring; and I am anxious again to behold the little unconscious unfortunates, who, in so remarkable a manner, have been consigned to our protection."

Mrs. Milford made no further observation, and they descended to the parlour, where they found Mrs. Morton, who had already prepared the breakfast.

She seemed struck by the alteration in their personal appearance; and greeted them very respectfully, trusting that they had rested well, and were recovered from the fatigue of the previous night. Milford and his wife returned a suitable reply; and they then directed their attention to the two children, who, with the infant boy of Mrs. Morton, were reclining on the sofa. They were more forcibly struck with their extreme beauty than they had ever been when they first beheld them; and they could not help both remarking to themselves, notwithstanding they were so young, that they imagined their features bore a most extraordinary resemblance to those of the lady delineated in the miniature; and who there could be very little doubt was their mother.

Mrs. Milford kissed the little strangers with the greatest affection, and the tear of sympathy started to her eyes.

"They are the loveliest children I ever saw," remarked Mrs. Morton; "and——"

She was about to add some opinion as to the nobleness of their birth, but perceiving the agitation of Mr. and Mrs. Milford, she checked herself, and they took their seats at the breakfast table.

There was very little conversation during the repast, and it was scarcely over when there was a knock at the street door, and a young woman of respectable appearance was ushered into the room, and presented Mr. Milford with a note, which, on opening, he found to contain the following words:—

" The bearer of this, Martha Alvin, is engaged to assist in the nursing of the children entrusted to your care. Her wages will be regularly remitted to you through an agent, and she fully understands the terms upon which she is hired. I need not remind you that the utmost secrecy must also be maintained towards her.

"Your Friend."

Mr. Milford shewed this letter to his wife, who could but feel satisfied with the arrangement which the gentleman had made, and, prepossessed with the appearance of Martha, it needed but few words to settle the business, and she immediately entered upon her duties.

Leaving Mrs. Morton and Martha to attend to the children, Mr. and Mrs. Milford retired from the room, not only with the intention of inspecting their new dwelling, but also to give vent to their feelings unobserved. It may easily be imagined that they were of the most extraordinary kind, but they could not but acknowledge that the gentleman so far had acted in every way to inspire them with confidence.

In going over the different apartments, they could not but admire the taste and even elegance with which they were furnished ; but the room which was fitted up as a drawing-room, more particularly arrested their attention. It was richly carpeted, contained a handsome piano, and everything else in strict keeping. But that which immediately attracted their whole notice, was the full-length portrait of a lady, painted in the first style of art, and in the features of which they instantly recognised the same likeness as that pourtrayed in the locket. The figure was graceful and majestic in the extreme, and the dress was of the most elegant description, which shewed that the lady represented was one of the most distinguished rank. The eyes bore the same melancholy expression that Milford and his wife had noticed in the miniature, and could not fail to excite a feeling of sympathy in the breast of the beholder for the lovely original.

Mr. and Mrs. Milford gazed at this portrait with the deepest interest ; indeed, it was some time before they could remove their eyes from it, and then Mrs. Milford, turning to her husband, said,—

" What a lovely woman does this portrait represent ; what consummate skill has the artist displayed ! One might almost imagine that the canvas breathed with life, and that we could hear the mournful sigh, proceeding from secret sorrow, issuing from the heart. It is no common individual that is depictured here. Majesty seems enthroned upon her brow, and to stamp the graces of her elegant form. Oh, who is the original ?"

" It is indeed a noble painting," said Milford ; " and I can entertain no doubt that it represents the mother of the children entrusted to us. Entertaining that opinion, and hoping that, together with the locket, it will be the means, at some future time, if the stranger does not think proper to reveal the secret, or should neglect to fulfil the promises he has made to us, of leading to some discovery, I shall never gaze upon this portrait except with feelings of the deepest interest. Our prospects at present, my dear Mary, are most promising : the change, however, is so sudden, that I must confess that it almost overpowers me. Heaven send that we may never again have to endure that misery it has been our lot for so many years to undergo."

" Oh ! James," said Mrs. Milford, again looking with admiring eyes around the room, " this is indeed a happy change, and Heaven grant that it is destined to last. We never, from any misconduct of our own, deserved the severe destiny that attended us."

" True, my Mary, but it was the will of Providence thus to visit us, and we must not murmur at its decrees. I regret that the gentleman should consider it necessary to maintain so much mystery as regards the fair little twins ; but, nevertheless, I trust that ultimately everything will be satisfactorily explained ; and I am determined to do my duty towards them ; and I know that you, my dear wife, will do the same, and guard them from danger and the temptations of the world, with the same watchful care and solicitude as if they were our own offspring."

" Oh, yes, James," replied Mrs. Milford, " I will indeed do all that you expect me. I will, if it pleases Heaven to spare my life, be the same affectionate mother to them as to my own dear child. I need not, I am certain, assure you, that their singular fate, and the extraordinary manner in which they have been placed under our protection, has excited my deepest interest and sympathy."

" I know it has, Mary, and depend upon it Heaven will amply reward us for all the care we may take of these children of misfortune. But I need not tell you that we must act with the greatest caution as regards Mrs. Morton and Martha, for should we by any inadvertency betray the real facts of the case, we know not how fatal the consequence[s] might be to those whom we have so solemnly promised to protect."

" You will find that I will ever be on my guard, James," returned his wife ; " I am fully aware of the necessity of acting in the way you have pointed out."

They now left the apartment, and after having inspected the other rooms, which from their commodiousness, and the taste and neatness with which they were furnished, equally excited their admiration, they returned to the one in which they had left Mrs. Morton and Martha, whom they found attending to the children.

The day passed away without anything particular occurring ; it was the happiest one that Mr. Milford and his wife had experienced for many, many years, and when they reflected upon their late wretched situation, the dreadful sufferings and privations they had been subjected to, they wondered how they had been able to bear up against them, and they could never be sufficiently grateful for the change ; and when at night they retired to their chamber, they poured forth the fervent feelings of their hearts to the most bountiful giver of all good, and earnestly supplicated His future protection.

CHAPTER IV.

REMINISCENCES OF THE PAST.—THE VICTIM OF DISSIPATION.—THE MURDER AND SUICIDE.—THE ORPHAN.

IT is now necessary, for the proper development of our plot, that we should refer back to events that took place several years previous to that epoch at which we have commenced our narrative.

At the period to which we are now adverting, there stood at the end of a pretty little hamlet, only a few miles from London, a small house of clean and neat appearance, which was the residence of Vivian Clavering, his wife Clemence, and their only child, a boy about four years of age.

Vivian Clavering was the ruin of a once handsome man, and at that time was not more than six-and-twenty, although, from habits of dissipation, he had more the appearance of a man of forty. His manners, however, still betokened him to have received the education of a gentleman, and no one could gaze upon him without feeling the deepest regret that a man so gifted by nature should have suffered himself to be led into those scenes of vice, folly, and extravagance which never fail to bring shame, misery, and ruin upon their unhappy votaries.

Mrs. Clavering was a bright, yet melancholy example of a suffering, patient, devoted, and affectionate wife. She was very beautiful, but constant care had dimmed the brilliancy of her eyes, banished the roses from her cheeks, and attenuated her graceful form ; and the troubles which she had so unmeritedly experienced from the misconduct of her husband had crushed her spirits, once so buoyant and playful, and rendered her sad and wretched.

Clemence Westbury had in early childhood been deprived of her parents, and was brought up under the protection of a maiden aunt, whose fortune was but small, but still sufficient to keep her comfortable, and she bestowed every care and affection upon her orphan niece, who well repaid her kindness, and looked up to her with the same veneration as if she had been her mother.

The house in which they resided was situated near the mansion of Mr. Clavering, a retired Indian merchant, and the father of Vivian.

Mr. Clavering was a widower, and his only children were two sons, of whom Vivian was the youngest. He was a gentleman who possessed many amiable qualities, with no small admixture of weaknesses, to call them by the mildest name. One of those was strongly evinced in the favouritism he ever showed towards his eldest son; not that he neglected Vivian, on the contrary he ever did a father's duty towards him, but while he was completely blinded to the faults of the former (and he early displayed some very glaring and dangerous ones, which needed the utmost parental care to destroy in their infancy), the most trivial error of the latter was swelled into offences of the greatest magnitude, and visited with the most unmerited severity. But in spite of this Vivian never murmured or attempted to act in disobedience to his father's will, while his brother, encouraged in every folly, grew up vicious, passionate, crafty, and revengeful.

THE ROYAL TWINS;

No. 4.

OR, THE SISTERS OF MYSTERY.

Vivian ever behaved towards him with the most brotherly affection, and although of course he could not be blind to the unjust partiality with which his father viewed him, he never evinced the least jealousy towards him, nor uttered the slightest allusion to him on the subject. Andrew Clavering affected to return the affection of his brother with equal warmth, but it needed no very penetrating eye to discover his insincerity. In fact, he hated Vivian in his heart, for, avaricious in the extreme, he could not bear the idea of his being a sharer in the fortune of their father, and would have been glad had he died in his infancy, and he yet hoped that something would occur to remove this detested obstacle to the gratification of his ambition.

Years passed away, and the brothers had arrived at manhood. Vivian had frequently been the companion and play-fellow of Clemence Westbury in childhood, and an attachment sprang up between them, which increasing years strengthened into a mutual affection.

This was another cause of jealousy to Andrew Clavering; the charms of Clemence had excited in his breast a dishonourable passion towards her, and the love she evinced towards his brother was perfect wormwood to him, and this ill-feeling was increased when he observed that his father (notwithstanding the disparity of their circumstances) showed every encouragement to their addresses, and when Vivian supplicated his consent to make Clemence his wife, he granted it without a moment's hesitation.

Vivian and Clemence were married, and from that day Andrew Clavering determined by the most artful means to effect the ruin of them both. How well, how fatally he succeeded will be presently shown.

Mr. Clavering advanced Vivian a large sum of money on his marriage, and provided him with a suitable establishment, and for some time the happiness of Vivian and his beauteous Clemence remained uninterrupted; but Andrew only waited a fitting opportunity to put his evil designs into execution; and it was not long ere one presented itself.

One child blessed the union of Vivian and his wife, and every day they looked forward with the brightest hopes to an increase of felicity. Andrew was a constant visitor to their house, and affected the greatest friendship towards them, but Mrs. Clavering always looked upon him with suspicion, and never felt easy in his society. She was certain that he bore her husband no good will at heart, and could not help entertaining some strange apprehensions towards him for which she was herself at a loss to account.

They had now been married about eighteen months, and Andrew Clavering became more frequent than ever in his visits, and introduced to them two or three of his most particular friends (as he denominated them), men of the world and excellent fellows, whose society he hoped would tend to enliven them, and cause them to pass many a happy hour.

The manners of these gentlemen were anything but pleasing to Mrs. Clavering, and they were far from being the individuals she would herself have chosen to be the companions of her husband, but, of course, as the friends of her brother-in-law, she was compelled to receive them with becoming courtesy, and she was pained to see that her husband was evidently prepossessed in their favour, and entered into the gaiety of their conversation (which sometimes bordered upon levity) with uncommon spirit and vivacity. Andrew also observed this with secret exultation, and anticipated the complete success of his villanous designs.

It is perhaps unnecessary to describe to the reader the real characters of these gentlemen; they were in fact men of the most reckless and dissipated character; votaries of every fashionable vice and profligacy; men who, having squandered away their own fortunes, preyed upon those of their unhappy dupes, when once led into their meshes, at the gambling table, and spread ruin and misery around them. Many were the once happy homes they had destroyed for ever—many a once honourable and amiable man whom they had reduced to poverty, wretchedness, and crime, while they themselves escaped with impunity, and laughed in triumph at the desolation they had spread around. Such were the men whom the designing Andrew had introduced to his unfortunate brother, such the men whom he had determined should be the means of working his destruction.

And well did they play their part, and Vivian became completely infatuated with them. In vain his wife ventured to express her suspicions of their real characters, and to caution him against them; he was blind to their faults, and gently chided his wife for imbibing what he believed to be such an ungenerous and unjust impression against them, and continued always to receive them as his most welcome guests. Andrew saw his triumph, and it emboldened him to proceed with redoubled boldness.

After much pressing and invitation, Vivian was at length persuaded to join their convivial parties away from home. Fatal weakness; what fears, what regret, what secret anguish and anxiety did it cause his gentle wife. And too soon she had ample reason for these cares and apprehensions. Vivian, who before this unfortunate acquaintance was formed, was seldom away from his domestic hearth, and was then accompanied on most occasions by his wife, was now frequently away for many hours together, and sometimes did not return home until long after the hour of midnight, and then his countenance too plainly betrayed the extravagant nature of the carousals he had indulged in.

How shocked was Mrs. Clemence at this melancholy change, and with what passionate feeling did she remonstrate with her husband upon his conduct, and implore him to abandon such dangerous companions ere it was too late ; he listened to her with impatience, and, on two or three occasions, he even replied to her with a degree of asperity that she could not have believed him capable of using towards her.

The villains had regularly entrapped him ; and Vivian Clavering, who was lately so prudent and temperate, was now the thoughtless and giddy votary of the bottle and the gaming-table. For some time they allowed him to be successful, and his good fortune, as he considered it to be, urged him on to greater extravagance ; he staked higher, and then the tide of affairs was changed, and he seldom left the company of his quondam friends a single night without being the loser of a large sum.

Andrew Cleverling now seldom made one of the party, for he had gained his point ; he had placed his unfortunate brother in the certain way to ruin, and he considered that it would not be prudent for him to be seen any longer in it. He placed every confidence in the men whom he had set to ensnare Vivian, and he had no doubt that they would not stop until they had succeeded in reducing him to beggary. But Andrew was at work to complete his ruin another way; he did not fail to represent everything to his father in the worst light, and Mr. Clavering was too ready to listen to his exaggerations, and to become more prejudiced against the deluded Vivian ; but instead of acting a father's part by remonstrating with, and advising him on his folly, he resolved to act as he thought proper, until useful experience should shew him the fatal consequences of his misconduct. Had he interposed at that time, as he should have done, the nefarious plans of Andrew would have been defeated, and Vivian saved from ruin.

In this manner six months elapsed, six months of such misery and anxiety to Mrs. Clavering, as she had never expected to experience ; and still Vivian continued to be the victim of the designing villains to whom he had been so unfortunately introduced. He seldom returned home unless he was under the influence of wine, and then his temper was to her testy and quarrelsome, and he was deaf to all her gentle expostulations. She could see plain enough that there was nothing but ruin before them, and she gave herself up to complete despair. She could not have believed it possible that ever so fearful a change could have been wrought in so short a time, in one who was before so remarkable for every manly virtue. Accursed vice! how quick and terrible are your results to those who by the tempter are led astray from the paths of rectitude!

At length the evil hour came. The blade was struck! The veil was drawn from before the eyes of the unfortunate Vivian when it was too late, and he found himself ruined! The wretches had completed their task, and swindled him out of every penny he possessed in the world.

What a terrible, what an affecting scene took place between Vivian and his wife, when he returned home in a state bordering upon distraction, and revealed to her the dreadful truth. He accused himself of being a heartless villain, in madly persisting in bringing ruin and misery upon the head of that devoted affectionate wife, whom he had sworn at the altar to love and cherish, and it was some time ere he was restored to anything like a degree of composure.

The heart of Clemence was full to bursting; but she offered not a word of reproach ; but on the contrary, she threw her arms around the neck of her husband, and endeavoured to pacify him by the gentlest words.

What a terrible night of suffering was that to them both! It would have been madness to have thought about sleep ; and they did not even seek their couch, but sat up all the dreary hours of night, Vivian upbraiding himself in the bitterest terms for the crime of which he had been guilty, and his affectionate partner exerting all her eloquence to soothe him, and to lead him to hope that something might yet be done to save them from the ruin which at present stared them in the face.

Vivian shook his head in despair.

"What a consummate fool, as well as a villain, have I been," he exclaimed, "to suffer myself to be so duped! Oh, why did I not listen to your advice, my Clemence! then should I be snatched from this terrible abyss. How shall I ever be able to meet my father? How can I endure his reproaches; and what pity can I expect from him? He will spurn me from him, and discard me for ever."

"Oh, no, my dear husband," said Mrs. Clavering; "I cannot, I will not believe that your father will ever act with such severity; since you have never before committed yourself, never given him cause to visit you with his displeasure. I will myself plead to him for his forgiveness; and I feel convinced that he will yield to my supplications, and once more restore you to happiness, confident that you will never again so commit yourself."

"Oh, Clemence, I have not deserved this kindness," said her husband; "on the contrary, all that I ought to expect from you are the bitterest reproaches. But, alas! I fear that you are too sanguine; I cannot expect, neither do I deserve that my father will so easily forgive me for the crime (for it is worthy of no other name) of which I have been guilty; and I shudder at the consequences of my folly, and blind and wilful infatuation, by which I have probably doomed you and our child to future misery and want."

"Oh, it is impossible that your father can ever condemn us to such a fate."

"My father never viewed my trifling faults with a very lenient eye," said Vivian; "and what am I to expect on this occasion, when I have so grossly abused his kindness, and permitted myself to become the dupe of designing knaves?"

"Calm your feelings, my dear Vivian; and do not thus anticipate the worst. But surely your brother was much to blame to introduce you to such individuals."

"He could not have known their real characters, or he surely would not have done so."

"I would fain believe that he did not," said Mrs. Clavering; "yet when I recollect that he declared them to be his most intimate friends, I must confess that it appeared to me to be strange and questionable. But Heaven forbid that I should judge him wrongfully; surely he will not fail to intercede for you with your father?"

Mrs. Clavering thought not so, although she thus expressed herself, for she had never entertained any very high opinion of Andrew Clavering, and his having introduced her husband to those who had plundered him of his property, confirmed her bad opinion.

"My brother, I hope, will act with kindness and consideration towards me," replied Vivian; "but I much doubt whether he even will be able to obtain for me my father's forgiveness. I have brought disgrace upon his name, and how can I expect that he can readily pardon me? Oh, my poor wife, for myself I care not, for I am deserving of every punishment; but it is the misery I have brought you and our innocent offspring to, that wrings my very soul with remorse."

"But have the wretches plundered you of all, dear Vivian?"

"All—all," replied Vivian, striking his forehead in despair. "Reputation, fortune, peace of mind, everything! oh, what a sorry, wretched beggar have they indeed made me!"

"But could you not move them to pity?"

"Pity from such unprincipled, such heartless miscreants as them!" said Vivian; "oh, how can you ask such a question, Clarence? When they found that they had entirely ruined me, they laughed and mocked at my madness and despair. Oh, God! if I had any deadly weapon with me, I should have committed murder."

"Oh, Heaven be thanked that you had not the means of perpetrating so dreadful a crime!" ejaculated Mrs. Clavering, shuddering with horror. "Pray endeavour to be calm, and to banish such horrible thoughts from your mind."

"Oh, Clemence, how can I be calm, when the heinousness of my guilt rushes upon my brain? I wonder that my senses have not entirely left me."

"For my sake, endeavour to conquer this intensity of anguish and remorse!" said Mrs. Clavering, again throwing her arms affectionately round her husband's neck; "and let us wait the result with patience."

"I should, indeed, act with patience, my too devoted Clemence," said her husband;

"for it is I who am the only aggressor; but I have no right to expect the same from you, upon whom I have brought such shame and sorrow. You should view me with disgust and reproach as a being unworthy of your regard. Methinks, I could better endure your hatred even than your most ardent love on this occasion, because I feel that I richly merit the former for not listening to your generous counsel, while I have forfeited all claim to the latter."

"Oh, forbear, forbear, dear Vivian," said the fond wife; "such words as these shock mine ears and render me doubly miserable. You have been misguided, my husband, but still this misfortune renders you, if possible, even still dearer to me than ever, and I see most clearly the necessity for all my utmost energies being exerted to arouse you from this abject state of despondency, and to enable us to struggle against the difficulties that at present surround us. Cheer up, Vivian; dark as the atmosphere at present may appear to be, the clouds, believe me, will disperse, and a bright sunshine of bliss awaken upon our future days. All that may be the affliction it may please Omnipotence to visit us with, I am prepared to meet with all the resignation and strength of woman's fortitude; but to see you thus give way to despair, drives me likewise to frenzy. Come, come, my Vivian; you will, for my sake, I say again, I know endeavour to compose your feelings, and to hope for the best."

Vivian Clavering dashed a manly tear from his eye, and for some few moments was unable to return any answer. How keen was the remorse which he felt; how bitterly did he upbraid himself for having neglected the excellent advice of his amiable wife, and cursed his own blind folly in being led to ruin by such shallow scoundrels as those by whom he had suffered himself to be deluded.

"Best of women and of wives," he said at length; "how have I deserved this,—this unparalleled forbearance, this unbounded affection? Indeed, it tortures me more, that, by your bright example, I am shown the villain that I have been. But — but I will say no more—but, indeed, try to calm my feelings to meet the crisis—the awful crisis I am afraid that is in store for us."

They then embraced again, and mingled their tears together; but those tears served in some measure to relieve them. They seated themselves by the fire, for neither of them felt inclined to retire to rest!—rest—there was no rest for them in their present state of mind; and a long silence ensued, during which they both of them gave free indulgence to the thoughts, the torturing thoughts that preyed upon their minds.

Thus drearily passed away the night, and when the morning's light streamed in at the windows, it found Vivian and his wife still seated by the dying embers of their fire in the same melancholy attitude. During the night the unhappy husband had made his wife acquainted with all the particulars of his ruin; and, although she shuddered at the idea of the fearful abyss into which he had plunged them, she tried all that she could to console and comfort him, and to inspire him with hope. Her mild forbearance—her patient fortitude, tortured him more than all, and intense, most intense was the struggle he had with his feelings.

After they had partaken of the morning repast, Vivian would have left the house, on the pretext of seeking by a walk to recover his spirits; but his wife, alarmed by the state of excitement she saw he was still in, strenuously exerted herself to prevent him from so doing, fearful that in his present state of mind he might be tempted to commit some rash act, and thus consummate that wretchedness which was already so threatening and overwhelming.

Andrew Clavering had received timely notice from his infamous colleagues of the success of their designs and the ruin of his unfortunate brother, and they did not fail to make a speedy exit from the neighbourhood, well satisfied with the booty which Andrew had put them in the way of fleecing from their unsuspecting victim.

As for Andrew himself, how he exulted in the success of his diabolical schemes, which he flattered himself would lead to the accomplishment—the final accomplishment of all his base designs, and he determined to follow them up with unabated spirit and perseverance until he had totally completed the ruin of his brother, and the removal of the only obstacle to the possession of the whole of his father's wealth. But still, he knew that it was necessary for him to continue to act with the utmost caution, and to continue to play the hypocrite, or all his designs might be overturned, and exposed to shame. He therefore determined to visit the unfortunate Vivian, pleading ignorance of what had happened, pretending to commiserate with him, and affecting to endeavour to bring about a reconciliation with him and his father, while he would take care, at the same time, insidiously to embitter the mind of the latter still more strongly against him.

Accordingly, not long after Vivian and his wife had partaken of their morning meal, on the melancholy occasion we have just been describing, the crafty Andrew, the real author of all their misery, made his appearance, and assuming an air of unusual gaiety, he said,—

"My dear brother and sister, I am most happy to see you, and hope that you are both well; I have come to press you to an invitation which—but how is this? Why these melancholy looks? You have been weeping, my fair sister-in-law; what has happened to cause this extraordinary change? No unexpected calamity, I trust?"

"Oh, Andrew," groaned his brother, looking up towards him at the same time with a ghastly expression of countenance, "how can I answer you? I am ruined, beggared, wretched!"

"What mean you?" demanded the hypocrite, with well affected surprise and anxiety.

"Mean!" returned Vivian; "how can I find words to explain? Andrew, I have been a mad, infatuated fool, and have been duped out of every farthing I possessed at the gaming-table, by those unprincipled villains whom I believed to be my friends."

"This is a sad disclosure, Vivian," returned Andrew Clavering, with a louring brow; "I am sorry to hear that you have been so imprudent; but who are the individuals by whom you have been thus duped?"

"Who are they? Good God! need you ask the question? Sir William Whiffles, and his base and rascally associates, are those by whom I have been thus shamefully plundered."

"I regret to hear that," remarked Andrew, "I should have thought that you would have known them better in a short time than to permit yourself to be made so ready a victim."

"Known them better!" repeated Mrs. Clavering, with unfeigned astonishment, and fixing upon him at the same time a penetrating look; "is it possible that you can make use of such observations, when you, sir, were the first who introduced them to my husband as your most intimate friends?"

Andrew Clavering rather winced under these observations, and the looks which Mrs. Clavering fixed upon him; but he concealed his confusion as much as possible, and with a tone of perfect coolness, replied,—

"'Tis true that I believed them to be persons who were worthy of my friendship, or you may rest assured that I should never have introduced them to my brother; but I afterwards discovered that which gave me cause to suspect them, and Vivian knows that I avoided their society, and not more than once or twice suffered myself to be a partner in their nocturnal revels; but afterwards, when I saw plainly that they were individuals of questionable character, I absented myself from their meetings, and I must say I felt rather surprised Vivian did not do the same."

"But you, sir, introduced them to us as *well known friends*," said Mrs. Clavering, pointedly, and fixing upon him a glance that again covered the villanous hypocrite with confusion; "and was the first to urge your brother to join you and them in those ruinous meetings which you now so much deprecate. Surely, Andrew, if you had discovered anything which gave you reason to suspect them, it was at once your duty to have cautioned and advised my unfortunate husband."

Andrew Clavering hesitated a moment or two for an answer, while Vivian covered his face with his hands, and in the agony of his feelings was almost unconscious of what was going on.

"Well, well," at length said Andrew, "I, perhaps, was wrong in not doing as you say, my good sister-in-law; but it was an inadvertency to which we are all subject to at times. Come, Vivian, do not thus give way to despair; although you have acted with this indiscretion, there has been nothing absolutely criminal in your conduct, and all may yet be well; our father, you know, is not a harsh or unjust man, and will, no doubt, act with forbearance towards you; as for me, you may depend upon my using all my best exertions as a brother in interceding for you with him."

This was spoken with so much apparent sincerity, that even Mrs. Clavering was deceived.

"Oh, sir," she ejaculated, "I pray you, for the sake of a brother who has ever shown the fond regard he bears towards you, to stand our friend upon this melancholy occasion, and to be our friendly advocate with Mr. Clavering."

"No, no!" ejaculated Vivian, "it is useless; I dare not, I cannot again show my face to my father, after the manner in which I have disgraced myself and him. He will not, he ought not to listen to my excuses."

"Nay, Vivian," returned his brother, "you must not reject my friendly offices. I will represent the whole unfortunate case to our father in the most favourable way I can, and I entertain the strongest hopes of a happy result. Therefore, seek to calm the anguish and despair of your feelings, and all may yet be well."

"Let me attend you, Andrew, to the mansion of our father," said Mrs. Claverling, "and on my knees will I plead to him for mercy and sympathy for my husband, and I feel convinced that he will not turn a deaf ear to my supplications."

"Oh, no," said Vivian, "that must not be, my poor Clemence; he will spurn you from him, and never can I suffer you to encounter such additional misery. I will myself accompany Andrew, seek an interview with my father, and at once know my fate."

"Pardon me, Vivian," returned Andrew, "but neither you or Clarence are in any tone of mind at present for such a task. Leave everything to me, and in the meantime do all in your power to compose your feelings; I will break the painful intelligence to him in the best manner I can. Wait patiently till to-morrow, when I trust I shall be able to bring you good news."

So well did the villain play his part, that both Vivian and his wife were deceived. The intensity of Vivian's anxiety and despair was in some degree abated, and he became more calm than he had been since the fatal night on which his ruin had been effected.

Andrew Clavering exulted in the success of his deep-laid schemes, and saw plainly that he had now his unconscious victims completely in his power, and at his mercy, and that his own ambitious, unnatural, and avaricious objects were certain of being accomplished. He passed some time with his brother and his wife, promising to see them again on the following day, and then took his departure towards home.

"They are my dupes," the villain soliloquized, as he walked towards the mansion of his father; "they are entrapped in a snare from which they cannot escape, and it will be my own fault if I do not accomplish the whole of my wishes. Oh, I have played my cards well, and richly merit the reward of my labours, which must and shall be the whole of my father's wealth. That will be ample revenge for the scorn with which the fair Clemence treated my advances, and the preference she gave to that brother I have always detested."

And well did Andrew Clavering act up to the diabolical plans he had proposed to himself. He did not fail to represent to his father everything in the worst light, at the same time that he was inflaming Mr. Clavering's mind against the unfortunate Vivian, pretending to pity him for his weakness and indiscretion, and beseeching his father to view them with every clemency and indulgence.

"You know, my dear father," said the crafty villain, "that poor Vivian is young and inexperienced in the world, and being naturally of a vivacious turn of mind, he was more likely to be lured into the vices of the designing and the improvident; certainly he ought, after the excellent example you have set us, and ——"

"Don't talk to me, Andrew," interrupted Mr. Clavering, passionately; "attempt not to intercede for him. You have ever been a good and dutiful son, but he with his pretended affection has proved himself to be a reckless spendthrift, an ungrateful scoundrel. He has brought disgrace upon my name; a gamester is one of the worst of characters, for he must be destitute of every honourable feeling; robbery, murder, are the certain crimes that accompany his guilty pursuits. Andrew, I tell you, I will no longer acknowledge him as a son of mine; I discard him for ever!"

"Oh, my dear sir," replied Andrew, with well affected emotion, "say not so, I beg of you; though, for his misconduct, Vivian certainly deserves to meet with strong marks of your resentment, I trust that you will not deal with him so severely."

"You plead in vain, Andrew. Forbear, lest you incur my displeasure. The ungracious boy! after all the kindness and indulgence I have ever shown him; the liberal provision I made for him on his marriage, and—and—oh! it will not bear a second thought. I have done with him for ever, and I beg, Andrew, that his name may never again be mentioned."

"But will you not see him, my dear father?"

" See him!—no. Has the ungrateful boy the audacity to expect such a thing ? Is he so hardened in crime as to dare to brave an injured father's resentment? I see,—I see, by your looks, my dear Andrew, that he has ; and that confirms at once the utter hopelessness of his character. Taking advantage of your brotherly affection, which you have ever so strongly evinced towards him, he has persuaded you to intercede with me. But it is useless, Andrew,—entirely useless; I will never see him again. Let him go to his dissolute associates, for not a shilling shall he ever receive from me. I have done with him, Andrew,—I have entirely done with him."

Thus saying, the hasty and thoughtless father rushed out of the room, leaving his designing and guilty son to exult in the complete success of his nefarious, his unnatural designs. All had turned out even much better than the villain had anticipated, and he flattered himself that every obstacle to the gratification of his desires was removed ; but still he found it necessary that he should act with the greatest precaution, lest he should excite the suspicions of his unfortunate victims, and thus thwart his plans.

Mr. Clavering remained secluded in his own chamber for the rest of the day ; and so prejudiced was he, by what Andrew had stated to him, against Vivian, that nothing whatever could abate the resentment he felt towards him.

In the meantime, the wretched Vivian and his wife awaited, in the most agonising state of suspense, the result of Andrew's disclosure to Mr. Clavering, though the former never for a moment anticipated anything but the worst ; and it was in vain that his amiable and devoted wife sought to inspire him with hope.

The following day, Andrew Clavering again visited them. He had masked his face in such hypocritical expressions of sympathy, that Vivian and his wife were completely deceived by them, and began to think that he was really their friend, at the same time that the villain was so insidiously plotting their destruction. He recounted to them the interview which had taken place between him and Mr. Clavering, to which they listened with feelings of anguish and despair we need not attempt to describe.

" Lost! lost! fool—villain that I have been," groaned Vivian, grasping his forehead with a look of the most intense agony, and sinking into a chair ; " name, fortune, a father's love,—all gone, through my accursed indiscretion. I deserve all ; I could expect nothing less than my father's greatest resentment ; but, oh! my poor wife, how can I look you in the face, after the misery I have brought upon you? There is nothing left for us now but beggary and want."

" Say not so, my dear brother," said Andrew, with the greatest apparent kindness and solicitude ; " my father's resentment will no doubt abate, and he will think better of this. Trust to me, and depend upon it I will do all in my power to bring about an amicable arrangement. In the meantime, I need not, I think, assure you that anything in a pecuniary way you may command from me."

" I see it is useless to struggle against the fate I have brought upon myself," said Vivian. " Clemence, we must go forth from hence ; it is no longer home of ours. Our father has discarded us, and we must no longer retain possession of the property that justly belongs to him. Heaven help us, for I know not what will become of us in this dreadful emergency."

" Patience, my dear Vivian," ejaculated the affectionate wife ; " all may yet end better than you expect ; but let whatever may be the miseries with which it may please the Almighty to visit us, I am prepared to meet them with fortitude and resignation, so that I can only see you aroused from this dreadful state of despair and self-reproach. Your father will relent ; he is too good, too generous, to visit you so severely with his wrath."

" Oh! no, I cannot,—I dare not flatter myself with such fallacious hopes," replied Vivian.

" A few days may work a wonderful change," remarked Andrew Clavering ; " till which time wait patiently and calmly. It is only natural that our father should feel greatly excited at such an unexpected disclosure ; but when he comes to think more calmly and dispassionately upon it, I firmly believe, as your wife has remarked, that he will relent, and receive you once more into his favour. But in the meantime, I will endeavour to prepare for any emergency that may arise ; and therefore, my dear brother and sister, endeavour to make your minds completely easy upon that subject."

What could be more specious than these observations ? Clemence was entirely deceived by them, and reproached herself for the opinions she had formerly entertained

OR, THE SISTERS OF MYSTERY.

to the prejudice of Andrew's character, and believed that he was now really acting the part of a sincere friend towards them.

"God speed you in your efforts, good Andrew," said Mrs. Clavering, "and rest assured that, whether they succeed or not, our most unbounded gratitude will ever be yours."

It was not without considerable difficulty that the guilty Andrew could conceal the real feelings which were passing in his mind at that moment; and, oh! could they but have read his thoughts, and known the dark designs he had in contemplation,—that he had made up his mind to be the author of their complete destruction,—how different would have been the sentiments with which they would have regarded him! with what disgust, indignation, and horror must they have looked upon him!

Vivian, indeed, felt somewhat tranquillised by his assurances, and in order to ameliorate the anguish of his wife, affected to be more calm and resigned than he absolutely was, and talked dispassionately to his treacherous brother. Andrew Clavering, however, having proceeded thus far, cut short the interview, lest, in the midst of his excited feelings of malignant triumph, he should betray himself, and took his departure, with many flattering promises of intercession in their behalf with Mr. Clavering, and promising that they should either hear from him, or he would visit them the next day.

"The poor fools!" he muttered to himself, as he retraced his steps towards home, "how completely have I gulled them; they now believe me most amiable and gracious, when, at the same time, I am their principal enemy, and have resolved that I will never rest until I have completely got rid of them, and secured to myself the undivided possession of my father's wealth whenever he dies. Nothing could possibly have been managed better, and I give—I must give—myself every credit for my consummate ingenuity."

After Andrew had departed, all the intense agony and despair of Vivian's feelings returned, and it was in vain that Mrs. Clavering exerted her utmost energies, and all the arguments she could call to her aid, to console him, or to bring him to anything like a degree of composure. Black despair had settled upon his heart, and nothing could remove it. He knew his father's temper too well to imagine for a moment that he would relent, and he could not bring his mind to think that he deserved it. And now he strongly remembered many instances in which his father had been accustomed to view his slightest errors in the severest light; and, therefore, what could he expect on the present occasion, when he felt that he had really transgressed and greatly disgraced himself? In reality, too, when he took all the circumstances of his brother's former behaviour towards him into consideration, notwithstanding his present apparent sympathy towards him in misfortunes, and the many kind promises he had made to him, he could not place that confidence in him that he would have wished, although he carefully concealed, as well as he could, his real thoughts upon the painful subject from his wife.

Another wretched day and restless night wore away, without any material change being wrought in the minds of Vivian Clavering and his wife. He was all mental anguish and despair, while she bore it all with that Christian fortitude, meekness, and submission, which could not have failed to have excited the deepest commiseration and admiration in the most insensible bosom. She tried to encourage hope; but, alas! when she reflected upon all the circumstances, she could not but entertain the most dismal prospects of the future; and not for the sake of herself, but that of her husband and her child she was truly miserable, which was rendered still worse by the hard struggles she had to conceal it from Vivian, apprehensive that, if he penetrated into her real feelings and sufferings, it would drive him to madness.

As soon as day dawned, Vivian would have left the house on the pretext of taking a walk, which he said he thought would revive him; but Mrs. Clavering most earnestly dissuaded him from it, for she dreaded lest, in his present disordered state of mind, he might be driven to commit some rash and desperate act; and he at length yielded to her persuasions, though it was not without evident reluctance that he did so.

When the morning, however, at length wore away, and Andrew did not make his appearance, they became uneasy, and could not help thinking that something serious had happened to prevent him from coming. The afternoon passed away in the same manner; night arrived, and still Andrew came not, and they now gave him up in despair.

It was with sad hearts that Vivian Clavering and his wife sought their chamber; various were the thoughts and conjectures that crowded upon their minds; but one fact appeared to them evident, namely, that Andrew had been unsuccessful, and that Mr. Clavering remained inexorable.

"Oh, how could I expect otherwise?" said Vivian; "why should I presume to look for forgiveness from that parent whose kindness I have so greatly abused, and upon whose head I have brought such disgrace?"

"My dear Vivian," remarked his wife, "you reproach yourself too severely—indeed you do, and I can never believe that your father will act with such undue harshness towards you. He cannot forget that you are his son, and never before this unhappy occasion gave him cause for offence. Wait patiently until the result of to-morrow, when I trust that all your fears will be dispersed."

But though that excellent woman thus tried to appease her husband's anguish by holding out such hopes, far, very far was she from encouraging them herself; in fact, she could not but view the future scene which broke upon her imagination with the utmost dismay, although she concealed her real thoughts from her afflicted husband, knowing that he was already suffering enough from the intensity of remorse, and fearful that he should for a moment construe it into reproach on her part for the misery into which he had plunged them.

She had now also again her doubts and misgivings as to the sincerity of Andrew Clavering, notwithstanding all his pretended sympathy in their misfortunes, and the professions he had made; and she could not at times help thinking that he was acting a treacherous part towards them, with what motives she had very little reason to find any difficulty in conceiving; for she had penetrated to the secret of his covetous disposition, and was well aware of the jealous eye with which he had ever viewed his brother. This base feeling, she was satisfied, had been greatly strengthened by the manner in which she had ever repulsed his advances to her favour, previous to her union with Vivian; and it needed not then be wondered that she had ever regarded him since with secret feelings of dread, and viewed his advances of friendship with a doubtful eye. His introduction of the villains who had effected his ruin, the reader may be certain did not tend to ameliorate those natural prejudices against him, and his present absence, after so faithfully promising to visit them again that day, knowing, as he must, the dreadful state of suspense they must be reduced to, served to add strength to her worst forebodings.

With these thoughts and feelings torturing her mind, the reader may well imagine the dreadful struggle the faithful and devoted wife had to contend with to hide her real apprehensions from her husband's eye; and it was wonderful to observe the fortitude and calmness with which she behaved under a trial so severe, that it would have broken some of the strongest spirits entirely down altogether.

Never had Vivian Clavering so strongly felt the full force of the love he bore towards his Clemence, as in this, the hour of their affliction, when the nobleness of her character was so prominently brought forth, and consequently his remorse at the sufferings he had brought upon her was the more acute and overpowering. These thoughts aroused him into action; and, for her sake, he determined to arouse himself as much as possible from despair, and to assume that appearance of calmness which it was impossible for him in reality to feel. It would be unmanly of him to seem desponding and inactive, when she was straining all her energies to make the best of their melancholy and alarming situation. Folding her, therefore, in his arms, and pressing her to his bosom, he ejaculated,—

"My beloved wife, my ever affectionate and devoted Clemence, you have set me a noble example, which I will endeavour to follow; if I did not, how unworthy should I be of your love. Yes, I will try to wait patiently the result of this unfortunate affair, and to hope for the best. Heaven help us, Heaven help us!"

"And I feel confident, my husband," replied Mrs. Clavering, "that while we rely upon the mercy of the Almighty, our supplications will not be in vain. Cheer thee, Vivian, cheer thee; though all at present is dark and gloomy as the valley of despair, something tells me that brighter days are in store for us, when we may look back upon the past with feelings of pleasure, instead of regret, as having taught us to properly appreciate and enjoy those blessings which the Supreme Being has lavished with so bounteous a hand upon all His creatures. Should Mr. Clavering still remain inexorable, let us ourselves seek his presence, and throwing ourselves at his feet, sue to him for forgiveness. Surely he will not, he cannot, turn a deaf, an insensible ear to our supplications."

Vivian shook his head, and sighed deeply.

"Alas! Clemence," he said, "would I could think as you do; but I fear there is little to hope for in that respect. You heard the message he sent by Andrew, that he would never behold me again—that he had discarded me for ever from his breast, and how dare I then, under such circumstances, venture to seek his presence?''

"But he will think better of that, dear Vivian, when his first excitement is abated. I cannot believe your father capable of such stern and cruel conduct. But let us retire to bed, and pray to Heaven that to-morrow may relieve us from our anxiety, and bring us happy news."

Vivian again embraced his wife, but made no reply, for his emotions were too powerful for him to do so. They then both sank on their knees, and in the most fervent and eloquent terms they implored the mercy of Heaven.

They felt more composed after this, and sought their pillow ; and at length, worn out with fatigue, both of body and mind, they soon sank into sleep.

But most troubled and unrefreshing it was. Painful visions flitted before their imagination, and they awoke at an early hour in the morning, more fatigued than when they had retired to bed.

They partook but slightly of their morning meal, for their hearts were too full to allow them to eat, and most anxiously did they await the arrival of Andrew ; but three hours passed away in the same tedious manner without his making his appearance, and the patience of both Mrs. Clavering and her husband was nearly exhausted.

At length, however, they heard a knock at the hall door, and they were in hopes that Andrew Clavering had at last arrived, but in that they were doomed to be disappointed. One of their servants entered, and presenting his master with a couple of letters, observed that the person who brought them had stated that he was only ordered to deliver them, and not to wait for any answer, which was not required.

Vivian looked at the superscription on both the letters with extreme agitation. One he discovered to be in the handwriting of his father, and the other in that of his brother. He opened the first with a trembling hand, and in a voice half choked with the power of his agitation, read the following words :—

"Your conduct has been such that I cannot easily pardon it, but that depends entirely upon your future behaviour. You have brought disgrace upon yourself and me, and I know of no punishment that you do not deserve for your ingratitude, and the shameful manner in which you have abused my kindness. You may thank your brother for his intercession with me for you, or I should never again have noticed you, or have recognised any tie as existing between us. I enclose you a cheque for one hundred guineas for present necessities, and you will receive twenty-five guineas quarterly through my agents in London. Do not attempt to see me, or to return any answer to this, but endeavour by repentance once more to deserve the regard of   "ERNEST CLAVERING.

"P.S.—I shall expect that you will quit the house you at present reside in, and the neighbourhood, as early as possible, and it is only by obedience to my strict commands that you can hope to convince me of your sincere remorse."

The letter fell from the hand of the unfortunate Vivian, and he clasped his forehead in despair.

"It is done !" he cried ; "my doom is sealed ; he casts me from him ; he discards me, he owns me no longer for his son. It is my mad folly has done all this, and what have I now to wish to live for ? But, if it must be so, let beggary, let misery come at once. I will send back this letter, and not accept the miserable pittance wherewith to eke out an existence which has now become hateful to me."

"Forbear, Vivian, forbear," interposed his wife, "and do not plunge yourself, me, and your innocent offspring into utter misery. Your father holds out hopes to you that by your own conduct you may yet regain his affection and forgiveness ; then do not rashly reject his offer, for I know that the time will not be long ere you will be enabled to convince him of your sincere penitence, and that you are worthy of being reinstated in his regard. Bear with it, then, with patience and submission, and we shall yet be happy. This allowance will be amply sufficient to keep us in comfort ; we will retire to some more humble dwelling in a neighbourhood where we are unknown, and the breath of scandal cannot reach us, and learn from this woful experience the source from whence true happiness alone flows ; but should we, on the contrary, act in disobedience to the commands of your father, however stern they may appear to be, all hope, depend upon it, is at an end."

This address somewhat calmed the ruffled feelings of Vivian, and throwing himself in a chair, he ruminated seriously and bitterly for a few minutes.

"The will of Heaven be done," he said, at length; "it is I who have been the aggressor, and I ought, I feel I ought to submit, and to endeavour to make atonement. But when I reflect, my dearest Clemence, that you also must suffer with me, it drives me almost to madness."

"Oh, think not of me, Vivian, only as your still loving wife, nor believe that I can ever for a moment reproach you for the past. If I can but behold you calm and resigned, I shall be happy."

"For your sake, best of women, tenderest of wives, I will, indeed, endeavour to be so," replied Vivian, reviving as he spoke, and seeming to have formed a resolution. He then broke the seal of Andrew's letter, and read the following words:—

"MY DEAR BROTHER AND SISTER,

"I need not, I am convinced, assure you of my continued affection, and the deep sympathy I feel in your misfortunes, which I trust to Providence you will soon be able to surmount, and that you will be restored to your former happiness.

"All my intercessions with our father proved ineffectual in persuading him to come to any other terms than those he has stated to you in his letter; but I feel satisfied that your own conduct will cause him to relent, and that in a short time you will be fully restored to his confidence and affection; you may depend upon it that no exertions on my part shall be wanting to bring about so happy and desirable a result.

"I would visit you, but I am prohibited by my father; but a letter left for me at the principal inn will be sure to reach me, and I shall be most anxious to receive one from you, informing me of every particular, and whither you have removed.

"I beg your acceptance of the inclosed fifty pounds, and will not fail to render you every assistance in my power.

"Praying you every happiness, and a speedy reconciliation with our father, believe me to remain

"Your affectionate brother,
"ANDREW CLAVERING."

What could be more plausible than this epistle? Oh, no, the hypocrite had played his villanous game well, and his unfortunate victims were completely deceived by it. Mrs. Clavering secretly upbraided herself for having entertained any suspicions of his sincerity, and endeavoured to persuade herself and her husband, that he would speedily be the means of bringing about a reconciliation with him and his father.

Vivian listened to her with more patience than he had ever done before, and after the first burst of emotion consequent upon the receipt of such a letter from the author of his being, he became comparatively tranquil.

"It is no more than I should have expected," he said; "for I have greatly offended, and have no right to murmur. I will endeavour to regain my lost character, and never again will I give my father cause to say that I have brought disgrace upon his name."

"Nobly resolved, my dear Vivian," said his wife; "but you give your indiscretion, notwithstanding, too harsh a name. Your character is not lost; you have merely been weak enough to be made the dupe of designing villains, whom you could not believe were capable of such nefarious practices, or were unworthy of your friendship. You have now received a severe but wholesome lesson, which I know you will profit by, and that though you now suffer, it will be afterwards for our future benefit."

Vivian was reconciled by her words, and after a short time he was so far recovered as to be able to sit down and write a long and affectionate letter in answer to that of his brother, in which he expressed his warmest gratitude to him for the exertions he had made in his favour, and expressed his willingness to submit with all the patience and resignation he could to the commands of his father, and stated that it was his intention to leave his present place of residence with as little delay as possible, and as soon as he could meet with a house better suited to his present circumstances.

Andrew Clavering read this letter with the most inward satisfaction.

"Poor fool!" he said, "your doom is sealed. It will be my fault if ever a reconciliation is brought about between you and your father. I have gained the point I have so long been studying for; you are banished from the home and the affections of your father, and I will not fail to take every advantage of it; the whole of that wealth which you would have shared shall now be mine."

A week elapsed, during which time Vivian and his wife had become comparatively resigned, and Mrs. Clavering attempted a degree even of cheerfulness, but which her husband knew must be foreign to her heart. However, most grateful to her was he for it, and in return sought to appear as contented as, taking all the circumstances into consideration, he could be expected to be.

They at length heard of a small house which was to be let a few miles off, and Vivian having been down to inspect it, and approving of it, he immediately entered into the necessary arrangements for it, and settled everything to his satisfaction.

The house was situated at the head of the peaceful and pleasant little hamlet we have described at the commencement of this chapter; and was possessed of every accommodation suitable to a small family; and the rent being moderate, was suited to the now limited means of Vivian and his wife. Although situated not far from the road-side, it was also very retired, and that rendered it more than anything a desirable dwelling for persons in their unfortunate situation.

To this new abode, therefore, Mr. and Mrs. Clavering prepared to depart; but, before they did so, Vivian addressed a letter to his brother, informing him of all the particulars of the arrangements he had made, and requesting him to correspond with him as frequently as possible; and begging him not to cease in his endeavours to bring their father to relent.

To this letter Andrew returned an answer, couched in the most brotherly language, and promising to be unremitting in his endeavours to bring about a reconciliation.

Vivian and his wife the next day removed to their new abode, with which Mrs. Clavering was very much pleased, and for some days amused herself by putting it in order. They hired a young girl to assist Mrs. Clavering in her household duties, and to attend upon the child; and in a short time the place wore an air of comfort that Vivian could not help appreciating. He tried to make himself as contented as possible; but in spite of all his efforts and those of his wife, he could not entirely banish from his mind the gloomy thoughts which the change in his circumstances, and the uncertainty of what would be his future prospects, gave rise to; and it could plainly be seen that he was enduring the deepest remorse.

Months rolled on without any material change taking place; they had received several letters from Andrew; but, although they were couched in the most tender language, and expressive of his unabated commiseration in their misfortunes, there was nothing in them to inspire them with hope. Andrew stated that unfortunately Mr. Clavering always felt the greatest reluctance to hear Vivian's name mentioned, and as yet seemed unabated in his resentment.

"Alas!" sighed Vivian, "it is no more than I expected; he will never forgive me; and, therefore, all hope of future happiness is at an end."

"Oh, no, Vivian," returned Mrs. Clavering; "do not encourage such gloomy apprehensions. Your father will never continue to visit your faults with such severity, when he finds how truly penitent you are, and how strictly you have acted in accordance with his commands. Let us wait patiently, and fear not but a reconciliation will yet be effected."

Alas! they little suspected the heartless villain who was secretly working to destroy their hopes, and to poison the mind of Mr. Clavering against them. Never did crafty rascal work his diabolical designs with greater ingenuity and with more success than Andrew Clavering. While he affected to intercede for his unfortunate brother, he never failed to throw out certain insinuations, in such a manner as was calculated to prejudice his father still more against him; while, at the same time, he looked upon the treacherous Andrew as one of the most dutiful, the most amiable, and affectionate of sons; and believed him to be perfectly incapable of one unworthy action. Andrew saw that his game was secure; and oh, how he exulted in his success, and secretly longed for the death of his deluded parent, that he might reap the golden harvest of his villanous toils.

At length Vivian and his wife began to think that they perceived a remarkable falling off in the warmth which had formerly characterised Andrew's letters; and they took alarm at it, and could not help fearing that even he had ceased to view them with that sympathy he had all along professed to do; and that he probably repented the interest he had formerly taken in their welfare.

Again did those suspicions she had once entertained of the sincerity of her brother-in-law, enter the mind of Mrs. Clavering; but she concealed them from her husband, and tried all that she could to quiet his fears, while her own were as powerful as those he experienced. But this was no easy task, and Vivian daily became more melancholy and reserved, and nothing whatever could at times arouse him from the gloomy reveries he was in the habit of indulging in.

At length Andrew Clavering ceased writing altogether, and then the truth burst upon them both with overwhelming force; he had either deceived them from the first, or had now abandoned them to their fate, and felt no further commiseration for them.

Vivian was now reduced to a state of absolute despair, and his wife became seriously alarmed for his health, but knew not in what way to ameliorate his sufferings, for indeed she stood in as much need of consolation herself, and it was wonderful how she was enabled to support such heavy trials with the fortitude she did.

Sometimes Vivian was half resolved to brave everything, and to seek the presence of his father himself, that he might hear at once from his own lips the determination he had come to, and whether he had indeed so steeled his heart against him as to resolve to discard him for ever. But still something withheld him from doing so when he reflected upon the contents of his father's letter, and he remained, for some few days longer, in a state approaching distraction, and undecided how to act.

Surely he was not deserving of such severity as this, and he could not have believed that his father could be capable of using it towards him. Indeed, the punishment he had been so long enduring, together with his innocent wife, he could not but consider was more than adequate to the faults he had committed, especially when his inexperience at the time was taken into consideration.

At length, by the persuasions of his wife, Vivian resolved to address a letter to his father, appealing to him for mercy; assuring him of his sincere penitence, depicturing the sufferings of himself and his wife, and pathetically supplicating his forgiveness.

He did so, and, in the most painful suspense that can well be imagined, they awaited the result; but when day after day elapsed, and still no answer was returned, their hopes were entirely annihilated, and their misery was rendered complete. They were at first inclined to think that something had happened to Mr. Clavering, or that he was ill; but then, if he had been so, surely Andrew would have let them known.

Resolved to be fully satisfied on this point, he employed a neighbour, an intelligent labouring man, to make inquiries on the spot, and he ascertained that both Mr. Clavering and his son were in perfect health, and were still remaining at the mansion. This satisfied them that they had resolved to hold no further correspondence with them, and threw poor Vivian into a state of frenzy, while the fortitude of Mrs. Clavering almost sank entirely under the shock.

It was some days ere they could sufficiently command their feelings to consult each other upon what was best to be done in their painful situation. At length Vivian determined to go to the inn where he had been accustomed to direct his letters to his brother, and endeavour to obtain an interview with him, so that he might receive an explanation from him, and at once be released from such a torturing and insupportable state of anxiety.

Mrs. Clavering saw him depart with a despairing heart, and when he was gone, she knelt down, and fervently implored the Almighty to interpose in their behalf, and to move the unrelenting heart of Mr. Clavering in pity towards them.

In the meantime, Vivian, with the most melancholy misgivings, pursued his way, and after walking for more than a couple of hours, at length arrived at the inn, where, having ordered some slight refreshment, he requested the use of writing materials, and immediately wrote a letter to his brother, in which he earnestly requested him to grant him an interview, so that he might receive from him an explanation of the cause of the silence of him and his father, and have the dreadful suspense, to which he and his unoffending wife had for so long been subjected, removed. This letter he delivered to the care of one of the ostlers, and awaited his return from the mansion with much anxiety.

Vivian could not but expect that his brother would respond to the appeal, and return with the messenger; how great then was his disappointment when the man came back with a mere cold verbal message from Andrew, stating that " he regretted that he could not see him, or enter into any explanation at present; but *probably he might hear from him before long !*"

The reader may well imagine the feelings of the unfortunate Vivian on receiving this message : to say that he was astounded, would be to use by far too mild a term. His eyes were at once opened to the base hypocrisy of his brother, and at first he was half determined to go to the mansion, and confront his brother and father, and upbraid them with the cruel and unnatural conduct they had practised towards him ; but after having given vent to his wounded feelings for a few minutes, he became more calm, and having written a keen and severe answer to his brother, in which he expressed his real opinion of his conduct towards him, which he dispatched by the same messenger, he departed from the inn, and, in a state of mind which we need not attempt to describe, retraced his steps towards home.

Clemence had been waiting his return with the greatest anxiety, and the most dismal forebodings had haunted her mind, and which were not in any way diminished when she saw the melancholy and disordered looks of her husband, and saw at once what had been the result of his journey. She threw her arms affectionately round his neck, and did all that she could to calm his feelings.

" There is nothing but despair left for us, my poor Clemence," he sighed ; " we are abandoned to wretchedness by those who at least ought to have regarded us with mercy ; and all this, by my own accursed weakness and folly, I have brought upon you, my innocent wife ; how, how can I ever forgive myself for the extent, the unpardonable extent of misery I have caused ?—Oh, Clemence, I feel myself unworthy of you, and would to Heaven that we had never met."

" Hold, Vivian," ejaculated his wife, alarmed at the wildness of his manner ; " do not, I beseech you, thus cruelly reproach yourself. You have erred, but not to the extent you accuse yourself, and have already, by the fervour and sincerity of your repentance, made ample atonement. Come, come, my dear Vivian, we will not yet give way entirely to despair ; black as our prospects are at present, they will brighten, they will brighten ; Providence will not entirely desert us while we put our trust in Him."

" Clemence," exclaimed Vivian, " I deserve not this from you ; however, in your affection and devotedness, you may seek to gloss over my errors, I feel, and most severely, my own unworthiness."

" Say not so, my husband, unless you would render me truly miserable. You have been deceived, betrayed, but the time will come when the really guilty will be unmasked, and justice will be rendered us."

" Oh ! I have indeed been deceived," cried Vivian, " and that by him whom I thought was entirely incapable of it, my brother ! His answer to my letter to-day unravels all, and shows me at once the blind fool that I have been. Oh, why did I not listen to your advice, Clemence, and avoid the society of the villains he introduced to me to effect my ruin, and accomplish his own diabolical end ?"

" But your father," said Clemence, " surely he cannot so far close his heart to every natural feeling as to banish you entirely from his affection or sympathy ?"

" What cause have we to hope otherwise, after the manner in which he has behaved towards us ?—what can be more harsh and unjust than the manner in which he has treated us, and that after promising that his pardon should follow my repentance ?—In what manner could I possibly have more evinced my compunction than I have done ?"

" He has been deceived, Vivian, his mind has been poisoned, depend upon it," said Mrs. Clavering.

" That I believe," answered Vivian,—" and also that my brother, at the very time that he was pretending to be my warmest friend, was the villain who was thus craftily working my ruin. But surely my father ought not thus to have been so strongly and so easily prejudiced against his own son. But listen, my poor Clemence, to the result of my mission."

Mrs. Clavering did listen with feelings of the most poignant sorrow and indignation, but she tried to control them as much as possible, for fear of adding to the excitement of her distracted husband. It was no more than she expected from the first, although there were times when she had endeavoured to imagine that her suspicions of the treachery of Andrew Clavering were wrong, and, as we have before stated, when she reproached herself for having ever entertained them. She saw now plainly that her first surmises had been correct ; she read at once the whole of the nefarious designs of her brother-in-law—that he had from motives of avarice taken the readiest way of effecting the unfortunate Vivian's ruin ; and nothing could surpass the disgust and abhorrence

OR, THE SISTERS OF MYSTERY.

No. 6.

with which she viewed the man who could be guilty of such infamous, such truly unnatural conduct. At the same time, she could but condemn in the strongest manner the
unjust severity with which Mr. Clavering had visited her husband, and the ready ear he
had given to the scandal of Andrew.

It was some time before either Vivian Clavering or his wife could sufficiently compose
themselves to talk in a dispassionate manner upon the melancholy circumstances that
attended their fate, a fate so uncalled for from any absolute misconduct of their own
(imprudence on the part of Vivian, it certainly might be termed); but it reflected much
discredit upon the natural feelings of Mr. Clavering, and likewise on his good sense and
propriety, saying nothing of his want of clemency and common justice, in visiting his son
with such undue harshness, and not affording him an opportunity of explaining the
whole of the facts, especially after the promise he had made in the first letter he had
addressed to Vivian, after the gross and cruel misrepresentations that had been made to
him by the crafty hypocrite, Andrew.

But need we say that Andrew had taken every advantage of the weakness and false
prejudices which we have before stated his father to possess?—while, in his communications with his brother, he had made it appear he was seeking to bring about a reconciliation between them, he was insidiously working the consummation of his ruin, and instilling
such notions into the mind of his father which placed his character in the darkest light.
By him he was led to suppose, in an indirect manner, that Vivian was abusing his generosity (if we can apply such a term to it), and upbraiding him for the conduct he still
continued to practise towards him; and Mr. Clavering was so far prejudiced in favour of
his eldest son, that he never took the pains to use his own judgment in respect to the
actual conduct of Vivian. In fact, he was completely blinded, and Andrew held him
entirely in his power, and used him as a ready instrument to work out his own nefarious
designs.

The letter which Vivian sent him from the inn, on his refusing to meet him, written,
as it naturally was, under a state of great excitement, gave him an excellent opportunity
of forwarding his base schemes, and he lost no time in presenting it to his father, who at
once, on perusing it, became exasperated, thinking that Vivian was not only acting in
direct disobedience to his commands, but most ungratefully reproaching his brother, and
seeking to make him as undutiful as himself.

He immediately despatched a letter to Vivian, in which he bitterly inveighed against
what he thought proper to term his gross ingratitude for his forbearance, and reduced
his salary to one half, intimating, at the same time, that it depended entirely upon his
future conduct whether he did not discard him altogether.

The reader may well imagine the state of mind to which poor Vivian and his devoted
wife were reduced on the receipt of the letter.

"The villain!" exclaimed Vivian, speaking of his brother; "he has worked our ruin.
Oh! cursed fool that I have been to permit myself to be so entrrpped! Father, father, I
do not deserve this. You should, at least, whatever my faults may have been, allowed me
an opportunity of an explanation."

"True, husband," said Mrs. Clavering; "I cannot attempt to excuse your father's
conduct, notwithstanding the crafty manner in which he has been deluded and imposed
upon by your brother. But be calm, Vivian; let us endeavour to submit to our misfortunes and the injustice that is rendered us as patiently as we can, and Providence, rest
assured, will not ultimately suffer us to become the victims of this unjust persecution.
Address a letter to your father in a cool and dispassionate tone, revealing everything, and
requesting an interview, when the merits or demerits of our case may be fully and satisfactorily proved, and surely Mr. Clavering will not refuse so reasonable, so just, and
natural a demand."

"My dear Clemence, ever my best adviser," said Vivian, looking up with more composure and confidence than he had done for some time, " I will do so, and for your sake
and that of our innocent offspring, may Heaven prosper the effort."

The letter was sent the following day, and a most eloquent and pathetic appeal it was,
in which nothing was exaggerated, but the whole plain and simple facts impartially stated;
but the villain Andrew had been upon his guard, naturally expecting that such a
course would be adopted by his much injured brother, and he had therefore taken his
plans accordingly. The letter was by him intercepted. He opened it, read the contents, and then, re-sealing it, returned it to his brother unanswered, at the same time

exulting in the complete success of his deep-laid schemes, which he was fully determined nothing should foil.

The anguish of Vivian and his wife on the result of this appeal may be imagined; they saw plainly that Andrew had obta'ned so much power over his father, that all epistolary correspondence would be useless, and, unless an interview could be obtained with him, no good could possibly be effected.

Two more days they passed in a state of the most inconceivable misery and anxiety of mind, and it was a most difficult task for Mrs. Clavering to keep her husband at all within the bounds of reason. She feared him to be out of sight for a moment, lest he should be tempted to commit some desperate act, and all her arguments to console him were almost exhausted. In fact, she saw that they had been so artfully drawn into the meshes spread for them by the base hypocrite, Andrew Clavering, that there would be the greatest difficulty, if any possibility at all, of escaping from them, and she trembled at the fate which she saw too evidently was in store for them.

But at length, as a last resource, Vivian made up his mind, whatever might be the consequences, to seek an interview with his father, and to confront Andrew face to face, and Mrs. Clavering, seeing that he was determined, and fearful of the result, should he be left alone, resolved to accompany him.

With melancholy and foreboding hearts they quitted their present humble home, Mrs. Clavering leaving her infant in the care of Rose until their return, and bent their way towards the mansion of their father. Tremulously they approached the porch of the venerable building, and rang the bell with the same diffidence as if they had been the veriest paupers. It was answered by Thomas, the faithful and long tried porter of Mr. Clavering, and who had always been strongly attached to Vivian. He started on beholding him and his wife, and the good old man could hardly refrain from tears. Vivian pressed his hand, for he well knew the honest heart he carried within his bosom, and requested that he should be immediately announced to his father and brother, and begging in the most urgent but respectful terms that they would grant him and his wife an interview.

Old Thomas shook his head in a melancholy manner, and, after expressing the sorrow he felt at seeing Vivian and his wife under such circumstances, informed them that Mr. Andrew was from home, and had been since the day before, but that he would deliver his message to his master, and he sincerely hoped that it would meet with success.

He showed them into the parlour, and the reader may easily judge of the feelings of anxiety and impatience with which Vivian and his wife awaited his return.

In a few minutes he came back with a verbal message from his master, declining most positively to see them; that he was engaged, and could not be disturbed. Vivian groaned aloud in the agony of his despair, and Mrs. Clavering knew not how to act in order to restore him to anything like a degree of composure. Although she had fully expected such a reception, the shock on this occasion was almost too powerful for her, and it was some time before she could recover from her emotion.

When she did so, she sought to arouse her husband, and to persuade him to submit at present with patience to the stern decree of his father, trusting that he would yet relent, and that they would have an opportunity of convincing him that he was in the wrong, and how shamefully they had been traduced. But this was no easy task to accomplish. She had the greatest difficulty in preventing him from rushing into the presence of his father, and demanding from him a thorough investigation into his conduct, and to have that full justice rendered him which was his due; but, at length, by her persuas'ons, and those of Thomas (who promised to communicate with him, and to inform him of all that took place), he was prevailed upon to desist from his first intention, and to leave the house.

" God bless you, Mr. and Mrs. Clavering," said poor old Thomas, as they left the hall; " times will mend, depend upon it they will, although they are black at present. You have been most sadly and unjustly treated, but he who has done all this (and I dare say you may guess who I mean, though I must not be so bold as to mention), will not always triumph. God bless you, God bless you, and may a change for the better speedily take place."

Mr. and Mrs. Clavering again pressed the hand of the good old man, and with melancholy hearts turned away from the mansion, and retraced their steps towards home.

For some days after this, Vivian was brought to such a deplorable state of mind, and constant anxiety had made such fearful inroads upon his constitution, that he was confined to h's bed, and Mrs. Clavering entertained the most serious apprehensions as to the results; indeed, it was wonderful how she herself found the strength to support so heavy a trial (under which many persons of even stronger nerve than herself must have sunk) with the fortitude she did.   But she put her trust in Heaven, and hoped that, although their circumstances were at the present time as gloomy as they could possibly be, the designs of their enemy would ultimately be frustrated, and that Mr. Clavering would be brought to a due sense of the unjust severity with which he was visiting them, and would restore them to his favour.

Vivian was at last enabled to quit his room, and struggled hard to conquer the feelings of despair and anguish that tortured h!s mind, but it was a task that he could not easily accomplish, and Mrs. Clavering saw with alarm the fearful change it was daily, nay, hourly making in his manners and his constitution.   His once fine, manly, and muscular frame was wasted to a complete shadow; his countenance became pale and haggard, and almost cadaverous, and there was a constant wildness in the expression of his eyes, which was quite alarming to look on.   In vain Clemence endeavoured to arouse him from this dejected state; the grief and remorse were too firmly implanted in his heart to be easily eradicated, and even the gentle remonstrances and supplications of his wife at last failed to have any effect upon him; in fact, he seemed totally lost to himself and everything around him; and Mrs. Clavering feared that his mind was fast sinking under the weight of anxiety that pressed upon it; and that his intellect must ultimately yield to the shock.   She watched all his actions with the most vigilant eyes, and was fearful of his being out of her sight for any time together.   But it was all to no purpose; Vivian would shun all society for days together, sometimes remaining in his own room, and at others wandering about, his wife could never ascertain whither.

Old Thomas had frequently communicated with them; but his letters gave them not the least room to hope for any favourable alteration in their circumstances.   Mr. Clavering still remained inexorable, and Andrew seemed entirely to have got him in his power, and to make him think altogether as he dictated, and as answered his nefarious views.

Thus wore on many dreary months, without any change for the better taking place. Vivian would now absent himself from home for days together; and when he returned he was sullen and morose, repulsed all the tender advances of his wife, and gave the most evident and alarming signs of his brain being affected.

It was what Mrs. Clavering had long predicted and foreseen; and many were the dreadful hours of anguish and suspense which she suffered; many were the tears she shed at the terrible misfortunes with which it had pleased Providence to afflict them; many were the prayers she offered up to Heaven to avert that still more awful calamity which she daily, nay, hourly, expected.   She often endeavoured to follow the footsteps of her husband, so that she might be at hand to prevent his committing any rash act; but he always contrived to elude her; and she would be compelled to return home to misery, anxiety, and fear.   Alas! little, however, did she anticipate the full extent of the awful fate that was in store for them.

We will now, having thus fully explained all these melancholy circumstances, return to the point at which we commenced this chapter.

The night was as lovely as could well be imagined; the moon was riding majestically on the bosom of her clouds of silvery light; and the mind might well become enchanted with the grandeur of the scene the eye gazed upon.

It was about nine o'clock, and the inhabitants of the peaceful little village had most of them retired to rest from their hard day's toil; and only a very few lights could be seen to glimmer in the casements of the different cottages; but suddenly those few individuals who had not sought their pillows, were aroused by the most awful shrieks, followed by loud cries of murder, which seemed to proceed from the top of the village, and rushing from their cottages, they beheld the girl Rose, the servant of Mr. and Mrs. Clavering, standing upon the door-step, wringing her hands, and exhibiting every other symptom of the greatest distress and horror.

"Oh, poor master and mistress!" she exclaimed, in answer to the questions that were put to her; "did you not hear the report of the pistol? For God's sake enter the house; they are both murdered!"

"Murdered!" repeated one of the men; "by whom?"

Rose was, however, unable to reply, and almost immediately afterwards fainted.

The persons who had thus been alarmed, entered the house in a body, and opened the bed-room door, from which they perceived a light gleaming; they started back in the utmost horror and dismay at the dreadful spectacle which presented itself. The unfortunate Mr. Clavering and his wife were stretched upon the fl or weltering in their blood, and by the side of the former lay a pistol, which plainly showed by what means the horrid deed had been prepetrated.

A surgeon who resided in the neighbourhood was sent for with the utmost dispatch : but he immediately pronounced life to be totally extinct in both of them. The child was quite safe, and reposing calmly in his little cot by the side of his ill-fated parents' bed.

CHAPTER V.

THE REMORSE OF MR. CLAVERING.—MORE STARTLING EVENTS.—THE SECRET MURDER, AND ITS FATAL RESULTS.

IT would be impossible to describe the sensation this horrible event caused in the peaceful village and surrounding neighbourhood. As soon as Rose could be restored to anything like composure, the whole facts of the dreadful case were elicited from her. It seemed that Mr. Clavering had been from home the whole of the day, and when Rose opene the door to him at night, she could not help noticing the particular wildness of his looks, and he seemed as if he was labouring under the effects of inebriation. She had previously placed the infant James in his little cot, and retired to her room, thinking that she would not be wanted again that night, and a short time afterwards she heard her master and mistress leave the parlour, and ascend the stairs to their chamber. She did not hear onny words pass between them, but they had not departed to rest, as she imagined. many minutes, when she was alarmed by a loud scream from her mistress and was rushing up stairs to ascertain what was the matter, when the report of a pistol smote her ears. She was horror-struck, and clung to the bannisters for a few moments unable to move a step, and her horror was increased when she heard a second report, followed by a sound as if something heavy had fallen upon the floor. She was now aroused to a desperate pitch of courage, and rushing up stairs, and bursting open the door, found her master and mistress extended on the floor, and weltering in a pool of blood. It was then that, horror-struck, the poor girl rushed from the house, and created the alarm she did.

The horrible catastrophe needed no further explanation ; driven to a state of madness the wretched Vivian Clavering had first murdered his wife, and then destroyed his own life !

As soon as possible intelligence of the awful event was forwarded to Mr. Clavering, who heard it with such feelings of horror and remorse which we cannot attempt to pourtray.

Andrew Clavering also pretended to be greatly shocked, while in secret the villain, exulted in the dreadful catastrophe, which had thus ridden him of two beings who presented the only obstacle to his covetous and ambitious views.

Most poignant was the remorse of Mr. Clavering, and for some time he was in a state of mind bordering on distraction. Bitterly did he reproach himself for the severe and unjust conduct he had pursued towards his unfortunate son and daughter-in-law, which had driven the former, there could be no doubt, to the perpetration of so dreadful a crime, but still he never for a moment suspected that the heartless miscreant Andrew had misrepresented facts to him, or had so cruelly poisoned his mind against his own offspring.

The bodies of Vivian Clavering and his wife were interred, the former without Christian rites, and the poor little orphan was removed to the mansion of his grandfather. For many weeks, ay months, Mr. Clavering was deaf to the voice of consolation, and at one period he was reduced to such a state of misery that he was confined to his bed, and his medical attendants entertained strong fears that he would never recover. The reproaches of conscience tortured him almost to madness, and he could not but accuse himself of being the sole cause of Vivian and his wife's untimely and awful end ; but the hardened Andrew bore everything with the greatest indifference, although he pretended to lament severely the dreadful fate to which his brother and his devoted and affectionate partner

had been brought, and expressed the greatest commiseration for their orphan child, while
at the same time he inwardly wished that it had shared the same fate as its parents, for
he saw plain enough that the affection of his father would now be attracted to him, and,
should he live, he might present the same barrier to the entire gratification of his avarice
that Vivian had done.

At length Mr. Clavering did become more calm, but the dreadful catastrophe, or rather
tragedy, which we have just related, left a melancholy impression upon his mind which
nothing could eradicate. Years flew away, and James Clavering was now a fine intelligent youth, possessing all the noble qualities of his unfortunate parents, and bearing so
extraordinary a likeness to his father, that it pained his aged grandfather to look at
him, and yet he was unhappy whenever he was out of sight. He employed tutors at
home to instruct him in every graceful and useful accomplishment, and did all that he
could in his behaviour towards him to make atonement for the cruel injustice with which
he had treated his parents. Need we say that this was a fresh source of jealousy and
uneasiness to Andrew Clavering, and that he viewed his nephew with the most deadly
hatred, while at the same time he affected to entertain the highest regard for him, and
admiration for his noble and amiable disposition.

Andrew Clavering remained a bachelor, which he pretended to do in consequence of
his reluctance to quit his father's roof, and that he might be in constant attendance upon
him, now that his great age and infirmities demanded such particular care; and his
father continued to be deceived by him, and to look upon him as the most amiable and
affectionate of sons with whom a parent had ever been blessed.

James Clavering had scarcely arrived at the years of manhood, when Mary Colburn
came to reside with her father (who was a small father) in the neighbourhood, and it
was not long before they became acquainted. He was immediately struck with the
modest graces of Mary's person and mind, and she was equally fascinated with the many
intrinsic qualities he displayed; friendship soon strengthened into love, and they were
never happy but when they were together. It was not long before Mr. Clavering became
acquainted with their attachment, and although he considered them both too young at
present to marry, he gave every encouragement to their suit, for he considered that Mary
was a maiden every way worthy of becoming his grandson's wife; and as Mr. Colburn
was also highly in favour of the match, it was finally settled that their union should take
place in due time, and the bosoms of the lovers were filled with emotions of the most joyful anticipation.

About this time it was that the unknown gentleman, whom we have introduced to the
reader at the commencement of this tale, suddenly made his appearance at the mansion,
and was ushered in the most mysterious manner into the presence of Mr. Clavering, with
whom he remained closeted for several hours, on the occasion of his first visit.

James Clavering was particularly struck with the nobleness of his appearance, and it
was quite evident that he was a person of distinction, from the deference with which he
had been received by his grandfather; but what his name was he could not learn, neither
could he imagine what his business with Mr. Clavering could be; but he thought from
the looks of Andrew that he knew him, and did not appear to be at all satisfied at his
visit. When he departed the elder Mr. Clavering exhibited no little degree of excitement, and motioning to his son, he followed him out of the room and remained closeted
with him for the rest of the day.

From that time the stranger's visits became frequent, and although the same air of
mystery was maintained as on the first occasion, he sometimes joined them at the din-
ner-table, and entered freely into conversation, from which it could be seen that he was
a man of superior education, and of vast intelligence; and James Clavering took much
pleasure in listening to him, and was more anxious than ever to become acquainted with
who he was."

To or thee times he ventured to question his grandfather upon the subject, but he
evinced much displeasure at his curiosity, and desired that he would never more put
similar questions to him, as they could not be answered. Of course James had no alternative but to obey, but his wonder and curiosity were more than ever excited to know
the reason for all this extraordinary mystery, and he determined to do his best to discover it.

But other events soon occurred to divert his mind, and to occupy the whole of his
most serious thoughts. Mr. Colburn, the father of Mary, was taken suddenly and dan-

gerously ill, and, notwithstanding all the skill and attention of his physicians, he gradually sunk under the malady, and breathed his last, leaving his daughter completely overwhelmed and distracted with grief, and filling the mind of her lover with the greatest alarm lest this calamity should be attended with fatal consequences to her he so fondly loved.

Mary Colburn was now left an orphan, and with but limited means for support, for of late years her father had been very unfortunate, and had suffered much from bad harvests and the failure of crops, and James Clavering was therefore the more anxious that their union should take place with as little delay as possible, so that Mary might have a lawful protector. His grandfather duly appreciated and commended his sentiments, and gave his consent to their union as soon as a decent time had elapsed after the death of Mary's parent.

It was some months ere Mary could regain anything like her accustomed spirits, but at length the violence of her grief was in some measure calmed, and she gave her consent for her lover to fix the joyful day on which he should lead her to the altar.

That happy day arrived, and James Clavering and his beloved Mary were united in the holy bands of matrimony, and their future prospects appeared to be those of the most uninterrupted bliss.

James Clavering wished not to lead a life of indolence, and having always had a taste for agricultural pursuits, his grandfather established him in a comfortable farm, not far from his own residence, and gave him a considerable sum of money to commence business with, and James entered upon his new course of life with energy and the brightest anticipations.

This was wormwood to Andrew Clavering, and he tried all in his power by the most artful and insidious means to prejudice his father against him and his wife; but in this he failed, and he was compelled to conduct his designs with the greatest caution, lest the suspicions of the old man should be aroused.

James and his wife had ever viewed the conduct of Andrew Clavering with suspicion; and regarded his pretended friendship towards them with anything but confidence and satisfaction; but of course they could not have any idea of his real thoughts and designs, or they would have shunned him with disgust, and looked upon him as he really was, their bitterest enemy.

A twelvemonth elapsed in this manner, and a year of uninterrupted bliss it was to James Clavering and his wife; everything prospered with them, and they were esteemed by all who knew them. Mary had presented her delighted husband with a lovely girl; but their joy at this addition to their happiness was not destined to last long; the infant was little more than three months old when it was seized with a violent illness, which baffled all the skill of the medical attendant, and death deprived them of the little innocent whom they had hailed with such feelings of transport, and watched with such tender and affectionate care.

This was the first interruption they had experienced to their happiness, and it was some time ere they could recover from it; but at length they became resigned, and submitted with patience to the will of Providence.

In the meantime, Andrew Clavering continued to brood over the guilty designs he had for so many years had in contemplation, and viewed the prosperity of his nephew and wife with the most jealous eyes, and especially as his father's affection towards them seemed daily to increase, and he was continually bestowing upon them some signal mark of his favour. But Andrew was determined that he would not be foiled in his avaricious views, and he had already taken one material step towards the accomplishment of his nefarious wishes, which he flattered himself could not fail to be crowned with success.

Soon after this Mr. Clavering received a letter, which he said would compel him to go to London; and, as he (Andrew) had been from home some days, James offered to accompany him, as from his great age he considered it not safe for him to travel without a companion; but as the journey was only a short one, his grandfather peremptorily declined his offer, and took his departure accordingly alone.

On the third night after this, a cry of agony, followed by half-stifled groans, might have been heard to proceed from an old uninhabited house, situated in a filthy street at the east-end of the town, and directly after a man, with his hat drawn over his brows for the purpose of concealment, and enveloped in a great coat, rushed hastily from the house and, having glanced eagerly up the street to see whether the coast was clear, he darted round the corner, where the watchman (as watchmen were wont to do) was asleep in his box, and was soon out of sight.

All was silent for an instant, when again the low moaning cries of agony might be heard, and then a groan still louder than any that had preceded it followed, and a noise as if of some person struggling.

At this juncture, three men, apparently mechanics, and, probably, returning home from their daily toil, passed through the street, and just before they had reached the old house, their attention was arrested by the faint cries of agony before mentioned, and they stopped to listen.

"Why, they are certainly human cries, Sam," said one of them; "what can all this mean? Hush! Some poor creature, I shouldn't wonder, has sought a shelter from the cold in this house, and perhaps is dying."

"Where's the watchman?" asked another of the men.

"Oh! no doubt, he is, as usual, taking a comfortable nap in his box," replied the first speaker. "Let's arouse him, and see into this, for it will not do to leave a fellow being here to die."

The watchman was quickly aroused, and, having been made acquainted with the particulars in a few words, accompanied the men to the house. They found the door open, for the stranger had not stopped to close it when he emerged from it, and they immediately entered. The old watchman held up his lantern, and they all started back in horror and amazement at the sight which presented itself.

Stretched upon his back, and bleeding copiously from several ghastly wounds about the head and body, was the figure of an aged man, whose dress betokened him to be a gentleman, and by his side lay a stout cudgel, with which the blows upon the head, no doubt, had been inflicted; and a little farther off the watchman picked up a large clasp knife reeking with blood, and which, no doubt, the brutal assassin had made use of to complete his bloody deed.

They raised the unfortunate man from the ground; life was not quite extinct, but he only breathed one faint sigh, and expired.

An alarm was instantly raised, and the whole neighbourhood was thrown into a state of the greatest excitement. The body of the aged and unfortunate victim was conveyed to the nearest tavern, and immediate steps were taken to discover the inhuman murderer, but with little prospect of success.

No money or other property was found upon the murdered man, which plainly showed that the crime had been perpetrated for the purpose of robbery; but a letter was discovered in one of his pockets which led to his identity. The unfortunate victim was Mr. Clavering.

No time was lost in making his friends acquainted with the dreadful circumstances, and the horror of James Clavering and his wife, on hearing it, may well be imagined.

Andrew Clavering was still from home when the fatal news arrived; but he lost no time in returning as soon as he received intelligence of it; and he appeared to be completely horror-struck and distracted at the dreadful fate of his father. The body of the poor old gentleman was conveyed to the mansion, and an universal gloom was thrown over the inhabitants of the neighbourhood (by whom Mr. Clavering had been much esteemed) by the horrible event.

All attempts to discover the murderer was ineffectual; it had been perpetrated in so secret a manner that it was impossible for suspicion to light upon any one. Several of the low characters who resided in the street were taken up, and underwent several examinations; but nothing could be elicited to implicate them in the dreadful crime, and, of course, they were discharged.

How Mr. Clavering could have been lured into that low locality in which the crime was perpetrated, it was difficult to conceive. The gentleman to whom the deceased had been on business informed them that on the afternoon of the fatal day on which the crime was committed, he had left him to go to the coach-office; and he had supposed that he was on his way home when he had heard of his barbarous assassination. Thus, all was enveloped in the most painful mystery, and which, at present, there seemed to be no probability of ever being unravelled.

James Clavering and his wife deeply lamented the untimely end of their aged relative, and felt that they had lost their best, indeed, their only earthly friend; for in Andrew

THE ROYAL TWINS;

OR, THE SISTERS OF MYSTERY.

No. 7.

Clavering they placed no confidence, and had ever viewed all the professions he had made with the strongest suspicions, which what they had recently seen of his conduct did not in the least tend to diminish.

No one evinced deeper sorrow at the untimely death of Mr. Clavering than Andrew ; in fact, for some weeks he appeared to be quite inconsolable ; but could the dark thoughts that were passing in his mind have been revealed, with what horror and disgust would his real character have been viewed.

The moment to complete his avaricious designs had now arrived ; the will of the deceased Mr. Clavering was read in the presence of James and his wife, when it was found that he had bequeathed the whole of his property to Andrew, and had not made the least provision for his grandson.

It would be false to say that James Clavering was not astonished and disappointed ; after all the affectionate regard and attention his aged relative had ev.r paid towards him, from his earliest childhood, and the promises he had upon several occasions made to him, it did indeed seem strange, unnatural, and incredible, that he should thus have forgotten him. He could not help thinking there had been some foul play ; and well knowing his uncle's avaricious disposition, his suspicions fell upon him. But he concealed his real thoughts, in the hope that time would unravel everything, and that justice would be rendered him. His circumstances were at present comfortable and prosperous, and he hoped that, by his own industry and perseverance, Providence would yet enable him to obtain an honest independence.

Andrew Clavering's covetous wishes were now fully gratified ; but at what a price had he purchased that gratification ! but could the villain be really happy with all the weight of guilt that pressed upon his conscience ? It was impossible that he could be so ; but yet he struggled against the dreadful thoughts that would at times rush upon his brain, and tried to enjoy his ill-gotten wealth.

He pretended to feel much regret that his father had neglected to make any provision for his nephew ; but he did not offer to so instead, though he said, " if James should at any time need assistance, he knew where he had a friend."

James received this insulting promise with proud indifference ; he could see through the shallow hypocrisy of his uncle, and he despised him for it, and determined to suffer anything rather than ask a favour of him, which he was confident he would not be willing to bestow.

The real character of Andrew Clavering shortly after the death of his father more fully betrayed itself. On the pretext that, in consequence of the declining state of his health, he found it necessary to reside in future on the continent, he sold off the estate ; and, scarcely condescending to bid his nephew adieu, quitted England, merely stating that he would furnish him with his address when he had fixed upon the place of his abode.

James Clavering and his wife saw him depart without regret ; they had never expected any favour from him, and did not wish to be under any obligation to him, and they hoped by their own industry to be able to realize every happiness they wished.

For some months everything went on prosperously, and James and his wife were indeed the most happy and contented of human beings ; labour was sweet to them, for it brought with it health and spirits, and they envied not their sordid relative with all his riches. They were certain that he enjoyed not the pure happiness that they did, and they would have been sorry to have exchanged situations with him ; indeed they would have had good reason to think so had they known all.

They had never received any communication from him since he had left England ; and they therefore considered that he intended to abandon them altogether, a circumstance which they did not at all regret, as they had nothing to expect from his friendship, and they had ever viewed him with suspicion and mistrust.

But now misfortune was about to lower upon the prospects of James Clavering and his faithful partner. A very bad harvest brought upon them a very great loss ; and to add to the calamity, a disease broke out among the cattle, by which Clavering lost the greater portion of his stock. As if evil fate had resolved to overwhelm them at once, the country bank in which the farmers principally deposited their money, failed, and James Clavering, nearly the whole of whose capital was deposited there, found himself to his horror and dismay, nearly reduced to beggary at one fell swoop.

In this emergency what was to be done ? They saw no other prospect before them than shortly to be deprived of house and home, and the means of existence, unless some friend would step forward to assist them in their difficulty; but where could they look for that friend? There was no one to whom they could apply but their uncle, and from the idea of being beholden to him they shrunk with repugnance. But they had no alternative, and surely he could not be so cruel as to refuse them on such an occasion, especially as their difficulties had not been brought upon them by any misconduct of their own. To him, therefore, after much hesitation, they at length determined to apply; and having obtained his address from his bankers in London, Mr. Clavering dispatched a letter to him with all speed, in which he laid before him a plain and unexaggerated statement of his situation, and the fatal and unavoidable circumstances that had led to it, and requested him most earnestly to fulfill the promise he had once been pleased to make him; namely, to render him assistance in his difficulties, now that he so urgently stood in need of it.

It was nearly a fortnight before Clavering received any answer to this appeal; and he and his wife, as may be imagined, were in a state of the greatest anxiety and suspense, for their circumstances were every hour becoming more desperate and pressing. But when it did arrive their despair was rendered complete. " Mr. Clavering was sorry to hear of their misfortunes, but regretted that, at present, in consequence of the embarrassed state of his own aff irs, he could not render them that assistance he would otherwise have been most happy to have done."

Thus had the sordid villain fully unmasked himself, and the unfortunate Clavering and his wife saw nothing but ruin before them. To stay the coming storm was impossible They were greatly in arrears; their creditors pressed for payment; they were unable to meet their demands; and in consequence a distress was put in the farm; and a few days beheld the once happy James Clavering and his virtuous wife homeless and penniless.

A few kind neighbours, who had ever esteemed the worthy young couple, and deeply commisserated with them in their misfortunes, subscribed together, and rendered them all the assistance in their power. They obtained shelter in a humble cottage, where for many days they were in a state of complete despair, and knew not what course to adopt. At length Mr. Clavering aroused himself, and procured employment as a labourer on the very far.n which had so recently been his own. It was a sad reverse of fortune, and it needed all the fortitude they could muster, to support it with becoming patience; but at last they resigned themselves to their fate, trusting that although Providence had thought fit at present to visit them with such heavy afflictions, in due course He would once more restore them to happiness, and that state of comfort which they had so recently experienced.

It was at this period that Mrs. Clavering gave birth to a son, which the fond parents hailed with delight, notwithstanding the distressing state of poverty to which they now found themselves reduced. But fresh troubles were about to overtake them. Poor Clavering, through some feeling of jealousy in one of the parties placed above him, was dismissed from the farm, and was also ejected by the same functionary from the cottage he and his wife had occupied.

The horrors of their situation were now complete. The winter was setting in, and they were deprived of shelter, and had only a few shillings in the world, which Clavering had contrived to save from his scanty wages, to prov de them food. What a dreadful prospect to contemplate! It was wonderful that they did not at once sink under it, for it was a trial that persons of stronger minds than they possessed even might not have been able to endure.

For some days they were sheltered and assisted by their neighbours, and were completely lost, and bewildered, and distracted, to know in what way to act. But at last, scorning to remain a burthen to those worthy individuals, who could so ill afford it, Clavering, with what few shillings he had got, determined to make his way to London, in the hope of being there able to procure some enployment,—he cared not what it was, so that by that means he should be enabled to avert the horrors of starvation.

They arrived in the metropolis, where fate still continued to frown upon them. We will not endeavour to describe the dreadful privations they underwent, for it would harrow up the fee.ings of the reader; but at length they were reduced to the abject state of misery and beggary, in which they were introduced at the commencement of our tale.

CHAPTER VI.

RETURNS TO THE ROYAL TWINS.—THE PROGRESS OF BEAUTY.

IN the course of a few days Mr. and Mrs. Milford (for we deem it prudent for the present to call them by their assumed name), when the excitement of those extraordinary events had somewhat subsided in their breasts, became quite at home in their new residence, and began to hope that their misfortunes were at an end. They could not, the more they reflected upon all the circumstances, and the statements which the stranger had made, regret having taken charge of the poor infant sisters, for they trusted that, by so doing, they had been the means of saving them from some untimely fate; but still they would have been better satisfied if the unknown had been more explicit as to their origin, and have given them the means of finding him, should anything occur which might render it necessary to see him. What necessity there could be for him to maintain so much secrecy, after the oath he had extorted from them, they could not imagine; and, if he had not done so, it would naturally have inspired them with more confidence.

Notwithstanding the injunctions of the unknown gentleman, Mr. Milford could not resist the curiosity he felt to discover the mansion to which they had been conveyed on that eventful night; and after a week had elapsed, he started one morning after breakfast with that object in view. He traced his way along the road which he remembered they had travelled, and noticed every object on the road with the hope of refreshing his memory; but when he came to the spot where the unknown had first permitted the blinds of the carriage to be drawn up, he was lost entirely in perplexity, and knew not which way to proceed. He was at the entrance of three roads which branched off different ways, and after hesitating for some time, he took the one to the right, because he remembered that it was in that direction the carriage seemed to turn in going to the mansion. It was a lonely road with a wide range of fields on both sides, and did not seem to be a place of much traffic. Milford proceeded along it for more than three miles, but saw no signs of a human dwelling; and it was wild and unfrequented, (for he had not met a single passenger), as if it had been situated in the most distant part of the country; but at length, tired of walking, and seeing no prospect of his curiosity being gratified, he turned back, resolved to abandon the task he had imposed upon himself.

Milford had proceeded some distance on his way back, when the sound of carriage wheels caused him to look up, and he perceived a carriage preceded, by two out-riders in scarlet liveries, coming along the road at a moderate pace. When it had reached that part of the road along which he was walking, the speed of the horses was somewhat slackened, and Milford beheld that the panels of the carriage door bore the royal arms. The windows were open, and Milford saw two gentlemen seated in the carriage opposite to each other. One of those persons was a particularly handsome man, in the prime of life, and the majesty of whose countenance most forcibly struck Milford; he had seen the portrait of the Prince of Wales, and he was convinced that this could be no other than that august personage.

While Milford was thus occupied in gazing on the countenance of the prince, the other person in the carriage leant forward to address him, and Milford, although it was only for an instant, had a full and distinct view of his features; but what was his astonishment when in them he recognized those of the unknown! The next moment the carriage dashed way at its former speed, and Milford, filled with amazement and perplexity, watched it until it was completely out of sight.

As Milford retraced his steps towards home, his thoughts were totally absorbed by this extraordinary circumstance; and his interest and curiosity respecting the stranger were now greater than ever. That he was a person of the highest distinction was quite certain, or he would not have the honour of being the companion of royalty, and the was the individual who had been on intimate terms with his grandfather, and between whom so much secrecy ever prevailed. He was lost in wonder, and felt himself still more deeply interested in the origin of the children committed to his care, fully satisfied that the most noble blood flowed in their veins, and of the vast importance and responsibility of the charge which he had taken upon himself.

On arriving at home he immediately made his wife acquainted with the whole particulars, and her astonishment, if possible, surpassed his own.

"But are you certain that you were not mistaken?" said Mrs. Milford; "and that it was really the unknown gentleman you saw in the carriage with the prince."

"It was impossible for me to be deceived," replied Milford; "I had a distinct view of his features, and I almost imagined that he saw me at the same time."

"This event is, if possible, still more wonderful than all the rest," remarked Mrs. Milford; "who can this stranger be?"

"It is is impossible to say," replied her husband, "but it is quite evident he is a person of the highest rank, and we may run ourselves into danger if we do not strictly obey his injunctions; besides the trouble to which we might expose these poor children and all connected with them."

They continued to converse for some time upon this subject, and the longer they reflected upon it, the more they became involved in perplexity and amazement, and looked forward to the time when the mystery might in some measure be explained, with the utmost impatience.

The next day, while Milford and his wife were seated at dinner, Martha entered the room, and presented Mr. Milford with a letter, which she said had been brought to the house by a livery servant on horseback, who immediately rode off on delivering it. Mr. Milford on looking at the superscription, instantly recognised the handwriting of the stranger, and breaking the seal, read the following words :—

"I saw you, yesterday, and am convinced that you recognised me. Remember your promise, and do not, as you value the safety of the children committed to your care and that of those connected with them, attempt to make any discovery. Idle curiosity may ruin all, and bring trouble upon your own head. Rest satisfied with what I have told, and wait patiently for what may at some future time be disclosed to you. Above all, be careful not to divulge to any one, excepting your wife, what you yesterday beheld, for if you do, you may depend upon it, it will not fail to meet my knowledge. Be prudent, be cautious, be faithful, and so you shall be rewarded, and earn the lasting gratitude of

YOUR FRIEND."

"This then will convince you, Mary," said Milford, when he had perused the letter, "that I was not mistaken, and that this unknown gentleman was the companion of the prince."

"I am satisfied," said Mrs. Milford; "and my wonder is still more excited than ever. But we must, indeed, act with prudence and circumspection, lest we should, involve ourselves and the innocent children we have undertaken to protect, in danger. It is quite evident that they are the offspring of noble parents, nay, perhaps even of royalty itself."

"Ah!" exclaimed Milford, "what strange thoughts and feelings does that suggestion excite in my bosom; I feel now to the fullest extent the heavy responsibility we have taken upon ourselves, and almost regret that we have been persuaded to undertake the arduous task."

"Nay," returned Mrs. Milford; "while we continue to act in accordance with the injunctions of the unknown, I do not think that we shall have much cause to fear; besides, what could we do, in the awful and abject state of misery and destitution to which we were reduced, and when comfort and independance were offered to us, for merely performing an act of humanity?"

"Very true, very true," said Milford; "we could not have acted otherwise, and I trust that Providence will enable us to perform our task with credit to ourselves, and advantage to these poor children."

"At least, my dear husband, we will have the satisfaction of knowing that we have acted from the purest motives, and we will never give our young charge future reason to say, should they become aware that they are not related to us, that we ever acted in any other way towards them, than as if they had been our own children."

"Well, spoken, Mary, I know you will do your duty with all a mother's fondness and attention, and I'm sure I need not tell you that in me the fair sisters shall ever find a father, watchful of their safety and anxious to guard them from the vices and the temptations of the world. I cannot help thinking that these little strangers are sent to be a blessing to us; and so we will view everything in the brightest light, and look forward to the future with hope and confidence."

"And we shall not be disappointed, James," said Mrs Milford; "my heart assures me that we shall not, and I feel more cheerful and happy than I have done for many a long day. How can I be otherwise when I contemplate the change which but a few short days have wrought in our circumstances, a change so great and so sudden that at times I can scarcely believe in its reality? Oh, how grateful ought we to be, when we reflect upon the dreadful state of misery and contamination from which we have been rescued."

And, indeed, they were grateful, and night and morning they poured forth their thanks to Heaven, which after such months of bitter and almost insupportable suffering had restored them to every happiness.

When Milford saw the roses return to the cheeks of his wife, her eyes resume their beautiful mild expresson of content, and no longer dimmed with tears, or sunken with torturing anxiety; when he beheld her lately emaciated form restored to its former vigour and grace; his bosom overflowed with delightful sensations, and he looked upon the infant sisters with feelings of the warmest affection as the little saviours of himself and all he held most dear in existence.

Mrs. Morton proved herself to be a most amiable woman, and bestowed upon the children the most attentive care, and Martha also performed the duties allotted to her in the most exemplary manner, and showed that she was every way worthy of the character which the unknown had given of her. The children throve amazingly, and although so young, the uncommon beauty, and it might almost be said intelligence of their features excited admiration in the bosoms of all who beheld them. Mr. and Mrs. Milford, however, avoided any intimacy with their neighbours, for they were fearful that it might prove dangerous, and they were satisfied would be sure not to meet with the approbation of the stranger, should it reach his knowledge, which they had no doubt it would.

In this manner five months passed away, and they heard nothing more of the stranger, though the first quarter's wages for her and Martha's services had been regularly forwarded, as promised, but who the agent was they had no means of ascertaining, and, after the caution which the unknown's letter conveyed, they did not think it prudent to make any inquiry.

The favourite room of Mr. and Mrs. Milford in their new dwelling, was that which contained the portrait which had so particularly attracted their attention, and excited their interest and curiosity when they first beheld it, and there they passed much of their time, contemplating that finely executed painting, and conversing upon the wonderful events which had in the short space of a few months occurred to them. The portrait being the counterpart of the miniature in the valuable locket found suspended from the neck of the little Augusta, convinced them that it was the resemblance of the mother of the little twin sisters, and therefore did they the more prize it, and could not help feeling a sensation amounting to the utmost veneration whenever they gazed upon it.

The nobility of the countenance, the commanding grace of the figure, and the elegance of the dress in which she was represented, left little doubt upon their minds that she was a lady of distinction, and they perplexed tkeir brains in vain to form even the least conjecture as to the cause which could have induced her to part with her tender offspring, to suffer them to be committed to the care of strangers, and to deprive herself of the performance of all those duties which it so delights a tender mother to bestow; but they were satisfied that it must have been some dreadful necessity that could compel her to such an unnatural step, and taking that merciful view of the subject, they could not but deeply symp thise with her in her unknown misfortunes. They remembered the sounds of sorrow they had heard on the night when the children were committed to their care, and they could not for a moment doubt but it was the grief of a distracted mother in being thus compelled to separate herself (perhaps for ever) from her tender babes. How terrible and mysterious must be the circumstances that could render such a desperate course necessary; Milford and his wife in vain endeavoured to conjecture them, but the more they did so, the more they became bewildered in the maze of uncertainty and perplexity.

And what connection did the unknown, whom Milford had seen in the company of royalty, bear to the mother of their tender charge? They well remembered his emotion on parting with them; it was an emotion of no ordinary kind; could such feelings spring from any other than a fathers's breast? and yet all his observations, vague even as they were, tended to shew that such ties of consanguinity did not exist between them. It was fruitless to ponder upon the ambiguous subject, for it only bewildered them the more, and left them in a still greater state of dissatisfaction. To one conclusion and resolution Milford and his wife could only come, namely to do their duty faithfully towards the poor children, so strangely placed under their protection, and to wait patiently for the unravelment of the secrets connected with them, perfectly confident that circumstances of the most extraordinary and important character were involved in their fate, and that the greatest circumspection was requisite on their part in all probability to prevent the occurrence of the most serious evils.

We should become tedious were we to dwell upon all the trifling incidents that occured in the family of Milford and his wife during the first twelve months of the remarkable change in their life. All proceeded calmly, and they had become completely settled in and attached to their new home; in fact, surrounded as they were with every comfort, how could they be otherwise? The twin sisters daily increased in health, and strength, and beauty, and their protectors looked upon them with the same fond affection as if they had been their own offspring, and blessed the strange incident which had placed them under their care.

But there was one circumstance at this period which caused them considerable regret, and that was an announcement from Mrs. Morton, that in consequence of the return of her husband, and his intention not to go to sea again, she must be compelled to leave them, as her own domestic duties would demand her attendance at home; but she promised to call upon them frequently, and expressed her sincere acknowledgments for the uniform kindness she had experienced from them since she had been in their service, and trusted that they and their little family would continue to enjoy health and happiness.

The loss of so amiable a woman as Mrs. Morton was a matter of the deepest concern to Mr. and Mrs. Milford, more especially as they had met under such peculiar circumstances, and they did not fail to express themselves to that effect, at the same time earnestly soliciting her future friendship, and likewise that she would endeavour to recomend them some respectable female to supply, in some measure, her place. This Mrs. Morton promised to do, and they parted with much regret on both sides. In a few days Mrs. Morton introduced a respectable female, a widow, to them, and every arrangement having been satisfactorily made, things went on much the same as usual.

The first three years rolled rapidly away, and the innocent prattle of the twin sisters and their own boy, George, formed a source of unbounded delight to Mr. and Mrs. Milford. The beauty of the little sisters daily expanded, and children as they were, they yet gave remarkable symptoms of intelligence, and put forth fair promise of future excellence. The likeness that existed between them was most extraordinary, but yet at that early age they evinced considerrble difference of disposition. The little Charlotte was always overflowing with innocent mirth, playful as a young fawn, while Agusta at times showed a seriousness of temper that was quite remarkable in so young a child. Every day their likeness to the portrait became more forcibly striking, and fully confirmed Milford and his wife in their first opinion, namely, that it could be no other than the resemblance of their mother.

And now the time having expired when they expected to hear again from the unknown, they awaited most anxiously that event; but when a month over the time had passed away without their receiving any communication from him, they began to feel uneasy, and to entertain doubts as to whether or not he would fulfil his promise. But another week having elapsed, all their apprehensions were dissipated by the arrival of a groom in rich livery, on horseback, who having delivered a letter to Martha, addressed to Mr. Milford, departed again immediately, without having spoken a word.

Milford having opened the letter, discovered a cheque for five hundred pounds, and a note addressed to himself, in the following words—

"You have hitherto acted prudently, and I am perfectly satisfied with your conduct. Continue to pursue the same, and all will be well; but once deviate from it, and horrible will be the consequences that will follow. Everything you do is known to me; there is nothing can escape my knowledge. Therefore beware, for on your faithful performance of your promise depends your own happiness, and probably the lives of those unoffending children whom you have undertaken to protect.

"This day week I shall visit you; I shall be accompanied; but seek not to know by whom; neither must you venture to address me. Three o'clock will be the hour at which I shall arrive. Place the children in the room which contains the portrait at that hour, and take care that the servants are not in the way. Remember, be silent, and be cautious!"

Nothing could equal the astonishment of Mr. add Mrs. Milford on perusing this singular epistle; every day produced some fresh mystery, and involved them still further in doubt and perplexity. They were at a perfect loss what opinion to form, and awaited the arrival of the day of the unknown's proposed visit with the utmost anxiety and impatience.

It came at last; and just before the hour at which the stranger had appointed to be there Mr. Milford sent Martha and her companion from the house, much to their amazement, and desired them not to return till the evening; they then awaited the coming event with the greatest expectation.

A few minutes before three Mrs. Milford led the two sisters to the portrait room, and having supplied them w th some toys, left them, knowing that they would not be alarmed, as they were often in the habit of playing there by themselves; she then returned to her husband, and the clock had no sooner struck three, than they heard the sound of a carriage rattling up the street, and the next moment there was a loud double knock at the street-door. Milford answered it, and perceived a handsome private carriage standing in the road. The footman was at that moment opening the door, from which the unknown gentleman immediately afterwards alighted, his tall form enveloped in a large military cloak, similar to the one which he had worn when he met Milford on the occasion mentioned in the first chapter. He merely exchanged a glance with Milford, but it was a most significant one; and then handed a lady from the carriage, and placing her arm within his, walked hastily past Milford into the house, and motioned the hall door to be closed after them.

The figure of the lady was tall and stately; she was attired in black, and a long black veil completely concealed her features and descended to her feet. Mr. and Mrs. Milford beheld her with the greatest curiosity, and a feeling almost amounting to awe; but the unknown, without uttering a word, led her towards the door which opened upon the staircase ascending to the chamber were the children were; and as she passed them they could hear her sigh deeply, and could plainly perceive that she was otherwise violently agitated. The unknown closed the door after them, and Milford and his wife heard them slowly ascending the stairs.

They looked at each other with amazement, and it was some time before either of them ventured to speak.

"What can be the meaning of this?" at length said Mrs. Milford, in a low tone; "and where will it all end? This surely must be the mother of the children, who has came to visit them, and there must be something very important to cause all this mystery."

"Would that we had an opportunity of seeing her features," said Milford, "that we might have known her again, and discover whether she at all resembles the portrait that has so deeply excited our interest."

"And if we did, what would that avail, as we should still be in the same state of ignorance as to who she absolutely is? The gentleman will surely address us before he goes, and give us some explanation."

";I should rather think, from the tenor of his letter, that he would not," returned Mr. Milford; "but hush! do you not hear something?"

They advanced to the door, which they even ventured gently to open, and listened attentively. They could hear that the gentleman and lady were in earnest conversation;

THE ROYAL TWINS;

OR, THE SISTERS OF MYSTERY.

but the observations they made were perfectly incoherent, until the following words spoken in the melancholy voice of the female, reached their ears,—

"What a dreadful trial is this! Oh, God, in mercy——"

They could not catch the remainder of the sentence, for it was delivered in a more indistinct tone, but it was succeeded by the most convulsive sobs, which it was quite agonizing to hear, and it was with the greatest difficulty that Mr. Milford could so far control the womanly feelings of his wife as to prevent her from breaking through all the injunctions of the gentleman, and from rushing up stairs to express her sympathy with, and offer her aid to the unknown lady.

A short silence now ensued, which continued for a few minutes, only interrupted at intervals by the sobs of the female, but at length they were again enabled to catch a few broken sentences.

"Alas! alas!" they heard the female ejaculate, "why should I be thus cruelly persecuted by——. Why am I not allowed to retire *there*, and to have those that are dear to me?"

"Need you ask that question?" returned the gentleman, "have you not brought this all upon yourself? and should you therefore murmur at the course we are adopting to prevent the world from being acquainted with the particulars. Recollect that the character of your future king is at stake, and submit with the fortitude that becomes you under the circumstances."

They could not distinguish the answer that was returned to these observations, but they could still hear the female's violent expressions of grief, and deeply did their hearts sympathise with her in her unknown sorrows.

During this time they never once heard the voices of the children, which somewhat surprised them, as they had naturally imagined that they would be alarmed at the sight of strangers, especially from the sombre dress of the lady.

Some minutes elapsed, when the lady and gentleman were on a more evidently immersed in the most serious conversation, though it was conducted in such tones that neither Milford or his wife could distinguish a syllable of it; much to their disappointment, their curiosity being so much excited. However, a short time afterwards a burst of the most powerful agony escaped from the bosom of the lady, which was followed by a cry of alarm from the children, and they therefore imagined that their singular visitors were about taking their leave. In a few moments the sound of their footsteps upon the floor covinced them they were right in their conjectures, and cautiously closing the door, they returned into the parlour.

Presently they heard them descending the stairs, and immediately afterwards the room door was opened and the unknown entered, leading in the trembling form of the lady who appeared to be suffering the most acute mental anguish. They endeavoured in a hasty glance to discover her features, but the veil she wore completely obscured them, and the stranger seeing that Mr. Milford was inclined to speak, silenced him by a significant and peremptory look, and led the female to a chair in which she sunk evidently quite overpowered by the violence of her feelings.

The stranger now motioned to Milford and his wife to leave the room, and to hasten to the children, whom they could hear sobbing and crying above, and they immediately obeyed, leaving their extraordinary visitors to themselves.

The little sisters flew to them on their entrance, and appeared much alarmed, but the kind efforts of Mr. and Mrs. Milford quickly pacified them, and they were about to take them down stairs, when they heard the hall door closed, and they were induced to go to the window. They now beheld the unknown gentleman about to lead his female companion to the carriage. She appeared to be in almost a fainting condition, and they now perceived for the first time that there was another female in the vehicle, who from her appearance, seemed to be a servant. She lent her assistance to that of the gentleman, and they having entered the carriage, it was driven off with the greatest rapidity, leaving Milford and his wife in a state of the greatest perplexity and astonishment.

CHAPTER VII.

THE DEPARTURE OF THE STRANGERS.—THE ALARM.

WHEN Mr. and Mrs. Milford returned into the parlour with the children, they remained for some time silent, completely bewildered by the extraordinary nature of the event. All that they could elicit from the lisping tongues of their innocent charge, was to the effect that, "The pretty lady and gentleman had kissed them, and the lady had cried so much that it frightened them and made them cry too."

All the circumstances of the case tended to convince Milford and his wife of one thing, namely, that the lady who had been brought to them in so singular a manner was the mother of the little twin sisters, but in what relation the gentleman stood to them, they had no means of arriving at any positive conclusion.

The observations of the unknown in answer to the melancholy complaints of his companion, were particularly impressed upon their memory, especially the following :—

"Have you not brought all this upon yourself? And should you therefore murmur at the course we are adopting to prevent the world from being accquainted with the particulars? Recollect that the character of your future king is at stake, &c."

These were indeed important observations, and gave rise to various conjectures in their minds, which were strengthened by what Mr. Milford had seen when he went to try to discover the mansion where he and his wife had been taken. But they were almost afraid to mention their surmises to each other, lest they should be productive of any evil consequences.

It was some time before the excitement consequent upon this adventure could be at all abated, and when they retired to their chamber for the night, their minds were in such a state of agitation, that it was some time ere sleep descended on their eyelids.

The next morning on descending into the parlour, Martha presented her master with a letter, which she said had just been delivered to her by the same servant who had brought the previous ones. He perceived it was in the hand-writing of the stranger and breaking the seal, read the following contents :—

"The unfortunate mother has seen and embraced her children for the last time, unless it be the will of Providence to change the fearful destiny which now surrounds her. Seek not to know who that hapless mother is, for it would be attended with the most incalculable danger, and frustrate all the plans that have been formed for the preservation of the children. However, I place sufficient confidence in your integrity and prudence to believe that you will not attempt to disobey my injunctions. I am satisfied with your conduct yesterday, and trust it will ever be characterized by the same wisdom and precaution, in which case you will ever find me

Your Unknown Friend.

"Our conjectures then were right," said Mrs. Milford, after the perusal of the letter, "the veiled lady is indeed the mother of those poor children. Oh, I was certain she could be no other from the emotion she displayed. How terrible must have been her anguish at again beholding her children, and on being compelled to tear herself away from them, probably, as this letter states, never to behold them again. What a strange and fearful destiny it must be that can thus deprive a mother of her tender offspring, and leave them to the mercy of strangers."

"True Mary," coincided her husband, "but torturing as all this mystery is, I cannot but rejoice that the dear children have fallen under our protection, for had they been committed to the care of others, how sadly different might have been their fate."

"But from the tenor of the present letter," said Mrs. Milford, "it seems most uncertain whether these children will ever know their real parents."

"And if they do not, Mary, if it please heaven to spare us, they shall never know the loss."

"Indeed they shall not ; they shall share our love and anxious care equally with our child."

It was some days before Milford and his wife could entirely banish from their minds the excitement which these events had naturally created, but at length they resumed their ordinary tranquility, and left the result of the peculiar responsibility they had taken upon themselves to the wisdom of Providence, not doubtnig that he would in due course of time bring about an explanation of everything to their mutual satisfaction, and the future happiness of the twin sisters.

We will pass over a period of two years, during which time they had received no further communication from the gentleman. Augusta and Charlotte were now five years of age, and nature never found too more lovely or engaging children. Their playful innocence was ever most captivating, and the love they showed towards their supposed parents rendered them doubly dear to them. To the little George they ever showed the most sisterly affection, but he from the earliest age evinced a passionate and hasty temper that created the utmost alarm in the bosoms of his parents, and which they did all in their power to check, knowing the fatal consequences that might arise if it should be allowed to grow upon him. He often repulsed the affectionate advances of his innocent companions, and refusing to join them in their playful sports, showed, although so young, that a feeling of jealousy had already taken possession of his childish mind. This caused Mr. and Mrs. Milford many an anxious thought, and they exerted themselves to the utmost by kindly admonition and advice to conquer a disposition, so every way fraught with danger, but with little success.

Mrs. Ashfield, the female who had succeeded Mrs. Morton, was a woman who had received an excellent education, which, added to natural good sense, rendered her an invaluable assistant to Mr. and Mrs. Milford in early forming the minds, and imparting instruction to their young charge, and it was astonishing to see the readiness with which they imbibed all that was taught them, and the precocity they displayed.

The twin sisters were never so delighted as when they were permitted to play in the drawing-room, the principal attraction of which was to them " the pretty lady," for so they called the portrait which has been before so frequently alluded to. They would sometimes put such questions to Mr. Milford and his wife, respecting this painting, which greatly bewildered them, and they scarcely knew what answer to make, and they could not but admire the instinctive power which so particularly directed the attention of the lovely children to that painting which they had every reason to believe was the resemblance of their mother.

But now an event occurred which created their greatest alarm, and from the effects of which it was some time before they recovere t.

It was beautiful summer weather, and Martha frequently took the children out for a walk, Mr. and Mrs. Milford seldom accompanying them. On a lovely morning in the month of June, Martha left the house with the twin sisters, George, being rather indisposed, remained at home on that occasion. Mrs. Milford had desired her not to remain from home more than a couple of hours, and therefore, when more than two hours and a half had elapsed, and they did not return, Mr. and Mrs. Milford began to feel uneasy lest any accident should have happened to them, and at last the former determined to go in search of them. He wandered everywhere he thought it was likely they would stroll to, but could see nothing of them, and he was at length compelled to return home in a state of the greatest consternation, but still not without a faint hope that they had returned home by some other way during his absence. His despair and that of his wife, however, may be imagined when they found that they were still absent.

Another hour of the most terrible anxiety elapsed, and Mr. and Mrs. Milford were worked almost up to a pitch of madness, and knew not what course to adopt ; in fact, so great was the agitation of Mrs. Milford that she several times fainted away. At length a loud knock at the street door alarmed them, and Milford flew to open it, when Martha entered alone, wringing her hands, her countenance ghastly pale, and sunk speechless in a chair.

Milford and his wife flew towards her, and in eager and distracted accents demanded where the children were. Martha looked up at them with an expression of the utmost dismay and consternation, but for a second or two was unable to return any answer. Mr. and Mrs. Milford repeated their questions with more impatience and emotion than before, and then Martha in a voice half choked with fear and anguish, ejaculated,—

"Oh, dear—oh, dear, what a poor miserable and unfortunate girl I am! How can I look you in the face, my dear master and mistress? What can I say ?—what shall I do? but indeed I am not to blame, I——"

"Where are the children?" again demanded Mr. Milford, with the most insupportable agony; "answer me, girl, what has become of your innocent and tender charge?"

"Alas—alas! that ever I should live to tell it; they are gone, stolen from me !"

"Oh, God !" groaned Mrs. Milford, and overpowered by the dreadful shock, she fainted.

"Gone! the children stolen," gasped forth Mr. Milford, turning ghastly pale; "gracious Heaven, what do I hear? I shall go mad! Wretched girl, tell me all the dreadful particulars, and quickly, as you value your life."

Mrs. Milford now recovered, and looked vacantly around her, as if imagining that all she had heard was only some fearful dream, but when she did not behold the children, she burst into a convulsive flood of tears, and sobbed as if her heart would break. Her husband although so violently agitated himself, sought to tranquillize her, and again demanded of Martha all the fearful particulars. In a voice of the most trembling emotion Martha complied.

"Oh! sir," she said, "little did I expect that this would have happened, or I would not have gone out at all this morning. We had taken our customary walk, and had reached the old mile stone down the road on our way home, when just as we were crossing the road, a carriage turned abruptly round the corner, and it was with difficulty that I saved Miss Augusta and Miss Charlotte from being run over. I uttered a loud scream, and the coachman stopped the horses, and a lady put her head out of the carriage window, and inquired if we were hurt ; but she no sooner beheld the two poor dear little children, than she uttered an exclamation of astonishment and emotion, and requested me to stop. The next moment she alighted from the carriage, and after gazing at the children for a minute with an expression of countenance that I shall never forget, she beckoned to the footman, who, descending from his place behind the vehicle, advanced towards her, and she addressed a few words to him in an under tone. I was so utterly confused and astonished at all that had taken place, that I could neither move nor speak, until the cries of the children aroused me, and I then beheld that the lady had re-entered the carriage, and that the footman at that moment had the little Augusta and her sister in his arms, and was handing them into the carriage ; before I could recover myself he had done so. The door was hastily closed, he took his place on the box beside the coachman, and the vehicle was driven off with the utmost rapidity, leaving me screaming for help in the road. There was, however, no one at hand, and if there had, it would have been of little use, for the carriage was very quickly out of sight."

"Great God of Heaven !" exclaimed Milford, when Martha had concluded; "who can have been tempted to commit this atrocious outrage? We are ruined—we are ruined !"

He beat his breast in despair, and Mrs. Milford was so overpowered by the horror of her feelings, that she could only give vent to the anguish of her feelings in the most heart-rending groans. The extraordinary nature of the whole affair rendered it the more bewildering and hopeless, and the misery of Mr. and Mrs. Milford cannot be wondered at.

"What is to be done?" cried Milford; "what steps can we possibly take to discover the unfortunate children? Whither can we go in search of them? Oh, God! this is indeed a dreadful calamity, which I never once anticipated. I shall go mad !"

"The poor little innocents, thus to be so cruelly taken from us !" sobbed Mrs. Milford. "Oh, what will now become of us? What on earth shall we say to ——"

"Hush !" interrupted Milford, in alarm, lest his wife in her agitation should betray the secret. "Let us try to be calm, and to think of some plan that may lead to the recovery of our children. Martha, tell me, what kind of a woman was this lady? Should you know her again?"

"Oh, yes, sir," answered Martha. "She was tall, apparently about six and twenty years of age, and very handsome. It struck me that I had seen her before, but where I cannot remember. Ah! the thought strikes me now. Gracious me, sir, she bears as strong a likeness to that portrait that is up-stairs, as if she had sat for it herself."

"Ah!" cried Milford and his wife, in a breath, "is it possible? It must be her, and if the children have fallen into her hands ——"

"Do you, then, know her, sir?" inquired Martha.

"No matter—no matter," returned Mr. Milford; and then desiring Martha to leave the room, he turned to his wife, and notwithstanding the violence of his own emotions, endeavoured to calm her feelings.

"This is indeed a horrible blow, my dear Mary," he said: "but we must bear up against it as well as we can, or we shall not be able to act with the necessary prudence, promptitude, and judgment in this emergency. If the poor dear children have indeed fallen into the hands of their mother, they will, no doubt, quickly be restored to us."

"But should she discover to them who they really are," said Mrs. Milford, "and that we are not their parents, all the plans that have been so nicely laid to save them from that danger which the stranger said threatened them, will be frustrated. Oh, why did not the gentleman inform us where we could find him, that we might consult him on such a terrible and alarming occasion as this?"

"Would to Heaven that he had," said Milford; "but let us not give way entirely to despair. It is more than probable that he will soon hear of the abduction of the children, and see them restored to us."

The remainder of the day was passed by Milford and his wife in the greatest state of anguish, and they could not come to any satisfactory conclusion as to the course it would be best for them to adopt. Had they been their own children they could not have experienced greater agony at their loss, and Mrs. Milford, in particular, was so overwhelmed with grief, that she was entirely deaf to the voice of consolation. If it was indeed the mother of the children who had thus deprived them of them, they could not marvel at her conduct, and yet it was strange that she should venture such a step, when she had been compelled to resign them, in order, as the stranger had said, to save them from some untimely and cruel fate, and the character, nay, even the lives of many individuals.

Milford having somewhat recovered himself, gave notice of the extraordinary circumstance to the proper authorities, in order that every means should be adopted to lead to a discovery; but from the vague information, there was very little hope of success, and Milford was rather doubtful whether he had done right in giving the circumstances publicity.

No sleep visited the pillow of Milford and his wife that night, and they arose in the morning with sad hearts, and the most dismal forebodings. What rendered it more distressing was that they had no means of making any inquiries, and the circumstances under which the singular abduction had taken place, precluded all possibility of obtaining any clue which might lead to a discovery.

In the most melancholy manner the day passed away, and the agony and suspense of Mr. Milford and his wife increased to an insupportable degree, and again night closed upon them without any tidings being obtained of the lost children.

The third morning dawned upon their misery, and Mrs. Milford was completely worn out with anxiety of mind, and gave vent to her grief in the most painful manner. Milford was scarcely more composed than her, but he struggled hard to control his feelings, lest it should render her worse; but their fears and anxiety were about to be brought to a termination.

The morning repast was scarcely over, when they heard a carriage drive hastily up to the door, and rushing to the parlour window, they beheld, to their amazement and delight, the stranger step from the carriage, and afterwards lift out the darling objects of their anxiety and their fears—the little Augusta and her sister Charlotte!

With an exclamation of joy, they immediately opened the door, and the next moment they held the beauteous twin sisters to their bosoms, and kissed them again and again with delighted fondness. And nothing could equal the delight of the little Augusta and her sister on again beholding their beloved and kind benefactors.

So completely absorbed were all parties by the pleasures of that moment that neither offered to speak a word. The stranger folded his arms across his chest, and seemed to contemplate the scene with no little degree of satisfaction; but at length he rang the bell, and Martha having made her appearance, he desired her to remove the children to another room, which order she obeyed, though the twin sisters parted from their supposed parents even for a short time with evident reluctance, and some misgivings that they would not be permitted to remain with them.

The stranger in the meantime had taken a seat, and although his eyes were fixed stedfastly upon Mr. and Mrs. Milford, his thoughts were apparently abstracted, and he frequently sighed deeply.

Mrs. Milford, however, who was overjoyed at the restoration of their tender charge, could no longer restrain her feelings.

"Oh, sir," she ejaculated, " how can I sufficiently express to you my gratitude for the restoration of these two precious children, whom I and my husband feared were lost to us for ever? Indeed, I cannot describe to you the anguish and suspense we have suffered since their disappearance, for indeed we love them as dearly as if they were our own offspring."

"Hush !" said the gentleman, placing his finger upon his lips in the most significant manner; " I place every confidence in your fidelity ; but the utmost caution should be used upon all occasions, and curiosity might prompt those about you to be listeners."

He then advanced to the door at which Martha had departed with the children, and opened it, but finding no one there, and hearing the voices of the servant and the children up-stairs, he once more closed it, and resumed his seat, satisfied.

"Clavèring," he said, in an under tone, " I come not here to reproach you, for I feel satisfied that you have hitherto performed your promise faithfully, but still I cannot too strongly impress upon your mind the necessity of using the utmost precaution, or the most serious consequences may ensue. Never again must you suffer them to walk out unless accompanied by yourself, for there are persons who must know their features well, who are constantly on the alert for them, and should they fall into their power, inevitable misery, if not entire destruction to many individuals would be sure to follow."

"And how, sir, may I ask," said Milford, " did you discover them, and be the means of restoring them to us ?"

"Fortunately they fell into right hands," replied the stranger, " though it might have been otherwise. The lady whom accident threw in their way is their unfortunate mother, and it was only natural that she should act in the manner she has done. Of course, the circumstances could not long remain a secret to me, and I lost no time in averting the dangers that threatened ; thus it is that the children are restored to you."

"Alas! poor lady," ejaculated Mrs. Milford, " although I am ignorant of the circumstances of her sad history, how sincerely do I commiserate with her fate."

The stranger sighed, and for an instant passed his hand across his eyes, as if to dash away the rising tear.

"How terrible must have been her anguish at being thus again compelled to part with her tender offspring," continued Mrs. Milford. " But, sir, since you have thus so far confided in us as to place these children under our care and protection, surely you cannot object to make us acquainted with some of the particulars of the mother's history, if you do not think proper to reveal her name."

"It is impossible," returned the stranger; " do not urge it. For the present it must remain a profound secret, but the time may probably come when everything can be explained without danger ; till then I must beg of you to wait patiently."

"And you still object to furnish us with your name, sir," said Mr. Milford, " or to inform us where we might apply to you for advice under similar circumstances that have just occurred?"

"I do, and I must request that you will be contented with the assurance that I act from the purest, the best of motives.   But of this you may rest satisfied, that I have made such arrangements, that nothing whatever can happen to you or the children placed under your protection without its reaching my immediate knowledge, and I shall always be ready and in a position to avert any dangers that may threaten.   You found a locket suspended from the neck of the child Augusta?"

"We did."

"What has become of that locket?"

"We have it secure, sir," answered Milford; "we thought it would not be prudent to suffer so valuable a trinket to be worn by the child until she should have arrived at years of maturity."

"You acted perfectly right," said the stranger.

"Do you wish it's restoration, sir?"

"No.   But treasure it as you would your own life, and never show it to the sisters, until you have my permission to do so.   Have you noticed that the minature enclosed in that locket bears a resemblance to anything else you have seen?"

"Oh, yes;" replied Mr. Milford, eagerly, " to the portrait of the lady which decorates the room up-stairs."

"True. true;" said the stranger, with a melancholy look and sighing deeply.

"And that portrait is the resemblance of—"

"No matter—" abruptly interrupted the gentleman, " seek not to know more at present.   But mark me, should you accidentally at any time encounter a lady whose features resembles that portrait and those of the miniature, I charge you, as you value the oath you have taken, and the welfare of the children you have agreed to protect, to evince no surprise, to court no explanation from her, to sedulously avoid her, and above all to attempt not to follow her footsteps, or to seek to discover who she is, and where the place of her abode.   Remember those injunctions, and obey them strictly, for they are most important, and any infringement of them might ruin all."

"I will act in accordance with your wishes, sir," answered Milford, " though I must acknowledge it is not without the greatest reluctance."

"It is absolutely necessary," said the stranger, "to prevent the frustration of my plans.   And now our interview must terminate; remember all I have said, and keep a watchful eye over your precious charge as you value your own safety, and their's; farewell.   I know not when we may meet again."

The gentleman arose from his seat as he spoke, and moved towards the door.   Mr. Milford was again about to address some observations to him, but he waved his hand, and opening the hall-door himself, stepped into his carriage, which was immediately driven off, leaving Milford and his wife in an increased state of astonishment and perplexity.

But all other thoughts and feelings quickly gave way to the joy they felt at the restoration of the children, and that joy was fully participated in by poor Martha, who had embraced the little sisters a hundred times during the time this conversation was going on below-stairs, and who could never be sufficiently grateful to Providence for having once more returned them safe to their home.

Mr. Milford and his wife, immediately after the departure of the gentlman, summoned Martha to bring them into their presence, and having embraced them tenderly, they desired the servant to withdraw, and then tried to elicit from them all that had happened to them after they had been seized in so mysterious a manner.   The few particulars they were enabled so gather from the children did not serve to enlighten them much upon the subject.   They talked much and fondly of " the pretty lady" who had taken them into the carriage, and soothed their tears and anguish by the most tender caresses, weeping over them all the time.   Then they said that they had been taken a long way, until they came to a large house, with a beautiful garden before it, and servants in splendid liveries waiting at the hall-door to receive them.   They were conducted by the lady through many spacious rooms, where there were fine pictures and handsome furniture, till they arrived at one more splendid than all the rest, and there " the pretty lady" again embraced them, and wept over them, and kneeling down, prayed to Heaven.   When night came, they wanted to be taken home, but the lady still endeavoured to sooth them, and at length they became more pacified, though they still cried for their " dear papa and mama."   At night when they retired to rest they slept in the

OR, THE SISTERS OF MYSTERY,

same bed with the lady, and when they awoke in the morning they found themselves clasped to her bosom, and that she was weeping and praying over them. The whole of that day the lady would not permit them out of her sight for a moment, and did nothing but cry incessantly, gaze affectionately upon them, and embrace them; but towards the evening there was a great bustle in the house, and soon afterwards a "fine gentleman" was ushered into the room, who no sooner beheld them, than he showed as much emotion as the lady, and caressed them with the greatest ardour. Some words passed between them which the children did not understand and could not recollect, and soon afterwards a female servant was summoned, who was ordered to take them into another room. When they were brought back to the room the gentleman was gone, and the lady was more agitated than before. The day, as far as they could gather from the little sisters, passed away in a similar manner to the previous one, but on the following morning the stranger made his appearance at the house, and after a long interview with the lady, a female servant came to them to dress them for a journey, and they were told that they were going home again to their papa and mamma.

The joy of the innocent Augusta and her sister at this intimation was unbounded, but when they were taken to the room in which the stranger and the lady were waiting to receive them, seeing the extreme grief of the latter, the ardour of their spirits was somewhat diminished, and they could not help feeling almost sorry to leave her. She pressed them frantically to her bosom, and wept hysterically over them; she uttered incoherent words, which they were too young to understand the meaning of or to remember, and when the stranger at length tore them from her embrace, she fainted, and was left in the care of her female attendants. They were conveyed to a carriage in waiting, by the gentleman, who treated them with great kindness, and nothing more occurred to them until they were restored to those whom they supposed to be their parents.

Such were the only particulars which Mr. and Mrs. Milford could elicit from the children, and they only served to involve them in still greater mystery, though they could not have the least doubt that the lady who had thus, for a short time, got possession of them, was their mother, and the same who had visited them at their house; and deeply did they sympathise with her in the heart-rending sufferings she must endure in being thus, by a strange and cruel fate compelled to part with her tender and lovely offspring.

CHAPTER VIII.

A CHANGE.—THE DISAPPOINTMENT.—THE ABANDONED ONE.—FUTURE HOPES BLIGHTED.

TEN more years have winged their rapid flight, and a change has come over the family of Mr. Milford, and care, anxiety, and disappointment usurped the place of former content, happiness, and cheerful anticipation. The stranger had broken his word, and from the time they had reecived the third remittance they had had no communication whatever from him, nor could they obtain any information respecting him. They could, therefore, come to no other conclusion than that he had deceived them, or that he was no more, and therefore that the secret connected with the sisters would ever remain undivulged. They were several times half tempted to reveal to them the truth, but they had so entwined themselves around their hearts, that they could not make up their minds to inform them that they were not their children, or to impress them with the idea that they were a burthen to them.

Augusta and her sister were now sixteen years of age, and they more than realized all the most sanguine expectations that had been formed of them in their earliest days of childhood. To say that they were pretty and interesting, would be to give by far too faint an idea of their captivating, their glowing charms; they were in point of loveliness, in fact, all that the most vivid imagination can conceive of perfection, while the accomplishments of their minds, and the sweetness of their dispositions, rendered them still more irresistable. The likeness they bore to each other was most remarkable, but Augusta was rather taller than her sister, and her manners were generally more staid and sedate than those of the vivacious, the ever cheerful, the ever smiling Charlotte. Towards their supposed parents they ever behaved with the most dutiful and unbounded affection, and Mr. and Mrs. Milford returned their love with the same fond ardour as if they had really been their own children, and watched the improvement of their minds with the some anxious care.

They had taken the greatest pains with their education, determined to fulfil the promise they had made to the unknown to the very letter, and should their real relations at any time claim them, they should have no cause to complain that they had neglected them in any respect. This had put them to great expense, and much impoverished their resources, and this circumstance rendered the neglect of the stranger the more annoying and alarming; but there were other circumstances that distressed them more than all.

George Milford from childhood had evinced a wayward and reckless disposition, and obstinately rejected all the advice and remonstrances of his amiable parents, who had never treated him otherwise than with the greatest affection and indulgence; and these evil passions grew and strengthened with his strength, and in spite of all their efforts to the contrary, his association with vicious characters threatened to work his ultimate ruin.

He was passionate, sullen, and vindictive, and when once he had received an imaginary injury, never forgot it, but brooded it over in his mind, and would never rest until he had in some way gratified his revenge.

Augusta and Charlotte always showed the most sisterly regard towards him, and frequently interceded for him with his parents; but he had ever viewed them with eyes of jealousy, and secretly hated them, for he imagined that his father and mother had always shown then more indulgence than himself, and he determined, if possible, at some future period to have his revenge.

We need not seek to describe the anguish of mind that Mr. and Mrs. Milford endured as they noticed these degrading vices in their only child, and they saw no prospect of being able to reform him. Many hours of anxious thought did it cause them, and many were the sleepless nights they passed ruminating upon this, their fast decreasing means of support, and the mystery with which the fate of Augusta and Charlotte was still, and seemed likely for ever to be enshrouded. It had a most serious effect upon Mrs. Milford's health, who had been for some months declining, and her husband began to look forward to the future with the most gloomy apprehensions.

At length George Milford did evince some signs of compunction, and expressed a wish that he might be placed in some situation where he might have an opportunity of providing himself with a respectable living.

Hailing this imagined reformation with feelings of the most unbounded delight, Mr. Milford lost no time in complying with his wishes, and shortly obtained for him the situation of a junior clerk, in a respectable merchant's office in the city, and supplied him with everything requisite for entering upon his new course of life.

For seme weeks George conducted himself to the entire satisfaction of his employer and his parents, and thhe began to hope that he had at length clearly seen through his folly, and would no more give them occasion to complain of his conduct. But alas! they were doomed to be most wofully disappointed. George had never forsaken his abandoned companions, and they at last gained such power over him, that they persuaded him to rob his employer, which he did of a considerable sum, and then absconded. His unhappy parents were distracted when they were informed of this, and saw now that the ruin of their misguided son was all but inevitable; but in consequence of their intercession, and the high opinion he entertained of their character, George's employer declined to prosecute him, and thus the abandoned youth escaped that punishment that would otherwise assuredly have overtaken him. It was several days before his father could discover the place of his retreat, and he then had the greatest difficulty to persuade him to return home; but at length he succeeded, and again Mr. and Mrs. Milford exerted themselves to the utmost to awaken him to a sense of his guilty conduct, and by kindness and persuasion sought to withdraw him from his profligate habits, in which they were most earnestly assisted by Augusta and Charlotte, and they at length flattered themselves that their efforts would at last be crowned with success. George remaided more steadily at home than he had done for some time before, and was less violent in his manners; but had they known the real thoughts that inhabited the abandoned youth's breast, they would have seen how little reason they had to hope.

George Milford was as shrewd and artful as he was badly disposed, and not with-standing all the precautions which his father and mother had used, and all the plans they had adopted to prevent the least possibility of suspicion, he could not but imagine that there had always been a marked difference in their behaviour towards Augusta and Charlotte and himself, for which he could not in any way account, though at times strange thoughts would steal into his jealous mind which he could not very readily define. Certain observations made by his parents, too, at different times, had not escaped his ear, particularly as they bore reference to the sisters ; and he treasured them in his memory, resolved to leave no means unemployed to gratify the anxious curiosity which had found a place in his bosom.

He had a perfect recollection of the stranger's visit to the house on restoring the twin sisters to their home, and the secret and cautious manner in which everything was on that occasion conducted, and this circumstances strengthened his suspicions, and made him more determined to probe the secret to the very core.

Besides, another thing which most forcibly struck George Milford was, that neither Augusta nor Charlotte bore the least resemblance to his father or mother, and that there seemed to be only a month or two's difference between his own age and theirs. Could they be his sisters? He began to suspect that they were not, and if so, who were they, and why were they placed under the protection of his parents?

George had also frequently contemplated the portrait in the room up stairs, and noticed its extraordinary likeness to the twin sisters ; and the confused manner in which his father evaded all the questions which were at different times put to him about it, convinced him that there was some secret connected with that painting which Mrs. Milford chose not to disclose, and with which Augusta and Charlotte were in some way associated. He determined to be watchful and wary, and to penetrate the mystery, if possible. It was not long after he had formed this resolution, ere fortune favoured his wishes.

He had returned home late one night, having had permission to go to the theatre; and having let himself in with a latch-key, and not wishing Mr. or Mrs. Milford to know the hour at which he had come home, he took off his shoes, to prevent him from making a noise, and cautiously ascended the stairs.

In passing by the bed-room door of his parents, however, which he had occasion to do, he perceived a light burning within, and heard them conversing in an earnest tone. Curiosity prompted him to stop to listen, and the nature of his father and mother's discourse quickly engrossed his whole attention, especially when he heard the names of Augusta and Charlotte mentioned. On that unfortunate occasion the young profligate elicited all that he had been so anxious to know, namely, that the twin sisters were in no way related to his parents, and the manner in which they had been placed under their protection. He also found that neither Augusta nor Charlotte were acquainted with the secret, and could not have the slightest suspicion that they were not what they were represented to be. The observations his father made use of convinced George that they were the offsping of parents of distinction, who would doubtless some day claim them ; and his plans were immediately formed.

He hurried to his chamber, where he gave free vent to his exhultation, and flattered himself with the prospects of future aggrand'zement which now opened upon his view. But it would require time and the greatest precaution to put his designs into effect ; and George Milford from that night resolved to change the line of his conduct altogether in order that his success might be the more certain.

In the course of a very few days, Mr. and Mrs. Milford beheld a most remarkable change for the better in the behaviour of their son, and we need not say how sincerely and fervently they rejoiced at it, and gave him every encouragement to continue the same. Augusta and Charlotte were no less delighted at the evident and promising change in the manner of their supposed brother ; and by their most affectionate atten-tions endeavoured to show him the pleasure it afforded them, and how anxious they were to share his undivided brotherly love. He affected to receive their advances with much avidity and grateful feeling ; and so well did the young hypocrite play his part that it was no wonder the innocent and unsuspecting girls were completely deceived, and felt the most unbounded gratitude towards Heaven for having changed the heart of that youth whom they imagined to be their brother, in time, and saved him from the ruin which must inevitably have followed the course he had been pursuing.

To his parents George expressed the utmost contrition for his past misdeeds, and implored their forgiveness for all the numerous pangs he must have caused them; and the reader may well imagine with what avidity they granted it, and bestowed upon him their blessing; and George Milford, in secret, triumphed at the success which had attended him so far, and which appeared likely to crown all his villanous designs.

Milford and his wife now felt happier than they had done for some time, notwithstanding the mystery with which the two lovely sisters were surrounded, and the double weight of responsibility which now rested on their shoulders, and from their increasing years; kept them in a constant state of suspense and anxiety. They firmly believed that the reformation of their son was sincere, and that idea removed a weight of care and apprehension which had before pressed upon their minds.

George was regular in his habits, kept good hours, abandoned his former associates altogether (at least so his parents believed); he never gave way to those fits of passion he had formerly done, and was cheerful, agreeable, and sociable, in the place of being sullen, uncouth and morose. The most experienced and consummate hypocrite could not possibly have performed his part better than he did, and it would have been impossible to have had the least suspicion of his sincerity. Towards Augusta and Charlotte he behaved with the most marked respect, and no one joined more readily than he in the merry laugh in which the playful Charlotte so delighted; he was almost their constant companion,, and seemed unhappy when away from them even for the shortest period of time.

Thus wore away several months, and still Milford heard nothing more of the stranger, and he and his wife now began to despair that ever they would. But fresh trouble was in store for them; Mrs. Milford's health daily became worse, and it was soon quite evident that her time in this world was but brief, that consumption was working its destructive effects upon her constitution, and that not all the skill of man could prolong her existence.

Mr. Milford prepared herself for the solemn change she knew she must so shortly experience, with the calm resignation of a Christian, and tried to comfort those around her: but that was impossible! Mr. Milford sought to bear up against it with manly fortitude; but he could not. Oh, what could ever replace that beloved partner who for so many years had been the companion of his joys and his sorrows?—nothing!—And now that he, if possible, needed her aid more than ever, in the protection and guidance from the snares of the world of those two fair beings, whom they loved as fondy as if they had been their own children, cruel death was about to snatch her from him. Surely it was a most awful trial, and who shall marvel at or reproach the violence of his grief?

The twin sisters were perfectly distracted, and every argument that friendship and sympathy could suggest to console them failed. How could they ever support the loss of so fond, so gentle a parent? Where could they ever find another that could equal her in affectionate attention; where look for those shining virtues it was their pride and study to emulate? Nothing but black despair was before them, and they feared that they must sink beneath the shock. They could not be induced to leave the bedside of the dying woman only for the shortest space of time.

Mrs. Milford would frequently gaze at them in an earnest and peculiar manner, with the tears glistening in her eyes, and seemed as if she wished to communicate something, but she had not strength to do so, and could only press their hands in her own, in silence, while the tears that forced themselves to those eyes which had ever gazed upon them with such gentle kindness, with such maternal love and anxiety, showed the intense mental feelings the dying woman was experiencing, not from any fear of death (for her life had been a spotless one, and she could have no fear of meeting her Almighty Judge) but doubtless from a dreadful presentiment of the troubles that were yet in store for them.

Augusta and her sister could not help observing, (although they could not account for it, no more than that her reason must be wandering), that whenever her son was present, Mrs. Milford appeared to be suffering the most extraordinary uneasiness, and that she

seemed to reject in a most unnatural manner, especially taking into consideration the
solemn situation in which she was placed, all the affectionate advances he made towards
her, and to view his grief and commiseration not only with suspicion but dread. Mr.
Milford, too, never seemed more at ease than when his son was away from the chamber of
his dying mother, and altogether the circumstances were such as to create the most extraordinary surprise and sensation in rthe bosoms of the sisters. Geoge Milford, however, seemed to be entirely insensible to, or unmoved at, these remarkable demonstrations,
and only appeared to be the more assidously attentive to his mother in her last
moments. But did he not feel them ? Was he not satisfied in his own mind that she
looked upon him with an eye of suspicion ? That, as she approached the verge of
eternity, she fathomed, with all the prescience of more than mortality, his secret thoughts,
and had a wish to warn the lovely sisters of the danger in which they stood from him,
and to reval the whole truth of the peculiar circumstances in which they were placed,
and that they had no claim upon her or his father than that which had been created by
sympathy and their own virtues. Oh, yes, George Milford was too shrewd a villain
not to know all this, and he watched the result with the deepest possible anxiety, lest
his own plans should at one blow be frustrated, and awful as it must appear, he even
wished that his mother's death might take place before she had the power of making
the important secret known.

Drearily the time lingered on, and the amiable sufferer gradually wasted out the
lamp of life, every day and every hour becoming weaker, and her senses almost continually wandering. The sufferings of Mr. Milford, and the two sisters, may readily
be conceived, more especially as not one ray of hope beamed upon them to assure
them that her they believed to be their parent would be spared to bless them. What
melancholly thoughts did this terrible certainty engender in their affectionate and
susceptible bosoms, and in vain they looked to Mr. Milford for that consolation which
he so much needed himself. They remained unremitting in their attentions upon the
suffering woman, and no consideration of the danger their own health incurred by such
unusual exertions could induce them to abandon their dutiful and affectionate offices,
even for the shortest period of time. Mr. Milford was alarmed, and in vain tried all
his powers of persuasion to prevail on them to seek at intervals that rest which was so
necessary to give them strength to bear up against the severe trial that was shortly in
store for them. If anything could have made him love the beauteous sisters, who had
been placed under his protection in so remarkable a manner, more, it was the gratitude
and self devotedness they evinced on that melancholy occasion.

When alone, George Milford would exult with all the inward malice of a demon
upon the probable success of the plans he had formed ; at the same time he feared lest,
in her last moments, his mother should be tempted to divulge the truth to the
sisters.

" My father and mother," he would soliloquise, " little imagine that I have become
acquainted with their secret, and the advantage that I am resolved to take of my
knowledge. So far so good ; and if fortune continues to favour me, the whole of my
wishes shall be accomplished, and wealth and power, at some future period, doubtless shall
be mine. One thing is quite certain from all I have overheard, namely, that the origin
of the girls is noble, and could I ingratiatè myself into the favour of one of them
(the gay and giddy Charlotte especially), I may yet become a man of distinction, and
of property, and laugh at the fastidious and too prudent portion of mankind to scorn ;
the game I seek to play is a high and a bold one, but I have sufficient confidence in
my own skill and determination to doubt that I shall meet with success. But I must
be cautious, and endeavour to discover who this stranger really is (if he still be living,)
and then my triumph is certain."

Thus the young villain in secret pondered over his nefarious plans, and already reck-
oned triumph as allbut certain. From the moment that his suspicions were excited
that Augusta and her sister were not related to him, he had felt an unlawful passion
for the beauteous Charlotte, and he now determined that nothing but death should
prevent him from ultimately gaining possession of her, though from the conversation he
had overheard between his father and mother, and which convinced him that the sister's
were nobly born, he was anxious that it should be in the character of his wife, for by

that means he flattered himself that he should secure fortune and power, and every means towards the gratification of his own covteous and ambitious views.

Weeks wore on, winter approached, and Mrs. Milford gradually became weaker and weaker; it was quite evident that before another spring could put forth its blossoms her gentle spirit would have winged its flight to eternity. But calm and resigned was the evening of her existence. She whose whole earthly career had been one of Christain rectitude, even under the most severe trials and visitations of Providence, who had never entertained a thought derogatory to the welfare of her fellow creatures, who had ever been the readiest to pour the balm of consolation into the bosom of afflicted humanity, and to suffer herself " for the weal of others," could have no terrors of the mysterious future, could have no torturing regrets in shaking off this mortal coil, only in the thought of those she should be compelled to leave behind her, and for whom she could not but apprehend there were yet many troubles in store. The long silence of the unknown, and the daily impoverished circumstances of her husband, filled her with much anxiety for the future, and greatly imbittered her last moments, which would otherwise have been so serene and happy; but yet the excellent woman withall sought to conceal her real thoughts, lest it should increase the anguish of a final earthly separation in the bosoms of those who were so dear to her.

With what anxiety did Mr. Milford and the two lovely sisters watch the waning moments of the amiable sufferer, and how dismal were the prospects which opened upon them when the grim messenger of death should finally snatch her from them. It was not without the greatest difficulty that they endeavoured to console themselves with the certainty of her future happiness, and Providence enabled them to do so much better than might have been expected.

At times the mind of Mrs. Milford wandered, and she then gave utterance to broken and incoherent sentences, which greatly alarmed her husband, lest she should divulge that secret, the knowledge of which might at present be fraught with so much danger, and create the most extraordinary and unaccountable surprise in the bosoms of the sisters. As they hung over her, and uttered the name of mother, a shuddering sensation would come over her, and her countenance would undergo such a remarkable change, that they would instinctively look to Mr. Milford, as if they thought that he could afford them some explanation, at which times he would endeavour to withdraw them from the chamber, but without effect, and Mrs. Milford, by her earnest and impresssives looks disuaded him from his purpose, and seemed fearful of loosing sight of them, even for a moment.

The melancholy day of trial at length arrived; the beam in the lamp of life was flickering in the socket, and it was quite evident that its last ray was shortly to be extinguished in the mysterious darkness of Eternity. The little family were gathered around the bed of death, and solemn was the silence that prevailed, interrupted only at intervals by the half-stiifled sobs of mental agony that escaped from the bosoms of those who were so soon to be deprived of that beloved being whose life had been one of such exemplary virtue. Yet the countenance and demeanour of the dying woman was calm and placid, and no boding anguish seemed to affect her exhausted frame. Her pale countenance, indeed, seemed to be animated by a chaste smile of confidence and hope, and for a time her eyes, which were so soon destined to close for ever, bore all that expression of joy and content that they had been accustomed to do in her hours of greatest happiness. One of her wasted hands, the sorrowing husband pressed alternately to his heart and lips (while he in vain sought to suppress the manly tears that would, in spite of everything, rush to his eyes) and the other was held with convulsive emotion by the fair sisters, who felt, with sensations of agony, such as no language, however powerful could do adequate justice to, that pulse which they were too fatally satisfied would ere long cease to beat for ever. George Milford stood on one side of the bed and pretended to be as deeply affected as any of the rest; but could they have read his real thoughts at that moment, with what horror and disgust must they have viewed him.

How awful and impressive is the stillness which prevails in the chamber of death; how solemn the prelude that characterises the earthly exit of those we hold most dear. We seem as if we almost feared to breath, lest we might hasten the departure of that breath so valued by us, and which every moment is rendering more short and painfully difficult.   Oh, it is surely in the chamber of the dying that the erring children of the earth ean, if anywhere, be brought to a sense of their own faults, and to form resolutions of good for the future.

"Put back the window curtains," at length said Mrs. Milford, in a calm but faint voice,—"my sight grows dim and I cannot behold you all distinctly."

Her wishes were obeyed immediately, and the sun (for it was a fine clear bright winter's day) streamed in at the windows, and fell upon the pale countenance of the dying woman At a sign which she made, they raised her gently in her bed, and she then fixed upon them all an earnest but calm look, and a faint smile of resignation and hope passed over her features.

"You weep," she said, "but why should you do so? I am about to leave this, I trust, for a better world, where we shall all shortly meet again, no more to part. Oh, why should we regret leaving a world of care, and sin, and sorrow, for one of uninterrupted happiness and purity? All praises to that beneficent Almighty in whose bright presence I must shortly appear, for inspiring me with such confident hopes of his love and mercy. And yet had it been his will that I should do so, I would that I might for your sakes, my beloved husband, my son, and those dear girls that I might have been permitted to have retained this mortal coil yet a little longer; but God's will be done; it is not for erring mortals to murmur at his all-wise decrees!"

"My Mary," sighed the heart-broken Mr. Milford, "and must I after all the years of mingled joy and sorrow we have passed together, now be doomed to part with you? Oh, God! it is hard!—Give me fortitude, or I know not how I shall find strength to support the blow."

"Bear up, my husband," said Mrs. Milford, in the same tranquil and collected tones as before; "much you know depends upon your fortitude and resolution. Live, for the sake of those dear children dependent on your guidance, love and protection. Augusta, Chalotte, I must leave you, but if it is permitted, my spirit shall watch over and protect you from any dangers that may threaten your youth and spotless innocence. Do not weep, my poor girls, you have nothing to reproach yourselves with; you have been good, affectionate, and dutiful, and however dark and foreboding your prospects may at present and at any future period appear to be, Heaven will be sure to reward you with that happiness which your virtue merits. There is a secret—but no;—I feel that at present, not even in this solemn hour, it must not be divulged. Bless you, children, bless you, and may the Supreme Being continue to watch over your safety and to guard you from every evil."

The words of Mrs. Milford made the deepest impression upon the sisters, and the allusion to the secret created the greatest astonishment and curiosty in their bosoms, but the solemnity of the moment, and the rapid approach of dissolution in her, they imagined to be their parent, completely absorbed every other thought, and pressing her damp hands alternately to their lips and their hearts, sobs for some moments choked all their powers of utterance.

George Milford, when he heard the observations of his dying mother in allusion to the secret, was in a state of much anxiety and alarm lest all should be divulged, but he concealed his thoughts as well as he could, and no one being aware of the knowledge he possessed, of course could not have any suspicion of them.

A pause of some moments ensued, during which interval Mrs. Milford seemed engaged in mental and earnest prayer; but at length a remarkable change came over her countenance, and it was quite evident that the final moment was approaching. Mr. Milford and the sisters beheld it with the most inexpressible agony and alarm; but again the dying woman, perceiving the intense emotion of those around her, struggled with the agonies of death, and endeavoured to smile tranquilly and encouragingly upon them.

"Mother, dearest, best of mothers!" ejaculated Augusta and her sister in a breath, and again pressing the fast-chilling hand of Mrs. Milford, with the most powerful, emotion to their lips, while scalding tears chased each other in rapid succession down their cheeks: "Oh, must you indeed be torn from us?—Will not Heaven in mercy spare you to us a little longer?—Mother, mother—"

For a moment or two the mind of the dying Mrs. Milford seemed to wander, and fixing upon the sisters a look which they could not easily forget, she interrupted them

THE ROYAL TWINS;

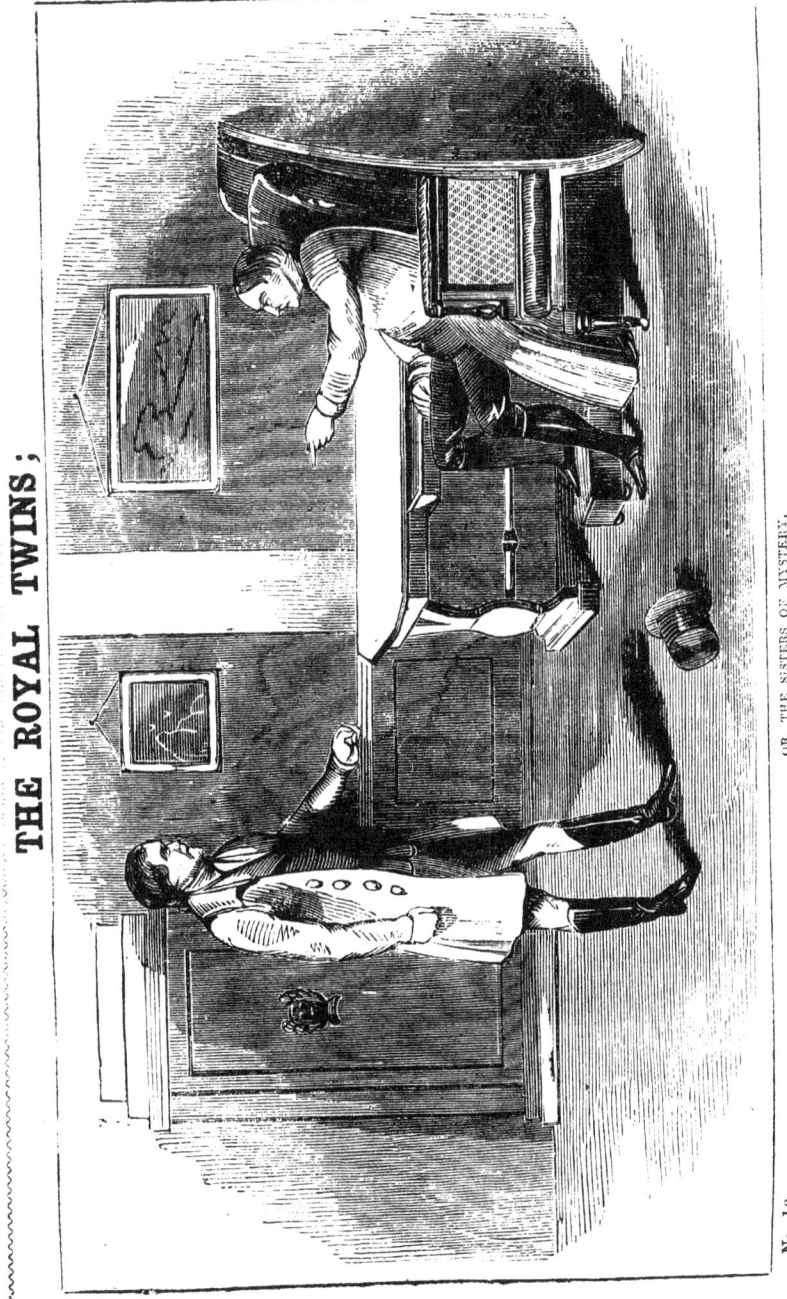

OR, THE SISTERS OF MYSTERY.

No. 10.

by the following words uttered in wild but expressive accents. "Mother, no, no, no, I can lay no claim to that title though heaven knows that I have loved ye both as fondly, as fervently as if—"

Her voice failed her, and she sunk back upon the pillow apparently exhausted. Augusta and her sister gazed at each other and then at Mrs. Milford, with the most indescribable astonishment.

"Good God," they exclaimed, "what can be the meaning of those mysterious words? Explain them to us, father, we beseech you."

Mr. Milford could with difficulty conceal his emotion and alarm, but he fixed upon the poor girls a significant look, as if to endeavour to persuade them that the mind of Mrs. Milford wandered, and she knew not what she uttered; and their attention was soon entirely engrossed by the fearful change which had suddenly came over the features of the sufferer, and which convinced them that her final moment was just at hand. The dew of death was upon her brow, her lips moved as if in prayer, but she was unable to utter a sound, and her eyes, which were fast becoming dim, were still fixed with an earnestness of expression upon the countenances of her husband and the weeping sisters, which was quite melancholy to behold.

With what intensity of agony did Milford and his youthful companions hang over the couch of Mrs. Milford, and watch the rapid departure of that life which they valued, if possible, still more than their own existence, and heart rending were the sobs that escaped their bosoms, and which they found it utterly impossible for them to subdue; while George Milford still retained the place he had at first occupied, and seemed to be enduring the same anxiety of mind as any of the other persons present, although very different were the feelings which even in that solemn and impressive moment, when the soul of one of the of women and of parents was rapidly winging its flight to eternity, predominated in that guilty young man's breast.

For a moment Mrs. Milford again seemed somewhat to revive, and made a sign for them again to raise her in the bed; they hastened to do so with as much care as possible. She stretched forth her arms, and embraced her husband, her son, and the sisters alternately; her lips moved, but words were denied her; one earnest **parting** glance she fixed upon them, her eyes then closed for ever, and sinking on the bosom of her husband with one soft sigh, she resigned her pure and gentle spirit into the hands of her Maker.

When the sisters became satisfied of the melancholy and irreparable loss they had sustained, unable any longer to bear up against the violence of their grief, they uttered a cry of the most distressing anguish, and immediately became insensible.

CHAPTER X.

THE FUNERAL.— THE GRIEF OF MILFORD. — THE MEETING IN THE CHURCHYARD.

VAIN would be the task to attempt to describe the anguish which reigned in the residence of the bereaved family that fatal night. Augusta and her sister, who were committed to the tender care of Mrs. Ashfield and Martha, only recovered from one fit to return to another, and so great was the shock that they had sustained, that there was for some time every reason to apprehend the most dangerous consequences.

And nothing could equal the distraction of Mr. Milford; he hung over the corpse of his wife all the night, and neither argument or persuasion could induce him to quit the chamber of death. He felt that he had suffered a loss which nothing whatever could replace, and deeply lamented that it had not been the will of Heaven that they should both die together. He seemed as if he were suddenly left alone in the world, and that there was nothing more left for him to live for, and he became completely deaf to the voice of consolation and hope. Where could he look for that sweet and gentle comforter he had ever found in the midst of all his greatest sorrows and afflictions in his deceased partner? Alas! he might look, but it would be all in vain.

He endeavoured to arouse himself from this intense agony of grief, and to support his melancholy bereavement with becoming fortitude, so that he might be able to impart some consolation to the fair sisters; but, alas! how difficult was this to accomplish. Mr. Milford shrunk from the task, and gave himself almost entirely up to despair.

It was not until three days after the demise of Mrs. Milford, that Augusta and Charlotte could recover the least degree of composure or were enabled to leave their chamber, and then they persisted in visiting the chamber of death, and weeping their tears of anguish and regret over the cold remains of that revered woman whom they supposed to have been their parent. It was hours before they could be induced to leave that dismal room, and when they did so it was with bursting hearts insensible to consolation. Never, never could they forget that final scene, and as they recalled to their memory the numerous virtues of the departed, their grief increased in strength and threatened to overpower them altogether. But for the sake of their supposed father, who so much needed the kind offices of consolation, they did endeavour to calm their feelings, and imploring the aid of the Supreme, they became much more tranquil and apparently resigned than could have been anticipated.

But not the least thing that perplexed and bewildered the sisters were the remarkable words that had been made use of by Mrs. Milford, and in which she had so nearly betrayed that secret which had been kept for so many years; but after racking their brains for some time in vain to define them, they abandoned the task, and came to the conclusion that the mind of the deceased had been wandering, at the time she had given utterance to them, and that she knew not what she said.

The day of the funeral arrived, and the remains of Mrs. Milford were conveyed to their final resting place. It was a day of severe trial to Mr. Milford and the beauteous sisters, and there was scarcely a dry eye in the the church-yard when the corpse of the lamented lady was lowered into the grave, and the earth closed for ever over the ashes of one who had been so justly revered by all who had known her in her life time. The grief of Mr. Milford and our two fair heroines was quite agonizing to behold, and it was some time ere their friends could tear them away from the dismal scene, and with sad hearts they returned to that home which was now rendered cheerless by the irreparable loss they had sustained.

Some weeks elapsed, but still nothing could assuage the violence of their grief, and Milford wandered about the house like a ghost, lost entirely to every hope and comfort. Even the society of the sisters failed to have its usual influence over him, and he would seclude himself for hours in his chamber, where he would give the most unrestrained indulgence to the violence of his grief, and wished himself in the same grave with her whose loss nothing on earth could ever replace. Dismal indeed was the change that had come over the once happy family. It scarcely seemed to be the same dwelling all was so silent and so sad.

In this melancholy feeling George Milford affected to participate, but in secret the young profligate only exulted in the probable accomplishment of his wishes, and resolved to lose no opportunity of putting them into execution.

Augusta and Charlotte for the sake of Mr. Milford endeavoured to assume that air of composure they were far very far from feeling in reality. And they struggled with their own grief, for the purpose of tranquillizing his feelings, but it was all to no purpose, the blow was such a severe one that he found himself totally inadequate to the task of supporting it with that manly fortitude he wished to do; and it was only occasionally that they could withdraw him from the solitude of his own chamber.

In Mrs. Ashfield and Martha the two fair sisters found their principal consolation, and those amiable women exerted themselves to the utmost to assuage the violence of their grief, though they knew that they had sustained a loss which it would be utterly impossible for anything to replace, and they could not expect that they could easily be restored to a state of tranqui l ty.

The death scene was ever present to the poor girls' minds, and particularly the ambiguous words which Mrs. Milford had given utterance to, and which seemed to insinuate that she was not their parent. This raised strange thoughts and surmises in their hearts but after all they tried to banish them from their minds, and to attribute the singular observations of their supposed mother to the wandering of her brain in that solemn moment.

The sisters had a perfect recollection of the extraordinary incident that had occurred to them in their childhood, namely, their being stolen in so mysterious a manner by the lady, and what had occurred to them afterwards. The features of the lady were vividly stamped upon their memory, also the emotion she had displayed on taking them to the splendid mansion, her fond endearments, the caresses she bestowed upon them, the tears she shed in such abundance, and the violence of her agitation when they were again forced away from her, and many were the reflections that this circumstance had at different times since given rise to in their minds. Who could she be? and what could be the cause of her betraying such extreme violence of grief at beholding them? It was quite evident that she must have known them, and probably was related to them; yet they had never been enabled to elicit from Mr. Milford whether or not they had such a relation in existence.

But what more than all surprised and bewildered the sisters, was the striking resemblance which the portrait bore to the lady; whenever they gazed upon it, they could almost imagine that she stood before them. They had frequently questioned Mr. Milford, and endeavoured to ascertain from him who that portrait was meant to represent, but he always evaded their enquiries, and seemed so confused and agitated whenever they put them to him, that they at last ceased their importunities, and left it for time to unravel the mystery.

Six weeks after the death of Mrs. Milford, Augusta and Charlotte prevailed upon Martha to accompany them, unknown to their beloved benefactor, to the churchyard, in order that they might pay their devotions at the grave of that amiable woman to whom they had been so greatly indebted during her life-time. Martha reluctantly yielded her consent, and Mr. Milford being in his room, they left the house together, and made their way towards the melancholy but revered spot.

It was a very fine and mild day for the season of the year, and after about half an hour's walk they arrived at the place of their destination. At the church door they saw a handsome carriage in waiting, and the livery of the servants struck Martha that she had seen it before, though where, she could not at that time call to her memory.

With sad and almost bursting hearts the lovely sisters walked into the old churchyard, and were soon kneeling, bathed in tears and engaged in earnest prayer, upon the grave of their supposed parent.

They were aroused from their solemn devotions by hearing the sound of footsteps, and looking up they beheld a lady and gentleman approaching towards the spot where they were, and they hastily arose from their knees, and turning round were about to retire, when the lady in a moment caught a full view of their countenances, and no sooner did she do so, than she uttered a loud scream and immediately sunk insensible in the arms of her companion; at the same moment the sisters and Martha, notwithstanding the lapse of years, to their utter astonishment recognised in their features and persons those of the lady who had taken them away in their childhood, and likewise the stranger who had restored them to their home.

The stranger seemed to be little less amazed and agitated than Augusta and Charlotte, and for a second or two fixed his eyes stedfastly upon the countenances of the lovely damsels, as if lost in astonishment, perplexity, and admiration, then in a voice of great emotion, but in accents of command, he exclaimed,—

"Confusion! to meet again thus; but begone, return home, for there is danger in remaining here!"

Before Martha and her fair companions could recover from their surprise, the unknown raised the insensible form of the lady in his arms, and bore her towards the carriage, which they immediately afterwards heard driven away, and when they looked in the direction where it had been in waiting, they found that the coast was perfectly clear.

It was several minutes ere the sisters or Martha could sufficiently recover from their amazement to speak, and then Augusta ejaculated,—

"What a remarkable adventure is this. What are we to understand from it? These are the same persons with whom we came in contact some years ago; I have a perfect recollection of their features, and it is quite evident from their behaviour that they knew us also."

"Oh, yes," said Charlotte, "it is; dear sister I am lost in mystery. Who can these strangers be, whom we have not seen before, for so many years ? Never did the likeness which the lady bears to the portrait we have so often gazed at in wonder and admiration, appear to me more striking. There is something that convinces me that they are in some way connected with us."

"But if they are," observed Augusta, "why should our dear father wish to conceal it from us? It is clear that they are persons of distinction."

"Come, my dear young ladies," said Martha, "let us return home. I fear that my master will be uneasy at our absence, and also that he will be very angry with me for suffering you to go out without his permission, especially after he has frequently cautioned me not to do so."

Augusta and her sister once more turned their melancholy gaze towards the grave of the deceased Mrs. Milford; their tears flowed fast, and having once more breathed the most fervent blessings on her memory, suffered themselves to be led away from the church-yard, and slowly retraced their steps towards home, reflecting deeply on the remarkable adventure they had met with.

When they arrived at home they were informed by Mrs. Ashfield that Mr. Milford had not yet quitted his room, and that he was not therefore aware that they had been absent from home, and at first Augusta and her sister were half resolved not to make him acquainted with their strange adventure; but, however, on considering that their supposed parent was the most proper person to be made acquainted with the particulars, and the most able to give them advice, they communicated the whole proceedings to him.

Mr. Milford heard their recital with evident interest, and his agitation was such that he could scarcely sufficiently command his feelings to make any observations upon the extraordinary adventure, but fearful of betraying himself and exciting the suspicions of his fair *protogees*, he assumed as much composure as he possibly could, although he found it most difficult to answer the questions which they naturally put to him, and was not a little confused to find that the sisters retained such a vivid recollection of the stranger and the lady (whom he was satisfied beyond the smallest doubt was their mother) after so many years had elapsed since they had seen them, and at which time they were so very young.

He was very cautious in the questions he put to them as to their having seen the parties before, but the remarks they made in respect to the extraordinary resemblance which the lady bore to the portrait they had so constantly admired, greatly bewildered him, and he scarcely knew in what way to evade them. After some further conversation he again warned them not to venture forth without he himself accompanied them, and took the earliest opportunity of again retiring to his chamber, to reflect in solitude on all these circumstances, and to endeavour to devise some plans for the future unravelment of the torturing mystery which enshrouded the origin of the sisters, more especially, as his own pecuniary resources were daily becoming more impoverished, and unless he received some assistance from those from whom he had a right to expect it, nothing but poverty stared him in the face.

Notwithstanding the long affected reformation of his son, Mr. Milford had now too much reason to believe that he had only been acting the part of the hypocrite, to forward his own secret and nefarious designs, and at times he threw out certain dark hints, which gave his unhappy father reason to suspect that he knew more than he at present thought proper to disclose, and which he was determined to take advantage of to forward his own dark purposes; and this, coupled with the loss of that amiable partner, who had been his solace under every affliction, rendered the unfortunate Milford one of the most miserable men in existence; and so rapid were the effects upon his constitution, that all his energies seemed at once prostrated, and it seemed as if he was about shortly to follow his wife "to that bourne from whence no traveller returns.",

CHAPTER XI.

THE DISSIPATION OF YOUNG MILFORD.—THE THREAT.—THE ALARM.—THE CONFLA-
GRATION.

VARIOUS were the distracting and conflicting thoughts which the adventure of the sisters in the churchyard gave rise to in the bosom of Mr. Milford; but if it were possible for him to derive any consolation from the circumstance, it was in the certainty that the unknown and the mother of the lovely sisters were still in existence, and the probability that after this rencontre the gentleman would no longer delay communicating with him, either to release him from the obligation he had imposed upon him, or to afford him counsel and assistance.

But Milford wished not to part with Augusta and her sister; oh, no, he loved them as fondly as if they were his own children; they were his only comfort, his props to existence, since his late melancholy bereavement, and the dutiful affection they had ever bestowed upon him rendered them doubly dear to him; but his own decreasing means and constitution rendered the prospect before him most awful to contemplate; should anything happen to him they would be left in poverty, and without a protector at the very period of life when they most needed one to guard them from the snares and vices of the world. What would become of them? He trembled, he shuddered to think. Their extraordinary beauty would render them the objects of envy and design of every unprincipled libertine, and without any one to guide them, ignorant as they were of the artifices practised upon unsuspecting and inexperienced innocence, how readily might they be ensnared into the meshes of ruin. This thought was torture to Mr. Milford, and vain were his endeavours to persuade himself that Providence would interpose to render his apprehensions groundless.

He had indeed hoped that the unknown, after seeing the sisters, and knowing how straitened he must be in his circumstances, through not hearing from him so long, would have lost no time in calling upon him, especially after the solemn promises he had so frequently made; but when week after week, and month after month elapsed, and he neither saw or heard anything of him, he gave up the idea in despair.

The neglect of the stranger, Milford could not but consider, absolved him from the oath he had taken, and he was frequently on the point of divulging the whole of the remarkable facts to the sisters, but some instinctive feeling prevented him; besides, what would be the misery of Augusta and Charlotte to find that they had no natural claim upon him, that they had been so long beholden to him and his late wife, and moreover that they knew not where to find those who were really their parents, and upon whom they had a claim for protection?—No, let whatever might be the consequences, Milford was determined to keep the secret, for the present, at any rate, inviolable, and trust to the kindness and wisdom of Providence for the result.

George Milford seeing that the means of his father were daily becoming more impoverished, and that there was no prospect of the mystery which surrounded the origin of the sisters ever being revealed, began to abandon his former designs, and resolved to take every advantage of the knowledge he had obtained to extort the remnant of his unfortunate father's little property from him, in order to support him in the career of profligacy he had so long entered upon. Callous to every proper feeling he cared not who suffered, what misery he caused so that he obtained the means of gratifying his vicious propensities, and he was fully determined that nothing whatever should daunt or retard him in the execution of his diabolical plans.

Mr. Milford was surprised and alarmed at the boldness of conduct he shortly assumed towards Augusta and her sister, particularly the latter; and they were no less shocked and astonished at it, and, unable to understand it, shrunk from him with a feeling of repugnance they had never felt before. Was this the conduct of a brother, they reflected, he whom they had a right to look up to for protection from insult, and who should be the last to give utterance to a word that should be calculated to call a blush upon their cheeks?—Oh, no, how different was it to what they ought to expect from one in whose veins they imagined flowed the same blood as their own.

Previous to this they had always courted his society with all the affection of sisters, but now they dreaded to meet him, and avoided his presence as much as possible.

Indeed George Milford was seldom at home until a late hour of the night, when he would always return in a state of inebriation, and make use of language that shocked the ears of all who heard it.

In vain his father remonstrated with him, and with tears in his eyes, sought to convince him of the misery he was causing, and the ultimate ruin and disgrace it must bring upon himself; George Milford only laughed at him, and made fresh demands upon his purse, which he had now become too weak to oppose, although he saw clearly that the destitution of himself and those poor girls who were so dear to him must be the ultimate consequence.

So limited had now become the means of the ill-fated Mr. Milford, that, much as he regretted to part from such old and faithful attendants, he found it absolutely necessary to dispense with the future services of Mrs. Ashfield and Martha, and with much anguish of mind he gave them notice that effect.

Although those two excellent and faithful servants were not surprised to hear it, the regret it caused them from their long attachment to that family, may readily be imagined. But nothing could equal the sorrow of the sisters at the idea of a separation from their old friends, whom they had ever looked upon with the same affection as if they had been their nearest relations, and it was only on the promise of Mrs. Ashfield and Martha that they would frequently visit them, that they could become in the least degree tranquillised, or reconciled to their parting.

For his own part, George Milford was very glad when Mrs. Ashfield and her companion quitted the house, for they possessed that influence over his father and the sister's which presented considerable obstacles to the execution of his designs, and he suspected that they penetrated far deeper into his intentions than it was convenient for him they should do.

The whole attention of Augusta and her sister were now devoted to Mr. Milford, and when they beheld him daily becoming weaker and weaker, and his spirits every hour becoming more depressed, they shuddered at the prospect which opened before them, when they should be left parentless and without a friend in the world to whom they could apply for assistance and advice, for to George they dared not look with any other feelings than those of dread and almost aversion.

The limited means of Mr. Milford was not the least source of uneasiness to them, for they felt satisfied that for their comfort, and in consequence of the continual demands upon him through his son's extravagance, he must deprive himself of many of those little enjoyments which were so necessary to him in his declining years and health. They revolted at the idea of continuing to be a burthen to him, and determined to do something that might tend towards their own support and the happiness of him to whom they were so much indebted.

"Dear father." said Augusta one day when they were seated in their little parlour, "you are poor, I see with the most sincere and fervent grief that your means are daily becoming more limited, and at the very time when you most require the means of comfort. I fear that you have much impoverished yourself in the education of me and my sisters, certain as we are that it is from no improvidence of your own. Charlotte and myself feel that we have too long been a burthen upon your hands, that we have too long been indolent, when by our exertions we might have contributed to your happiness and our own benefit. Let us no longer continue to be thus inactive, but by our future exertions endeavour to make up for the time we have lost. We are willing to work, and.—"

"To work, child," interrupted Mr. Milford, with a look of emotion, "my girls descend to the drudgery of work, never, never."

"And why not, dear father?" said Charlotte, "why should we feel too proud to do that which others circumstanced like ourselves are compelled to do?"

"Ask not the question," replied Milford, "for you know not the tender chord you touch upon. What would you do?"

"Go to service, father, anything," said Augusta. "to release you from the burthen which has pressed too long and too heavily upon you."

"Go to service!" ejaculated Mr. Milford, looking upon Augusta, at the same time with an expression of gentle reproach,—"What leave me here alone in my solitude, and to the mercy of that young profligate, who, I fear, is determined to break my heart?"

"Oh, no, no, dear father!" cried the beauteous sisters in a breath, and entwining their fair arms around his neck; "we will never, never leave you, Heaven forbid; but we must not, we feel that we ought not longer to remain in idleness, when fortune thus frowns upon you—thanks to your affectionate attention to us, we are accomplished, and may by exertion procure such employment at home as we may be competent to undertake, and which, while it contributes to our general welfare, will afford us both gratification and amusement."

"Talk no more of this my dear girl," said Mr. Milford; "for I cannot consent to it. I have got sufficient left to support us in comparative comfort (Heaven knows it is little that I myself want now), and ere long something may occur to place you in a situation you little anticipate."

The sisters looked at Mr. Milford with astonishment and perplexity, as he uttered these remarkable words.

'Dear father!" ejaculated Augusta, "what can you mean by those observations? What reasonable anticipations can you entertain as to our future circumstances?"

"Question me not," said Mr. Milford, with some confusion, "for I cannot answer you. Perhaps I have already said too much. However, I will take the present opportunity of confiding that to your care which I have long treasured with the utmost anxiety, and I trust that you will do the same, for on it much—oh, very much may depend. I must leave you for a few minutes, but will quickly return."

With these words Mr. Milford slowly quitted the room, leaving the sisters completely overwhelmed with amazement, and at a loss to imagine what was about to take place. In a few minutes he returned, his countenance exhibiting considerable emotion, and having resumed his seat, remained for a few minutes silent.

At length he took a small crimson velvet case from his bosom, and opening it, drew forth from it the locket which had been found suspended from the neck of Augusta when they had been committed to his care. The sisters started at the sight of the valuable trinket, and more especially when they beheld the miniature, which in every respect bore so striking and so remarkable a likeness to the portrait in the room up stairs.

Mr. Milford beheld their emotion without surprise, and after a few moments pause to regain his composure, he presented the locket to Augusta, saying;—

"This, my dear girl, belongs to you, and I now commit it to your care, solemnly charging you to treasure it as you would your own life, and never to part with it on any occasion, but to suffer anything in preference. Above all, I caution you not to let it be seen by George."

"Gracious Heaven!" ejaculated Augusta, "what can this mean? Oh, surely my dear father, you will give me some further explanation? This trinket is evidently of great value; what claim have I to it, and whom does this miniature represent!"

"All these are questions that I must not answer you," returned Milford, "let it suffice that you have a claim to it; remember my words, and at some future period it may lead to some great and as I trust happy discoveries."

Augusta involuntarily pressed the locket to her lips, and Charlotte stood by entirely bewildered by astonishment.

"I will strictly obey your injunctions, my dear father," said Augusta, as she placed the locket around her neck, "and no circumstance whatever, let it be ever so pressing, shall induce me to part from it."

"Enough, enough, my dear child" said Mr. Milford, tenderly embracing her and Charlotte; "and may Heaven prosper and protect you when I may be no more."

"Oh, talk not thus, beloved father," ejaculated Charlotte, "God I trust will, in his infinite mercy, prolong your valued life for many years to come to bless us."

Mr. Milford shook his head mournfully, as a melancholy presentiment crossed his mind, and he then arose from his seat.

"I must leave you children," he said, "and for a while seek the retirement of my own room. Heaven bless you, Heaven bless you."

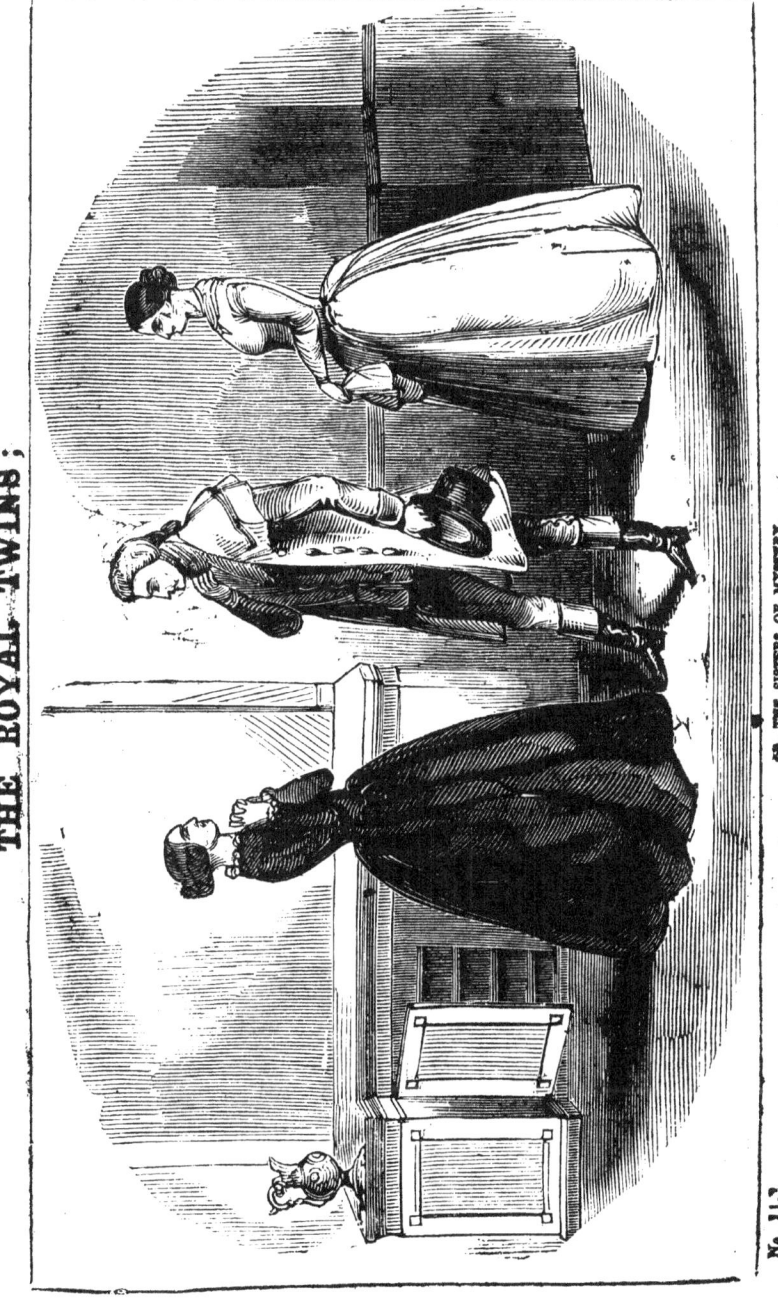

With these words Mr. Milford retired and left the sisters to themselves. We need not say that they were quite lost in amazement and perplexity at all that had happened, and the remarkable observations which Mr. Milford had addressed to them, but more than all were they astonished at the valuable trinket which he had delivered to Augusta, in so mysterious a manner, and the strict injunctions he had impressed upon them respecting it. Augusta took the locket from her bosom, and for some time they continued to gaze upon it, and the miniature it contained, with increased interest; but in vain they endeavoured to conjecture its history, or to form the least idea who the individual was it represented, although its likeness to the portrait up stairs and the lady whom they had encountered upon two such remarkable occasions was unquestionable.

Some days elapsed after this conversation had taken place, and Augusta and Charlotte were glad to perceive that Mr. Milford appeared much better in health and spirits than he had seemed to be for some time before; and they sincerely hoped that time and attention would completely restore him to convalescence.

Now that Mr. Ashfield and Martha had left their service, all the domestics duties devolved upon the fair sisters, and most cheerfully did they perform them, and exert themselves to the utmost to afford their supposed father satisfaction. Could they win but a smile of approbation from him, they felt more, far more than amply rewarded.

Mrs. Ashfield and Martha did not fail to fulfill their promise, and several times called to see them, and most welcome visitors they were, and by their excellent advice and expressions of approbation, urged the sisters on to fresh exertions.

George Milford continued his course of dissipation; indeed he was now so deeply plunged in vice as to be past reclaiming, and good reason had his unhappy father to regret that he had ever been born, for what but shame and ignominy could be the termination of guilt like his? Having extorted some money from his father, he had been absent two or three days and nights from home, passing his time with his abandoned companions at a low public-house situated in Whitehart Yard, Drury Lane. In that house some of the most depraved and notorious characters of both sexes were wont to congregate, and amidst their noisy carousals, all sorts of crimes of the most abominable description were concocted, and the terrors of the law were laughed to scorn.

George Milford was always a welcome guest among those wretches, when he had money, but he had hitherto avoided taking any part with them in their depredations, not from the want of inclination so to do, but from fear, for notwithstanding all his boasting and empty bullyings, a George Milford was at heart an arrant coward.

At length, his money being exhausted, he left his guilty associates, and bent his way towards home, with the determination of frightening his father out of more. He had not yet recovered from the effects of the drink he had taken to such excess, and he was therefore in a very fit humour for his purpose.

On arriving at home, he found his father seated alone in the parlour, Augusta and her sister being up stairs engaged in their domestic duties, and it was therefore a good opportunity for him to put his plans into execution.

Mr. Milford gazed at his son as he staggered into the room, with a mingled expression of pity and reproach, and mournfully shook his head, which only excited from the hardened profligate a vulgar laugh of scorn.

"So, old man," he said, "you see I have returned, and I dare say it affords you much gratification."

"George, George," said his father with much emotion, "is this the reward for all the care, the anxiety, and affection I have bestowed upon you from childhood? Are you entirely lost to every feeling of propriety and rectitude? Misguided youth, I am ashamed of you."

"Oh," returned George. "if you are going to moralize, it may just be as well to advise you at the onset to hold your tongue, for I can tell you I am not now exactly in the humour to listen to any such nonsense."

"Beware, George, beware, you are on the brink of ruin, another step, and you are lost for ever."

"Well, I suppose I must take my chance, as many others have done before me."

"Boy, reckless boy," exclaimed Mr. Milford, in a voice half stifled with the power of his feelings, "are you determined to break my heart?"

"No," answered the hardened youth, " I do not wish to do that exactly, because I do not know that I should gain much by it. The whole of it is, my money's gone, I have promised to meet a few friends in an hour or two, and as I am always very particular in keeping my word, I must draw upon your good nature for the requisite to do the thing that's handsome."

"George," said Mr. Milford, rising from his seat, and looking sternly and reproachfully at him, " you have already by your extravagance nearly reduced me to beggary; I cannot in justice to myself and others submit to allow myself any longer to pander to your extravagance and dissipation."

"Ha, ha, old man," laughed George Milford ironically, " I see you are inclined to be jocular. Very well, no matter, I can allow you to indulge your humour for a few moments, so long as you afterwards produce the mopusses."

With what feelings of shame, regret, and disgust did the unfortunate Mr. Milford gaze upon the besotted countenance of his still half inebriated son, as he gave utterance to these words; but pity predominated over every other feeling, and in a voice half stifled with emotion he said,—

"George, George, you torture me; can you so recently after the death of your poor mother, that mother that was ever so kind and indulgent to you, persist in this course of iniquity, and treat the advice I offer you with so much levity. Repent, repent, and all that a father then can accomplish to advance your well being in society, as far as his limited means (which Heaven knows are limited enough now) will allow him, shall be done for you."

"Psha! this is all humbug," exclaimed the abandoned youth, impatiently, " I came not here to listen to a sermon, but to replenish the exchequer. I must have money, that's the plain English."

"I will not give you any," returned his father, resolutely, " to go and squander upon your dissolute associates, and to afford you the means of entering into fresh vices which must ultimately end in your ruin."

"You will not?"

"I will not!"

George Milford gnashed his teeth, and biting his lips, and making two or three hasty strides across the room.

"Father," he said at length, with a stern and determined look, " you had better reflect before you come to any hasty decision, which you might afterwards have good reason to repent. I am driven into a corner, and am in no humour to be trifled with."

"Oh, God!" groaned the distracted Mr. Milford, " is it then indeed come to this that I should be threatened by my own son? Misguided young man, what would you have."

"I thought I had sufficiently explained myself, money."

"I will give it you; and mark me, George, henceforth you must endeavour to get your own honest living by your own industry. I have no longer the power, and if I had it would not be just, to support you in idleness, but towards establishing you in any way which may procure you an honest and respectable livelihood, I will render you all the assistance I can. This is all you have a right to expect from me, and if you reject my offers, you must take the consequences."

"So," said George Milford, with a bitter and malignant look, " you, old man, would punish me for your own folly and injustice; having neglected giving me the means to earn an honest and respectable living, as you facetiously call it, having brought me up in ignorance and indolence, you would now turn me adrift upon the wide world to get that honest and respectable living in the best way I can. Oh, this is most kind, most parently, but it so happens that it does not exactly meet my views of what is right and what is wrong, and consequently, I reject it. George *Clavering* has never been instructed to work, and now that he has arrived at the years of manhood, he does not intend to commence his apprenticeship."

"George Clavering!" exclaimed his father, turning ghastly pale.

"Aye, that is my name, is it not?"

"Good God! how know you that?"

"Oh, I know much more than you imagine. I know that I am the only one who has any natural claim upon you for support ; and that those girls who have always shared so much of your affection and indulgence, whom you have forged upon me as my sisters, are alike strangers to you in blood and origin !"

Mr. Milford was thunderstruck ! his limbs trembled violently, and he stared upon his son in stupified amazement and consternation. George perceived his triumph, and he inwardly chuckled at the confusion and agitation into which he had thrown his unhappy father.

"George, George," he gasped forth at length, "how have you obtained this knowledge ?"

"Can you deny the truth of it, old man ?" coolly demanded the profligate. His father was unable to return any answer, and George Milford went on :—

"You do not answer me, father, I suppose for one very good reason, because you cannot to your own satisfaction. Perhaps then it may be necessary for me to convince you that I do possess that knowledge. I shall commence then by reminding you of the old street or rookery near the Dog-Row, Whitechapel ; who was one of the vagrants who some twenty years ago sought with his wife and child a shelter in that fashionable part of the town ?—Was it not James Milford, alias Clavering ?—One day he walked forth and encountered a certain individual whom he had frequently seen before at the house of his grandfather, but knew not by name ; an appointment was made, and the following night this James Milford, alias Clavering, with his wife, were conveyed in a carriage by the before mentioned individual, in a most mysterious manner to a certain old mansion, situated they knew not where, and where after being ushered into a splendid apartment two infant girls were introduced to them, whom they pledged themselves, upon certain conditions to adopt and bring up as their own. They kept their oath, although the stranger did not fulfil his promise quite so faithfully, and the fair Augusta and her sister Charlotte——"

"Great God of heaven !" interrupted Mr. Milford, in an agony of despair, "how is this ? After all the precaution that has been used, how, how have you acquired this fatal knowledge ?"

"Then you cannot deny the authenticity of my interesting little narrative ?" said the abandoded young man with a malicious look of triumph.

Mr. Milford groaned in the anguish of his feelings, and covering his face with his hands, was unable to return any answer.

"No doubt," said George, with the utmost coolness, "the fair twins would be equally interested by hearing a repetition of the same story."

Mr. Milford started on hearing these observations, and gazed at his son with a look of terror.

"George, George," he ejaculated, in a hoarse voice, "you would not, you surely could not think of communicating these important facts, which by some unaccountable means have come to your knowledge, to these poor girls ?"

"You know the way to stop my tongue."

"Have you become entirely insensible to every proper feeling of duty ?"

"My friends are waiting for me, and I must, as a man of honour, keep my appointment ; "was the laconic reply.

"What would you have ?"

"I told you, money."

"Then you are determined to ruin me," groaned Mr. Milford.

"Oh, the gentleman, your patron, no doubt will supply your necessities," returned his son.

"Cruel boy," ejaculated Mr. Milford, " can you indeed be so destitute of feeling as to thus delight to torture me."

" My friends are waiting for me," repeated the guilty youth, with a sardonic grin of triumph.

"But you will promise me not to betray this secret to any one ?"

"On certain conditions."

"What is now your demand ?"

"Why, let me see," replied George Milford, with the greatest possible effrontery, "oh I think ten guineas will do at present."

"Ten guineas."

"Aye, I'm sure you cannot grumble at that, seeing it is so very moderate; so let us have the blunt, and then I will be off, unless you prefer my remaining to pay my respects to my dear sisters; ha, ha, ha!"

"Abandoned, heartless youth," exclaimed Mr. Milford, flashing upon him a look of shame, reproach, and indignation; "you are lost, you are lost entirely, nothing whatever it seems, can bring you to a sense of the enormity of your conduct."

"Will you give me the money or not?" peremptorily demanded George Milford. "I am tired of waiting here; and besides, you know, or at least you may guess what will be the consequences should you obstinately decline."

"Rash, unfeeling boy," said the broken hearted father, "do you again threaten me. Will no sense of shame or proper feeling induce you to relent?"

"Again I tell you I must have money; morality is not palatable to me at present. I have no wish to threaten you, old man, but I can tell you that my patience is nearly exhausted. Why should those girls who have no claim upon you, share all your favours, while I——"

"Hush," interrupted Mr. Milford, with alarm, as his guilty son raised his voice, and he feared that his observations might reach the ears of the sisters; "you do not wish to betray this secret, which by some most unaccountable manner has come to your knowledge, to Augusta, and her sister."

"You know the way to prevent my doing so," replied George Milford. "Are you willing to purchase my silence or not?"

"And am I indeed thus spoken to by mine own son? By him whom I have behaved to with so much affection and indulgence? Oh, George, shame upon you. Mark my words, you will bitterly, you will most keenly, at some future period, repent this."

"Bah, bah!" growled the young profligate, "the money, the money, that's all I want."

Mr. Milford saw plainly that it was useless to attempt to expostulate with his hardened son, with a sigh, therefore, he drew forth his purse, and counting out the sum he demanded, placed it in his hand, and motioned him to be gone, for his emotion was too great to suffer him to speak, and he motioned him to be gone, fearful lest the sisters should enter the room, and he should betray all. George Milford deliberately counted over the money, and then with a malicious smile of satisfaction, he quitted the house, and once more hastened to join his dissipated associates.

On the way he exulted in the success of his plans, and blessed the lucky chance which had put him in possession of the important secret, and of which knowledge he was determined to take every advantage. Callous to every natural feeling; completely abandoning himself to his own vicious propensities, he cared not how much misery he caused his unhappy parent, or whether or not he might bring him to ruin, so long as he could extort the means of indulging in his guilty and dissipated course; but there were one or two circumstances which he was still most anxious to fathom—namely, who were the parents of Augusta and Charlotte, and likewise who the strange gentleman was, and in what manner he was connected with the twin sisters; and this secret he resolved to lose no opportunity which might present itself to unravel.

After the departure of his son, Mr. Milford threw himself into a chair, and covering his face with his hands, for some time gave himself up to the most overwhelming and distracting grief, and could not help bitterly lamenting that George had ever been born, or that he had not died in his infancy. He saw plainly enough that he had now given himself up entirely to vice, and that he was past redemption; what else could be the consequence of the guilty course he was pursuing, but shame and ruin, and fervently poor Milford wished that it might please Heaven to take him, ere that fatal day arrived.

But little had Mr. Milford been prepared to hear that which had been revealed to him by George at their recent interview, and it gave him the greatest alarm, and caused him the most painful suspense, for he saw that the young profligate was resolved to take every advantage of it, and he could not help shuddering when he reflected upon what might be the consequences.

How the secret had come to the knowledge of his son he could not imagine, since himself and his late wife had ever used so much precaution, and for some time he racked his brain in reflecting upon this perplexing subject.

When Augusta and her sister re-entered the parlour, they could not help noticing the extreme agitation of Mr. Milford's manner, and eagerl y inquired the cause. However, he evaded their questions as well as he could, and they, knowing that George had been there, naturally attributed it to that; for they well knew the extreme anguish of mind which Mr. Milford suffered from the wild, the reckless, the dissipated and ruinous course his misguided son was pursuing; and the regret of the fair sisters was almost equal to his, although there were times when they could not help viewing George with sensations almost amounting to fear, and when the boldness of his manners towards them and the singular looks he would fix up on them, excited their utmost astonishment and disgust.

Mr. Milford, however, was in no humour to enter into conversation with the sisters on this occasion, and he therefore excused himself and retired to his own apart-ment, where he might give indulgence to the various thoughts which crowded upon his mind, and to seek to devise some means to avert the evils which might otherwise arise from the unfortunate knowledge his son had acquired; but this he felt certain would be a task that it would not be easy to accomplish. George Milford had now become quite lost to every feeling of shame; it was evident that he looked upon his father with no more regard than as if he had been an entire stranger to him, and that he would not rest until he had brought him to entire ruin. Unless he received some further assistance from the stranger, and of which, after such a long silence, there did not seem to be the least likelihood he could ever long withstand the system of extortion he had commenced against him, and the destitution of himself and the fair sisters must inevitably follow.

This was a fearful picture to contemplate, and Mr. Milford shuddered at it. But the conduct of the stranger astonished and bewildered him more than all. What could be the reason of his h aving so shamefully broken his solemn promise, and how could he expect him to be faithful to his trust when he had acted in so treacherous a manner? Could it be possible that he had made up his mind to abandon them to their fate? Circumstances were certainly in favour of such a conclusion. After the meeting of the sisters with the stranger and the lady in the church yard, Milford did indeed fully expect that he should either have received a visit or a communication from him; but his con-tinued silence was sufficient to excite his worst suspicions, and added much to the anxiety of his mind.

There were indeed times when Mr. Milford was half resolved to make the sisters acquainted with the whole particulars, for he considered that it would be much better for them to hear the remarkable story from his own lips than those of his son; but still there was a certain feeling, which he could not exactly understand, that prevented him from doing so, and he resolved to leave it to the will of Providence, not doubting that He would not see the innocent suffer through the vicious designs of the guilty. One thing, however, was certain, that the secret could not remain for any great length of time longer concealed, for George Milford' would not fail to divulge all he knew, as soon as his unfortunate father no longer had the means of pandering to his wishes.

Day after day passed away, and week after week elapsed, and still Mr. Milford neither saw nor heard anything of the stranger, and he could only come to the conclu-sion that he had resolved to desert the two fair beings whom he had in childhood com-mitted to his care, and that he should receive no further assistance from him. This thought, as may well be imagined, greatly distressed the mind of Mr. Milford; for in his present precarious state of health, he knew not how soon it might please Heaven to take him from them, and then they would not only be left without a protector, but without the means of support.

And yet surely the stranger could not be so cruel, so treacherous and unjust, as to leave those poor girls in whose fate he had expressed so deep and extraordinary an interest, to the mercy of the world?—Such a thought seemed opposed to all reason, and Mr. Milford sought to discard it from his breast, and to encourage hope, gloomy and unpromising even, as everything at present appeared to be. This, however, was much easier suggested to the mind than put into effect; and with this variety of conflicting thoughts torturing his brain, Mr. Milford daily became more miserable, and apprehensive. He dreaded every time when his son came home, lest anything should transpire to betray all the painful and extraordinary particulars. But in that respect he was not frequently annoyed, George remaining from home, gambling and drinking with his depraved associates, until he wanted a fresh supply of cash; and when he did make his appearance at the residence of his unhappy father it was generally at a late hour, and after Augusta and Charlotte had retired to their chamber. So that there was no fear of their overhearing anything.

But these repeated demands upon his purse had so impoverished Mr. Milford's means, that at length he had not more than three hundred pounds in his possession, and without further aid, in the extravagant manner that his son was going on, that must soon be exhausted, and then what was to become of them? Several times Mr. Milford had serious thoughts of disposing of the house and furniture, and taking one more humble and better suited to his means; but he could not make up his mind to do so; the house had become endeared to him from the number of years he had resided in it; besides should he remove from there the stranger would not be able to find him, should he be desirous of doing so, and that might be the means of retarding the discovery he was so anxious to make, and probably leave the sisters in ignorance of their origin for ever. He therefore abandoned the idea, and endeavoured to wait patiently the result; resolving to struggle with his own feelings as much as possible, for the sake of those whom he had undertaken to protect, and who had ever shewn him the same dutiful regard as if he were their father! in fact, they had never known any other, nor could they have the least suspicion that they had no claim upon him by the ties of consaguinity.

There were many circumstances, however, in the lives of the twin sisters, which to them seemed most extraordinary and inexplicable, and they frequently when alone discussed them. Most anxious were they to learn who the stranger and the lady were, and whether they were in any way connected with their destiny, which from all that had transpired seemed most probable, but they found it impossible to elicit anything from Mr. Milford that was calculated to throw the least light upon the subject, and the more they reflected upon it, the deeper they became involved in perplexity. They often contemplated the valuable locket which Mr. Milford had so recently placed in the possession of Augusta with the deepest interest. It was quite evident that both the miniature and the portrait represented the lady whom they had twice encountered in so remarkable a manner, and that gave rise to a variety of conjectures in their bosoms, although they were unable to come to any one of a satisfactory nature. It seemed perfectly clear to the sisters that this lady, whoever she was, must have some peculiar claim upon them, or why had she exhibited so much emotion on both occasions when she had seen them, and why was the locket inclosing a likeness of herself placed in their possession, with such strict injunctions to treasure it as carefully as they would their own lives. From all that they had seen, and also from her own personal appearance they were satisfied that she must be a lady of distinction, and taking all the circumstances into consideration they could not but imagine that she must be in some way related to them, and why their supposed father objected to make them acquainted with all the particulars, they could not conceive.

Another month wore away without anything worthy of particular notice occurring, and as the mild weather had now set in, there was an improvement in the health of Mr. Milford which was highly gratifying to Augusta and Charlotte, who trusted that he would yet be spared many years to bless them by his affectionate attention and advice.

Mr. Milford had now given up all hopes of again hearing from the stranger, and he contemplated the future with a fearful eye; for daily were his limited pecuniary means becoming smaller, and he could see no other prospect but ruin before them, unless Providence should interpose to save them.

Many a sleepless night did these reflections occasion Mr. Milford, and he in vain sought to devise some plan to avert the coming evil, for that it must ultimately come he could not entertain the least doubt. The conduct of his son was also a source of incessant anxiety to him, and he could anticipate nothing but disgrace and ignominy for that misguided young man. It was in vain to seek to remonstrate with him, or to offer him any advice; it has been before shown that he had become so completely hardened as to turn a deaf ear to those who would counsel him only for his good, and he cared not what torture he inflicted upon his unfortunate father, so that he could obtain the satisfaction of his own selfish wishes.

About this time, however, when Mr. Milford was plunged into a state of great anxiety and knew not what course to pursue, he was agreeably surprised on receiving a packet, the superscription of which he immediately recognized to be the handwriting of the stranger. It had been brought to the house by a livery servant, on horseback, as all the other communications had been, and who had no sooner delivered it into the hands of Mr. Milford than without saying a word he rode off with the greatest speed.

Mr. Milford having retired to his own room, with a trembling hand he opened the packet, in which he found a considerable sum in gold, and a cheque for one hundred guineas, and a note which on opening, Mr. Milford found to contain the following words:—

"FRIEND CLAVERING—No doubt you have been surprised at my long silence, but circumstances which I cannot here explain have been the cause of it, and have rendered it impossible for me to keep my promise so faithfully as I could have wished. Inclosed I send you some more cash which no doubt will be acceptable to you, but I cannot undertake to say when you will hear from or see me again. I am perfectly satisfied with your conduct; continue to watch over your tender and beauteous charge with the same care that you have hitherto done, and fear not but that at some future period, perhaps not far distant, you will be amply rewarded. Remember my injunctions, and betray not the secret to Augusta and her sister.   FAREWELL".

The receipt of this communication, afforded some relief to the anxious fears of Mr. Milford; but still he was left involved in the same state of mystery as regarded who the stranger was, and what was the origin of the sisters, as he had been before; and there seemed no more prospect from the tenour of his note of his now becoming satisfied upon a subject which absorbed his complete interest than there had been the first hour that the fair twins had been placed under his protection.

The arrival of the servant at the house and the delivery of the packet to Mr. Milford (for being in the parlour at the time, they observed everything), created considerable surprise and curiosity in the bosoms of Augusta and her sister, and after Mr. Milford had retired to his own apartment they conversed long and seriously upon the subject. They had not failed to notice the extraordinary emotion he had betrayed on the arrival of the servant, and various were the ideas they formed, but without deciding upon anything to their satisfaction, and could not venture to question Mr. Milford lest he should be offended at their curiosity. Who could the messenger have come from? and what necessity was there for this secresy? The longer the sisters thought upon the subject, the more uncertain and bewildered they became. But when Mr. Milford returned to the room, the change in his appearance afforded them the greatest satisfaction, and convinced them that he had received some good news. It was long since they had seen him in such excellent spirits, and when they separated for the night, Augusta and Charlotte were buoyant with hope that happier times were yet in store for them, and endeavoured to be content to remain in ignorance of all the particular circumstances which had been the cause of this gratifying change.

It happened fortunately that George Milford was away from home at the time the messenger arrived, therefore he knew nothing of the circumstance, or there is no knowing what might have been the consequences; and Mr. Milford cautioned Augusta and Charlotte not to mention anything to him upon the subject; but he had no occasion to do so, for since the conduct of George had become so entirely disgraceful and depraved, the sisters avoided him with feelings of disgust and alarm, and it was not likely, therefore, that they should make him acquainted with the fact of the communication which his father had received, and which he seemed so much to value.

Their own curiosity, however, was greater than ever, and they listened attentively to the observations of their beloved guardian, in the hope of hearing something which might throw a light upon the subject. In this they were disappointed; Mr. Milford was on his guard, and while he gave them to understand that the communication he had received was of a highly satisfactory nature, and would release him from those immediate difficulties which had before threatened him, he most sedulously avoided

THE ROYAL TWINS;

No. 12.

OR, THE SISTERS OF MYSTERY.

throwing out the least hint which might arouse their suspicious, and give them any idea of that he wished to conceal from them.

Had their revered protector then received some pecuniary assistance, and if so from whom had it come ? They had it never heard him speak of any relation save his uncle and from all that they had gathered of his character from Mr. Milford, he was the last person who would assist him or ,from whom he would condescend to receive an obligation. From whom then could it emanate ? They were at a perfect loss to form even the slightest conjecture though they had noticed the rich livery of the servant and felt satisfied that he had come from some individual of exalted rank. However, it was useless for them to rack their brains in seeking to fathom this mystery, and they contented themselves with noting the favourable change it had so quickly wrought in the health and spirits of Mr. Milford, and left the other circumstances for time to unravel.

CHAPTER XII.

THE ACCIDENT.—AN INTRODUCTION FRAUGHT WITH DANGER.—THE CONSEQUENCES. —THE CONFLAGRATION.—THE RESCUE.

GEORGE MILFORD continued the same career of profligacy, and indeed it would have been madness to have thought of reclaiming him, so completely hardened had he become in guilt. His anxiety, and curiosity to become acquainted with the whole of the secret connected with the sisters, remained unabated ; but at present he saw very little chance of that wish being gratified, although he had not yet abandoned his designs of placing them completely in his power, and in a position to profit by his knowledge, should their relations ever be discovered. He kept his father in a constant state of dread, by threatening to divulge everything to Augusta and her sister, if he did not comply with all his demands ; but that, of course, he knew better than to do, as such a disclosure would be more calculated to defeat his plans than to promote them. At length Mr. Milford was released from the importunities of his abandoned son for a time. George Milford having been engaged with some of his infamous associates in an an assault of a violent description, was apprehended, and being taken before the magistrates, was committed for three months to prison.

The two sisters deeply commiserated in the sorrows of Mr. Milford, and lamented the unfortunate and degrading propensities of him whom they believed to be their brother. They sought to console him all they could, and most fervently did they pray to Heaven to work a reformation in George Milford, ere an ignominious fate should overtake him. They could not, however, help feeling a great release at the absence of George Milford, from the house, for the abuse he was heaping on the head of his amiable father was a source of the bitterest anguish to them ; the more so if they ventured to expostulate with him, they were sure to receive some brutal retort from him which disgusted their ears, and shocked their feelings. There was something too, as we have before stated, so preliminary bold and repulsive in his recent bearing towards them, that they shrunk from his presence with a feeling almost amounting to abhorrence.

At length Mr. Milford became somewhat more reconciled to the fate of his abandoned son, for he had nothing whatever to reproach himself with ; Heaven knew that he had always done his duty as a father to him, had ever been most affectionate and indulgent to him, had brought him up in the paths of virtue, and given him the most excellent parental advice, but he had scorned it all, and seemed determined to bring disgrace and misery upon his declining years. His misconduct had shortened the days of his poor mother, and surely sooner or later his conscience would bitterly reproach him, and he would be brought to a full sense of the enormity of the course he had pursued. These and similar were the reflections that continually tortured the mind of Mr. Milford, and cast a perpetual gloom over his spirits. Besides, he often thought what would become of Augusta and Charlotte should it please the Almighty to deprive them of his protection, and they should be left to the mercy of George Milford? He fervently prayed to Heaven to avert such a calamity, until the mystery connected with the fair objects of his care and solicitude should be unravelled, and they should be placed under the protection of those on whom they had a natural claim, and in that station of society they were assuredly born to, and which they were so well calculated to adorn.

It was a beautiful summer afternoon about this period, when invited by the fineness of the weather, Mr. Milford had resolved to take the two lovely sisters out for a walk in the neighbouring fields, and having completed the necessary preparations, they were about to leave the house, when they were startled by the furious noise of a horse's hoofs, followed by the shouts of several individuals, and going hastily to the door, they beheld to their alarm, a horse galloping that way with frightful speed, the rider of which (a young man fashionably dressed) had evidently lost all command over him, and was in danger every moment of being precipitated to the ground. The terror of Mr. Milford and the fair sisters may readily be imagined, and more so when just as the affrighted animal with his unfortunate rider had reached nearly opposite the door, the former stumbled and fell, throwing the young man from his back with considerable violence, indeed so much so, as immediately to deprive him of his senses. Augusta and her sister uttered a scream of terror, but Mr. Milford being more collected, rushed forward, and the horse being secured, the rider was rescued from his perilous situation, Mr. Milford assisted by one or two of the bystanders, carried him into his house, and placing him on the sofa, despatched a person immediately for a surgeon.

He was still quite insensible, and the blood was flowing pretty freely from a slight wound on the right temple, and the gentle sisters were afraid that he had in the fall received a mortal injury, and all the tenderest sympathies of their nature were in consequence aroused. Mr. Milford, however, endeavoured to pacify them, and continued to bathe the temples of the young man with vinegar until the doctor arrived.

During this brief interval Augusta and Charlotte could not help contemplating with feelings of the deepest interest and curiosity the countenance of the young stranger. He was very elegantly dressed, and was evidently a person in the higher rank of life. His figure was tall, and elegantly formed. He did not appear to be more than three or four and twenty years of age, and his features though now pale were regular, manly and extremely handsome. His hair, which was black as jet, was most tastefully arranged, but fell in a profusion of ringlets over his shoulders, and added to the pleasing effect of his general appearance. His fingers were adorned with several rings, apparently of great value; altogether no doubt could remain on the minds of those who beheld him that he was a person of distinction.

The surgeon having arrived, he examined the stranger's injuries, and although he said, he had received several severe bruises, he was by no means dangerously hurt, and would, no doubt, shortly recover. However, he thought it would not be prudent to remove him for a few hours, in the course of which he trusted he would be sufficiently restored to return to his own residence.

Augusta and her sister felt extremely glad on hearing the favourable condition of the young man, and it happened fortunately that just at that juncture Mrs. Ashfield arrived at the house on a visit to Mr. Milford and the sisters, and immediately tendered her assistance, which could not have arrived more opportunely.

In the course of a quarter of an hour the stranger was restored to sensibility, and gazed around him with astonishment at the singularity of his situation, having but a confused idea of what had happened. But more than all his attention was attracted to the lovely sisters, and the earnest looks he fixed upon them caused the blushes to mantle in their cheeks (for brilliant and expressive were the eyes that were fixed upon them) and they averted their gaze in confusion.

" Pray where am I?" he asked, in a soft and pleasing voice.

Mr. Milford explained to him, and having expressed the pleasure he felt at having been the means of releasing him from his perilous situation, inquired whether he felt himself much hurt.

"No," answered the young man; "I am merely slightly bruised, and was stunned by the fall. To you, sir, I do not know sufficiently how to express my gratitude for the service you have rendered me."

"Do not mention it, sir," returned Mr. Milford; "I have done no more than what it was my duty to do, and it is very gratifying to me that you are not seriously hurt."

"I thank you, sir," said the stranger, "indeed I feel so little the worse for the accident, that, if you will do me the favour of procuring a vehicle, I will return to my hotel, to which I was on my way, when my horse took fright at some music in the street."

"I would advise you, sir, at any rate to rest here for an hour or two, when you may be sufficiently recovered from the effects of the accident to depart;" said the doctor.

"Well, well," said the gentleman, after a pause, and again glancing towards Augusta and her sister; "since you thus advise me, my worthy friend, I will, if I shall not be intruding upon the kindness of this gentleman, do as you desire. But as I have some important business to transact this evening, I trust my stay will not be protracted more than a couple of hours at farthest."

The doctor now took his leave, and the gentleman continued to recline on the sofa, and entered into conversation with Mr. Milford, the latter having desired the sisters to retire into another apartment, which they did with Mrs. Ashfield, deeply interested by the adventure of the afternoon.

Mr. Milford found from the conversation of the stranger that he was a perfect gentleman, and a most accomplished man, and he was altogether highly pleased with his appearance and manners.

In the meantime the sisters on retiring to their room could not help conversing most eloquently on the adventure of the afternoon, and expressing their satisfaction at his being rescued from the untimely fate with which he had been threatened. Nor could Charlotte in particular help expatiating in language which somewhat surprised her sister and Mrs. Ashfield, on account of its warmth, upon the elegant and handsome appearance of the stranger, and expressing at the same time a most ardent wish to know who he was, though, she added, she was convinced from the nobilty of his countenance and demeanour he was a person of no common rank.

"Gracious me, Charlotte," said her sister, with a smile, "how you talk; why, any one to hear you would actually think that you were smitten with this young man at first sight."

"They might, my dear Augusta," replied Charlotte, laughing, "but I do not know that I should be altogether willing to plead guilty to the charge. However, you confess, I think, that the stranger is very handsome.'

"To be sure he is well enough," said Augusta, carelessly, "but we must not always judge people by their looks; many a base heart is enshrined in a fair exterior."

"Nay, Augusta, this is surely uncharitable."

"I do not mean to insinuate that the stranger is not all that he appears to be;" returned Augusta; "of course not; I should be ungenerous and unjust to do so, but I still maintain that it is not prudent to jump to hasty conclusions respecting the individuals who are by accident introduced to us. However, in this case, it is a matter of indifference, as it is not at all probable that we shall ever behold this gentleman again."

We will not say that a sigh escaped the bosom of the beauteous Charlotte, as her sister gave utterance to these observations, but certainly the smile which had before brightened her features became overcast, and had it not been for the gentle raillery of Mrs. Ashfield and her sister, she would have become absolutely gloomy.

In this manner about an hour and a half passed away, when they were summoned by their father to the parlour, the gentleman having requested the honour to bid them adieu previous to his departure.

Charlotte herself could not account for it, but her heart palpitated with more than its usual emotion, when she received this message, and it was some time since she had felt so much confusion as she did on that occasion.

On entering the parlour, they found the gentleman, apparently suffering little or no ill effects from his recent accident, and ready to depart, a hackney carriage being waiting at the door. He received them with much gallantry and politeness, and was evidently much struck with the extreme beauty of the sisters, though, of course delicacy compelled him to conceal it as well as he could.

"I am extremely obliged to your father and yourselves, fair ladies," he said, "for the attention that has been paid me, and I trust that on some future occasion. I may be allowed the honour of cultivating the acquaintance of those to whom I am so greatly indebted."

Mr. Milford bowed, and after some further observations the gentleman took his leave, and stepping into the coach was driven off towards the hotel where he was stopping.

This adventure served Mr. Milford and the sisters to converse about for the remainder of the afternoon, and the former passed the highest eulogiums upon the stranger, to which Charlotte could not help listening with pleasure.

"He is evidently a perfect gentleman and a most accomplished scholar," said Mr. Milford, "and I must say that I have been highly gratified by the conversation we have had together. The accident might have been attended with serious consequences, and I am very glad that it turned out no worse than it did."

"Yes, it was very fortunate," remarked Augusta; "but in the course of conversation did you elicit from the gentleman what station of life he fills?"

"Yes, my dear father," added Charlotte, "or his name and——"

"Well upon my word, girls," interrupted Mr. Milford, with a smile, "you are mighty inquisitive respecting this handsome young stranger. Well then I will even make you acquainted with all I know myself, with which, of course you must rest satisfied. From all I could gather, his name is Henry Stirling, and that he is highly connected, and is the only son of aristocratic parents, who are at present residing abroad. He himself is putting up at an hotel near Bond Street, and has promised to call again in a day or two to pay his respects to me and yourselves. But I must acknowledge that notwithstanding I am greatly prepossessed in favour of this young man, I do not think it would be prudent in me to give any encouragement to his future visits, as the difference of our station in society is an in surmountable obstacle to our ever being on intimate terms."

Charlotte, in spite of herself, and notwithstanding she could not understand the feeling, found it impossible to conquer a sensation of sadness and regret when Mr. Milford made use of these observations ; and she was surprised to find the strong impression the stranger had made on her even on their first meeting; and she was very dull and less talkative for the rest of the evening than she was accustomed to be, and in spite of all her efforts to the contrary, notwithstanding she really felt vexed with herself, she could not banish the form of the handsome and interesting Henry Stirling from her imagination. She could not but also entertain a secret wish that he would fulfil his promise and visit them again shortly. Pure and innocent as it is possible for mortal to be, Charlotte could not for a moment suppose that there was any harm or danger in encouraging these thoughts ; but alas, woful experience was destined to teach her otherwise.

Never was man more deceptive or dangerous than he who called himself Henry Stirling (for that was not his real name); handsome, accomplished, wealthy, and nobly connected, he possessed the most unbounded power either for good or evil, and unfortunately his vices predominated over his good qualities. He was wild, giddy, and thoughtless, and, was accustomed to look upon the fair sex with too careless an eye (though an enthusiastic admirer of female beauty) and to view them merely as the ready tools, in fact the common property of mankind, which should be made subservient to all his passions and caprices. Although so young, numerous were the intrigues in which Henery Stirling had been engaged, and which redounded so highly to his discredit; and numerous were the innocent females whom he had tempted from the paths of virtue, and given reason to curse his name.

Henry Stirling had mixed himself up in every fashionable vice of the age, and in others of even a more low and questionable nature. He was a gambler, a libertine, and a profligate ; yet he could so well assume the mask of the hypocrite that it was only those who were most intimate with him that could entertain the least suspicion of his real character.

Henry Stirling was a great sporting character, and several of his transactions on the race course would not bear the closest inspection. The reason of his assuming the name

^by which we have introduced him to the reader will be explained in the course of the narrative.

As he bent his way to his hotel, he could not help reflecting with pleasure and admiration upon the extreme beauty of the sisters, and he could not help feeling satisfied with the accident which had introduced him to them; and he determined to take the earliest opportuntity of seeing them again. But he was more particularly struck and captivated with the playful beauty of Charlotte, and indeed he did not remember ever before to have seen a female who had made so powerful an impression upon him at first sight.

Added to all his other faults, Henry Stirling possessed no ordinary allowance of personal vanity, and he usually flattered himself that he was all but irresistible in the eyes of any female who had once beheld him. He could not but think that Charlotte had viewed him with anything but indifference, and this thought gave him encouragement, so that by the time the young libertine had arrived at the hotel, he began to flatter himself with the idea that he had already made a conquest of a female to whom he had scarcely spoken half a dozen words; and resolved to lose no opportunity of presenting his lawless passion, thinking that in this respect he should be equally as successful as he had been on former occasions.

But notwithstanding his numerous faults, Henry Stirling, as we have hinted, had also his good qualities, which had he had any one to counsel and direct him, might have made him an ornament to society, and completely have counteracted his vices ; but his parents had ever given him too much indulgence, and being their only son, had winked at those faults, which, had they been corrected in early youth, would have saved him from the crimes and excesses into which he afterwards so deeply plunged. Such was the man whom an unfortunate accident had introduced to Mr. Milford and the fair damsels over whose happiness he had ever watched with such anxious care. Oh, how deeply would Mr. Milford have lamented, had he but known the trouble it would bring upon him, and what ready steps he would have taken to avert the evils with which the beauteous Charlotte and all connected with her were threatened.

It is a most extraordinary thing, but it is nevertheless true, that Charlotte found that the more she attempted to banish the image of Henry Stirling from her mind, the stronger became the impression on her memory, until she blushed for herself, and she dreaded to enter into conversation with her sister upon the subject, lest she should betray herself. It even followed her in her dreams, and when she awoke in the morning it was, if possible, stamped more vividly upon her imagination. She felt uneasy and anxious, and Augusta, who, of course, could not help noticing it, though she did not for a moment suspect the real cause, was very much surprised, for she had never seen her so serious before, since the death of Mrs. Milford. She, however, did her best to arouse her from it, and at length she partially succeeded, and Charlotte became somewhat more cheerful.

The third day after the accident, which had happened to Henry Stirling, while the two sisters, with Mr. Milford and Mrs. Ashfield were sitting in the parlour, they were aroused from the conversation, in which they were deeply engaged, by the sound of two horses galloping up the street, and immediately afterwards there was a loud knock at the hall-door, and Mr. Stirling was announced. Charlotte felt greatly agitated, and thinking that her companions must notice it, she became more confused, but before she had time to recover herself, Henry Stirling was ushered into the room. He greeted them with much cordiality, appeared to be in excellent spirits, and seemed to have recovered entirely from the effects of his recent accident. Mr. Milford welcomed him with the same warmth of feeling, as if they had been on intimate terms for many years, and the young man seemed not a little gratified with his reception, as indeed, he in reality was, encouraging him, as it did, to a latent hope of being able ere long, to make a favourable impression upon the mind of the lovely Charlotte, and thus to add another victim to those whom he had already ensnared.

Never did Henry Stirling exert himself more to render himself agreeable, than he did on this occasion, and with perfect success. Mr. Milford could not but entertain a most favourable opinion of the qualities of his mind, whilst Charlotte and her sister, particularly the former, listened to the noble sentiments he constantly enunciated, and which bore all the appearance of the greatest sincerity, with the warmest admiration, and to feel a pleasure in his society, and in listening to the arguments he treated with such uncommon eloquence, with a pleasure they had never experienced before.

Secluded as the life of the beauteous sisters had been, and inexperienced as they were in the ways and artifices of the world, it is not to be marvelled at, that they should be dazzled by the glowing qualities of mind and person which were so eminently displayed by Henry Stirling, and he saw full soon the advantage he had obtained, and fully resolved to avail himself of it to the fullest extent. The beauty of Augusta had excited his admiration, but the volatile disposition of Charlotte, added to her incomparable charms, and the simple artlessless of her conversation were a source of far greater attraction to him, and he resolved to use every exertion in his power to obtain the gratification of those unholy passions which the first sight of her had excited in his bosom.

It afforded him the utmost satisfaction to find the favourable impression he had made upon them, but more particularly that fair being to whom he had dared to raise his guilty thoughts. He saw the confusion she evinced whenever their eyes met, and already the young libertine flattered himself with the idea that her conquest was secure.

And indeed, that interview was a fatal one to poor Charlotte, for it made sad havoc in her peace of mind, and threatened to ruin her prospects for ever. She listened with transport to every word he uttered, and when he ceased speaking, she felt an unaccountable depression of spirits, as if some sudden calamity had befallen her. She almost feared to raise her eyes towards him, le t her looks should betray the strange and secret feelings which were passing in her mind, and she entertained the greatest apprehensions that Mr. Milford and her sister should notice the extreme confusion of her manner, yet she found it utterly impossible to conquer her feelings, while, at the same time, she was afraid to trust herself with a solution of them.

Henry Stirling prolonged his visit to the latest moment, and when he arose to take his departure, he had so completely won upon the good opinion of Mr. Milford, that he warmly invited him to honour them with a visit, whenever he might feel so disposed, or if it suited his convenience. This was just what the young roue wanted, and he left the house well satisfied with the success which had attended him so far, and thoroughly convinced in his own mind that he had created a sensation in the mind of the beauteous Charlotte, which she would find it difficult, if not impossible to conquer. Alas! he had calculated but too correctly ; when he quitted the house, the heart of poor Charlotte almost unknown to herself, went with him, and many were the troubles that were in store for her in consequence.

After Henry Stirling's departure from the house, Charlotte became dull and thoughtful, and Mr. Milford and Augusta could not but notice a change in her so unusual, with considerable surprise, though they were far from imagining the real cause from which it sprung ; and having pleaded slight indisposition, she retired to her chamber at an early hour, leaving her sister and Mr. Milford, in the drawing-room.

Glad to find herself alone, Charlotte gave free indulgence to the perplexing thoughts which crowded with such rapidity upon her brain ; and recalled to her memory, with feelings of pleasure, every word to which Henry Stirling had given utterance, and the deeper she reflected upon them, the stronger became her mingled feelings of delight, admiration, and astonishment. However, she endeavoured to compose herself before her sister joined her ; and by dint of considerable exertion, she succeeded much better than could have been expected.

Several days elapsed, and they saw no more of Henry Stirling, and the spirits of Charlotte became so much depressed, that Mr. Milford and Augusta could not but notice it ; and with the greatest solicitude they questioned her upon the subject, which only seemed to increase her agitation, and they were unable to elicit from her any satisfactory explanation. Every knock that came to the door, caused her to start and tremble, and she would frequently sit for a considerable time together at the window, gazing listlessly up the street, and apparently wrapped in thought, from which all the efforts of Mr. Milford and her sister failed to arouse her.

Whenever the name of Henry Stirling was mentioned, she would start, blush, and otherwise betray the greatest emotion and confusion. It was impossible that Mr. Milford could long help noticing this extraordinary behaviour; and it excited his suspicions, and created some alarm in his bosom. Could it be possible that the many accomplishments of the handsome young stranger (for such he really was to them), had made too favourable an impression upon the sensitive heart of his lovely protogee? —There was nothing at all unreasonable in such a conjecture; but he resolved to watch her narrowly, and then if his surmises should unfortunately prove to be correct, he must adopt prompt and energetic measures to prevent the evils which might arise from such a hopeless passion.

Mr. Milford, however, could not help blaming himself for having been too ready to give encouragement to the visits of a young gentleman of whom he knew so little, and especially considering the peculiar circumstances in which the fair sisters were placed, and he determined the next time he saw him, to beg to decline the honour of his future intimacy, on the plea that the difference of their stations in society, and the necessity which himself and his daughters had always found for retirement, rendered such a resolution unavoidable. He had already broken through the injunctions of the unknown by admitting a stranger into his house, and he knew not what danger might arise from Henry Stirling's having once beheld the beauteous sisters.

And Charlotte herself could not help seeing the folly, the imprudence, and even culpability of encouraging the strange thoughts which she had suffered to take possession of her breast, and the real nature of which she could no longer conceal from herself. She exerted herself to the utmost to conquer them, and to re-assume her wonted cheerfulness. But this she found to be a much more difficult task than she had at first calculated upon, for in spite of all her efforts to banish it, the too interesting image of Henry Stirling would too frequently occur to her mind, and the more she reflected upon him, the stronger was the hold that he gained upon her affection, and she could not but feel the greatest anxiety till she beheld him again.

More than a week, however, passed away, and Henry Stirling did not call again, much to the satisfaction of Mr. Milford, high as was the opinion from what little he had seen of him, that he entertained of his character, and he hoped that something would occur to prevent him from renewing his visits, trusting that if he had really made any impression upon the susceptible heart of Charlotte, which he had too much reason to fear he had, that time and absence would enable her to banish him from her thoughts, and to resume her wonted cheerfulness of disposition.

The term of George Milford's imprisonment had now expired, and he returned home, much to the alarm of his unhappy father, and Augusta and her sister, for they saw plainly that punishment had completely failed to work any reformation in him, and they apprehended the most painful and ruinous results from the reckless, depraved, and profligate habits, which had already brought his father to the very brink of ruin.

Mildly and fervently Mr. Milford remonstrated with his guilty son, and offered to assist him all that was in his power, if he would abandon his disgraceful ways, and endeavour to turn his thoughts to some way of getting an honest living, as it was impossible for him to support him in indolence, and that if he continued in his present career, nothing but an ignominious fate could possibly await him. It was all to no purpose, George only laughed at the admonitions of his father, and treated his advice with scorn and vulgar abuse.

Three days after the release of George Milford from prison, while he, his father, and the sisters were seated below, to the confusion of all present with the exception of George, who evinced an expression of countenance that created the greatest surprise, the name of Henry Stirling was suddenly announced.

Charlotte turned pale and trembled, and Mr. Milford felt a glow of shame and alarm mount to his face as he glanced at the dissipated countenance of his son, whom he hastily endeavoured to persude to retire, but he only laughed ironically, and seemed to enjoy a secret triumph, which they were at that time at a loss to understand.

Nothing could be more inopportune than a visit from Henry Stirling at such a time, and Mr. Milford would fain have excused himself, but before he could do so Henry Stirling had already entered the hall, and the next moment he stood in their presence.

THE ROYAL TWINS ;

No. 13.

OR, THE SISTERS OF MYSTERY.

He did not at first perceive George Milford, but when his eyes fell upon him, he started, his countenance became pale, and he exhibited in other respects, the greatest confusion. They, however, exchanged significant glances ; Henry hastily put his finger upon his lips, which was not observed by Mr. Milford or the sisters, and he then resumed his accustomed demeanour, and after exchanging compliments with Mr. Milford, and those fair beings whom he supposed to be his daughters, he took his seat, and entered into conversation with the utmost gaiety and freedom.

George Milford did not remain long in the room after the arrival of Henry Stirling, and after having bade him good day with mock politeness, at the same time exchanging another secret and significant glance with him, he retired, much to the relief of them all.

It was not without the greatest difficulty that Henry Stirling could remove his eyes for a moment from the lovely countenance of the blushing and trembling Charlotte ; but he could plainly perceive fron the altered demeanour of Mr. Milford that his visit was far from being so agreeable as it had formerly been, and he felt confused and ill at ease, which was not by any means diminished when Mr. Milford desired that he would favour him with a private audience in another room, and Henry, excusing himself to the ladies, followed him to the apartment up-stairs.

What passed between him and Mr. Milford, when they were alone, may be briefly told. The latter commenced by expressing his regret to be compelled to decline the honour of the friendship of a gentleman whom he was convinced, was every way so deserving of esteem, but that peculiar circumstances, which he could not explain, rendered such a course necessary, if the difference of their positions in society had not made it prudent ; and although he should always entertain the most lively sense of the honour he had done him, he must in future request that he would discontinue his visits.

Henry Stirling, as may well be imagined, was quite astounded and disappointed, on hearing this, and endeavoured to remonstrate with Mr. Milford on the unreasonableness of such a step, and to induce him not to persist in his demand, but all to no purpose, and Henry therefore had no alternative than to submit with the best grace he could, though the vexation of his feelings may easily be imagined.

After some further conversation, Mr. Milford and Henry Stirling returned to the parlour, where the latter shortly afterwards took a respectful leave of the sisters, observing that he trusted, although he was at present prohibited from visiting them, the time would come when he should have the honour and pleasure of beholding them again.

Charlotte's heart sunk within her, when she responded to the farewell of Henry, who having been permitted to press the hands of the fair sisters respectfully to his lips, after bidding Mr. Milford good day, abruptly took his leave.

Augusta was astonished at this unexpected termination of the interview, and the agitation of Charlotte was so great that she could not conceal it ; but it was not a little increased, when Mr Milford informed them of the course which he had deemed it prudent to adopt, and Charlotte could scarcely refrain from tears at the disappointment, while her confusion was equal to her emotion, for it seemed evident to her that her father had penetrated her thoughts, and had thus been induced to adopt the plan he had in order that he might nip her passion in the bud. But should she then never again enjoy the pleasure of Henry Stirling's society ? Had she seen him for the last time ? The thought was agonizing, and she longed to be alone, that she might give free and unrestrained vent to her feelings.

Henry Stirling left the house with his mind filled with vexation and disappointment. After the warm reception he had previously met with from Mr. Milford, he had never anticipated such a result as this, and he could not endure it with any degree of patience. Mr. Milford could surely not have penetrated his real character and designs, and yet he was at a loss to understand his peremptory conduct. But could he resign his hopes of possessing the beauteous Charlotte, who had made a more powerful impression upon him than any he had ever experienced before ? He felt that to be impossible, and he was resolved to give himself up entirely to despair, especially as he was satisfied that the lively damsel, even in the short acquaintance they had had, viewed him with a favourable eye.

His meeting with George Milford in so unexpected a manner, filled him with no little astonishment, he knew him well to be a villain, and in fact he had assisted him in some of his nefarious transactions, and it was necessary that he should secure his secresy. But could it be possible that he was the brother of that fair being who had so completely captivated him ? The very idea seemed unnaturally preposterous, and he could not bring his mind to believe it.

He had not proceeded far from the house, when he heard a well-known voice calling upon him to stop, and turning round, he beheld George Milford advancing rapidly towards him. He stopped and George came up to him, an expression of malignant satisfaction overspreading his features.

" I thought you understood the look I gave you, and would have waited for me at the end of the street," said George.

" Who would have thought to have met you, George, under such circumstances ?' remarked Stirling.

" Why, to be sure it was rather singular," returned George, " but perhaps it is fortunate for both of us. The old man, I see by your looks, has said something to vex you ?"

" Aye, indeed he has ; he has prohibited me from visiting his house, though for what reason I know not, any more than that he seems to consider the difference of our station in society ought to prevent any intimacy arising between us."

" Very awkward that, Mr. Stirling."

" Awkward !" repeated Henry Stirling, ". it is most provoking, quite unbearable ; especially when there in such an attraction as your beauteous sister, Charlotte."

" Ah ! I thought that was the magnet that attracted you. Well, well, l cannot but admire your taste, though the prize might, without assistance be a most difficult one to win."

" Let us retire into yonder tavern," said Stirling, " for I have much to say to you, and we might be observed in the street."

George Milford nodded assent, and they entered the tavern, which his companion had pointed to, and were shown into a private room at the back of the house, where Stirling called for refreshment, and then remained silent for a few minutes, and gazing earnestly upon the countenance of George.

" Now then, at once to business," at length exclaimed the latter, " there is no one to listen to us."

" You were away from home when I was first introduced to your family ;" commenced Henry Stirling,

" Yes," answered his companion, " I was rusticating in Bridewell, and have only been out three days."

" Did you hear my name mentioned by your father or sisters after your return home ?"

" Not till it was announced to-day, and you may well imagine that I was not a little surprised."

" You know me, George ?"

" Why, I believe I do know *something* of you. I once *borrowed* a trifle of you which might have lagged me, but you acted like a trump, and have on several occasions rewarded me pretty handsomely for some little services I rendered you."

" True, true," returned Stirling, hastily, " but there is no occasion to dwell upon those particulars now. George, you will not reveal what you know of me to your father ?"

" Certainly net, on conditions ;" answered George.

" I understand you, and you shall have no cause to grumble."

" That's enough, and I could not have met you at a better time, for I am devilish hard up, and the old man will not come down at all. Now then, what is it you want ?"

" The beauteous Charlotte has completely captivated me ; I have thought of nothing else since I first saw her, and —"

" And I suppose, you would fain add her to the list of your other victims, eh ?"

" I should be the happiest fellow in the univese, if I had her in my power. I would keep her like an empress ; there is nothing that I would consider too much to do to contribute to her happiness; no sacrifice that I would not be prepared to make, with the exception of tendering her my hand."

"And that I presume it would not be convenient for you to do ?" said George Milford, sarcastically.

"Certainly not.   You know, George, that I am a nobleman, and am restricted from marrying any woman whose birth and property are not equal to my own; or, by Heaven, there is not a damsel in the world   I would sooner make my bride than the lovely and fascinating Charlotte Milford."

"I'm sure I ought to feel highly flattered by the compliments you so lavishly bestow upon my sister;" said the profligate with an ironical grin.

"Nothing I can say can sufficiently express the admiration I feel for her ;" remarked Henry Stirling; "but I am fearful that I must abandon all idea of getting her in my power."

"Not at all," replied George Milford, "[that is if you only act the thing that's right towards me."

"Is it possible," exclaimed Henry Stirling, with astonishment, and even he could not help feeling a sensation of disgust as he listened to the observations of his guilty companion, "that you are ready to connive at the ruin of your own sister?"

"What matters that to you?" demanded George; "I suppose I know my own business best, and if the girl is placed in your power, I do not suppose you will be very particular by what means it is accomplished."

Henry Stirling looked at him for a moment or two in silence, and could scarcely believe his sincerity, the offer was so unnatural, so perfectly monstrous.

"George," he said at length, "you are not trifling with me, are you, or attempting to deceive me ?"

"Well," he answered, "if you think I am, there is an end of the matter, and we may as well end this interview."

He rose from his seat as he spoke, and made a sign as if to go, but Henry Stirling detained him.

"Nay," he said, "do not take my question amiss; you must admit that I have plenty of reason for astonishment and doubt at such an undertaking coming from the lips of a brother."

"I have good reasons for not being particular on that point," returned George, with a significant look ; "but there is no necessity to enter into any further explanation. So that you have your wishes complied with, I suppose that is all you have to care about ? Leave me to answer for my own sins, and to settle my actions with my own conscience in the best way I can."

"George," said Stirling, still looking steadfastly at him, and unable to conquer his feelings of disgust, "you are an arrant villain."

"Agreed!" returned the former, coolly, "and who else but a villain can you expect to aid you in your nefarious plans?"

Henry Stirling somewhat winced under this just retort, and he hesitated.

"Well, well," he said at last, "it is no use entering into any tedious or lengthy arguments upon this subject ; then you think it is not impossible for me to get this fair damsel in my power?"

"Not at all," answered George, "that is with my assistance, which you say you are willing to purchase ?"

"Yes, yes, we shall not quarrel about the terms, I dare say."

"Well then, as that is all settled, we may as well at once enter upon our plans."

Stirling opened the door and looked out, to satisfy himself that there was no one within hearing, and then resumed his seat, and he and his guilty companion continued to converse with each other in an under tone.   We will not here enter into the particulars of their discourse, which probably would not be at all interesting to the reader; it is sufficient to say that when they both arose to depart, they seemed perfectly satisfied with each other, and separated, Stirling most sanguine on the ultimate success of his plans, and George perfectly satisfied with the terms on which he had agreed to assist him.

Supplied with cash, George Milford sought his old associates, with whom he spent that night and several other days in riot and debauchery, exulting in the favourable prospect he had of mending his fortune, and resolved to make the best of it. His absence from home created no surprise, though it was a source of the greatest anxiety and anguish to his father, who expected every hour to hear of his apprehension on some dreadful charge, which would bring an ignominious fate upon himself, and shame and misery to all who were connected with him.

Mr. Milford felt perfectly satisfied with the course he had adopted towards Henry Stirling, though he still entertained the highest opinion of his character, and under any other circumstances than the peculiar ones by which he was surrounded, he would have felt proud to have cultivated his friendship; but it was a source of the deepest regret to him to observe the heavy depression of spirits which Charlotte manifested since his last visit, which thoroughly convinced him that the mental endowments and personal attractions of Henry Stirling had made a very strong impression upon her heart. However, he forbode to mention his suspicions to her, lest it should torture her the more, and he trusted that time and absence would banish him from her thoughts, and restore her to that elasticity of spirits by which she was so strongly characterised.

Augusta, however, did not hesitate to question her sister upon the subject, so anxious was she to know what was the cause of her melancholy, and with the hope that she might by her sympathy and advice be able to ameliorate it. Charlotte endeavoured to evade the questions her affectionate sister put to her as she could; but Augusta fully satisfied as to the real cause, was not to be thus defeated in her purpose, and in as gentle and affectionate a manner as she could, she expressed to Charlotte her real suspicions, and begged that she would not hesitate to make a confidant of her, certain as she must be of her deepest sympathy, and important as all that affected her happiness, must necessarily be to her. Little expecting to have been so closely interrogated, Charlotte could hold out no longer, and throwing herself upon her sister's neck, with streaming eyes, she acknowledged that the many intrinsic qualities which Henry Stirling displayed, had proved too dangerous for her peace, and that from the first day that accident had introduced them to each other, his image had never been absent from her thoughts; but she begged of Augusta not to disclose her secret to their father, and promised to exert herself to the utmost to conquer the unfortunate passion she had suffered to take possession of her bosom, certain as she was how hopeless it must ever be, not only from the disparity of their rank in society, but also in consequence of the marked objection with which Mr. Milford seemed to view it, if that was his object in declining the visits of Henry Stirling, which she could not help thinking it was.

Augusta again expressed her sympathy with her beauteous sister, and then exerted herself to the utmost to compose her spirits, and to lead her to hope for happier days; in which she at last succeeded, and Charlotte became more tranquil than she had been for several days before.

      *   *   *   *   *   *   *   *

Summer was o'er, the leaves of autumn had been dispersed before the winds, and hoary winter once more resumed his cheerless career.

The health of Mr. Milford still continued very indifferent, and the fair sister's became alarmed lest the inclemency of the season should prove too severe for his debilitated constitution. They could not but look forward to his dissolution with the most dismal forebodings, for to whom then could they apply for protection and consolation? Where could they seek a home? George Milford was an abandoned outcast, and they had everything to dread instead of to hope from him. The thought was a terrible one, and many were the wretched hours it caused the affectionate sisters.

Charlotte had lost all that vivacity of spirits which had once been so charming in her, and it was seldom that a smile was seen to irradiate her countenance. She was almost constantly wrapped in thought, from which nothing seemed to have the power to arouse her, and it was too painfully evident that notwithstanding all her endeavours she had been unable to banish the image of Henry Stirling from her memory. Oh, if she had been aware of the real character of that man who had first kindled the fire of love within her gentle breast, had she been aware that he was at that very time, and had been for months past, plotting her destruction, with what horror and disgust would she have viewed him, and how quickly would she have plucked his image from her pure heart, where one so utterly abandoned was so unworthy to reign.

During the summer Charlotte had two or three times absented herself from home, and when she returned home, she would most carefully avoid answering all the questions which were put to her by Mr. Milford and her sister, as to whither she had been, though she always appeared more melancholy than usual on such occasions.

Mr. Milford gently reproached her for thus acting in disobedience to his wishes, and warned her of the danger that might be attending on it. He resolved to keep a strict watch over her, and enjoined her as she dreaded his displeasure never again to venture forth alone without his permission.

Poor Charlotte, with tears in her eyes, promised to obey, and she kept her word, though it was quite evident that it was not without the greatest anguish and regret that she did so.

It was on a dreary night in the month of January that Augusta and) t ster had retired to their chamber, and were just sinking into their first sleep , hey were suddenly aroused by a suffocating smell, which was immediately followed a crackling sound, and their bed-room was illumined by a broad glare of light, which left no doubt upon their minds that the house was on fire.

Terrified to the utmost, the sisters screamed aloud, and jumped out- of bed, hastily threw on their clothes, and hurrying to the window, which they threw open, the scene which burst upon their view filled them with horror and despair. The fire was raging fiercely below, and the flames were fast ascending towards their chamber, threatening to envelope the whole of the house in the destructive element. There were several persons in the street, and numerous others were hurrying to the scene of destruction, but as far as regarded assistance there seemed to be none at hand.

The sisters wrung their hands in despair, and in frenzied accents shrieked for help; but even in that awful situation, their own danger was only a secondary consideration to that of Mr. Milford, and loudly they called upon his name, and implored the by-standers to rescue him from so horrible and untimely a death.

And now they quitted the window and rushed to the room-door, thinking to make their escape that way, but when they forced it open they were met by a body of flames, which drove them back, and rendered all hope of their escaping down the stairs mpossible. The room was also filled with smoke, which almost suffocated the unfortunate sisters, and their awful fate seemed to be inevitable.

What a moment of horror was this. The unfortunate sister threw themselves into each other's arms, and breathing a brief prayer to Heaven for mercy, resigned themselves to their fate. At this critical juncture, when all hope seemed at an end, for the flames were spreading rapidly on every side, and threatened not only to destroy the residence of Mr. Milford, but the whole of the immediate neighbourhood; a loud shout rose 'rom the spectators, who had hitherto been afraid to approach the doomed building in consequence of the intense heat of the flames, and then the rattling sound of two or three engines approaching the scene of devastation might be heard.

Quick as lightning, Stirling bounded into the burning room, and raising the insensible form of Charlotte in his arms, began to descend the ladder, amid the loudest shouts of admiration at his heroic conduct from the assembled multitude, and having arrived at the bottom, he deposited his precious burthen in the arms of the distracted Mr. Milford, (who had in vain endeavoured to reach the chamber of the poor girls, and had nearly lost his own life in the attempt), and then, without the delay of an instant, he again ascended the ladder, although he was completely surrounded by flames and smoke. He reached the room; the flames were within a yard of the insensible form of Augusta, and in another moment she must have fallen a victim to the devouring element. The courageous young man raised her also in his arms, and with much difficulty, for he was nearly exhausted, emerged from the window, and descended the ladder in safety, and scarcely had he reached the ground, when the flooring of the apartment gave way, and sank amid the ruins of the burning pile !

———

CHAPTER XIII.

THE EFFECTS OF THE CATASTROPHE.—THE FATAL PASSION OF CHARLOTTE FOR HENRY
STIRLING.—THE SEDUCER TRIUMPHANT.—THE ELOPEMENT.

IT was some time before Augusta and her sister recovered their sensibility,
but when they did so, they found themselves in a strange room, attended by a medical
man, and Mr. Milford and Henry Stirling hanging over them with looks of the most unspeakable anxiety.

"Father! father!" they both exclaimed in a breath. "Gracious Heaven! you are
saved, and we are content."

"My darling children," ejaculated Mr. Milford, frantically clasping them to his bosom,
while the scalding tears of mingled joy and sorrow streamed fast down his pale cheeks,
"my soul's whole hope, ye are rescued from a horrible fate, and though our comfortable
home, and all that it contained, has fallen a prey to the devouring flames, I will endeavour to be content. But to this gallant youth you owe the preservation of your lives; to
him I am indebted for the preservation of those who are far more precious to me than my
own existence."

Charlotte timidly raised her eyes towards the countenance of Henry Stirling,
but she could not speak, and that one look spoke a volume of love and gratitude,
which filled his breast with the most unspeakable feelings of transport. His eyes
beamed with delight, and pressing the delicate hands of the beauteous sisters to his lips,
he said—

"Fair damsels, how grateful must I ever be to Providence, who has made me
the fortunate instrument of saving two such amiable and innocent beings from
so dreadful a fate. I need not say how deeply I lament this frightful calamity,
but I trust to God that you will quickly recover from it, and depend upon it that
if in anything I can be of service to you, you may command me. In this house
you will find every comfort and accommodation that your hapless case requires
for the present; to-morrow I have Mr. Milford's permission to call upon you
again, when I hope to see you nearly recovered from the alarming effects of
this awful night. Farewell, sweet ladies, till we we meet again. Mr. Milford, good
night, and sincerely do I hope that this calamity may be the last you may have to experience."

Again he pressed the hands of the sisters, and then without waiting for any reply from
Mr. Milford, he hurried from the room.

How the conflagration at the house of Mr. Milford had originated it was impossible at
present to ascertain, but it was entirely destroyed; as well as the houses on either side
of it. Mr. Milford, as we have before stated, had in vain endeavoured to reach the
chamber of the sisters, and it was not without the greatest difficulty that he had himself
escaped into the street, having fortunately secured his cash-box. Here he stood wringing his hands, and calling on the spectators to save his darling children, in accents which
were truly heart-rending to hear, but the flames were raging with such fearful fury that
no one would venture to approach the building. What was the maddening agony of
Mr. Milford when he heard the despairing shrieks for help of the sisters, and indistinctly
through the smoke beheld their fair forms at the window! Language must fail to give
an adequate idea of his sufferings; it was not without the greatest difficulty that the
crowd could prevent him from again rushing into the burning building in the mad attempt to save them, or to perish himself in the effort. It was at this critical moment
when all hope seemed to be at an end, that the figure of a man was seen forcing his way
through the crowd towards the spot were Milford stood. That man was Henry Stirling,
and Milford beheld him with looks of astonishment and despair. Stirling pressed his
hand, and speaking a few hasty words of consolation and hope to him, called loudly for a
ladder. In a very few seconds one was procured, though to make any attempt to enter
the building, which was now nearly one body of flames, seemed little short of madness.
Stirling, however, was deaf to the voices of those who expostulated with him, and placing
the ladder as close as he could beneath the window, proceeded to mount it. What followed has already been related.

With the assistance of some of the by-standers, Henry Stirling and Mr. Milford bore the insensible forms of Augusta and Charlotte to the nearest tavern, where they were received with every feeling of sympathy and humanity, and all that could possibly be done for them under the painful circumstances was immediately put into operation.

The home of Mr. Milford was destroyed; he had lost everything that he possessed, with the exception of the cash he had secured, and nothing could be more awful than the prospect now presented to him; but the lives of those dear girls who had in so wonderful and mysterious a manner been placed under his protection, were preserved, and that enabled him to bear up with more fortitude against the calamity than he would otherwise have been enabled to do. But how did his heart overflow with gratitude to Henry Stirling, who by his heroic conduct had saved the lives of those so dear to him? Could he refuse to receive his future friendship, after such a marked proof of his magnanimity and courage? No, he could not; neither could he feel surprised if Charlotte or her sister should, after such signal service, imbibe far warmer than mere sentiments of gratitude towards one who had so distinguished himself in their welfare.

If such were the thoughts and sentiments of Mr. Milford, what must have been the feelings of the sisters on the occasion, but more especially Charlotte? Could she, with all the generous admiration that she had previously entertained of his character, view him as anything but one of the most noble of individuals, and if not before, she was now prepared to devote to him, (although it might never be returned, or there might be no opportunity of its being gratified) her very soul's most ardent affections.

And what were the reflections of Henry Stirling, as he wended his way on that eventful night to his hotel? They were conflicting and torturing. His good principles were struggling violently with his wild and reckless passions, and for some time it was questionable which would gain the ascendancy. He had hitherto been plotting for the destruction of the innocence of that fair being whose life he had by accident, and so miraculously preserved, and for whom he could not deny to himself, he felt a passion of a far, a very far different nature to that he entertained for any other of his previous victims, and could he continue to seek to win her pure affections, and thus sacrifice her at the shrine of his base passions. It was a severe struggle with his feelings, but, alas! his evil ones prevailed. There was not a woman in existence, whom he had yet seen that he would have felt so happy to have made his wife, as the gentle, the lovely, the confiding Charlotte Milford. She had every grace, both personal and mental to adorn a throne; but then the humble position she held in society, completely precluded the possibility of his ever making her his bride, and at the same time he could not form the resolution of resigning all his hopes of her. No, unfortunately the young libertine finally came to the determination of taking advantage of the opportunity thus afforded him of achieving his lawless object, which far superseded all the diabolical plans which he and George Milford had for weeks past been concocting together, although to do so he must still retain that unprincipled young man in his pay, lest he should be induced to betray him, and there would not only be an end to all his projects, but his real name and station (for George Milford by accident had become acquainted with them) would be revealed, and thus not only would all his future schemes be rendered abortive, but shame and obloquy would for ever attach themselves to his name.

Mrs. Harlingford, the worthy hostess of the Peacock, which was the sign of the house in which Mr. Milford and the sisters had sought a shelter after the dreadful calamity related in the previous chapter, was a widow and a woman of a most excellent and benevolent disposition, and she did all that she could under the painful circumstances, to render them comfortable, at the same time endeavouring to tranquillize their feelings, and seeking to inspire them with the hope that although it had pleased Providence to visit them with so terrible a calamity, the time was not far distant when those clouds of adversity would disperse and happier days open upon them.

Mrs. Harlingford was one of those happy individuals, who always look on the sunniest side of events, and she endeavoured to induce others to do the same, and it was not seldom that the good woman had been successful in her efforts.

Comfortable chambers were prepared on that fatal night, for the reception of Mr. Milfold and his two supposed daughters, but it was not until after much intreaty that they could be prevailed upon to separate. And when the lovely sisters retired to their

OR, THE BROTHERS OF MYSTERY.

apartment, and sought their couch could they sleep ?   Oh, no, could it be imagined
that the drowsy god would shed his soothing influence over their senses after the dreadful events of the night ?   That home which had sheltered them from their earliest days
of infancy was destroyed, that home with which their dearest feelings were associated,
and what was to be their future destiny ?   They looked forward to it with the most
gloomy forbodings. The means of their poor father, they felt satisfied, were nearly exhausted, and how would he again be able to provide a home?   What was to become of
them ?   These reflections were most agoni: ng, and f: : some time after they had retired,
Augusta and Charlotte could do nothing but give v: t to their feelings of anguish and
despair.

At length they sought their pillow, and Augusta, worn out with fatigue and thought,
at length fe.. into a sound sleep, but not so Charlotte.   Her mind was too busily occupied to allow her that temporary respite from anxiety.   The sight of Henry Stirling, and
his noble and her::c conduct were sufficient of themselves to keep her mind in an uninterrupted state of excitement, and she found that sleep was utterly impossible.   She
dwelt upon his image; it was still vividly present to her mind's eye, and the more she
reflected upon him, and his conduct in the late awful catastrophe, the greater was the
power that she felt, in spite of herself, he gained over her affections.   Could she feel
anything else but the warmest sentiments of more than gratitude towards the preserver
of her life and that of her beloved sister?   She could not ; and why should she be
ashamed of the feeling, when the object who excited it was possessed of every mental
endowment?

Such were the thoughts which crowded upon the mind of Charlotte, as she tossed about
on her restless bed on that eventful night, and when sleep at length alighted on her
eyelids, they were repeated to her in dreams of the most varied and conflicting
nature.

Sleep, however, visited not the pillow of the unfortunate Mr. Milford, nor could it be
expected after the dreadful catastrophe which had befallen him, and which at present
threatened to prove his utter ruin.   That home which had so long sheltered him, and
which contained so much that was precious to him, and in which the mystery connected
with those dear girls whom he had so long protected, was involved, was destroyed, and
what could ever redeem so great a loss ?   Where could he now seek another asylum ?
The money he had preserved from the flames would be scarcely sufficient to support
them for many montes, and when that was exhausted, what was to become of them ?
For himself he cared not ; he could alone have suffered any privation which it had
pleased the Almighty to visit him with ; but he felt his health and strength daily decreasing, he felt convinced that his time in this world would be short, and when he was
no more, what would become of Augusta and Charlotte, left as they would be without
a protector, without means of support, and at the mercy of the cruel world ?   He shuddered at the thought, and his mind was wrought up to a pitch of madness.

But surely the unknown when he became acquainted with the calamity that had
befallen him, as he undoubtedly would, would not delay a moment in coming forward
to his relief, and he would then insist that the mystery which had been so long maintained should be unravelled, so that in case of anything befalling him, they at least
should not be left [destitute, confident as he felt that they had claims upon the most
noble, the most wealthy, and distinguished.   The circumstance recorded in the early
part of this tale of his beholding the stranger in the same carriage with the Prince of
Wales, had ever been fresh in the memory of Mr. Milford, and many were the perplexing
and conflicting reflections to which it had given rise ; but of one thing it had satisfied
him, namely, that the unknown must be a person of the most illustrious station of
society, or he would not have been chosen as the companion of royalty.   But was he
related to the twin sisters?   This was a question that he often put to himself, and
the more he did so, more strongly did he become convinced that he was, or otherwise
why should he take such a peculiar interest in their fate ?   Sometimes when Milford
reflected on the emotion he had evinced when parting with the sisters on the night
that he had committed them to his future care, he was inclined to believe that he was
absolutely their father, and he had half made up his mind whenever he should behold
him again, to challenge him with being so.   But surely, there could be no sufficient

reason for his persisting in maintaining such profound secrecy towards him, after having tried him for so many years, and found how faithfully he had adhered to that promise which he and his late wife had made him on the eventful night when the children were committed to their care. Besides, he had promised that all should be revealed to him at some future time, and he could not see why that revelation should any longer be delayed. If the stranger did not keep his promise how could he expect that he would his?—He was often half inclined to make the sisters at once acquainted with the important secret; but at length he determined to await patiently, and see the result of the calamity that had befallen him, trusting that the stranger would come forward as he ought to do, to his assistance, and to consult with and advise him how to act. He was the more anxious for this, as his health was declining so rapidly, and he saw the absolute necessity of some arrangement being at once made for the future protection of Augusta and her sister; and it would be monstrous to imagine for a moment that the relations of the beautious girls, could be so lost to all proper sense of feeling and of duty as to suffer them to be cast friendless, homeless, and destitute upon the wide and cheerless world; exposed to all its insults, vices, and temptations.

Such were the thoughts which distracted the mind of the unfortunate Mr. Milford, on the fatal night of the conflagration, and it was not without the greatest difficulty that he could find strength sufficient to bear up against such an accumulated weight of misfortune. The morning dawned without sleep having for the shortest period come to his relief. Sleep! how was it likely that he should do so under such appalling circumstances'?

How shall we describe the meeting of Mr. Milford and the sisters in the morning?— Their emotions were so powerful that for some time they were unable to give utterance to a word, and could only mingle their tears of anguish and regret together; but Mr. Milford struggled hard with his feelings, and endeavoured to impart that consolation to them which he, in fact, stood so much in need of himself.

"Terrible as this calamity is," he remarked, " how much more dreadful might it have been. Good God! my children, had you perished in the flames, how could I ever have withstood so awful a blow!—Madness must have seized upon my brain, and death have speedily put a period to my sufferings. To the heroic Mr. Stirling, who at the risk of his own life preserved all that was precious to me, I owe a debt of gratitude that it will never, never be in my power to repay."

How the heart of poor Charlotte palpitated as Mr. Milford thus warmly but justly eulogized the noble conduct of Henry Stirling. She felt that he deserved all the praises which could be bestowed upon him, and much more, and fervently did her heart respond to those sentiments which at the same time she was afraid to give utterance to.

Nothing could surpass the kindness which the worthy hostess, Mrs. Harlingford shewed towards the unfortunate family; she had prepared breakfast by the time they left their chambers, and did all that she could to render them as comfortable as ti was possible to be under such peculiar and trying circumstances, and endeavoured to impart to them consolation and hope; but alas! it was little they could entertain at present.

In the course of the morning several of the neighbours called in at the tavern to express the deep sympathy they felt for the terrible misfortune that had befallen them, and all were ready to offer them every assistance in their power.

The breakfast over, of which none of them had been able scarcely to partake, nothing could dissuade Mr. Milford from visiting the ruins of his late comfortable residence, and the sisters fearful that his emotions would overpower him, prevailed upon him to allow them to accompany him.

The fire had made fearful ravages; only a tottering portion of the walls of Mr. Milford's house, and the adjoining premises, were left standing, all else had been destroyed, only an heterogeneous mass of smoking rubbish was left remaining, and fearful was the scene of desolation that met the gaze of the spectator.

Mr. Milford beat his breast in despair, and Augusta and Charlotte shed scalding tears of bitter anguish and regret. There was a great crowd of persons assembled at the scene of destruction, and great was the sympathy excited for the unfortunate family, who had thus at one fell swoop been rendered houseless, and probably reduced to beggary. It was some time before the sisters could persuade the distracted Mr. Milford to leave the melancholy scene and return to the tavern, and when they at last gently forced him away, the expression of his eyes was wild, and he was in a state of almost utter unconsciousness.

They had not long returned to the tavern, when Mrs. Ashfield arrived, she having only a few hours before heard of the dreadful calamity that had befallen her esteemed friends. We need not seek to pourtray the grief of that amiable woman at what had taken place, but she did all that humanity could suggest to mitigate their sufferings, and to tranquillise their feelings, and to inspire them with the hope that something would ere long transpire to release them from their present difficulties, and restore them to their former state of comfort. In the meantime, she warmly urged them for the present to make her humble house their home, until Mr. Milford should have made some arrangements for the future. Mr. Milford was most grateful for this kind offer, and immediately accepted it, for he did not hesitate to place himself under an obligation to one whom he had known for so many years, and whose friendship he knew to be so sincere and disinterested.

Some time was passed in conversation upon the melancholy and awful events of the previous night, and at length Mr. Milford and the sisters. by the arguments of Mrs. Ashfield, did become more reconciled, and offered up their supplications to the Almighty to watch over and protect them in their present severe trials. While they were thus occupied, Henry Stirling was announced, at the mention of whose name Charlotte trembled and could not conceal her emotion, but it created no wonder when it was remembered that to the) heroic conduct of that young gentleman, she and her sister were indebted for the preservation of their lives.

On entering the apartment he greeted Mr. Milford and his supposed daughters with much respectful commiseration, and his eyes involuntarily wandered to the lovely girl who had so captivated him, but she averted her looks, unable to trust herself to meet his glances. Still with what transport did she listen to the tones of his voice, and every word of sympathy he uttered added strength to the fatal passion he had engendered in her breast. How could she feel other than the warmest regard towards the preserver of her life and that of her sister ?

Mr. Milford again in the most fervent manner expressed his gratitude to Henry Stirling for the service, the invaluable service he had rendered him, while Sterling begged that he would cease to lavish upon him so many praises for merely doing that which was no more than his duty, and expressed the delight he felt to think that he should have been led to the scene of destruction in time to rescue the beauteous sisters from the dreadful fate that had threatened them.

After some time passed in conversation, he requested Mr. Milford to retire with him into another room, as he had something particular to say to him, Milford complied, and when they were alone, after a pause, Henry Stirling thus addressed him—

" I am convinced, Mr. Milford, that I need not assure you how deeply I sympathise with you in the terrible misfortune that has so suddenly and so unexpectedly fallen upon you. The subject I am about to speak upon is a delicate one, spoken upon by a person who is almost an entire stranger to you, but I hope you will fully appreciate the motives I have for so doing, and do me the justice to believe that I am induced to make the offers I am about to propose to you from no other feelings than those of humanity and friendship."

"Proceed, sir," said Mr. Milford ; " after the noble conduct you have displayed towards me and those who are more precious to me than my own existence, after having, in fact, snatched those dear girls from the jaws of a horrible death, I must indeed be most ungenerous, most ungrateful did I not place every confidence in your friendly motives."

" Enough, my dear sir, ' returned Stirling, with a look of satisfaction, " you do me ne more than justice, I assure you. This dreadful calamity, Mr. Milford, there can be no doubt, has greatly distressed you, I mean not only in mind, but in a pecuniary point of view. You have lost considerable property, you are rendered houseless; it is not my place or my intention to make any impertinent inquiry into your circumstances, but if I can be of any service to you in replacing you in a comfortable situation, you may command me."

It was impossible that Mr. Milford could feel otherwise than grateful for this generous offer, but his pride revolted at the idea of receiving any such favours from a young man who was almost an entire stranger to him, and he accordingly replied—

. "Mr. Stirling, your generous and disinterested offers do honour both to your head and heart, but at the same time (and I hope you will not be offended at my doing so,) I must beg leave to decline them. It is true that I have suffered a severe loss, and that my circumstances are far from being prosperous, but at present I have enough that with economy will keep me and my children in comfort, and I trust that when they hear of the calamity that has befallen me, those upon whom I have a just claim, will come forward to release me from any difficulties by which I may be surrounded. As regards a home, my amiable friend Mrs. Ashfield, has generously afforded me the use of her house, until I have arranged my affairs, and been able to provide myself with a dwelling, certainly a more humble one than that which is destroyed. Again I most cordially thank you, Mr. Stirling for your generous sympathy, in my misfortunes, and believe me I shall ever entertain a lively sense of the obligations I am already under to you."

Henry Stirling could not conceal the disappointment he felt at this rejection of his offer, but finding it was useless to urge it further, he dropped the subject, and merely requested that he should sometimes be permitted to call upon them, which, of course, Mr. Milford could not refuse.

They returned to the room in which they had left Augusta, Charlotte, and Mrs. Ashfield, and Henry Stirling having remained with them about an hour longer, took his leave.

Charlotte felt sad and wretched when he was gone, and in vain her friends endeavoured to arouse her. The more she saw of Henry Stirling, the more deeply did her heart become impressed with his noble qualities, and she longed for the time when she might behold him again.

Having at length somewhat tranquillised their spirits, it was determined that they should depart to their new and temporary home without delay. A coach was procured and the unfortunate family with Mrs. Ashfield having stepped into it, were driven off to the humble, but neat residence of the latter. Mr. Milford first having in vain endeavoured to prevail upon Mrs. Harlingford, the good hostess, who had behaved so kindly to them in their fearful difficulty, to receive some remuneration for her trouble.

George Milford, who had been from home for several days, did not hear of the destruction of his father's house until two days after the conflagration, and his rage and disappointment may then be readily conceived. For some time he did nothing but give vent to the most dreadful curses, for he could not endure with patience the destruction of that dwelling and its valuable contents which he had flattered himself would one day be his, and moreover, his father was probably now reduced to a state of beggary, and would no longer have the means to pander to his wants, should he find it necessary again to apply to him. Latterly, however, Henry Stirling had frequently given him large sums of money, to aid him in his plans against Charlotte, and he determined that he should continue to do so, or he would betray him, and thus render his designs abortive, and hold him up to disgust and shame.

Stirling and George Milford had their places of assignation where they met at certain times, and the latter on hearing of the conflagration immediately sought him out, and from him heard the whole of the particulars, and his astonishment was great indeed when he was informed that Stirling had rescued Augusta and Charlotte from the flames.

. "This is indeed lucky for you, Stirling," he said, "for it cannot fail to fix you still deeper in the esteem of my father and Charlotte, and thus to forward your wishes. But this confounded fire is a bad job for me; that which would have been my future property is destroyed, and I am confident that my father's means must now be so exhausted, or will be so in providing himself with another home, that I shall stand but little chance to extort more money from him. What am I to do under these circumstances?—I must either beg, steal, or starve, and you know I like to get my living in the easiest manner possible. At present I am close run, and have scarcely a sixpence left, but I suppose you will not see me want, when you take into consideration the services I have rendered you, and am still ready to render you."

"George," said Henry Stirling, "I must confess that I feel some hesitation in pursuing my designs against the lovely Charlotte. She is so gentle, so artless, and so innocent, that she has created in my breast a far different passion to that which I have felt for any previous object. Surely it would be monstrous to destroy the virtue and happiness of that pure being, and to bring the grey hairs of her father with sorrow to the grave."

"Pshaw!" exclaimed George, impatiently, "what, are you going to reform then?—After all the hopes you have formed respecting this new conquest, and the trouble you have been at to carry your designs into effect, are you now going to resign her at the eleventh hour, when the favourable impression you have undoubtedly made upon her, plainly shows that she would become an easy victim."

"And you can thus talk, calmly talk of and encourage the ruin of your own sister?" said Stirling, with a look of disgust.

"Enough of this," said George, "I have before answered you sufficiently upon that subject. The whole of it is, have you made up your mind to pursue the accomplishment of your wishes, or have you come to the determination to abandon your designs?"

"No, no," replied Stirling, "I cannot think of resigning all my hopes of the lovely Charlotte Milford, for the more I see of her, the firmer she rivets my very soul. Were her rank equal to my own, I would not hesitate a moment wooing her in an honourable manner, and could I but win her heart, which I flatter myself that I could, I would make her my bride."

"Humph!" exclaimed George Milford, with a sarcastic grin, "then as her rank don't happen to be so distinguished as your own, I suppose you will be content to honour her by making her your mistress?"

Henry Stirling looked at the hardened villain before him with astonishment and almost incredulity. Could these be the observations of a brother respecting his own sister?—It seemed scarcely possible that there could be such a heartless miscreant in existence; and yet he had so far degraded himself as to become the associate of that villain, nay more, he had even employed him, and was then employing him as the instrument to effect the gratification of his guilty wishes. Then must he not be as great a miscreant as himself?—For a few minutes Henry Stirling was shocked at the enormity of his own guilt, and felt disgusted with and thoroughly ashamed of himself.

"Well," remarked George Milford, after a pause; during which he had been contemplating the countenance of Stirling narrowly, "I see how it is, you repent, and have no wish to proceed any further in this business; so I may as well make my father acquainted with your good intentions towards Charlotte, and what has induced you to abandon them.

"Hold, Milford!" ejaculated Stirling, alarmed, and grasping his arm, "you cannot be in earnest, or know not what you say. Would you then, after the many solemn promises you have made me, and the manner in which I have rewarded you, mean to betray me?"

"Why, I have no wish to do so, but——"

"I would not have it for the world. Come, come, let us properly understand each other; I do not mean to abandon my designs against Charlotte; I cannot make up my mind to do so, and I will still continue to reward you handsomely for any assistance you may render me in carrying those designs into effect."

"Oh, that is enough," said George, "now you speak like a man, and I am your's to command. The girl is worth winning, and you would be foolish to give up the task now that you have proceeded so far, and having made a powerful impression upon her, have everything in your favour. But this confounded fire has upset me, and I need something to cheer my spirits, but I have no money, and must therefore get you to lend me a trifle."

Henry Stirling placed some money in his hand, and then enjoining him to be faithful and cautious, they separated, Stirling glad to be rid of his guilty companion.

Mrs. Ashfield had been a widow for many years, and inherited a small annuity, upon which, with the addition of some needle work, she contrived to live very comfortably, and indeed, more happily than thousands of her wealthy fellow-creatures, for she possessed that greatest of human blessings, a contented mind. The house she resided in, was situated at the East-end of London, and at that period was surrounded by fields and pleasant walks, which have since been covered with densely populated streets. It contained six-rooms, remarkable for their neatness and cleanliness, and there was a pretty little garden at the back of the house, which formed a source of amusement to Mrs. Ashfield in her hours of relaxation. An orphan girl about fourteen years of age, whom she had taken out of charity, assisted her in the domestic duties, and also in the labour of the needle, and altogether there was not a happier woman in existence, than Mrs. Ashfield.

Mrs. Ashfield usually let out three of her apartments furnished, as there was more accommodation than she wanted, but at present they were unoccupied, which she hailed as a fortunate circumstance, she being thus enabled to afford Mr. Milford and the sisters a shelter in their present distressed and melancholy situation. But there was one thing that she could not, and, had she been able, would not have considered it safe or prudent to do, and that was to accommodate George Milford. His wild and profligate habits would completely upset all the arrangements she had made, and render them all wretched.

Mr. Milford was very much distressed at this, and knew not scarcely what to do. Base and guilty as his misguided son was, he could not bear the idea of refusing him a home, nor relinquish the hope of yet being able to reclaim him; he must give him the means of providing himself with a lodging, and yet how could he afford to do so, so small, so very small was the property he now possessed, and with so faint a prospect of his purse being replenished when his present means were exhausted.

George Milford lost no time in calling upon his father, when he had accertained from Henry Stirling Mrs. Ashfield's address, and the scene which took place between them we will not attempt to describe. Instead of commiserating with his unhappy parent in the calamity which had befallen him, he vented the most dreadful curses on the accident, attributed it entirely to their carelessness, and threw out certain dark hints respecting Augusta and Charlotte, which alarmed Mr. Milford, and excited the greatest astonishment in the minds of the poor girls. He could not be prevailed upon to leave the house until his father had given him a sum of money, and intimated his intention of calling upon him again when that was exhausted,

Mr. Milford had taken the precaution of leaving his address with Mrs. Harlingford, in case any inquiries should be made after him: for he could not but suppose that the stranger would be most anxious to find him out, as soon as he heard of the fire, and to afford him prompt assistance; but day after day, and week after week elapsed, and still Mr. Milford neither saw nor heard anything of him, and he gave himself up to despair, thinking that the stranger had made up his mind to abandon him and the lovely objects of his care to their fate.

This thought was indeed most agonizing, for when the money he had in his possession was exhausted, what would become of them? He looked forward to the worst, and almost sank under the gloomy contemplation.

Mrs. Ashfield did all in her power to render them comfortable, and constantly tried to inspire them to hope for better days; but Mr. Milford saw no prospect of them, and all her efforts at consolation were lost upon him.

Henry Stirling was a frequent visitor, and by degrees, as they became more acquainted with him, the sisters felt less restraint in his company. Alas! his influence over the affections of the unsuspecting Charlotte daily became stronger, and to her he appeared one of the most perfect of individuals. Stirling had long seen with feelings of exultation, the power he had obtained, and he did not fail to take advantage of it, and even Mr. Milford was so wrapped up in his own sorrows, that he did not foresee the danger of encouraging the too close intimacy of the young libertine, who from his general conduct he believed to be possessed of every feeling of honour and virtue, and that the attentions he shewed to himself and the objects of his care and affection, merely had their origin in friendship and sympathy. Stirling, who could plainly perceive how limited were the pecuniary resources of Mr. Milford, had frequently in the most delicate manner possible, for fear of wounding his feelings, offered him assistance, but Mr. Milford always rejected it, for he could not bear the idea of becoming beholden to one of whom he had so limited a knowledge, although he thought Henry Stirling a very different man to abuse any confidence he might repose in him.

The hours were sad and dreary to Charlotte when Henry Stirling was absent, and even the society of her friends was annoying to her. At such times she would seek to be alone, where she could brood over her own thoughts without interruption. She no longer attempted to deny to herself that she loved Henry Stirling, and that it was useless to attempt to destroy that passion which had gained such a strong hold on her heart. That Henry also viewed her with something more than admiration, she was also, by his looks and his behaviour towards her thoroughly convinced, in fact, could she have thought otherwise she would have been doubly miserable.

"Oh, that kind fortune had placed us both in one situation of life," she would soliloquize, "then might we have encouraged our love without hesitation or fear! but now, alas! what hope is there for us? Unhappy accident that introduced us to each other, for it has destroyed my peace of mind I fear for ever."

Her tears would flow fast as these reflections arose to her mind, and she would seek in vain for consolation.

Six months have gone, and nothing more particular had occurred to them in that period. Mr. Milford had heard nothing of the stranger, and the constant care and anxiety of mind he was enduring had continued to make the most alarming inroads on his constitution. His body was bent and debilitated, his cheeks furrowed; his eyes sunken, and only a few months had given him all the appearance of a man at least twenty years older than he actually was. And his grief was greatly increased by the brutal and profligate conduct of his son, who never came to the house but to abuse and threaten him, and so he held him in a constant state of dread. What would have been his horror and disgust had he known that Henry Stirling, whom he looked upon as such a man of honour and a sincere friend, was actually pandering to the vices of that abandoned son, and what was more, paying him for assisting in working the destruction of the innocent and beauteous Charlotte.

By dint of the greatest economy, Mr. Milford had been able to husband his little money remarkably well, and he had still a sufficient sum to keep them from want for some time; but the day of trouble must come, and when it did, the shock must prove overwhelming. He trembled at the thoughts of it, not so much for his own sake as that of Augusta and her sister, who would then be left destitute.

During the time they had resided with Mrs. Ashfield, Augusta and Charlotte had occupied their leisure hours in assisting her in her business, and notwithstanding all the objections of Mr. Milford and the sisters themselves' she would persist in paying them to the full for what they did, which money they immediately gave over to their father, with a feeling of the most exquisite delight to think that they at last were able to contribute something (however small) towards their support.

But another calamity was about to befal them, which again changed the prospects and situation of the unfortunate family. The good Mrs. Ashfield, who had usually enjoyed a good state of health, was taken suddenly ill, and notwithstanding all the attention that was paid to her, it very soon assumed the most alarming aspect. The grief of Mr. Milford and the lovely sisters may very well be imagined, and all that humanity could suggest was done to save her, but it was soon quite evident that it was all hopeless, and that the days of the amiable Mrs. Ashfield were numbered. The good woman bore her sufferings with fortitude and resignation, and the only regret she felt was that of leaving friends so dear to her in such melancholy circumstances. The little property she possessed descended to her nephew at her decease, or how happy would she have been to have given them some substantial proof of the friendship she entertained towards them. Had Mrs. Ashfield been a near and dear relation, Mr. Milford and the sisters could not have felt more grief than they did on this melancholy occasion, and they constantly offered up their prayers to Heaven to restore her to health; but it was all unavailing, and in little

THE ROYAL TWINS;

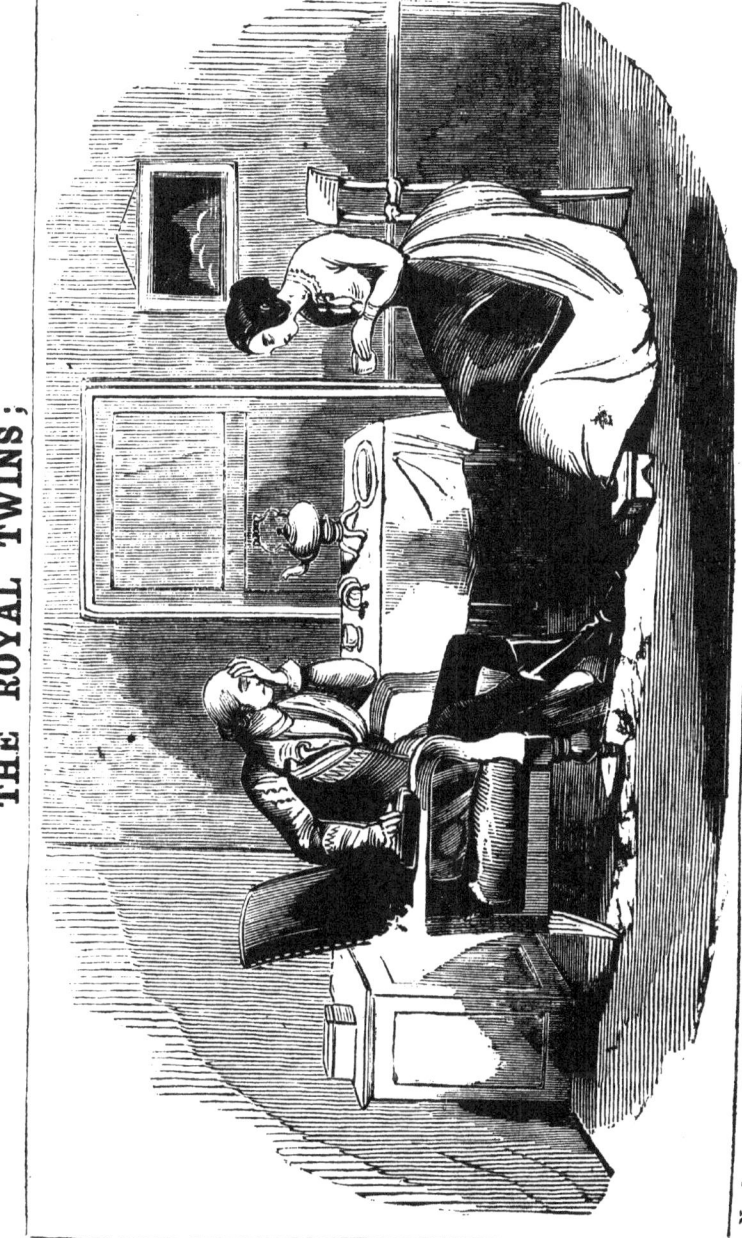

OR, THE SISTERS OF MYSTERY.

No. 15.

more than a week after the first attack Mrs. Ashfield calmly and almost without a sigh, breathed her last; and thus were the hapless family deprived of their only friend. It was a sad epoch in the lives of the beauteous sisters, and recalling to their minds the death of that amiable and affectionate being whom they imagined to be their mother, they felt a renewal of all that intense grief which they had experienced on that occasion.

The nephew of the late Mrs. Ashfield was an ignorant and dissipated character, and consequently the death of his most amiable aunt made no other impression upon him than the knowledge that it brought him so much per annum, as well as a freehold house, and all the useful, if not absolutely valuable furniture, it contained. He did not visit her more than once or twice, during her illness, and it required no very keen penetration to discover that so far from feeling any regret at the melancholy situation of his venerable relative, he was looking with the utmost anxiety to her decease; and his ideas upon that subject were quickly made apparent after the death of Mrs. Ashfield, by his intimating to Mr. Milford that he should feel obliged to him if he would furnish himself with other lodgings as soon as possible, as it was his intention to dispose of the house and furniture, having an objection to keeping it in his own possession.

Notwithstanding this put Mr. Milford at the present time to the greatest inconvenience, he had long, in his own mind, been prepared for such a circumstance, should any calamity befal Mrs. Ashfield, and consequently he met it with more, much more calmness, than might otherwise have been anticipated. To provide himself with a home in his present embarrassed situation was no easy task to accomplish, but Mr. Milford met it with fortitude, and replied to the young spendthrift accordingly. Here again Henry Stirling came forward to offer him pecuniary assistance, which Mr. Milford thought proper, respectfully, as on the previous occasions, to decline, much to the disappointment of the former, who had hoped by that means to advance the nefarious designs he had against the peace and innocence of the unsuspecting Charlotte.

Mr. Milford and the sisters remained in the house until the funeral of the much-lamented Mrs. Ashfield, which they attended, and sincere was the grief with which they followed, and saw the remains of that excellent woman deposited in their final resting place. They returned to the residence of the deceased under the most melancholy auspices, for Edward Ashfield had rudely informed them that they must provide themselves with another home in a week at farthest, as he had already disposed of the house and all it contained, and the purchaser intended to take possession in the course of a few days. Mr. Milford made it his business to see this individual without delay, and made to him a candid statement of his peculiar situation, requesting only to be permitted to reside in the house until he had the opportunity of providing himself with another habitation, suited to his present limited means; but the party he appealed to was a broker, possessed of all the bad qualities of the most worthless of that profession, and he therefore heard his application with indifference, and insisted upon his leaving in three days at the latest, as he intended to remove into the house himself, and should require the whole of it for his family.

Mr. Milford had, therefore, no alternative, and he was compelled to exercise all the energy he had left, to provide himself and those who were so dear to him with a home. It was a difficult and a melancholy task, and he had to use the utmost precaution, with the scanty means which were now at his command; still he felt too much honest pride to accept of the aid which Henry Stirling offered, uncertain as he was that it would ever be in his power to liquidate any debts which he might incur, for it seemed evident to him that the stranger was either dead or had abandoned them altogether, and, therefore, when his present means were exhausted, he would have no way of replenishing them. This thought was most torturing to Mr. Milford, the more so as he felt his own health so rapidly declining, and he was satisfied that a very few months must terminate his earthly career. And, oh, what would then become of Augusta and Charlotte, left, as they would be, entirely unprovided for, without a friend, protector, or adviser, at the most precarious time of life, with all those charms both personal and intrinsic, which hold out so many temptations to the world? He shuddered at the contemplation, and earnestly and fervently did he supplicate the aid of the Supreme Being in so painful, so terrible an emergency.

It was many years since Mr. Milford had had any communication with his uncle, but he knew that he was still living, and continued to reside on the continent, carrying on the career of profligacy which had characterised his earliest days. To him for assistance, he knew it would be useless to apply, had his pride permitted him so to humble himself, and he therefore found himself completely witho ut a friend in the world. But it was necessary that he should exert himself to the utmost of his energies in this emergency, and to conceal as much as possible from Augusta and her sister the mental anguish he was suffering, and he succeeded in this effort much better than might have been expected.

But could he disguise from the fair sisters the distress of mind he was enduring? could he blind them as to the real cause of his anxiety? Oh, no, that was impossible. Too keenly sensitive were they of the deplorable situation in which they were placed, and bitter were the pangs it cost them to think that they had not the means of trying to alleviate that distress they saw daily, hourly accumulating around them, and which made such dreadful havoc upon their suffering father's already so greatly impaiied constitution. How much greater would have been their anguish had they been aware that they had no other claim upon him than that of friendship and s ympathy.

Sad indeed was the retrospect that the sisters had to look back upon ; their lives had hitherto been those of gloom and sorrow ; very few rays of sunshine had irradiated their path! calamity had succeeded calamity, and now the prospect which presented itself to them was one of the most dismal aspect. They saw themselves without a friend in the world but he whom they imagined to be their father; that father reduced to poverty, almost to beggary ; his health rapidly, frightfully declining, and with every prospect of their shortly being deprived of him ; and when it should please the Almighty to snatch him from them, oh, what was to become of them, deprived of a home, a friend, a protector, an adviser ? Could they look to George for commiseration and advice? Could they expect that he would endeavour to supply the place of that beloved parent they must shortly lose? Oh, no, was he not one of the most abandoned of mankind? And had not his profligacy been one of the principal causes of his father's at present distressed situation ? Did he not seem to exult, aye, absolutely to exult in his misfortunes, and the strange and dark insinuations that he frequently threw out, filled their minds with terror and apprehension.

But had Charlotte been aware of the infamous plot he was carrying on with Henry Stirling for her destruction, what would have been her feelings?

Mr. Milford aroused himself as well as he could from his despondency, and praying to Heaven to assist him in his laudable efforts, he set himself about providing them with a future home. This, however, must be humble, very humble, and it required the greatest care not to overstep his means. He procured apartments at the house of a respectable widow in the neighbourhood, and having purchased such articles of furniture as were indispensable for their use, the unfortunate family removed to their new residence under the most melancholy auspices.

With a heavy heart Mr. Milford entered their new dwelling, for the most melancholy forebodings filled his mind; but Augusta and Charlotte bore the change much better than could have been expected, and tried their utmost to inspire Mr. Milford with the hope that gloomy as their prospects at present appeared, happier days were yet in store for them. Milford shook his head disconsolately, and showed by his manner altogether (although he sought to conquer his feelings) how little he entered into the ideas of Augusta and her sister. They made their new home as comfortable as possible, and indeed there was nothing wanting on the part of those two amiable and lovely girls to alleviate the misfortunes with which it had pleased Providence to afflict them. It was a source of much satisfaction to them, that the person for whom the late Mrs. Ashfield had worked, at their solicitation transferred the employment to them, and although the weekly amount it brought in was very small, it was a source of infinite delight and gratification to them to know that they contributed in some way to their support, and that it tended in some measure to ameliorate the pecuniary difficulties of their beloved parent.

They had not been more than two months in their new residence, when they were surprised by the same livery servant who had called upon them on previous occasions, and who having placed a letter in Milford's hand, rode rapidly away from the door before he had the opportunity of addressing a single question to him.

With a throbbing heart and a trembling hand, Mr. Milford broke the seal, and found inclosed in the letter a cheque for two hundred guineas. The epistle was in the handwriting of the stranger.

"Thank God! thank God!" he exclaimed, " then he still lives, and has not deserted us !"

Augusta and her sister heard these words with the most unbounded amazement, and looked at him for an explanation. Mr. Milford immediately saw that he had committed himself, and making a hasty excuse to the sisters, he retired from the room, that he might peruse the letter alone, and give indulgence to the feelings it was sure to excite, without observation.

Augusta and Charlotte reflected upon the words of Mr. Milford, and they were unable to penetrate their meaning, or to come to any satisfactory conclusion upon the subject. Who was the party to whom he had alluded, and what was the nature of the communication he had received, and which had thus elicited those observations? They were at a perfect loss to conjecture. They had always noticed the extraordinary visits of the servant with surprise, and had in vain endeavoured to ascertain to whom he belonged ; and what added not a little to their astonishment was, that he always brought some pecuniary assistance to Mr. Milford, which plainly shewed that he was not entirely without friends, and that the party from whom he received relief was in no mean station of society ; but who that individual could be, and why their father should hesitate to make them acquainted with him or her, they were at a loss to imagine. But the arrival of the letter (which they had no doubt contained that aid which they so much needed) was at this time a source of peculiar gratification to them, and they hoped that it would be productive of the most favourable r esults.

Mr. Milford on entering his room hastily proceeded to read the contents of the letter, which were as follows :—

"CLAVERING,—Although it is some time since you have before heard of me, do not suppose that I am unacquainted with your misfortunes, or am unmindful of your interests ; but circumstances over which I have at present no control, compel me to pursue the line of conduct I have done. Heaven only knows when (if ever) we shall meet again, but the secret must be maintained ;—on your fidelity in that respect depends the future welfare of those dear beings entrusted to your care. Oh, continue to watch them I implore you, with all a parent's solicitude, and as you so do, will Heaven reward you.

"I regret that unforseen circumstances have compelled me partly to break our contract, and prevented me from sending you that pecuniary aid which I promised, and you so much require, but depend upon it, I will render you all the assistance in my power. Bear up against misfortune ; live, live for the sake of those poor girls whom you have for so many years protected, and whose lives are so precious.

"But there is one thing against which I must solemnly warn you; beware of intro-ducing strangers into your family. I know that you have already done so in one instance, which might prove fatal to your peace and that of your lovely charge. You must command the discontinuance of the visits of the individual calling himself Henry Stirling. He is not your friend; he is not what he appears to be ; ruin and misery follow in his path; beware of him, I say, and banish him from your house. More at present I am not permitted to explain, but I enjoin you to do as I desire, or the conse-quences will be far more fatal and dreadful than you can at present form any conception of. Mark well my injunctions, and obey them.

"YOUR FRIEND."

It was with the utmost amazement that that Mr. Milford perused this letter, and it was some time before he could recover from the emotion which it excited in his bosom.

"When will this torturing mystery be unravelled?" he exclaimed; "what am I to understand from the tenour of this epistle? Surely there can be no more necessity for any longer secresy? Henry Stirling too; what can be the meaning of the warning which the unknown has held out to me respecting him? ' He is not my friend; he is not what he appears to be; ruin and misery follow in his path.' What strange observations are these, and what bold accusations to offer against one who has hitherto shewn himself to be so noble and so generous. And I am not permitted to make him acquainted with the charge which is thus brought against him. What reason can I assign for discarding him from my house? I know not."

The longer Mr. Milford deliberated upon this painful subject, the more he became bewildered, and it was some time before he could sufficiently compose his feelings to return to the room in which he had left Augusta and Charlotte. When he did so they immediately noticed the agitation of his manner, and eagerly inquired the cause. He evaded their questions as long as he could, but at length was forced to reply;

"My dear girls, it grieves me to have to state that from the communication I have this day received, I shall be compelled to decline the future visits and intimacy of Mr. Stirling. This the more afflicts me, when I recollect the vast obligations I owe him, and the high opinion I have ever formed of his character."

Charlotte turned ghastly pale, as her father thus spoke, and sunk powerless in her seat, while Augusta looked with astonishment at him as she said,—

"Oh, my dear father, what can be the cause of your coming to this severe and apparently unreasonable determination? What can be the nature of the charges brought against Henry Stirling, who has always proved our friend, and to whom myself and dear sister are indebted for the preservation of our lives?"

"I am not permitted to explain farther," said Mr. Milford, with much emotion, "than that I am informed that Mr. Stirling *is not really our friend*, that he is not what he appears to be, and that danger threatens us while we continue to cultivate his acquaintance!"

"It is false!" exclaimed the distracted Charlotte, with a burst of emotion she was unable to controul; "it is a base calumny. You will not, you cannot believe it, my father; Henry Stirling is the soul of honour and virtue, and he must be a base and cowardly villian who thus secretly seeks to traduce his character. Henry Stirling is——"

She could not proceed farther, for sobs checked her utterance, and sinking back in her chair, she covered her face with her hands, and gave herself up entirely to the agonising emotion that struggled in her breast.

With what mingled feelings of pity, regret, and agony did Mr. Milford gaze upon her; the whole painful secret was at once revealed to him, the suspicions he had for some time entertained were confirmed; he saw that Henry Stirling had made an impression upon her young and susceptible heart, which it would be difficult to destroy, and he foreboded the greatest trouble in consequence. Tenderly he approached her, and in his mildest and most impressive accents, endeavoured to compose her feelings; but the poor girl had received a shock from which it would be difficult to recover, and which was strengthened by the knowledge that she had betrayed the tender secret which she had so long kept locked within her own breast. Augusta understood her feelings, and sincerely did she pity her and sought to impart consolation to her; but unfortunately her efforts were attended with very little success; and unable to enter into any further conversation, she requested permission to retire to her chamber, whither her sister accompanied her. When they were alone Charlotte gave unrestrained indulgence to her anguish, which Augusta did not attempt to interrupt, for she thought it would afford her some relief.

"Oh, Augusta," sighed Charlotte, "I have been most weak, most culpable; but why did Providence ordain that I and Henry Stirling should ever see each other? Before we met, I was cheerful and happy, but now there is not a more wretched being than your unhappy sister."

"Need I assure you, my dear sister, (though I am sure I need not)" said Augusta, "how sincerely I pity you? Your happiness is so immediately connected with my own, that they cannot be divided. I wonder not, although I deeply regret the favourable impression that Henry Stirling has made upon your mind. He appears all that is amiable and virtuous, and——"

"Appears so;" interrupted Charlotte, vehemently, "oh, it is a base slander to say that he is otherwise! And who is his anonymous accuser? Why, if there is any truth in his assertions, has he not the manly boldness to come forward and confront him? But no, he dare not do so, and nothing shall ever induce me to entertain a different opinion of Henry Stirling, than that I have already formed of him."

" And you love him, Charlotte ?"

" If to admire him above any man that I have ever seen; to be happy only in his society, and wretched when he is away, be love, then indeed does Henry Stirling hold a paramount place in my heart."

" Poor girl, poor girl," said Augusta tenderly embracing her, " how sincerely are you to be pitied, and may Heaven give you fortitude, and resolution to banish such thoughts from your mind. Reflect, Charlotte, had other circumstances even not arisen, and if even you were convinced that Henry Stirling returned your passion, the difference of your stations in society would have precluded all hopes of your ever becoming his wife. Forget him, Charlotte, at least endeavour to think of him only with esteem, which I cannot help thinking that he still deserves."

" Forget him," gasped forth Charlotte, sobbing bitterly, " oh, that is impossible. And his future visits are to be forbidden ; I shall perhaps never behold him again. Surely our father will never act so ungenerously upon the mere assertions of an anonymous writer, towards one who has ever shown himself so noble and so virtuous, and to whom we owe such a vast debt of gratitude. The heroic preserver of our lives ?"

Her hysterical sobs choked her further utterance, and Augusta had the greatest difficulty to prevent her from fainting. It was some time before she could regain the least composure, and then she felt herself too ill to rejoin her father below, and she requested Augusta to apologize to him. Her sister complied, and having stated the facts exactly as they stood, to Mr. Milford, she returned to her suffering sister, with whom she remained for the rest of the evening.

A miserable night did poor Charlotte pass, for sleep never once closed her eyelids, nor was the image of Henry Stirling ever for a moment absent from her thoughts. The morning found her too ill to leave her bed, and Augusta continued to watch by her with the utmost solicitude and alarm.

The sufferings of Mr. Milford were not less intense than those of Charlotte. He saw at once the strength of the fatal passion she had imbibed for Henry Stirling (a passion which he had every reason to believe that he returned) and he feared that such a severe disappointment to her young hopes would be productive of the most fatal results. But how could he avert the evils he apprehended. The commands of the stranger rendered him powerless, and even under any circumstances he could not have undertaken to encourage a passion which could never be gratified.

But could he believe the assertions of the unknown, after all the noble examples he had witnessed of Stirling's integrity and honour? Could he imagine that he was not really their friend, that he was a man who was not to be trusted? That he had in fact been acting the part of the hypocrite towards them all along? It was no easy task for him to bring his mind to that conclusion, and how then could he refuse his future visits? What reasons could he assign for so doing? He was lost and bewildered, and deeply lamented that the stranger had not been more explicit. He feared, however, to disobey his injunctions, severe and disagreeable though as they were. Deeply, too, did he regret that Henry Stirling and Charlotte had ever met, for he clearly saw the evil consequences which might follow to them both.

That day and the next passed away, and Henry Stirling did not make his appearance, and Mr. Milford dreaded the time when he should do so, and shrunk reluctantly from the disagreeable task which had been imposed upon him. He exerted himself to the utmost to compose the feelings of Charlotte, in which he was assisted by her affectionate sister, Augusta ; but all their efforts had but little effect, and Charlotte became more wretched and melancholy the longer she reflected upon the dismal prospect before her. How could she again behold Henry Stirling without betraying the sentiments she entertained towards him ? And with what anguish must she witness the unexpected reception he would meet with from her father? These thoughts were of themselves sufficient to torture her to distraction, and she dreaded the next visit, which would be the last, of Henry Stirling.

Mr. Milford knew not how he should address him ; what explanation he could give of having come to so sudden a resolution, and which must make him appear so ungenerous, so ungrateful, and unreasonable in the eyes of that young man, who had rendered them such inestimable service. Had he known his address he would have sent him a letter, to have avoided, if possible, an interview, that must be so unpleasant to all parties, and several times he hesitated whether or not he should or not comply with the injunctions of the stranger, which he could not help thinking were not only extraordinary, but somewhat unreasonable, unless he had clearly explained his motives.

On the third day after the receipt of the letter, Henry Stirling came to the house, and was much disappointed at only beholding Mr. Milford, he having insisted that Augusta and Charlotte should remain in their own apartment till after he had gone.

The sufferings of Charlotte during this interview may be easily imagined; she resisted all the efforts of her sister to console her, and gave unrestrained indulgence to her tears, with a throbbing heart listening to hear the departure of Henry, knowing that probably that was the last time that ever she would be permitted to behold him.

Henry Stirling immediately perceived, from the manner in which Mr. Milford received him, that he was about to communicate something disagreeable to him, and not perceiving the sisters present, he eagerly inquired whether or not they were well ?— This afforded Mr. Milford an opportunity to commence his ungrateful task, and after some preliminary remarks, in the course of which he warmly expressed his gratitude to Henry Stirling for the friendship he had always shown towards them since their short acquaintance, and the eminent services he had rendered them; he regretted that certain circumstances would compel him to decline all future intimacy with him, and that although he should always remember him with esteem, he must request him to discontinue his future visits, as something had occurred to prevent his receiving them.

Henry Stirling was completely astounded on hearing this, and nothing could equal his chagrin and disappointment. He could at first scarcely believe that Mr. Milford was in earnest, but the seriousness of his looks soon convinced him that he was; and after expressing his astonishment at Mr. Milford's having come to so extraordinary a decision, he earnestly begged to be informed why he had done so.

"I must confess, Mr. Stirling," he said, "that I feel I have a most unpleasant duty to perform, and I deeply lament that it should have fallen to my lot. Doubtless I appear very unreasonable, but indeed, I am not so, and could I explain further, you would I am sure acquit me of any intention to insult you, or of not entertaining a proper sense of the deep obligations I am under to you."

"Has there ever been anything in my conduct, Mr. Milford," said Stirling, "that should render my visits unwelcome or annoying to you?"

"On my honour, nothing;" answered Mr. Milford.

"What then can be your reasons for declining my friendship?" demanded Henry,

"Excuse me, Mr. Stirling," returned Milford, "I cannot enter into any explanation; but I must request that you will comply with my wishes, and rest assured that although we may never meet again, I shall always think of you with the utmost respect."

"You surely will not persist in so preposterous a determination, Mr. Milford?"

"I have no alternative. But spare my feelings for the present, Mr. Stirling, and probably at some future period I may be at liberty to explain more."

"I am lost in amazement," said Henry; "and I cannot see the least reason you have to come to such a remarkable determination. Had I committed myself in any way, I should not of course, have felt any surprise."

"I cannot say more than I have already done," said Mr. Milford, "and as this interview cannot but be most unpleasant to us both, the sooner it is terminated, I think, the better."

Henry Stirling bit his lips, and could not conceal the extreme vexation he felt at an event so totally unexpected.

"Have you heard anything, Mr. Milford," he demanded, "which may appear prejudicial to my character? You cannot, I think, in strict justice and impartiality to myself, refuse to answer me that question."

" I must decline doing so," replied Mr. Milforc, with some confusion ; " but I wish us to part on the same friendly terms as those on which we met.' '

" This is most provoking," ejaculated Mr. Stirling, " and I cannot at all understand it. I had hoped that you had by this time seen enough of my character to have honoured me with your confidence, but it seems I was much mistaken, and since it appears that I cannot induce you to abandon your extraordinary resolution, suppose I must submit, though I need scarcely tell you with what feelings of deep regret I do so. However, I trust that you will suffer me to see your fair and amiable daughters before I go, that I may bid them farewell ?"

" I am sorry to say that I cannot comply with your request, Mr. Stirling," said Mr. Milford, " such an interview could only be distressing and embarrassing to all parties and is much better avoided."

Henry Stirling could not but again express his regret and disappointment ; and after some further conversation, he reluctantly took his leave, much to the relief of Mr. Milford. As he walked away from the house, he looked up at the windows, in the hope of catching a glimpse of Augusta and Charlotte, but his wish not being gratified, he hurried on, muttering curses at the unexpected disappointment he had that day experienced.

That Mr. Milford had come to such a strange determination he could not understand; and he in vain tried to conjecture the cause. Had he penetrated his real character ? He thought that was almost impossible, for he had ever been so cautious in his conduct, that he considered it was most unlikely that Mr. Milford could entertain the least suspicion of him. Had any one spoken against his real character ? There was no one that knew him except George, and he was satisfied that he could depend on his secresy. Altogether he was completely lost in amazement and perplexity, and his rage increased the more he reflected on it. But could Charlotte have been willing to resign his future friendship ? Oh, no ; her looks must indeed have much belied her if she had. He was confident from the pleasure she had ever evinced in his society, that he had made a most favourable impression upon her, if he had not actually won her heart's warmest affections, and he could not but flatter himself with the idea that she could never banish him from her memory, or help feeling the deepest regret at the harsh and unjust resolution her father had come to.

" And shall I suffer my plans to be thus frustrated ?" he soliloquized, as he walked on ; " shall I at once resign all my hopes of ever possessing that beauteous girl who has so captivated my heart! By my soul, never! I will proceed in my designs, let whatever may be the consequences. I must see George Milford, and consult him upon this disagreeable business. He will doubtless be able to afford me valuable assistance, and in spite of all the precautions of the old man, my triumph over the lovely Charlotte shall be yet complete."

With this determination, he walked on towards the hou e where George Milford usually resorted, with the hope of seeing him, and he had not proceeded far when he had the satisfaction of seeing him advancing that way.

" Why, how now, Mr. Stirling," said George, eying him narrowly, " you look sad this morning, and to judge from your aspect and demeanour altogether, you do not appear to be in the best of humours. Has anything occurred to vex you ?"

" Yes," answered Stirling, " something has indeed occurred to aggravate me, and I am glad I have met you, George, for I never needed your aid more than I do at present."

" Indeed ?" said George ; " well, what has put you out of temper, eh ?"

" I have just left your father's house."

" Well, what of that ?—You have not met anything to vex you, have you ?"

" Indeed, but I have ;" replied Henry Stirling : " your father has got some strange crotchets into his head which I cannot understand ; however, he has desired me never again to visit him ."

" Ah, how is that ? You have not offended the old man, have you ?"

" I gave him no cause for offence ; but he says that circumstances compel him to decline my future visits and intimacy, and refuses to give me any explanation of his motives for such extraordinary conduct."

THE ROYAL TWINS;

OR, THE SISTERS OF MYSTERY.

"Humph!" ejaculated George, "that is strange, sure enough, and rather unfortunate too. Do you think that he suspects your real character."

"I do not see how he can, for you know I have always acted with the greatest prudence and precaution."

"True;" said George, "I cannot make it out."

"You have not inadvertently let fall any hint, I hope?"

"Oh, no, you may be sure of that. But I think it is most likely that he has noticed your marked attentions to Charlotte, and the favour with which she viewed you, and being averse to the encouragement of such a passion, he has adopted this course in order to destroy it."

"That certainly is the most probable conclusion to come to," remarked Stirling; "but if your father thinks to put a stop to our passion by such a course he will find himself most wofully mistaken. This opposition only renders me more anxious to gain the gratification of my wishes than ever. Charlotte Milford must and shall be mine, though it cost me a fortune to get possession of her. I presume I may depend upon your assistance?"

"Certainly you may," replied George, "have I not already promised, and I will not fail to keep my word, if you do not break yours."

"That is enough, I am satisfied, and will still entertain the most sanguine hopes of getting the beauteous Charlotte in my power."

"If you will be guided by me, you shall not be disappointed, I'll warrant."

"I will follow your advice to the very letter, and shall consider no reward too great for any assistance you may lend me in accomplishing my designs. But we had better not remain talking in the street, or we may be seen by some person who knows us. Let us retire into the nearest tavern, and talk this important subject over further."

George Milford consented, and they walked into a house where they had often been before, where they sat down to consult upon the course it would now be best to pursue in order to bring about the gratification of Stirling's guilty wishes; and here we will leave the two worthies, and return to the hapless Charlotte. The decision of Mr. Milford had the most serious effect upon her health, and he and Augusta became considerably alarmed. How severely it grieved Mr. Milford to be compelled to act with such apparent harshness, and keenly did he feel the necessity of thus being compelled to blight her young hopes and prospects; but still he trusted that time and the absence of the object who had made so favourable an impression on her susceptible heart would have the effect of ameliorating her grief and disappointment, if it did not entirely banish the image of Henry Stirling from her memory.

It was a source of extreme annoyance to Mr. Milford that he should be compelled to decline the friendship of a young man of whom he entertained so high an opinion, and who had preserved the sisters from the frightful death by which they had been threatened; and he thought that in this, as in all other matters, the stranger had not been sufficiently explicit. His statements were most ambiguous, and after all Milford was really not inclined to place any particular confidence in them; and must still look upon Henry Stirling with feelings of respect, admiration, and gratitude. Nevertheless, the injunctions of the unknown were imperative, and he did not feel disposed to venture to disobey them.

For several days after this occurrence poor Charlotte continued in a most melancholy state of mind, and turned a deaf ear to all the efforts of Augusta and her father to console her. She no longer attempted to conceal the sentiments which glowed in her breast towards Stirling; in fact, it would have been useless for her to have sought to have done so, and she declared that let whatever might be the consequence she felt that it would be impossible for her ever to banish him from her memory, and that although it might not be the will of Heaven that they should ever come together, she was satisfied that he must continue in possession of her heart, and that no other man could hope to obtain her affections.

This declaration grieved Mr. Milford exceedingly, for he had no argument to oppose against it, except the disparity of their stations in society; and this he did with a very bad grace, when he recollected that the unknown had always given him to understand that the birth of those fair beings who had for so many years been entrusted to his protection was most distinguished; and it probably equalled if it did not surpass that of Stirling. He, however, remonstrated with Charlotte in his gentlest accents, and tried his utmost to reconcile her to the course he had adopted, assuring her that he had been compelled to do so by circumstances over which he had no control. But then he was placed in a most awkward dilemma, from which he found it a most difficult task to extricate himself. What were the questions which Charlotte naturally put to him? They were, what had he recently observed in Henry Stirling's conduct, to cause him so suddenly to change his good opinion of him? Could he deny that he was most intelligent, affable, and accomplished? That they owed him a debt of gratitude it would be impossible for them ever sufficiently to repay? He was completely bewildered how to answer those interrogatories. He could not explain that it was in consequence of information he had received in the letter which had recently been forwarded to him, because it would then naturally be expected that he should reveal to them such facts as he was prohibited from doing, to acquaint them who his correspondent was, and likewise upon what authority he founded his accusation. Every day Mr. Milford felt the position in which he was placed as regarded the sisters become more perplexing and difficult, and unless the stranger should think proper ere long to unravel the torturing mystery, he was at a loss to imagine in what way he should proceed. He thought it would be utterly impossible for him to conceal the secret from them much longer, especially when he considered the rapidly declining state of his health, and how soon they might be left without a protector, and without knowing to whom they might apply for advice and assistance; and surely it was now time that their friends should take that responsibility on themselves, unless indeed they meant to abandon them altogether, which after the solemn assertions and promises of the unknown he could not suppose them to be capable of doing. He was in constant dread of his son, lest he should betray the secret which had so unfortunately come to his knowledge, and which he would be sure to do in such a manner as would be productive of the most painful consequences; but although George frequently visited the house, another change for the better had taken place in his manners, and he conducted himself with much greater propriety than he had done for some time before. We need not say what satisfaction this afforded them all, but had they known the villanous designs he had in view, how great would have been their horror, indignation and disgust!

Time, however, did bring about a more favourable change in the health and spirits of Charlotte than they had anticipated. She seemed to be struggling hard to conquer the fatal passion which Henry Stirling had created in her breast, and to banish his image from her mind; and although she had lost all that volatility of spirits which was before one of her principal and most interesting characteristics, she seemed to be calm and resigned.

Mr. Milford and Augusta, delighted to see this promising change from the hopeless and melancholy condition she was recently placed in, did all they could to encourage her in it; and though they often reflected with regret on the painful necessity which had compelled them to resign the friendship and society of the apparently amiable, generous, and accomplished Stirling, they avoided as much as possible mentioning his name in her presence, lest it should arouse all the feelings she had so recently entertained towards him, with redoubled and overwhelming force. Alas! they little thought that the mind of the poor damsel was really occupied in the manner it was—that so far from her affection towards Henry Stirling being stifled in her bosom, it glowed with tenfold strength and unconquerable power—that so far from banishing him from her memory, he had gained by absence an ascendancy over her which threatened her future peace and innocence. They little imagined that although separated, they almost daily, through the agency of George Milford, corresponded together—that they had exchanged mutual vows of affection, and solemnly promised unalterable constancy; and that so well had the seducer succeeded in his artifices, that he entertained the most sanguine hopes of a speedy and complete triumph. Yet so it was, and such was the fatal influence that Henry Stirling had gained over her, that Charlotte was completely blind to the fearful and destructive precipice upon the very brink of which she stood.

But did she never reproach herself for the part she was acting? Did she never shudder at the idea of the deceit she was practising towards her beloved benefactor and her sister. Oh, yes, there were times when she hesitated, and was half inclined to make them acquainted with the whole truth, and to throw herself upon their generosity and sympathy, but an irresistible feeling prevented her.

She had earnestly implored Henry Stirling to seek another interview with Mr. Milford, notwithstanding his prohibition; to confess to him the mutual and unutterable affection that existed between them; to assure him of the honour of his intentions, and to endeavour to gain his sanction to their paying their addresses to each other. But Stirling always combatted these persuasions with that consummate skill of which he was complete master, and pointed out an elopement and a private marriage as the only chance of obtaining the gratification of their wishes; and he stated his firm belief that a reconciliation, and the forgiveness of Mr. Milford might afterwards be speedily obtained.

Charlotte shrunk from this proposition for some time with the greatest repugnance. To act in so clandestine a manner—to deceive that amiable being who had ever behaved towards her with such unbounded affection and indulgence, was most revolting to her nature; and she could not for a time persuade herself but that such conduct would have the most fatal effect upon the mind of her father, who had ever reposed such affectionate confidence in her. Besides, the connections of Henry Stirling were noble and distinguished, while she was humble, friendless, and almost destitute, could never approve of such an unequal marriage, and contracted under such circumstances; and what, therefore, could she anticipate would be the result? Nothing but ruin and misery to them both and all related to them.

These reflections had a most powerful effect upon the mind of Charlotte, and almost induced her to abandon all hopes of a union with Henry Stirling, since it was fraught with so much difficulty and danger. But alas! he had gained too strong a hold on her heart to permit her long to encourage this idea; and Stirling, perceiving his advantage, followed it up with unabated perseverance and success.

Weeks, months flew by without any change taking place. The summer had now set in, and Mr. Milford and the sisters frequently took long walks for the benefit of the air, though sometimes Charlotte would excuse herself on the plea of indisposition; and they never entertained the least suspicion of her.

What would have been their thoughts had they been aware that generally on those occasions Henry Stirling was a secret visitor to the house? That in such moments the libertine was using all his powers of persuasion and eloquence upon the innocent and unsuspecting Charlotte, to gain the final accomplishment of his designs, and that daily the fatal influence he had gained over her affections was increasing in strength, and threatened ere long to plunge them in the deepest misery and despair?

It was a beautiful afternoon, and Milford and Augusta (Charlotte having excused herself) had prolonged their walk to a much greater extent than was their usual custom. But the approach of evening warned them to return home with speed, as they had no doubt that Charlotte would begin to feel surprised and uneasy at their long absence.

They had reached within a few streets of their humble dwelling, when a post-chaise and four passed them at a rapid rate. The windows were only partially closed; and although it was only for an instant, Mr. Milford thought he could perceive the figures of three persons seated in the vehicle, namely, a gentleman and two females; but as the chaise rolled rapidly away, both him and Augusta plainly heard a faint scream proceed from it, and the next moment it had turned swiftly round the corner of the street, and was out of sight.

Mr. Milford and his companion could not help pausing, and gazing in the direction which the chaise had taken, and the former felt a strange sensation come over him, for which he could in no wise account.

"Did you not hear that cry, Augusta?" he said.

"Yes," replied the latter; "it proceeded from the voice of a female; and from the rapid rate at which the chaise was travelling, I should almost be inclined to suspect that there was something unfair in the business."

"It is strange," remarked Mr. Milford; "but it can be no business of ours; so let us get on our way home. Some elopement or abduction, I shouldn't wonder; and if so, what ruin and misery to numerous persons may it not be the cause of."

They were about to proceed on their way, when, turning round, they beheld an old woman, who resided in a miserable, dirty alley in the neighbourhood, and who eked out a wretched existence by telling the fortunes of the ignorant and credulous, standing before them.

Mother Alder, for so she was called, was very aged and shrivelled, and there was something particularly frightful and disgusting in her whole appearance; but on this occasion she looked even more disagreeable than usual.

Mr. Milford, who pitied the old woman, whom he imagined to be half crazy, smiled kindly upon her, and bidding her good evening, was passing on, when she detained him; and fixing upon him a very singular look, which he was at a loss to understand, she said,—

"You smile, friend, but your smiles will shortly be changed to looks of grief and despair. You need not be in such a hurry to return to your deserted home, for sorrow alone awaits to greet you there. She was most fair—most amiable—most lovely; but even the most fair and innocent cannot always resist the artifices of the tempter."

In spite of themselves, Milford and Augusta could not help feeling a shuddering sensation steal through their veins as the old woman spoke; and the former, in a tremulous voice, demanded what she meant, and why she addressed them in the manner she had done.

"The plot was cunningly contrived," replied the old fortune-teller, "and the young man almost deserves to win his fair prize for his perseverance and ingenuity. They thought no eye watched them when they departed, but I beheld them; and as I gazed upon that lovely face, I could not but sigh to think how soon that fair face would be pale and haggard with shame and remorse. Ah, well-a-day! ah, well-a-day!"

And having given utterance to these singular words, the old woman hobbled away, before Mr. Milford and Augusta had sufficiently recovered from their astonishment to offer to detain her.

"Good God!" exclaimed Mr. Milford, at length, "what are we to conclude from this strange old woman's insinuations? My heart misgives me, though I know not for why. Come, Augusta, let us hasten home; I regret that we have remained away so long."

A few minutes more brought them to their residence, and Mr. Milford hastily knocked at the door. It was answered by one of the lodgers.

"Where is my daughter?" he hastily inquired.

"She left the house more than half an hour ago," replied the lodger, "and I thought she had gone to meet you on your way home, as the evening was so fine."

"Left the house!" faltered out Milford and Augusta, in a breath; and remembering the words of the old fortune-teller, and the circumstance of the post-chaise they had seen, a cold, shuddering sensation of fear came over them. "Did she not say anything? Did she not leave any message?"

The woman answered in the negative; and Mr. Milford and Augusta rushed into the house, in a state of the greatest agitation. Everything in the parlour was the same as when they had left it, but the first things that met their eyes was a letter lying on the table, and a canvass bag standing beside it, which seemed to contain money. With a trembling hand Mr. Milford seized the letter, which was in the handwriting of Charlotte, and breaking the seal with appalled eyes, in a voice choked with emotion, read the following words:

"Beloved father and sister, yes, still most beloved although I have for a time abandoned you. Oh, how shall I venture to address you—how express my feelings—how implore your forgiveness on this solumn occasion? when ungovernable love for that one object who could never otherwise have been mine, has tempted me to take a step which I fear will wring your affectionate hearts so bitterly? Feel for me, pity me, pardon me for this my only act of disobedience. But I was left no alternative, I could not abandon all thoughts of that man on whom I had fixed my heart's warmest affections; without rendering myself miserable for ever, and in whose honour I place every confidence.

Would that we could have obtained your sanction to our love without, being compelled to adopt this desperate course, what bitter suffering would it have saved us all.

"My beloved father, oh, bear this unexpected event with fortitude, I implore you, and we shall shortly meet again. In a few hours I shall be the wife of Henry Stirling, for I cannot doubt his truth and honour, and oh, what future happiness I trust will then be in store for us.

"Dearest Augusta, do not reproach your poor sister for this act, or for having so long deceived you! Believe me my heart still beats with the warmest affection towards you, and must ever continue to do so, though your sentiments towards me may unhappily change, which Heaven in its infinite mercy forbid.

"My future husband begs me, dear father and sister, to supplicate your forgiveness for him, and to assure you of the honour of his intentions, which a very short time will prove. He craves your acceptance of the accompanying, trifle my dear father, which he trusts may be of service to you until further arrangements of a pecuniary nature can be made.

"And now my ever revered parent and sister, once more humbly but earnestly imploring your forgiveness for this my first dereliction from the path of duty, and trusting that in a short time we may meet again under happier circumstances than any we have yet experienced, bless you, bless you both, and farewell, and that All Bountiful Heaven may keep you in its preservation, is the fervent prayer of your affectionate

"CHARLOTTE."

Augusta could scarcely hear this letter to the conclusion, when shocked and overpowered with emotion, she fainted and was committed to the care of the lodger who had opened the door to them, and who apprehending that something serious had happened, was waiting handy to render any assistance in her power.

But what language can do adequate justice to the feelings of the unfortunate Mr. Milford? Madness almost seized upon his brain, as again and again with wild and vacant eyes he continued to gaze upon Charlotte's letter.

"Gone! gone!" he cried; "fled! abandoned me, who have ever behaved with even more than the affection of a father towards her, for the arms of a stranger; oh, wretched, misguided, ungrateful girl; you are lost, ruined for ever! The wily villain only seeks the destruction of your innocence, and perhaps ere now you have become the thing of shame and degradation! Alas! alas! most true was the character the stranger gave me of him, but what other course could I adopt to guard myself and Charlotte against him than that which I did? and who would have thought she could ever have found the heart so cruelly to deceive me? Alas! too cleverly and successfully has the youthful libertine devised and executed his diabolical designs. And, heartless as he is, has dared to add insult to injury! The miscreant; thinks he then that I am so lost and guilty as to sell my Charlotte's honour at a price? Curses light upon his gold! I would not touch a coin of it were it even to save my existence! Oh, Charlotte, Charlotte, thoughtless, infatuated, imprudent, misguided girl, what shame and misery have you brought upon yourself and all connected with you! My God! and had I but known that you and your seducer were in the chaise which I encountered; that it was your voice I heard! Thought will drive me mad! Charlotte, Charlotte, you have done that this day which nothing can ever redeem!"

He beat his breast and groaned with agony and despair, and it was indeed most painful to observe the intense suffering he was enduring, and which, if possible, was greater than if the unfortunate Charlotte had been his own daughter.

Augusta now recovered and turning her streaming eyes towards Mr. Milford, she ejaculated:—

"Oh, my poor father, what a terrible blow is this! Heaven help us, I can scarcely believe in its reality! Good God! and is it possible that my beloved sister can have fallen into the snares laid by the tempter, to entrap her? Is it possible that she has abandoned us? Eloped with a man who is almost a stranger to us, and deserted those in whom I thought her whole affections were centered? It seems like some frightful, hideous dream. Oh, Charlotte, unfortunate girl, could the beloved, the gentle mother who bore us, have been living to have witnessed this terrible day!"

"Ah!" groaned Mr. Milford, striking his burning temples, "could your mother indeed witness it, but she——" He checked himself suddenly, and after a paus of the greatest agony, added:—"It is a maddening reality, Augusta; your sister has shamefully deceived, and abandoned us, and voluntarily placed herself in the power of a villain, who seeks and will effect her destruction ! He make her his wife ! poor deluded victim ; too soon will you discover 'tis false, false as the black heart that could conceive it ! Horror ! perhaps ere this, she whom I have ever watched with such anxious care is brought to degradation and everlasting shame ! But I will pursue them to the extremity of the world and snatch her from the villain's power ! I am mad ! Whither can I go in search of them ? They are far enough away by this time and can elude my vigilance. It is too late to save her, oh God !"

He threw himself back in his chair groaning heavily, while the distracted Augusta being over him almost in a state of utter unconsciousness, and her tears mingled freely with his.

——

CHAPTER XIV.

MORE SUFFERING.—THE FATAL RESULTS OF THE ELOPEMENT.—THE DECEIVER UNMASKED. —THE RETURN.—THE DEATH.

IT would be a fruitless task to endeavour to describe the sufferings endured by Mr. Milford and Augusta that night, but to retire to their chambers they could not for a moment think of. Sometimes he raved incoherently, and gave utterance to strange observations, which Augusta was at a loss to understand, and more than once he was on the point of betraying the important secret he had for so many years kept inviolate. What course to pursue they knew not; they had no means of discovering whither Stirling and his unfortunate victim had directed their footsteps, nor had they the least advance of tracing any clue to them. The thought was horrible ; they could neither of them help looking upon poor Charlotte as lost, and despair settled upon their hearts and drove them almost to madness. And yet did the gentle Augusta struggle against the violence of her feelings (for the sake of that revered being whom she supposed to be her father) with a fortitude that could not have been expected in one so young, and under the dreadful circumstances, and tried to impart some little degree of consolation to him, though at the same time her own heart was bursting. The lodgers in the house being all respectable, though humble people, deeply sympathized with them in their misfortunes, and did all that they could to assist them, but the shame to which they were exposed by the conduct of Charlotte afflicted her sister and Mr. Milford more than all.

That night passed away, and the morning found Mr. Milford and Augusta in a most deplorable state. They anticipated the worst to have befallen the unhappy Charlotte, and pictured to themselves the horror and remorse she was probably now enduring when it was to late too recal the past. And what course to adopt Milford knew not. Where could he find the stranger ? where communicate with him, so that he might acquaint him with what had happened, and receive his advice and instructions how to act ? He could not but feel more forcibly than ever the imprudence of the stranger in not furnishing him with the means of finding him on any occasion of emergency, and his conduct appeared, if possible, more painfully inexplicable to him than ever. It was certain, from the tenour of his last communication, that he knew who the quondam Henry Stirling really was, and that if he was aware of what had taken place, and promptitude was to be used before the danger which threatened the betrayed and unfortunate Cnarlotte, she might be rescued from his power. Placed in this awkward dilemma what could he do ? He was completely lost, distracted and bewildered, and Augusta from being ignorant of the real thoughts which occupied his mind, was in no position, had she even possessed the power, to advise him.

The old fortune-teller was requested to call upon Mr. Milford, and by the offer of a reward to inform them of all the particulars of the elopement which she had observed ; but the information they could gather from her, was not of the slightest importance ; she had merely seen the post-chaise waiting at the corner of one of the most obscure streets in the neighbourhood, and suspecting that something was wrong, curiosity had prompted her to stand aside and watch. Presently she beheld Charlotte approaching, leaning on the arm of a young gentleman, and apparently much agitated. She cast two or three anxious glances towards the turning that conducted to her home, and seemed to hesitate, but the young man whispered a few words in her ear, and conducting her towards the carriage, into which he handed her, and following himself, he gave the word to the postillions, and the chaise was driven off with the greatest speed.

Such was all the further information they could glean from the old woman, and it left them in the same state of agony and perplexity. When Milford had, however, become a little more cool and collected, he bethought him, that probably giving information at the offices of the different magistrates, might assist them in the discovery of the fugitives, and accordingly, being too weak himself, he got one of his neighbours to perform this task for him. He also gave directions for a number of placards to be printed and posted about, hoping that perchance they might meet the eyes of the stranger, and cause him to come forward to their assistance. But surely Charlotte could not long remain silent herself!—She could not rest, knowing the dreadful state of anguish and anxiety they would naturally be in, without making them acquainted where she was, and whether Henry Stirling had indeed fulfilled his solemn promise to her?--But, alas! had he meant to betray her (of which there could be little doubt) he would take good care to prevent her from communicating with them, and if she had unhappily fallen a victim to his nefarious designs, shame and remorse would prevent her from being the herald of her own ruin.

With such racking and conflicting thoughts as these torturing their minds, it may well be imagined how dreadful were the sufferings of Mr. Milford and Augusta. It was with difficulty that the latter could support herself with sufficient fortitude to attend upon that unfortunate and revered being who so much needed her assistance, and to whom this terrible shock seemed likely to prove a death blow. How awful was the prospect which opened upon the poor girl's eyes. Should Mr. Milford be snatched from her, she would be left alone and unprotected in the world, and without one friend to whom she might apply for consolation and advice. The idea was too dreadful to contemplate, and it almost drove her to madness. When alone, many were the scalding tears she shed, and fervent were the prayers she offered up to Heaven to avert so dreadful a calamity, and to restore her poor sister, uninjured to them.

But when a week had elapsed, and they still received not the least tidings of the fugitives, their anguish became insupportable, and Mr. Milford was reduced to a most pitiable state, and was unable to leave his bed—at times being quite delirious, and raving in a manner that it was quite melancholy to hear. Sometimes he imagined that Charlotte was still near him, and then he would weep over her imaginary form, and upbraid himself for having for a moment supposed that she could abandon him, or do aught that should call a blush of shame upon her lovely and innocent cheek. Then the delusion would quickly pass away, and he would reproach her with ingratitude, and call down the most bitter maledictions upon the head of her seducer.

George Milford had only called to see them once or twice since the elopement, and as may be expected, he expressed no sympathy for his father's deplorable situation, neither did he express any surprise at the conduct of Charlotte, but on the contrary, seemed to exult in it, as in fact, he did, as it not only gratified his feelings of jealousy and hatred, but had paid him so liberally into the bargain.

It was, indeed, a relief to the wretched Augusta when the abandoned villain took his departure, and the suffering Mr. Milford appeared more easy when he was gone, as he could only contemplate him with feelings almost amounting to horror; and how much more would his horror and disgust have been increased, had he been aware of the active and treacherous part he had taken in the intended destruction of the innocent Charlotte. How Augusta shuddered when she thought of the painful situation in which she would be placed if it should please the Almighty to take her father, left to the mercy of such a man!

The illness of Mr. Milford hourly increased, and nearly all his faculties were prostrated. He was conscious that his end was approaching, and the only regret he felt at

quitting a world in which he had experienced so much trouble and so little happiness, was the lonely, unprotected state, in which he must leave Augusta, and the uncertain fate which had befallen her unfortunate sister.

The continued silence of the stranger augured the worst; and it seemed but too evident that he had deceived him, and had made up his mind to abandon them altogether. And yet it seemed impossible that one who had made such solemn promises, and who was evidently in some way or other so closely connected with the sisters, could act with such injustice and cruelty. Surely he must be in ignorance of what had taken, place, or he would immediately have come forward to their assistance in so precarious and alarming a situation, and especially at a time when it was absolutely necessary so much should be explained.

In his moments of consciousness, Mr. Milford, feeling that his demise must take place before long, was often on the point of revealing to Augusta the important and extraordinary secret connected with her; but still some unaccountable feeling of repugnance prevented him, and he deferred it from day to day, with the hope that Providence would still permit him to behold Charlotte again before he died, and that he might in the presence of both the lovely sisters have an opportunity of disclosing to them that mysterious secret he had so long and so faithfully kept concealed within his own breast throughout the severest trials, and notwithstanding the stranger had broken his promises in so many instances.

Augusta saw plainly that something pressed upon Mr. Milford's mind, which he yet hesitated to divulge, and in vain did she rack her distracted brain to discover what it was, but her thoughts were too painfully and busily occupied another way to suffer her long to dwell upon this circumstance. Her only friend, her revered parent was hastening to the grave; she would have no one to console or advise her when he was gone, and that of itself was sufficient to drive her almost to madness.

And he so near his end, and Charlotte not there to assist her in smoothing his dying pillow, and mingle her tears with her's. Oh, God! what would be the sufferings of that unfortunate girl, did she but know her father's awful situation? And it was her conduct that had been the cause of it. Alas! how bitter must be her pangs of remorse whenever it should reach her ears! Would to Heaven that Providence would restore her to them before his death, that she might give them the blessed assurance that she was still pure and innocent, and receive his forgiveness. With what anxiety did she watch by the couch of that expiring individual whom she believed her father, and pray for the accomplishment of all these desires. But, alas! there was no hope, no consolation for her, for no intelligence could be obtained of Charlotte, and hourly she saw the strength of her beloved protector wasting away, and fearful proofs that he must soon be snatched from her altogether. And the poor suffering Milford, in his moments of consciousness saw the agony that she whom he had ever loved as fondly as if she had been his own child, was enduring, and it added of course to his own mental anguish, though he did his best to conceal the facts from the penetrating eye of his fair and anxious attendant.

Thus the time wore drearily on; dreary indeed, to poor Augusta, who had to contend with so many torturing and conflicting feelings, and it was marvellous how that delicate frame supported with so much fortitude and apparent composure such an unnatural weight of affliction that might even have weighed down a giant constitution.

Heaven knows that the loss and probable ruin of a beloved sister was sufficient to reduce the poor girl to a state of the most abject despair and mental incapacity, but Providence was kind to her, and supported her, although the dreadful certainty that she must speedily likewise be deprived of her only earthly protector was every moment made more apparent to her tortured and nearly worn-out mind. She scouted the black picture of the future from her brain, as well as she could, but still, in spite of all her efforts, it would rush upon it, and could not remain concealed from the tender and suffering object of her anxiety. At times he looked upon her with such intense feeling and solicitude that it wrung her heart almost to bursting to contemplate it, and at such moments, when the dreadful thought would arise to him, in what a fearful situation she would be placed when he was taken from her, the secret so long concealed arose to his lips, but some instinctive power prevented his giving utterance to it. He could not reveal it, now that she was so lonely and so wretched ; he could not utter it unless in the presence of that unfortunate girl whom he could never hope again to behold in this world. But where was the stranger? Where were those friends upon whom they had a natural claim ?—what had become of all the solemn engagements which the unknown had made to him? Surely if living he or they must have heard of what had taken place, and if they were sincere in their affection towards the two unfortunate beings they had cast upon the world, or at least, under the circumstances represented in such an ambiguous manner committed to the care of a stranger, they could not help coming forward to their relief, and to save them from the destruction which otherwise threatened them?

Drearily, drearily three more days wore on; still no intelligence of Charlotte; still no communication from the stranger; still no hope for poor Augusta! She saw her beloved father hourly wasting away, and all her tender attentions, all the skill of his medical attendants were unavailing ; she knew, and so did he, and he did not seek to disguise the truth from her, or to inspire her with false hopes, that his hours, his moments were numbered, that his end was rapidly approaching, and yet with all she supported it with a fortitude that was truly wonderful, though all before her was blacker, far darker than the darkest midnight. It was a dreadful trial for the poor girl, both bodily and mentally, and Mr. Milford in his moments of consciousness, keenly felt that, and it sharpened the pangs of death, which otherwise would have been calm and unruffled.

The third evening came ; the day had been warm, sultry, and oppressive to the senses, even under ordinary circumstances, and the reader may well imagine what must have been the effects upon the spirits of the broken hearted and despairing Augusta in that chamber of dolour, and with all the awful and unprecedented weight of cares which pressed upon her brain. The thunder which had long been murmuring at a distance, now rolled in fearful peals immediately over the humble dwelling, while the vivid flashes of lightening darted in at the windows of the chamber in which Milford was lying, rendering his countenance, bearing all the awful impress of death, still more ghastly, and adding to the terrors of poor Augusta's almost worn out mind. She struggled with her feelings as well as she could, but the storm speedily became so frightful that even under ordinary circumstances, it must have imparted a degree of horror and awe to even the stoutest heart, and can it then be wondered that Augusta in her dismal watching by the couch of that revered being of whom she knew she was so shortly to be deprived, upon whom the hand of the grim tyrant death was already laid, should feel more than commonly affected ? She drew the blind closer, but still the lightning played vividly in at the windows, at intervals illumining the chamber with a lurid glare, whilst the voice of the thunder every moment became louder, and the rain descended in showers that might almost have been compared to a second deluge.

Augusta was terrified, and even the presence and kind efforts at consolation of Mrs. Barton, the lodger before mentioned. and who had rendered such valuable aid during the illness of Mr. Milford, failed to restore her to anything like composure. In fact, the poor girl was completely worn out from long anxiety, constant watching by the bedside of the invalid, and deprivation of rest, and it was only wonderful that she did not sink entirely under such an extraordinary trial. The chair tottered beneath her, and it was only with the greatest difficulty that she could prevent herself from fainting. Mrs Barton, however, administered some restoratives to her, and in a short time she partially recovered.

Still the storm raged with increased instead of abated violence, and the face of nature seldom presented a more frightful aspect than it did in that melancholy hour. Peal after peal roared from the heavens in rapid succession; flash after flash lighted the sky, and the rain continued to dash down with the most impetuous fury. Every door in the slenderly built house shook on its hinges, and the windows rattled in their frames. To add to the melancholy of the season, the dismal howling of a dog, apparently immediately beneath the window of the chamber (and according to an old English superstition the certain harbinger of death) was heard at the intervals between the pauses of the tempest.

It was indeed an awful time for Augusta, who had been watching for hours the unfavourable change which had taken place in her father, and when the medical attendant had as feelingly and as delicately as he possibly could, assured her he was past all hope of recovery, and could not survive many hours. Although she had from the first been prepared for the worst, and had scarcely ever encouraged the least ray of hope, the shock came so powerfully upon her that it almost deprived her of her senses, and indeed of every faculty.

And Charlotte still silent, still absent! Oh, what a terrible addition was that to the affliction she endured. How dreadful was it to reflect upon the probable fate that had befallen her, which her silence seemed to render the more certain. She had fallen into the snares of the tempter, had become a degraded being, and was ashamed to divulge the fatal truth! Yet surely, if she was aware that her unfortunate parent was so near his last moments, nothing whatever could keep her from his dying couch; no power could restrain her from seeking his forgiveness ere his soul should be called to eternity!

. " Oh, that she would come," sighed Augusta to herself, " even though fallen, that she would come to assist me in closing the dying eyes of her poor father, and to hear from his lips his pardon. Surely some villanous power must prevent her, or she would ere this have communicated with us, and divulged the truth, however fatal it may be. Charlotte, Charlotte, my only sister, the twin offspring of our parents love, what accursed fate has caused this dreadful estrangement ? Oh, what a dark game must your seducer have played, thus to have imposed upon your innocence and unsuspecting confidence, and to have tempted you to abandon those who were, and must be still so dear to your affections."

Scalding tears chased each other down the pale cheeks of the beauteous girl as these sad, these distracting thoughts arose to her mind, and had it not been for the exertions of Mrs. Barton she must have been completely overpowered.

Still fiercer and fiercer raged the storm, and no probability of its abating presented itself. Night came on, dark and dismal, save when the lightning imparted a transient glare, still more awful than the darkness.

But in spite of the fearful raging of the tempest, Milford had till now been wrapped in an apparent calm sleep, so calm indeed that he scarcely seemed to breathe at all, and several times when Augusta beheld the ghastly change in his countenance, she became dreadfully agitated and rushing to him placed her hand upon his heart, and her ear to his mouth, fearful that the vital spark had fled. But at length he opened his eyes, and beholding Augusta affectionately hanging over him, for a few seconds, gazed at her wildly, and in seeming unconsciousness.

" Do you not know me, dear father?" said Augusta, pressing her lips to his in the greatest state of mental agony, for she could too plainly perceive that the life so precious to her was near its close, and all the despair of the moment rushed upon her with maddening effect.

" Oh, Charlotte," he ejaculated with sudden energy, and extending his feeble and wasted arms to embrace her, " you have then, my poor deluded child returned ; you have not abandoned me in my last moments. You have not fallen, you still are faultless, pure, and—and—I pardon you."

" Father, dear father," sobbed Augusta, convulsively, and throwing her fair arms around his neck : " oh, speak to me, to your own affectionate and broken-hearted daughter !"

" Ah !" ejaculated Mr. Milford, with a shudder, and withdrawing himself from her embrace, " who calls me daughter ? I have no daughter, no child who loves me. I—I—never had a daughter. I want none, for they are all deceitful, treacherous ! Yes, I had one fair thing that I used to love and call my daughter, and behaved to her with even more than a father's affection, expecting no other return than duty, but she dceived me, deserted me ; fled to the arms of a villain, repudiated the claim which I had at least upon her gratitude and ——"

" Father ! beloved father !" again cried the distracted Augusta, " do you, oh, do you not know me ?"

" Ah !" he exclaimed, as recollection seemed to flash across his brain. " I know you now ; you arr Augusta, my own fond Augusta, but no child of mine."

"Oh, God!" groaned the poor girl, wringing her hands in agony, "his mind wanders; he knows not what he says. Heaven help me in this moment of bitter trial! Father!—"

"No, no, no," he feverishly interrupted; "call me not by such a name; I have no claim to it!"

"No claim to it;" exclaimed Augusta, "Oh, my honoured parent, you know not what you say; have I not ever been to you—"

"Yes, yes," again interrupted the dying man, "you have ever been most kind, most dutiful, and affectionate, and so was she, until accursed fate introduced the tempter to our house, and blighted all my hopes. But where is she?—She will not come!—I must die and never behold her again. Oh, surely this is cruel, and ungrateful, although she is no daughter of mine."

Augusta heard these words uttered with such apparent sincerity, with the most unbounded astonishment and perplexity, and again throwing her arms around her supposed father's neck, implored him to explain himself. He looked at her for a few moments with a vacant stare, and then said;—

"What a dreadful night; how the thunder roars, and the lightning flashes, Heaven frowns upon the delinquencies of the hapless Charlotte. But she has no home;—oh, what an awful night for the friendless one to be exposed in. She will not come; she will not come, and I must die without once more embracing her, and revealing to her——"

Then apparently for the first time beholding the presence of Mrs. Barton, he added, as recollection seemed to dawn upon him—

"But we must be alone, Augusta;—my time is short;—I feel that my final moment is fast approaching, and while reason and recollection are left me, I must reveal a secret which has perhaps been too long concealed by me, and on which the future prospects and welfare of yourself, dear Augusta, and your unfortunate sister, probably depend. I repeat, we must be alone."

Mrs. Barton immediately withdrew, and Augusta awaited what the dying man had to say, with the most indescribable impatience and curiosity.

"Raise me gently in the bed, darling," he said, in a faint voice, "and Heaven give me strength to perform my duty."

With feelings of emotion of which the reader may form a much better conception than could be conveyed to them in language, Augusta assisted Mr. Milford to a sitting posture in the bed, and he then passed his thin hand across his aching forehead, as if endeavouring to recall his scattered senses, and sighing deeply, looked eagerly around the chamber.

"Oh, would that she were here;" he ejaculated, "though fallen, would that she were here, to hear my dying revelation, and receive my farewell blessing!—But you are here, Augusta, and should fate ever ordain that you and your unfortunate sister should meet again, assure her of my pardon, and communicate to her the extraordinary secret I am now about to impart to you. Oh, God! would that it had been thy Almighty will that I should have lived till I saw you placed beneath the care of your natural protectors, but——"

"Our natural protectors!" interrupted the still more astonished Augusta; "oh, my revered parent, you know not what you say, you cannot;—what do you mean?"

"My poor girl," said Mr. Milford, in calmer accents, "this is no time for concealments, and believe me I am perfectly conscious of what I am saying, and what I speak shall be nothing more than the truth. The secret I am about to divulge to you, and which I probably should have done before this, under all the circumstances, is one of the utmost importance to your future welfare, and upon which, as I have been given to understand, in all probability may even affect your life and that of your misguided sister."

"Gracious Heaven! What can you mean?—What extraordinary intelligence am I destined to hear?"

"Listen to me patiently, calmly, and without interruption, dear Augusta," replied Mr. Milford, arousing all his energies for the peculiar task he had imposed upon himself in such a solemn hour, and mustering more fortitude as he proceeded; "You ever looked upon me and my sainted wife, and loved us as your parents?"

"Love you," repeated Augusta, "oh, why put such a question to me? Did I ever give you reason to doubt me? Has it not been the whole study of my life to shew you, to convince you that you were dearer to me than my own existence?"

"True, true, Augusta, dear Augusta," replied Mr. Milford, with a faint smile, and pressing her to his bosom;—"Oh, you have ever been most kind, most affectionate, and dutiful, and so was that poor girl, your sister, until untoward fate introduced her to a villain, God help, and preserve her!"

He passed his hand again across his brow, and his bosom heaved with the convulsive emotion which that thought engendered. Augusta's tears started to her eyes, and she was unable do give utterance to a syllable. A silence of two or three minutes ensued, in which short interval Mr. Milford seemed to have completely conquered his feelings, and to have prepared himself for his task.

"Augusta," he resumed, "you and your sister loved me and my late amiable wife, and looked upon us as your parents, but——"

He faultered, and his strength again for the moment failed him. Augusta threw her arms around his neck, and looked eagerly, and with the most agonizing suspense in his pale countenance, as she ejaculated:—

"But what, my father?—Oh, speak, and dissolve at once this extraordinary and insupportable mystery!"

"*Your father!*" replied Milford, in the most emphatic manner, and fixing his eyes with an intensity of meaning upon her countenance;—"Oh, would——"

The conclusion of the sentence was interrupted by a loud knock at the street-door.

"Ah!" exclaimed the dying man, starting and staring wildly about him;—"who is that?—Who comes to me in this hour?—Is it she, the poor deluded one?—Oh, Heaven grant that she has escaped the power of the seducer, and has returned to see me in my last moments; oh, what a blessing would that be to me!"

The unfortunate Milford had not seen his guilty and heartless son for several days, but agonising had been the thoughts he had excited in his bosom, and most anxious was he to behold him ere he died, with the hope that in such a solemn moment he would succeed in moving his heart to repentance, and yet he could not think of him without a shuddering feeling approaching to horror. His emotion may then be well imagined when the chamber door was thrown violently open, and that abandoned young man abruptly presented himself. His father gazed at him for a moment with an expression of impressive feeling, which the son treated with the utmost indifference, and walking up to the bed, took a newspaper from his coat pocket.

George Milford could not have arrived at a more inopportune time for Augusta, her feelings being wound up to the utmost pitch of anxiety by the observations of his father, and she was fearful from the demeanour of George, that even the awful situation of his parent would not restrain his evil passions, and that the interview would be productive of the most fatal results. She looked at him imploringly, but he was evidently as usual, excited by drink, and returned her look with one of scornful and insolent derision, deliberately at the same time, unfolding the paper, and referring to a particular passage.

"George," said his father, in a fain andt hollow voice, "you have then come to see me ere I die?"

"Die!" re-echoed the profligate, with a brutal laugh; "what's the use of talking about dying? Psha, old man, you are worth fifty dead uns yet, though to be sure you do look rather queer; but I have something to tell you that will put new life into you. Nothing like mopusses to mak a man happy in this world. Care be d——d, while you have got plenty of them."

"George, George, forbear," cried the horror-struck Augusta, "how can you give utterance to such language in such a moment as this?"

"There, none of your mummery and nonsense, young lady," replied the ruffian; "keep that for ears to which it is more agreeable, my business is with my father, and as it cannot concern you, I should thank you to retire for a few minutes, while I communicate it to him."

"Remain, Augusta," said Mr. Milford in a firm voice, "I command you. Oh, George, George, unhappy, guilty young man, can nothing move your stubborn heart? Have you come here to embitter the last moments of your unfortunate father?"

"Not I, old man," returned George, with the utmost indifference, "I have come here to sweeten them, and as I said before, to put new life into you. I tell you I have good news for you."

"Good news for me," said Mr. Milford shaking his head, "I have now no earthly hope, for the few hours I shall remain here, but one; the restoration of the unfortunate and betrayed Charlotte, and——"

"Oh," interrupted the ruffian, never mind her; "what is she to you? I dare say she will come back when her and Henry Sterling are tired of each other."

"Cruel, heartless boy, whom no sense of shame can move to repentance," ejaculated his father in a tone of voice, and with an expression of countenance that might have moved even the most obdurate heart; "I cannot, I will not listen to language such as this. Leave me, and may Heaven when I am gone bring you to a proper sense of the guilt, the enormity of your present conduct."

"Psha!" exclaimed the determined young man, "what's the use of talking in this manner; I knew very well that you never had any particular regard for me, but that you lavished it all upon others, and perhaps, it was only natural after all, considering you were so well paid for it; however, I dont bear any malice, so we'll let that matter drop, and I'll come at once to the business which brought me here. A large slice of good luck has befallen us, old man, and it is not before we wanted it? I intend to come out in first-rate style now, and I'll be bound to say that I'll take the conceit out of some of the nobs."

"What do you mean?" demanded Mr. Milford, in a faint voice.

"Mean, why that we are up in the stirrups, that we have got a windfall; that we are rich, that's all about it; and if that is not news good enough even to resuscitate a corpse, I don't know what is."

"Rich!" ejaculated his father, with a mournful shake of the head, "alas! what will riches avail me now? Can they delay my passage to eternity one moment? Can they restore to me pure and unsullied that fair being whom by the most villanous artifices has been decoyed away? Oh, no, no, no! But you come here only to mock me, George."

"So, that's all the return I get for my trouble and information. But I do not come here to mock you, which I will soon prove. Happening yesterday, by accident, for it is a thing I seldom do, to glance over the newspaper, my eye happened to encounter the following advertisement: 'If the next of kin to the late Andrew Clavering, Esq ——."

"Andrew Clavering!" cried the astonished Milford, while Augusta now listened with the utmost impatience and curiosity.

"Yes," returned George with a satirical grin, "my late much respected grand uncle. 'If the next of kin to the late Andrew Clavering, Esq., for many years past residing on the continent, or their heir will apply to Mr. Sparkhall, Solicitor, Clements Inn, London, they will hear of something to their advantage.' I believe there's no mistake in that. But here is the advertisement and you may read it yourself if you are not satisfied."

"My uncle dead," said Mr. Milford, with a shudder, as he recollected his vices, and the many injuries himself and his father had experienced from him, "may Heaven pardon him, for alas, I fear he has much to answer for."

"Aye, he was not one of the best of men," said George, carelessly, "so it's a good thing he has kicked the bucket. Had he done so some years since it would have been much the better. However, better late than never, and we have every reason to be satisfied, as he has left no trifle of money behind him."

Mr. Milford listened to the brutal observations of his son with horror and disgust, and the looks he bestowed upon him sufficiently expressed his feelings, but they had no effect upon that hardened young man, and he continued in the following words:—

"Knowing that you could not very well visit this Mr. Sparkhall, and thinking it was best not to lose any time about the business, I called upon him myself this morning, at his chambers, and on making myself known to him, and giving him satisfactory evidence of the truth of my statements, he entered into every particular, and a very pretty story it is ; but I dare say you will not be surprised to hear it. I believe your grandfather was found murdered in an uninhabited house in one of the low streets of the metropolis—is not that correct ?"

" Yes, yes ;" answered Mr. Milford.

" And that his murderer was never discovered ?"

" True."

" Well, that is known now, or at least at whose instigation the crime was perpetrated."

" Ah !" gasped forth Milford, with emotion, " who, who was the villain ?"

" Your much respected uncle, Andrew Clavering," replied George.

" My uncle ! Oh guilty, wretched man ! but how know you this ?"

" From his own dying confession, which the solicitor communicated to me. It seems that about three months since since he met with a dreadful accident by the upset of his carriage, and when he found that the injuries he received were sure to prove mortal, like a sensible man as he was, and much to our good fortune, he confessed all, and moreover that he had forged the will of the old man, who had bequeathed to you a very handsome annuity. However, his murderer is no more, all that he possesses is ours, and if that is not a slice of good luck enough to made any heart glad, I don't know what is."

" Wretched, guilty man !" said Mr. Milford, " may Heaven pardon him his sins."

" Well I don't care much about that," said George, " all that I have got to say is, that I am much obliged to him for dying, and wish he had taken it into his head to have done so before; for as I am your only son and heir, of course I may expect no more to be put to those confonded shifts that I have so long been."

" Hold !" cried his horror-struck parent, " can you, when you see me on the verge of eternity talk thus ? Oh, George, George, will nothing whatever move your heart to compunction ?"

" Why, what would you have me do ? What's the use of continually schooling me in this manner ? I have brought you good intelligence, and this is all the return I get for it. If you are ill, I am sorry for it, and that's as much as I can say; so as I suppose you cannot make it convenient to see this Mr. Sparkhall, you will leave it to me to settle the business with him. Good night, you will see me again to-morrow or the next day, I dare say."

" George," groaned the unfortunate Mr. Milford, " can you leave me thus ?"

" Why, what the devil good can I do by stopping," demanded the hardened ruffian; " besides if I may judge from the reception I have met with, my presence is not want ed here, and so the sooner I go the better."

" My God !" exclaimed the agonised father, while Augusta looked at George with feelings of the most indescribable horror and disgust, " can this really he my own son to talk to me thus ? George, you will never see me alive again. The hand of death is already upon me, and I am sinking fast."

" Oh, don't say that," returned George in the same reckless tone, " but you will find yourself mistaken I have no doubt, and will live for many a year yet. Good by, I cannot stay any longer, as I have got a little business to transact to-night."

With these words the guilty young man, without so much as pressing the hand of his dying parent, or deigning to look at Augusta, stalked abruptly from the room, and quitted the house, and no sooner was he gone than Mr. Milford sunk back on his pillow with a deep groan of anguish and immediately became insensible.

The terror and agony of poor Augusta were most intense, for she thought that the vital spark had fled, and that her loved benefactor was snatched from her for ever.

She threw herself frantically upon his bosom, and her shrieks alarmed Mrs. Barton and the physician, who were quickly in attendance, and who rendered all the prompt assistance in their power, and did all that they could to pacify the grief of Augusta, assuring her that her father was not dead but had only fainted. But she could admit of no consolation under circumstances so trying and distressing, and as she looked upon the ghast y countenance and almost rigid features of that revered being; she feared

THE ROYAL TWINS;

In this condition things remained for some hours, Augusta a prey to the most distressing feelings, and Mr. Milford in a state of stupor that seemed the sure forerunner of death. At length he sank into a slumber, the consequence of a draught administered by the physician, during which no persuasions could induce Augusta to leave his side. When the soporific effects of the medicine went off, poor Milford awoke, somewhat refreshed, and with returning senses, although evidently weaker.

"Augusta," he said at length, "hear with patience and resolution the extraordinary facts I have to disclose, and receive my dying advice as to the future course you should pursue under the peculiar and trying circumstances in which you will find yourself so unexpectedly placed."

Augusta did indeed listen with breathless attention, and her heart presaged the worst of terror. Mr. Milford moistened his lips with a cordial which Augusta had presented to him, and he was then about to speak again, when he was once more interrupted by a violent knocking at the street door, and Augusta started from her seat, and looked about her with amazement, but was unable to walk to the casement to ascertain who it was.

"Again interrupted," ejaculated Mr. Milford, "am I never destined to reveal this painful secret? Who can this be? Ah, it is most probably that wretched, guilty boy again, come to insult and torture me in my last moments! But I will not, cannot see him. Summon Mrs. Barton here, and let her prevent his intrusion upon me."

At that moment the street door was heard to close with a loud bang; there was a brief pause, then a loud cry of agony and despair was heard, followed by hasty footsteps ascending the stairs, the chamber door was thrown open, and with a countenance ghastly pale, her hair hanging wild and dishevelled over her shoulders, and her dress disordered and dirty from exposure to the wet and cold, Charlotte rushed into the room, and staggering up to the bedside of the dying man, sunk insensible and inanimate on the floor ere she could repeat more than "father!" in a tone of agony.

"Ah! it is her voice!" cried Milford, raising himself in his bed with a sudden strength and energy, which, considering his exhausted state, was truly surprising; "it was no wild delusion of the brain! Providence has heard my prayers, and the poor lost and deceived one is restored to me ere my eyes are closed for ever in the sleep of death!"

"Father, father!" shrieked Charlotte, recovering herself, and sinking on her knees by the side of his couch; "it is your wretched, unfortunate child, whom the voice of the tempter lured to abandon you. Augusta, dear sister, plead for me; though I have erred, I am still pure and innocent as when I quitted this humble dwelling. Gracious Heaven, and have I been the guilty cause of all this? Pardon, pardon!"

"Father, beloved father!" ejaculated Augusta, "oh, speak, I implore you to my unfortunate sister, and assure her of your forgiveness. You hear the blessed statement she has made, that she is pure and innocent; the seducer has not triumphed, and you may still press her to your bosom without a blush of shame!"

"God of Heaven! for this I thank thee!" cried Mr. Milford, straining the poor girl to his heart, while his tears fell fast upon her pale but beauteous face, "and now I can die happy! Charlotte, Charlotte!—I pardon and bless thee!"

We must pass over the scene which ensued, for the reader will be much better able to form a conception of it than we can describe it; but it was almost too much for the exhausted strength of Mr. Milford, and the doctor was obliged to interpose, and to advise Augusta to lead her sister into an adjoining apartment for a short time, until they should somewhat have recovered from the effects of such a severe trial.

When they were alone, Charlotte threw herself upon her sister's neck, and for some time they mingled their tears together, without being able to give utterance to a word.

"Oh, God! Augusta," at length ejaculated Charlotte, "how terrible have been the consequences of my indiscretion; cursed fate that ever introduced me to Henry Stirling; our father is dying, Augusta, I see it plainly; we shall shortly be left alone in the cheerless world; and I have been the fatal, the guilty cause of all this? It is I who have broken the heart of that revered being, and hastened his passage to the grave. Oh, how can I ever, ever forgive myself?"

"Cease, my dear Charlotte," replied her sister, in a soothing voice, "to reproach yourself so severely; our beloved parent's constitution has been for some time declining, and if it is the will of the Almighty now to take him from us, it is our duty, dreadful though the trial will be, to submit. Providence, I trust will yet raise us up a friend where we might least expect it. Oh, my sister, what you must have suffered on discovering the treachery of that man who won your young and susceptible heart, and seduced you from your home!"

"Alas!" replied Charlotte, "I cannot describe it. How bitter were my pangs of remorse, and how insupportable my terrors at the threats which he who held me in his power held out to me. But Providence did not forsake me, Stirling was taken suddenly ill and confined to his chamber, and it was then that I contrived to escape from the house, and after much difficulty and suffering, being in a part of the country to which I was an entire stranger, I found my way once more to that home which I had so unfortunately forsaken; my heart racked with the most torturing forebodings, which, alas! I find are too fatally realized. But come, Augusta, let us return to the chamber of our poor suffering parent; I cannot rest away from him, and much I fear that the time is fast approaching when we shall be deprived of him altogether. Oh! God!—oh, God! how torturing is it to anticipate that dreadful calamity!"

Augusta endeavoured to compose her, though she as much stood in need of consolation herself, and they then, with trembling steps, returned to the chamber of the suffering Mr. Milford, whom they found wrapped in a calm sleep, which the doctor predicted would have the most beneficial effect on him after the excitement he had undergone, and desired the sisters to keep as quiet as possible and not to disturb him.

Charlotte and her sister pressed a gentle kiss of affection on his thin pale lips, and then sitting down by the side of the bed, watched him with the most tender anxiety.

It was nearly two hours before Mr. Milford awoke, and beholding Charlotte and Augusta hanging over him, he uttered a faint cry of joy, extended his arms, and pressed them to his bosom. What a moment of poignant anguish was it to them all, and their hearts throbbed with such emotions as they had never before experienced.

"It was then no dream;" ejaculated Mr. Milford, in a faint voice; "no, no, I behold her; I clasp my Charlotte again to my throbbing heart, that heart that must soon close to beat for ever, and I am happy and resigned."

"Oh, most beloved, best of parents," sobbed Charlotte, "talk not thus; surely Heaven in its infinite mercy, will yet spare you to your poor children, for deprived of you, what oh, what will become of them ?"

"God will watch over you and protect you from danger when I am gone," said Milford, in a calm voice; but," he added, as a sudden recollection seemed to flash upon his brain;—" why do I waste that time which is so precious ? Why do I delay the disclosure of that secret which is of so much importance to your future welfare ?"

"A secret, father," ejaculated the astonished Charlotte, eagerly.

"Aye," returned Mr. Milford, "and one that will fill you with amazement and anxiety. And yet do I hesitate to reveal it. We must be alone, for I feel my strength rapidly failing me, and that there is not a moment to be lost. Heart be firm! my conscience assures me that I have ever done my duty."

The physician and Mrs. Barton having retired from the room, and the two lovely sisters having assisted Mr. Milford to raise himself in his bed, awaited the disclosure he was about to make with the greatest suspense.

"Augusta, Charlotte," exclaimed Milford at length; "you ever looked upon and reverenced me and my late wife as your parents."

"Oh, my father!" cried the sisters, in a breath, "how can we properly describe the affection with which we ever beheld you and that beloved mother who is now in Heaven?"

"Bless you, bless you for this; I never doubted your affection, but hear me while I declare to you that the love you bore us, was due alone from gratitude, and not from the ties of nature !—"

"Gracious Heaven!" exclaimed the poor girls, looking earnestly in his face, and thinking that his senses wandered, "not from the ties of nature?—What strange and painful mystery is this?"

"The secret must come out!" replied Milford, mustering all his fortitude, " Augusta Charlotte, children of my love and anxiety, I am not your father!"

No words could properly describe the startling effect which this extraordinary announcement had upon them; they could scarcely credit the evidence of their senses, and stared upon him with speechless amazement.

"Great God!" they cried at last, "you know not what you say ;—your senses must wander, adored being."

"Be calm, be calm, my poor girls," sighed Milford, with a look of compassion;— "indeed my reason has not deserted me; I repeat that you are not my offspring, neither am I in any way related to you."

Augusta and Charlotte tried to speak, but for a few seconds they could not, and their emotions were of that intense and agonizing character that they had the greatest difficulty in saving themselves from fainting.

"Not your children—not related to you?" said Charlotte, "oh, it seems to be impossible."

"It is true, as I hope for mercy from that Almighty in whose presence I must soon appear.   You were committed to the care of myself, and that amiable woman whom you ever supposed to be your mother, in your infancy, and we bound ourselves by a solemn oath to bring you up as our own."

"Astounding revelation !" ejaculated Augusta.   " Who then were our parents?"

" 1 know them not, no more than that I have been given to understand that the lady whose likeness is delineated in the miniature contained in the locket which you wear, and the original of which you may remember more than once to have encountered, is your mother."

Augusta and her sister uttered an exclamation of the most indescribable astonishment and clasped their hands vehemently together.   All the events of the past rushed immediately on their memory ; the circumstance of their being taken away in so mysterious a manner when they were children, by the lady, and their afterwards encountering her in the churchyard, and the feelings which predominated in their bosoms may be with little difficulty imagined.

"Mysterious Providence!" cried Charlotte, " what an extraordinary discovery is this!   But is it possible, my dear father (for such I must ever continue to call you and to look upon you), is it possible that you are really ignorant of the names of our parents, or where they are to be found ?"

"I am," answered Milford, "but I am informed that they are persons filling the most illustrious and exalted stations of life."

"Mystery upon mystery," ejaculated Charlotte, " and what could ever have induced the authors of our being to desert us ?"

"Listen my dear children," replied Mr. Milford, " and I will relate to you all the particulars."

With breathless attention Augusta and her sister obeyed, and their wonder increased as he proceeded and recounted to them all those remarkable particulars with which the reader is already acquainted, being several times compelled to interrupt him to give expression to their emotions; but when he had concluded, they threw themselves on his bosom, and gave vent to their feelings in a flood of tears.

"Alas! alas !" they cried, " what a remarkable and bewildering fate is ours. Surely it must have been some fearful misfortune that could compel our parents to part with their infant offspring ?—Oh, revered being, what do we not owe to you and that excellent woman whose soul is now in Heaven ?—But the stranger, who can he be ?   Can it be to him that we owe our existence ?"

"I know not;" said Milford, " but I have often suspected that he is, or some one nearly related to you, or he would not h ave taken such an interest in your fate."

" But," said Charlotte, " surely if our parents are still living, they cannot longer delay when they learn our friendless condition, coming forward and revealing themselves ?"

"God grant that they may," ejaculated Mr. Milford; "I have performed my duty, my beloved girls, and I feel my mind now greatly relieved.   The only regret I feel in leaving the world, is in the thought of parting from you, and leaving you so miserably provided for, and without a protector. My guilty son, you cannot, dare not hope to look to, in fact you must avoid him, for there is danger and contamination in his path, and I know he views you even with feelings of hatred. But I grow faint—here is the key of my desk, in it you will find the remainder of the cash forwarded to me by the stranger, and which justly belongs to you. It is not much, but it may with economy prove sufficient to support you until it may please Providence to send those upon whom you have a claim to your aid. I——"

Here Mr. Milford suddenly paused, for a deathly faintness came over him, and he could not speak. He sunk back exhausted on his pillow, his eyes closed, and such was the sudden and awful change that came over him that the distracted sisters screamed with terror, thinking that the vital spark had] fled, and that death had snatched from them the only friend (with the exception of Mrs. Milford), whom they had known in the world. Hastily they summoned the physician and Mrs. Barton, who pronounced that Mr. Milford was not dead, but was sinking fast; and knowing that it would not only be dangerous, but cruel to buoy the poor girls up with false hopes, he candidly assured them that it was impossible the sufferer could survive many hours. What terrible agony did this announcement impart to their bosoms. They wrung their hands, and wept bitterly, and then they threw themselves on their knees, and fervently supplicated the Almighty to avert so dreadful a calamity, and yet to prolong the life of that revered being, whom till now they believed to be their father. The physician would fain have persuaded them to retire from the chamber for a short time, until they should in some measure have recovered themselves, but nothing whatever could prevail upon them, and poor Charlotte forgot all the uncommon fatigue she had suffered for the last day or two in travelling, in the anxiety she felt in the deplorable and hopeless situation of her dying benefactor.

Mr. Milford once or twice opened his eyes, and seemed perfectly conscious of their presence, and all that was passing around him; but he could not speak, and it appeared but too probable that the wretched sisters had listened to his beloved voice for the last time in this world.

He noticed the agony they were enduring, and by a faint smile, endeavoured to inspire them with consolation and fortitude. Alas! how was it likely that the poor girls could encourage either under such melancholy circumstances?

Thus the hours waned slowly and dismally away, and Mr. Milford remained in the same speechless state, and his breathing gradually became more difficult, and fainter and fainter, while the appearance of his countenance, and the heavy perspiration that stood upon his brow, shewed too plainly how rapidly the grim destroyer was approaching. The sisters stood on either side of the bed, and pressed the hands of the dying man to their heart, while he looked calmly in their countenances, and his lips moved, and although no sound was permitted to escape them, it was evident that his soul was engaged in prayer, and that he was invoking the blessings of the Almighty upon the heads of those beloved beings from whom he was so soon about to be taken.

Oh, how solemn and impressive was the silence which reigned in that chamber of death; it was only broken by the sobs of the sisters, and the hollow and difficult breathing of the dying man. Evening set in, darkness was upon the earth, and still Mr. Milford lingered, though from the tranquil manner in which he lay, and the serenity of his countenance, he did not seem to be suffering any particular pain. Still the sisters watched with dreadful anguish and anxiety, expecting every moment would be his last, were completely worn out with fatigue and the agony of their feelings. At length just as the hour of ten had ceased striking from a neighbouring clock, a most significant change came over his features, and two or three convulsive paroxysms agitated his frame. Again he made a powerful effort to speak, but he could not. He stretched forth his arms, and looked in the countenances of the weeping sisters with an expression which they could never forget, he folded them to his bosom with a last convulsive effort; suddenly his arms relaxed their hold;—a gentle sigh escaped his bosom, and Mr. Milford's soul was summoned into the presence of his Almighty Judge. A simultaneous cry of the most heart-rending agony escaped the lips of Augusta and her sister, and they sunk insensible upon the bed by the side of the corpse of him who had been their best, nay only earthly friend.

CHAPTER

THE BRUTAL CONDUCT OF GEORGE MILFORD.—THE FUNERAL.—THE GUILTY PROPOSAL,
AND THE FLIGHT OF THE SISTERS.

IT was some hours before Augusta and Charlotte were restored to their senses, for fit succeeded fit, and had it not been for the unremitting exertions of the physician, who remained in the house, and the kind attentions of the humane Mrs. Barton, the most fatal consequences might have ensued. Weak and ill as they were, it was with the utmost difficulty they could be prevented from entering the chamber of death, and weeping over the cold remains of him they had so fondly loved in life. What a dreadful night of suffering was that to the unfortunate girls; Mrs. Barton and another of the female lodgers, sat up with them the whole of the night, and did all that was in their power to ameliorate their affliction, and to persuade them to call the power of Christian resignation to their aid; but alas, as could only have been expected, with but little if any effect. They were now indeed alone in the world, without any one to whom they could apply for counsel and protection, and if their parents did not come forward to claim and receive them to their bosoms, they knew not what would become of them. Although they had both for some time been prepared for this dismal event, it had now come with such terrible effect upon them that they felt as if they could never withstand the shock, and Charlotte's anguish was particularly keen, for she could not help reproaching herself for the conduct she had recently pursued, and which she feared had been the primary cause of hastening the death of the unfortunate Mr. Milford.

The following day, notwithstanding the poor girls were so heart-broken and ill, and should have confined themselves to their bed, nothing whatever could dissuade them from visiting the chamber of death, and to weep their anguish over the ashes of him whose voice was silenced for ever, and to offer up their prayers to Heaven for the repose of his soul. We will pass over that dismal scene, for it needs no description of ours to impress it upon the imagination of the reader; but at length after they had been thus occupied for about an hour, Mrs. Barton entered the room, and informed them that George Milford had just arrived and wished to see them. They heard this with a sensation of horror and repugnance, and would fain have excused themselves from the interview, especially in their present distracted state of mind, but they knew it would be useless, and fixing an agonizing look upon the corpse, and impressing a kiss upon the lips, with trembling steps and foreboding hearts, they followed Mrs. Barton from the chamber, and descended into the parlour, where George was awaiting them, and who greeted them on their entrance with coarse familiarity, and with an air of as perfect indifference as if nothing unusual had happened. They trembled, and their disgust was increased.

"So the old man has gone, I understand;" said the heartless ruffian. The sisters looked at him with feelings of the most indescribable horror, but could return no answer.

"Well," continued George; "it's what we must all come to, so it is not much use fretting about it. Young lady, you have got tired of your spark, I see, and have thought proper to give him the slip, eh?"

"Mr. Milford," returned the indignant Charlotte, fixing upon him a withering look of reproach; "did you send for me and my sister merely to insult us with your brutal observations? Shame on you, to talk with such inhuman levity here, and while the corpse of your unfortunate parent is scarcely cold!"

"I tell you what it is, young lady," said George, "I did not come here to have a lecture read to me by you, and so the sooner you alter your tone the better. I have got some business to settle with you and your sister, and so the sooner we enter upon it the better. I suppose my father before he died did not neglect to inform you exactly how you are situated, and the future prospects that are before you?"

"Your father informed us of everything," sighed Augusta; "and we ask but permission to see to the interment of his cold remains, and to follow them to their final resting place, and then we shall be prepared to seek another asylum, for we do not expect or desire to receive one from you."

"Indeed," sneered George, "you are mightily independant, considering how you are situated ; but you will tell a different story by-and-bye, or I am much mistaken. Of course you are then aware that you are not related to me ?"

"Oh, yes, thank Heaven !" ejaculated both the sisters fervently. George bit his lips, and could not conceal his vexation, notwithstanding he attempted to treat the observations of the sisters with indifference.

"Such being the case then," he said, "I need not remind you that you have no claim whatever upon me ?"

"Oh, no ;" replied Augusta, "and none, I assure you, do we wish to make, We lament that Mr. and Mrs. Milford were not our real parents, but still we must ever revere their memory the same."

Sobs choked her utterance, and turning away her head, she laid it on the shoulder of her weeping sister.

"Come, come," said George, "I do not like to see so much of this snivelling, it all won't bring the dead to life again."

"What is the purpose of your visit to us ?" demanded Augusta, conquering her emotion, and resuming all her natural dignity, while she still continued to contemplate the ruffian with the most ineffable disgust.

"My visit to you !" repeated George, with a look of scorn; "come now, I like that, seeing that I am master of all the contents of the place, and that your only dependence for a home and shelter is upon me, your mysterious friend having apparently deserted you."

How the bosoms of the unfortunate sisters swelled at these brutal remarks; but they quickly recovered themselves, and viewing him with the contempt he so fully merited, Charlotte, who had hitherto been overpowered by her emotions, ejaculated,—

"Mr. Milford, or Mr. Clavering, (which I now understand to be your real name) whatever sufferings and privations myself and my poor sister may in future be destined to endure, matters not to you ; it may be satisfactory for you that we scorn to place ourselves under an obligation to a man who has never shown us common respect, upon whom, as you have so unnecessarily reminded us, we have no claim, and who can act in such a brutal and unnatural manner, only a few hours after the death of his parent, and our only earthly friend. We only request that you will at least have the common decency to spare our sufficiently tortured feelings for the present, and allow us to follow the remains of our lamented benefactor to their last resting place, and then——"

Tears gushed to her eyes, a deathly faintness came over her, and she was unable to finish the sentence.

"Well," said George Clavering, in the same tone of indifference as before, and inwardly exulting with all the malice of a fiend at the mental torture the poor girls were enduring; "although you have not complimented me very highly, I do not wish to act in any way unfairly towards you. I am now a man of fortune, thanks to my old scoundrel of a grand-uncle, for dying, and I do not know but that you and I may yet come to terms, by which we may be friends. You will find me not a bad fellow after all, I'll warrant. As for the funeral of the old man, I will give the necessary instructions to the undertaker, and leave you at liberty to make such arrangements as you please. I shall not follow, for I have other business to attend to, and I am not very partial to such dismal business as that. Good day, I shall see you again shortly, when I shall have such business to propose, as I have no doubt will meet with your mutual approbation."

Thus saying, the rebrobate fixing upon the heart-broken and horror-stricken sisters a most peculiar and disgusting look, abruptly quitted the house, much to their relief, though they could scarcely believe that any one, however stepped in crime, would be so utterly callous to every sense of feeling, while the corpse of his only parent was lying in the house. They threw themselves into each other's arms, and for some time the horror and anguish of ther feelings deprived them of the power of speech. Brutal as they had ever found George to be, they could never have imagined him capable of such conduct as that he had thus displayed, had they not witnessed it, and the dark insinuations he had thrown out, and the insolent boldness of his conduct altogether, filled them with tenfold astonishment and alarm. They feared he had some deep laid designs in contemplation, which they feared it impossible to penetrate, and that they should be compelled to abandom their present place of residence as soon as possible, for that they would not be safe from some insidious and villanous persecution while he knew where they were.

But where were they, two young and innocent, and defenceless girls to go ? Where seek any asylum, inexperienced as they were in the ways of the world ? By what means obtain a living? Nothing could be more forlorn and torturing than their situation, and they looked in vain for even some faint ray of hope and consolation. What a mysterious, what an unprecedented fate was theirs ! Providence seemed to have marked them out, to be the children of continued misfortune. And could their relations, their parents, if still living, refrain from coming forward to their rescue, when they knew their present friendless and deserted situation ? Alas, they could not help entertaining the most fearful apprehehsions when they reflected upon all the melancholy and extraordinary circumstances of their life.

Mrs. Barton, who though a poor woman, and one who had not had the advantages of education, was still a most humane and naturally sensible person, and deeply commiserating with the unfortunate girls, who deemed it prudent to confide to her the particulars of their peculiar situation, did all she could to comfort them under their heavy affliction, and was ready to assist them all that was in her humble power. We need not say that both Augusta and Charlotte duly appreciated her good intentions, and thanking her most heartily for her kindness, did indeed feel somewhat more tranquillised. George Clavering sent an undertaker on the following day after his visit to the sisters, to see after the funeral obsequies of his unfortunate father, and Augusta a Charlotte, mustering much more fortitude than they had anticipated they should be able to have, made all the necessary arrangements for the melancholy ceremony, which they had resolved even should it cost them the last shilling they had in the world, should be performed with all the respect that was due to the innumerable virtues of the deeply lamented deceased.

According to the dying request of Mr. Clavering, they had determined that his remains should be deposited in the same grave as those of his wife, and George had the decency to have given instructions that a monument should be erected to their memory.

Almost immediately after his interview with Augusta and her sister, George Clavering having administered to the will of his late guilty uncle, departed from London to take possession of certain estates in the country. He now suddenly found himself a wealthy man, and determined to enjoy it (in his way) to the fullest extent. So far from lamenting the death of his father, he looked upon it as a peculiar turn of good fortune, particularly as he had died without a will, thus leaving him the sole possessor of that property which he otherwise, from his attachment to Augusta and her sister might have been induced to divide between them, his conduct having been such as to lead him to expect only a small portion of it.

But still, George Clavering had determined not to lose sight of the sisters ; the guilty passions which had formerly been excited in his breast now burst forth with redoubled vigour, and he resolved, now that he had the power, to avail himself of the opportunity to gratify them. He was also most anxious to become acquainted with the secret of their birth, and resolved to leave no means untried to discover it, for he could not help thinking that some remarkable advantage was to be derived from it.

The melancholy day of the funeral arrived, and the unhappy sisters in a state of mind bordering upon absolute despair, and accompanied by the physician and Mrs. Barton, followed the remains of their beloved and affectionate benefactor to the silent grave, that grave which also contained the ashes of that revered, that amiable being, who in her unsullied lifetime had been to them even more than the most affectionate of mothers. We must hurry over that mournful scene ; it was with the greatest difficulty that the unhappy twins could be persuaded to leave that narrow space of earth that enclosed all that was so dear to them, and they were then borne away to their humble place of residence, in a state bordering upon insensibility.

The remainder of that day and night they remained in a most deplorable condition, and, in fact, it was not till three days after the funeral that they were restored to any-

thing like a degree of composure, and then indeed their situation was most alarming. They found themselves alone in the world, without a friend from whom they could seek advice and protection, while the dark hints of George Clavering, and his depraved character, convinced them that they had everything to fear from him, that it would not be safe for them to remain where they were any longer than they could help, and that they must also retire to some place where he could not discover them; but where could that be? Whither could they go? They sought the advice of Mrs. Barton, but for some time she was unable to counsel them. She well knew the danger of two young and inexperienced girls being left by themselves to buffet with the snares and dangers of the world, but her own circumstances were too humble to allow her to afford them any assistance, although her will was so good to do so. The money which the late Mr. Clavering had left behind him, and which he had bequeathed to their care, amounted to little more than thirty guineas, and when that small sum was exhausted what was to become of them? Unused as the poor girls had been to labour, how willing were they to do it could they only procure it, and how grateful would they have been to any human being to obtain it for them, though the occupation should be ever so humble, but unknown as they were, what chance was there for them to meet with such a friend? It was indeed a most dismal prospect, and no wonder that the two poor girls almost sunk under it, and in the bitterness of their feelings regretted that they had ever been born.

It would be an irksome task for us to relate at greater length the distress of mind which the fair sisters continued to endure for several weeks, during which George Clavering was fortunately detained from them by the course of dissipation into which he had plunged. We gladly turn to the more pleasant labour of recounting in few words, the events which at length threw sunshine over their once desolate prospects.

They were agreeably surprised one morning by the appearance of the stranger, whom we may designate at once as the Duke of M——, and the uncle of our heroines. He had been long engaged in the search for them, and when to his extreme joy he succeeded in tracing them out, he hurried to their abode, and lost no time in conveying them to their mother, that dear parent of whom they had as yet been able to form but a vague idea.

On their way to St. James's-square, where the mansion of their mother was situated, the duke made them aware that they were the offspring of the Countess of C——, and the highest personage in the realm, next to the King—the Prince of Wales. The astonishment of the sisters at this announcement was most profound, and they were all anxiety to learn the reason why, with such a distinguished origin, there should have been any necessity for so much mystery—mystery which had been productive of the deepest misfortune. Poor girls, they had yet to be informed of the existence of a Royal Marriage Act, which rendered the Prince's marriage with their mother illegal, and which, in conjunction with other circumstances, with which the reader will presently be made acquainted, had rendered secrecy imperative.

The meeting with the countess was of the most tender description. The sisters, of course, recognized in her the lady who had been so agitated on her former meetings with them, and toward whom they had been drawn by the mysterious impulses of nature.

The joy of the countess was fully reciprocated by her children; and this was if possible enhanced in a few days by a private visit paid them by their father, who was anxious to embrace his lovely daughters whom he had not beheld since infancy. The fair twins were charmed with the graceful and affectionate manner of the Prince, who appeared to them perfection itself; while he was no less delighted with his daughters, whom he declared with truth to exceed in grace and beauty all the ladies of the court. The Prince parted from them with reluctance, and with a promise of paying them frequent visits whenever he could escape from the prying eyes of those who surrounded him.

Another surprise awaited the sisters. In the drawing-room of the countess's mansion they observed a portrait, so strikingly resembling Henry Stirling, that Charlotte could not refrain from an exclamation of astonishment on beholding it. Augusta had calmness enough to enquire the name of the person for whom it was intended, and was informed that it was the young Earl of B——, their cousin! They were further promised an introduction to him on an early day.

We need not attempt to depict the surprise and confusion of Charlotte and the earl when the meeting took place—for it was Henry Stirling himself! To be brief, suffice it to say that his influence over Charlotte's heart was not extinct, and that on the countess being satisfied of his penitence for past misconduct, and his determination to make amends for all by future propriety of behaviour, he was received as the accepted lover of the fair girl who had bestowed upon him, under his assumed name, her hearts's first and purest affections.

CHAPTER XVI.

A BRIEF EXPLANATION.—THE ACTORS IN THE DRAMA DISPOSED OF, AND THE CONCLUSION.

ALL was now happy and cheerful at the mansion in St. James's Square; the earl and Charlotte looked forward with the brightest of hopes to the future, and Augusta in witnessing the felicity of those so dear to her felt her own happiness doubly increased.

Hitherto there had been no company at the mansion, but the countess now gave a grand party for the purpose of introducing her two charming daughters, and nothing could equal the admiration they excited in the bosoms of all present.

Charlotte and her sister had frequently requested the countess to favour them with the particulars of her history, which it was necessary to know, but she had always avoided it, as she felt it would be too great a trial to her feelings; at length she requested her brother to gratify their curiosity, which he did at the earliest opportunity.

The particulars are shortly these:—Lady Helena, was the daughter of the Duke and Duchess of M——, and was as remarkable for her surpassing beauty as she was for the polished elegance of her mind. The Earl of C——, having become enamoured of her, and having also made a most favourable impression on her heart, he submitted his suit to her parents, and being every way their equal, was accepted, though it was arranged that the union should not take place for two years, when Lady Helena would be of age.

On being presented at court, Lady Helena for the first time, beheld the Prince of Wales, and the impression that the personal attractions, and intrinsic accomplishments of that illustrious individual's mind made upon her, were of the most fatal description. The prince was also completely captivated with her, and exerted himself to the utmost to ingratiate himself in her favour.

The passion of the Prince and Lady Helena daily increased, and she found it utterly impossible to conquer it, and yet the bare idea of straying in the least from the paths of virtue filled her with disgust. The Prince, however, was not the man to abandon all his hopes so easily, he put all his consummate powers of persuasion into operation, and in order to quiet the virtuous scruples of the Lady Helena, he proposed a private marriage, although he knew, and so did she too know, that such marriage in the eye of the law would be nothing better than a mockery, and could never be publicly acknowledged. She yielded, at length, and became in the face of Heaven, the wife of his Royal Highness the Prince of Wales.

She repented immediately after she had yielded to the persuasons of the Prince; her anguish of mind increased; she saw that she had plunged herself into a dilemma which would probably terminate in shame and ruin, and she knew not in which way to act. She dared not divulge the secret to her parents, for she knew well that they would never forgive her, and how could she consent to become the wife of the earl, when she had already plighted her vows with another at the altar. To add to her agony ard dispair, she found herself in a situation to become a mother, and how could she conceal the fact from her parents?

In this dilemma, she applied for advice to her royal paramour, and he at length begged that she would allow him to divulge the facts to her elder brother, who was a particular friend of his, and who, he had no doubt, would for that reason, assist him in keeping the secret concealed from the public.

The marquis, who was very much attached to his sister, was greatly shocked when he was made acquainted with these painful particulars, and keenly reproached the Prince for the part he had acted; but at length he was somewhat appeased, and promised them all the aid in his power.

Fortunately at this time the earl was summoned to Italy on business of importance, so that for a time, at any rate, Lady Helena was released from his importunities; but as the time of her *accouchement* approached, her situation became more critical and dangerous.

Her brother had an estate only a few miles from town, and as he stated that he had invited some ladies and gentlemen of his acquaintance to pass a few weeks with him there, and the duke and duchess were too feeble to go visiting, he prevailed on them to suffer his sister to make one of the party. Instead, however, of his taking her to the place he had mentioned, she was conveyed to an old house only a few miles from town, and known as the Old Manor House at the present day, where it was resolved she should remain until after her confinement, when it was farther arranged that the infant should be placed under the care of some trustworthy person, until such time as it might be acknowledged by at least one of its parents.

This house belonged to the Prince, and therefore everything could be carried into effect with the greatest security. But how bitter were the sufferings of the unfortunate Lady Helena at the thought of being compelled to part with her innocent babe. We need not dwell upon it, for the reader may easily imagine the extent of her anguish.

In order to quiet the suspicions of her parents, Lady Helena wrote to them, stating that she had received so many pressing invitations from her brother's friends, that she must beg their indulgence for a few weeks, particularly as she found that change of scene had the most beneficial effect upon her health. Only five weeks after her arrival at the Old Manor House, Lady Helena was safely delivered of the lovely sisters who have formed the heroines of this story.

Lady Helena, having recovered from her confinement, returned home with a sad heart, although she affected to be much more cheerful than usual; and the earl shortly afterwards returned to England, and resumed his addresses. It may be readily imagined with what increased anguish Lady Helena now received them, which was not diminished by the urgency of her brother and the Prince, (who probably had got tired of his unfortunate victim) who impressed upon her the absolute necessity of her marrying the earl to save herself from shame, at the same stating that the secret of the birth of the children need not be divulged until some favourable opportunity offered. Lady Helena had no alternative; she was forced to yield, and became the wife of the man she respected, but could no longer love. Only a short time after this, the duke and duchess were simultaneously attacked with a dangerous illness, which baffled all the skill of their medical attendants, and they died in less than a week from the time of their first being taken bad.

The countess was afterwards frequently upon the point of divulging the whole truth to her husband, who behaved to her with the greatest affection; but there was something that prevented her, and it was not until he was seized with a violent illness, and given over by the physicians, that she formed the resolution to confess the truth to him, and to solicit his forgiveness. He was very much shocked and astonished when he was made acquainted with the facts, but he did not withhold his pardon from that wife he had loved with such devoted affection, and died in peace with all mankind.

Our "round unvarnished tale" draws towards its conclusion, having thus explained all those facts which were involved in perplexity. In due time the Earl of B—— led the beauteous Lady Charlotte to the altar, where she was resigned to his future care and protection, by no less an individual than her royal father.

It was not likely that the charms of Lady Augusta should long remain unnoticed; she was seen, and loved, and admired by the son of one of the most distinguished noblemen in the kingdom, and returning his passion with equal fervour, all the preliminaries being settled, Lady Augusta became the happy bride of one of the best of husbands.

It is not many years since the twin sisters have been summoned " to that bourne from whence no traveller returns," but they have left a numerous family behind them, who are at once an honour and ornament to the country.

George Clavering soon squandered away the whole of his property, and being reduced to want, became concerned in several daring burglaries, and was ultimately transported for life.